LONE STAR CRIME SCENE CLEANUP

by Fergus Hinely

Copyright ©2025 Line By Lion Publications
www.pixelandpen.studio
ISBN: 978-1-969677-33-5

Edited by Dani J Caile
Cover Design by Fergus Hinely

PART ONE:

Peanuts

CHAPTER ONE

Ghost Station

HE fell into consciousness like someone jerking awake at the wheel of a car.

That split second of not knowing when or where you are. Except, that feeling didn't leave Robert Dievs. It stuck around. And after a few moments of searching in his mind, he realized he truly had no flippin' idea where or who he was. He remembered his name. *Yes… Dievs… Robert Dievs… or Swiss? No, that's cheese. From… er- Waco? Wait a spot.*

He was sitting on a bench in the middle of a train platform. It wasn't Grand Central, but it was well done, he had to admit. *Wait, have I been to Grand Central?* He couldn't remember. The ceilings were high and domed, with beautiful pastel paintings of biblical shit and pudgy, naked babies. *Perty.*

He had a strange and sudden sensation that he'd been here before. As if he'd only just sat down again. The sensation fled just as quickly as it had come, though a series of disjointed images flashed through his mind, rapid and unprompted, like secret frames spliced into a movie. *A briefcase, and inside… a terrible, dark blue light, like shadows cast on the bottom of a pool. A man in a white suit with yellow gloves- a cleaner. A St. Bernard, and a man with green eyes.* Those green eyes seemed to linger in Dievs' mind for a time, then fled with the other images to wherever forgotten memories go. Dievs smacked his dry mouth.

The bench he sat on was bolted to a raised platform, and just now a train was rolling in from the right. He turned his head to look at the incoming locomotive. *Oof.* A crackling sound exploded from his neck like he'd twisted a roll of bubble wrap. *Little stiff. Goodness.* The feeling was that good kind of pain. Like sore legs after a big run, or pinching off a big no-wiper.

The incoming locomotive was beautiful and terrible, its front face dominated by a mean-looking black-iron cowcatcher and a single round headlight. The station was brightly lit, but even under the strong white light, Dievs could see the headlight burning a deep orange. *Like fire. Hellfire and brimstone sorta look.*

The train rolled in with a heavy *CHUGG-A-CHUGG-A,* slowing down only once it'd passed the bench Dievs was sitting on. Its carriages were similar to the engine: done in the style of a new century steam train, boxy, but full of exquisite details. Yellow trim on black carriages. The trim, windows, doors, wheels — *everything* — looked brand spankin' new. The only strange thing was the writing on the side. Where usually there would have been the name of a rail company or line, painted in big blocky letters, was:

#

DO NOT EAT THE PEANUTS

#

Dievs read the words and blinked. His neck popped again. *Ow.*

He was still pondering the strange slogan on the side of the passenger cars when the carriage doors clicked open, hissing. The train whistle blew twice, and steam rose from the engine in a great, billowing white cloud, obscuring the pastel scenes painted on the ceiling. Misty breath from a great steel monster.

Dievs sat patiently, waiting for the disembarking crowds, but after a few seconds, he realized no one was coming. *It's empty. Completely empty.* It was only then that he noticed the other folks around him. *Well…*

A crowd of vaguely human-shaped, translucent white shadows milled about the platform. There was even one sitting next to him on the bench. He turned his head, forgetting to be gentle, and set off another string of firecrackers in his neck. *Oohhh.* The ghostly shadows were definitely people, but in his peripheral vision, they seemed to fade out, until they were little more than the *outlines* of people. *Ghosts. Shadows. Color-inside-the-lines people.*

Further inspection revealed that focusing on one of these ghosts would render it solid, at least briefly. A *mostly* normal stranger. A whole bustling conglomeration of these phantoms swirled on the platform, silently squishing past one another like wet balloons, fading in and out of reality. Some carried great big duffel bags, others, old-style trunks, and some, no bags at all. But all these ghostly strangers kept their heads down. Their faces blurred and fuzzy. *Not mean-looking like the train,* Dievs thought, *but not happy either. They look kind of sad, actually.* And then Dievs felt kind of sad himself, and the urge to get up and leave grabbed him tight.

Upsy-daisy.

#

HIS knees popped worse than his neck. Two shotgun blasts. Two rusted out, un-oiled bolts being twisted for the first time in a good long while. *A **good** long while.* He thought of the tin-man from the wizard of Oz. He actually felt his kneecaps clicking back into place, like weak magnets on ball bearings. It didn't *hurt* exactly, but it wasn't pleasant either. Then he was up, swaying on feet he didn't recognize.

Though the realization he was in some kind of ghostly train station should have been alarming, the strangeness wasn't what bothered Dievs, but the sadness. The travelers' shadowed faces. The way they moved, as if carrying a great weight of some kind. That sadness felt somehow eternal, as if it had been happening for a long time, and yet, for no time at all. *How long have I been here?* The answer seemed irrelevant. Maybe there was no answer — at least, not one that mattered. *Maybe forever. Maybe I just got here.*

Dievs looked down at his own arms and legs. Everything felt completely natural and solid, except for the fact that he did not recognize this body at all. *God, my arms are hairy.* It was uncomfortable to look down at a body he didn't know, but when he thought about it, no image would come to mind as to what he *ought* to look like. *I guess this is what it's supposed to be. Could be worse.*

Dievs looked up, away from his body and back to the stopped passenger train in front of him. He saw that the ghost people on the platform were thinning out. They were all piling onto the train — slowly and orderly squeezing on board, like human caviar squishing into a can.

Alright. Dievs took a big breath and stepped. He snapped, crackled and popped like a fresh bowl of Rice Crispies. The sound was distressing, but he kept his feet underneath him. *Whooo- head rush.* A fit of dizziness hit him, but he got his breathing under control and did some stretches. *Toe touches. Trunk twisters. Arm circles…* A few of the ghost passengers looked at him strangely as they passed by, hauling their great duffle bags. *Don't mind me…*

A few stretches later, Dievs felt almost like a functioning person. *Now, some coffee. Wonder how I like it…* He turned back around to the bench and saw his ghostly neighbor staring at him. An old lady with a pinched face and primly clasped hands. She was looking at Dievs like he'd just reached in the cookie jar without permission. *Okay, lady.* Sitting next to her on the bench was a small leather sling bag. Somehow, Dievs knew it was his.

The thought came so effortlessly, he wondered why he was having such a hard time remembering the more important things. *Like, maybe, how I got here… Or, I dunno, who I am. I'll find out soon enough,* he told himself. *It's just a bout of temporary amnesia, that's all. Totally normal. Right. I'm sure there's a perfectly reasonable explanation. Right…*

Dievs reached down and grabbed his bag. He eyed the pinched-faced old lady, and contemplated asking her for help, then decided he'd rather not. Her face read, *you are a disappointment. Yeesh.* He threw the bag over his shoulder and turned around to get a better sense of his surroundings.

The station was cleanly built. Smooth white stone and polished marble- big columns and sharp lines. He turned and looked down to both ends of the platform. In the direction the train had come from, the raised platform ended, and a set of train tracks led out into… *whiteness.*

A dense fog hung in the air outside the station, obscuring any kind of view. Dievs could see the tracks for a few meters as they trailed off into the emptiness. *Hm.* There was something very *definite* about that fog. It gave no answers and asked no questions. Dievs stuck his tongue out and blew like a taunting child. *That's not very helpful.* He felt the old lady's eyes boring into the back of his head. *Up yers, ya old bat.* It occurred to Dievs that thought wasn't very nice, but it felt right. *Familiar.*

Turning in the other direction, the station opened up before him, a towering building, with neck-breakingly high ceilings. Dievs had thought this place had nothing on Grand Central, but now, after giving it a proper look, he saw it was much, *much* larger and more detailed than he'd been able to see from the bench. Everywhere he looked was some kind of mural or carved stone. *It's like Rome or Prague or something, maybe?* Then Dievs saw a sign hanging from one of the iron lampposts on the platform that read, "TICKETS."

He took a moment to read the sign, then it occurred to him to check his pockets. *I have a bag I don't remember. Might be something in the pockets.* His pants were gray linen, and scratchy. Another feature he did not recognize. He dug his hands deep down into his pockets and rummaged around. In the right, he found nothing but lint and a crumb of some unidentifiable food. In the left, he found the same, plus a small, stiff piece of cardstock, serrated on two ends. He pulled it out and looked at the words written on the yellow paper's front face:

#

WESTERN LINE - ONE WAY
DIEVS, ROBERT

#

And that was it. Nothing else except for the black border lines around the edges. Nothing on the back either. Dievs looked up from the card to the train. Something deep in his gut told him this *was* the Western line. *And maybe, every other line too.* But there was a war in his tummy. One part told Dievs he *needed* to board this train, and the other screamed, *I don't wanna, and you can't make me.*

In the end, the latter voice won. By the time he'd made his decision, Dievs realized he was totally alone on the platform. The ghostly passengers had all boarded the black and yellow Western line. A few stared out at him from behind glass windows, waiting for the show to get on the road. Dievs put the ticket back in his pocket, did one more swivel, then started off towards the ticket sign.

I'mma get me a refund.

(HAPTER TWO

Line-Cutters Get It

A set of stairs plunging down from the train platform led Robert Dievs to a long, plain hallway that stretched out to his left and right for what looked like miles. *Ah- hmm.*

Several signs adorned the wall at the bottom of the staircase, each pointing left or right. The signs seem to be written in multiple languages, and Dievs didn't even recognize all the *English* words written there. At least he thought they were English. What he did recognize was "LOBBY," and "TICKETS," and so he began his long walk leftward.

After five minutes of strolling down the barren hallway, he realized there were no lights, and yet the hallway remained brightly lit. A white glow permeated the long corridor, seemingly from within the walls. He took this in like a tic-tac — just sucked on it for a minute, enjoyed the flavor and kept walking.

Ten minutes later, he came across a few ghost passengers huddled on the ground and leaning against the wall. They looked to be sleeping. Almost like a small homeless encampment — gray black blobs of canvas and despair. Dievs strolled quietly past. They raised no objection. It was another fifteen minutes of walking before he finally reached the exit.

Oh my.

#

IT was a colossal domed room, made almost entirely of white stone. It gleamed and glowed with that same pearly whiteness. Something about it was attractive, he had to admit, but at the same time… *cold*. The floor was vast. Dievs couldn't actually see where the boundaries of the room ended. Huge stone pillars obscured his view, so he couldn't tell if there was a wall behind them or if the room just kept going.

Laid out in front of him was a wide-open plaza of polished marble. Dotting the empty expanse were several kiosks and desks labeled with big, glowing overhead signs reading, "TICKETS," and "HELP." In between these stands milled hundreds of the ghostly travelers Dievs had seen back on the platform, except here, many of the specters weren't as translucent.

Somehow it made him feel a little more comfortable, having other *opaque* people about. *And animals.* Dievs watched as a massive St. Bernard bounded across the floor to go sniffing around a marble pillar. *That's the biggest dog I ever saw. Must weigh 200 pounds. Jeezus.* There was a little tingle in his tailbone, like a feather had brushed lightly across the small of his back. *Weird.*

Dievs felt for the ticket in his pocket. *Still there.* He didn't know what his plan was, but he thought talking to someone would be as good a first step as any. He made his way toward the kiosk labeled "HELP." *Hey, that's me.*

As he moved through the crowds of milling ghostly figures, Dievs noticed just how packed the plaza was. It seemed like people were popping in out of nowhere, just *appearing* in his vision. Almost like eye floaters — there, then gone, then back again. He would blink to find more people had entered the lobby from some unseen doorway. Many of them, however, were also flooding *out* of the plaza through doorways like the one he had entered through. None were labeled. *Different platforms, I suppose.*

There was something else that struck Dievs as strange. *Everyone is ignoring each other.* Small groups, it seemed, stuck together. *Families, partners.* But mostly, everyone moved as if they were completely unaware of the rest of the crowd. A few people gave Dievs quick looks, but only a few. It was like walking through a bowl of drunk, meandering goldfish.

#

WHEN at last Dievs broke out of the crowd and got a clear view of the help desk, his heart sank. There was a line. A line at least two hundred people long. And there was only one man working the desk. A short fellow with a blue cap and uniform. He didn't appear to be in any great hurry.

"God," Dievs said in exasperation.

At that moment, he felt that tingle in his tailbone again, like some unseen hand had used his last vertebrae to ring a little bell. He turned and saw nothing. When he swung back around, he saw that the St. Bernard had found his way through the crowd as well and was sitting in front of him wagging its tail.

"Holy, Moly. Hello big fella. You're a handsome one," he said.

Dievs' voice sounded foreign to his ears. It was a strange feeling, having his outer voice not match the inner. Like talking on a half-second delay. He felt mumbly and rusty.

The dog just looked up at Dievs and panted. His green tag glittered in the glowing white light of the lobby. Dievs reached out and gave him a cursory pat on the head, then looked back up at the line for the help desk. *I wonder how they feel about line-cutting here.*

#

TURNS out they didn't like it much.

The twisty human line that stretched out into the wide plaza and terminated at the small help desk was moving at an absolute snail's pace. Dievs watched the person at the front of the line from his vantage point off to the side and saw that neither the man seeking help, nor the man giving it, seemed to be aware of the horribly long line of people waiting for their turn. *It's like they're talking about the weather.*

Dievs watched this interaction for a few minutes until finally the man at the front nodded thanks and stepped away from the counter, still looking slightly confused. *Welcome to the club, pal.* The next person in line, a tall woman in a blue suit, stepped up to the desk. *Good God, this is going to take a fortnight.* That tingle again. The line jiggled forward slowly, like a massive human caterpillar taking two hundred little steps.

Well. I am in a bit of a hurry. Right? Yeah. **Yes.** *Maybe someone will let me cut. I have uh…* The truth was: Dievs just didn't want to wait. *Who does? Too bad they don't sell fast passes.* He began by going up to the person second in line and asking politely if they minded.

"Excuse me, sir. I wondered if I might step in front of you? I have an urgent obligation; I don't expect my query will take long. Would you mind?"

He used his politest tone. His gentleman's voice.

No answer.

The man stood facing straight forward, still as a statue. He either did not hear Dievs, or was ignoring him. After a moment of expectant waiting, Dievs said, "Well. There's no need to be standoff-ish about it, man. Just say no." Another moment of waiting. *Nothing.* "Okay, then… I bid you adieu, good statue."

Dievs had a similar experience with the next ten people in line. It seemed they could not, or *would not,* hear him. He gave up after his eleventh failure, letting his hands fall in exasperation. And then, he spied her: an old woman, maybe twenty-five people back in line, standing stone still, with her eyes closed. *No… don't do it.* Dievs looked up at the sprawling line. *I'm gonna do it.* And he did. Dievs snuck quietly back to where the old woman was standing in line and stepped lightly in front of her. *Perfect.*

Except maybe it wasn't so perfect, because a few moments after he stepped into line, a moan gurgled up from behind him. A throaty sound, like someone being strangled while mic'd up. Dievs spun to see that the old woman had not only opened her eyes, but was glaring right at him, her mouth open so wide he could see her molars. One had a black spot.

Tears were streaming from her squinted brown eyes and rolling down her lined face. Her head looked too big for her body, like a melon on a loosely skinned broomstick.

Then Dievs realized *everyone* was looking at him. The ghostly bustle of the lobby had ceased. The only sound was the old woman's horrible, ragged cry. All eyes were fixed on him. The people in front of him in line had turned back to look as well. Even the help desk attendant was staring.

"I'll um... I'll just..." Dievs stepped out of line.

The old woman followed him with her beady brown eyes as he stepped out. The quiet remained for a few moments, and then everyone... *resumed*. Dievs stood in silence, looking around at the station and all the ghost people who apparently had *quite* the issue with line-cutters.

Ah- hmm.

CHAPTER THREE

Help Desk

HE couldn't say how long he waited in line. It felt like days, though it couldn't have been more than a few hours. Time was acting a little funny here. At least it felt that way to Robert Dievs.

It had taken waiting in line, doing nothing but staring at the back of a bald head, to notice it. But when he'd gotten within twenty spots of the help desk, time slowed to a withering crawl. He could almost hear the seconds ticking by on some invisible clock. *Tick. Tock… Tick……
Tock………Tick……………Tock…*

But he waited just like everyone else — *quietly, obediently* — and finally, he found himself one person away from the help desk. The bliss of stepping forward to speak with the attendant was extraordinary. He cleared his throat and was about to speak when the attendant turned away and reached under the desk. The man in the blue uniform brought out a little triangular paper sign, like one you might see at Cracker Barrel.

It read:

#

OUT TO LUNCH

#

Dievs gaped at the attendant, who seemed not to recognize the brutality of what he'd just done. He was even smiling a little as he gathered some papers from under his little desk. *Like he's taking muffins out of the oven. Oh, no. No, no, no…*

Dievs looked behind him and saw the line was not only still there, but *longer* than when he'd initially queued. None of them were paying any attention to the man at the desk.

"Hey, man. There's a heck of a long line here. Someone else coming to take over?"

Dievs felt that foreignness in his own voice again. *Strange.* The attendant didn't even look up; he just continued packing and organizing his desk.

"Hey… Excuse me. *Sir?*"

The attendant did not acknowledge Dievs' presence. He wasn't sure what kind of person he was — *quite literally* — but he had a feeling, one of those gut things, that told him he wasn't a mean one. *But this…*

Dievs reached over the wooden desk and slapped it hard with his hand three times. *BANGBANGBANG.* This got the man in the light blue uniform's attention. He looked up, startled and confused, and squinted at Dievs curiously, like one might inspect a bug they've never seen before. He was young and kinda squirrelly looking. Think discount Steve Buscemi.

"Can I… help you?" he asked hesitantly.

"Yes, man! *Jesus!* You deaf or something?" Dievs' tailbone twitched hard. It made him jump.

"Oh… No need for language, sir. I'm, uh… sorry about your wait. I was about to go to lunch, but…"

"Do you not see this line?" Dievs gestured back to the two hundred plus people waiting patiently behind him.

"Yes, but I…"

"*Yes, but…* And you're just gonna go to lunch?"

The attendant stared blankly. Dievs returned the look, slowly reached over the desk, picked up the little paper sign and casually threw it over his shoulder. The attendant watched it tumble to the floor sadly.

"*No…* But… it's 12:30…"

"No. It's 12. Tell me what the hell is going on, man. Why is everyone all see-through? And also, who am I? I just waited, I don't even know how long, in that goddamn line, and…" Dievs' tailbone did that tingly thing again, but this time it hurt. "…ow."

The attendant gasped and whispered, "You really shouldn't talk like that. Bad karma."

"Huh?"

"Bad karma," the attendant said, as if that explained all.

Dievs looked confused for a moment, then blinked.

"Look, if you can't help me, could you just show me where the exit is? I'll get out of your hair so you can go to lunch. I think I may need the hospital… I *can't*… I can't remember anything."

The attendant leaned in closer and gave Dievs a contemplative look.

"Do you have your ticket, sir?"

"Yes." Dievs dug into his pocket and pulled out the little yellow paper. He handed it to the attendant.

"…Mr. Robert Dievs, is it?"

"That's what it says. I think it's right," said Dievs.

"And you don't, er… remember anything? Like how you got here?" asked the attendant.

"No… I, uh, just woke up on a bench."

The attendant's eyes widened in surprise. "Mr. Dievs, would you just wait a few moments? I'll get a supervisor over here and we'll get you sorted."

Dievs flipped his hands up in an *okay, but I'm still kinda frustrated* gesture. The attendant picked up a blue corded phone from under his desk and dialed. He made nervous, furtive glances at Dievs as he punched in the numbers. He finished his dialing and waited. Dievs could hear the ringtone.

"*Meeeep. Meeeeep. Meeeep. Meeep. Meeeep. Meee- mewo?*"

"Um, Charlie?" said the attendant quietly.

"*Mawomp pu wah.*"

"Hey, uhehm…" he coughed. Whispering now, "Yeah, we've got a straggler out in the lobby. I think I'm gonna need a supervisor."

Dievs could hear all this.

"Hey, man. I'm literally right here. A straggler?"

The attendant just smiled at Dievs and listened intently to the voice on the other end of the phone.

"*MMAWaoop ie womp? A maguwa?*"

"That's right, sir," said the attendant. The phone went silent.

The attendant gave Dievs another big, nervous smile. Two minutes later, a short, portly man in a blue uniform came waddling hurriedly across the lobby towards the help desk. *Wonderful.*

\#

THE two men in light blue mechanic-style coveralls stood together with their backs to Dievs, hunched over his ticket. They spoke in low tones and shot uneasy glances over at Dievs, who stood, more calmly now, leaning on the poly-board desk. He saw a smudge on the countertop, licked his thumb and rubbed at it. He could hear the heavy huffing of the portly supervisor, out of breath from his breakneck waddle across the lobby floor. After a minute-long huddle, the attendants turned to face him.

"Well. Mr Dievs. I've been told you're a little… lost?"

"Well, not exactly *lost*, but kinda…"

"You'd like to know what's going on here though, right?"

"That'd be great. And maybe… I dunno, the nearest hospital?" Then, more to himself, "I probably should have just gone straight there… don't know what I'm doing *here*."

The portly attendant had taken the lead, and the squirrelly one stood behind him, smiling.

"Well… you do seem a little out of sorts. I don't blame you. This is the *help desk*, after all. We're here to help."

"Then help," said Dievs.

"Mr. Dievs, please don't be alarmed… but you've died."

\#

THEY stood looking at each other in silence for a few moments. The general hum of the station seemed to grow in Dievs' ears. He looked away from the attendant and up at the high marble ceiling.

"Mmm. Oh, yeah," said Dievs. He sounded like someone who'd just seen a pink car on the road. Like, *oh, say, would you look at that.* Suddenly, the white glow emanating from the walls got a little brighter. The ghost people milling about in the lobby seemed less like ghosts, and more like just… energy. "I guess that, uh… makes sense."

"Ah, so you remember how you got here then?" asked the attendant.

"No, no. Just… makes sense. I guess."

"Well… I can pull up your file, Mr. Dievs, if you'd like… Give you a little, erm, *closure?*"

Dievs looked plaintive. A little sad, and a little curious. He pursed his lips and nodded. The portly attendant turned to the big beige cube of a Dell computer sitting behind the desk and began clacking away on the keyboard. After a moment, he shook his head and smiled anxiously at Dievs.

"…ah, what a piece of… Sorry. Old computer. I hate Dell. They keep telling us we'll get i-Pads next quarter. I'll believe it when I see it." Dievs blinked at the attendant. "Oh, *right.* Little before your time. Never mind."

Discount Steve Buscemi coughed nervously. The portly attendant shrugged and continued clacking away at the keyboard.

"Here we are. Dievs, Robert. Okay, umm-mu-mu-mu… 48, from, *Waco?* Sound right?"

Dievs did not know if it sounded right.

"May…*be?*" he said.

"This is all just information we collect at ticket issuance, for a personalized experience, you know. It looks like… looks like you were, uh… murdered. with a, uh… a spoon."

The attendant looked up at Dievs blankly. They stared at one another. Dievs nodded his head slowly.

"A spoon." he said.

"That's right… oh, no… wait… No. *No.* My bad. Wrong file."

"What kind of…" Dievs said, shaking his head.

"Here you are… umm… says you chose not to disclose the manner of your death."

"Chose not to… What kind of help…" Dievs shook his head, as if to shake off disbelief. "*Okay, well…* Is there *anything* else?"

"Um…"

The second attendant broke in.

"Says you used to be a good bowler." The squirrelly man looked up at Dievs like this was going to make all the difference.

"It says I was a good bowler, but not how I died. *Alrighty.* Or how long ago? Or where it happened? Exactly what kind of operation you fellas runnin' here?"

The portly man answered, not unkindly, "Time doesn't really matter all that much here, as you might imagine… Also, this information is only what *you volunteered* at tickets when you arrived."

"You're telling me *I* said this?" Dievs asked, incredulous. The attendants nodded. "Why can't I remember it then?" The attendants both shrugged. Dievs sighed and lowered his head in exasperation. "So… what is this? Like heaven, or…"

"We don't like the binary conception of Heaven and Hell. We tend to think of it more as a *continuum.* This is just… *a starting point. A way station.*"

"Good band name," said the squirrelly attendant.

"What?" asked the portly attendant.

"Way station," the squirrelly attendant reiterated.

Dievs took a few seconds in silence to soak it all up. It settled into his brain pretty easily. He felt a little punch-drunk, even though he knew he ought to be… *what, angry? No.* He looked back at the attendants.

"So, where is my ticket for?"

"Well, that's more of a personal discovery kind of thing… we don't really have that information. However, you do have a yellow ticket… *ahem…*"

"Hey, why'd you cough like that? What does a yellow ticket mean? Is it bad? Was I bad? Am I going… *down there?*" Dievs pointed at the floor quickly. The attendant didn't stop to listen to Dievs' breakdown.

"I can tell you, you'll be on the W-line, though what stop…" The portly attendant shrugged, then glanced around and leaned over to Dievs, whispering, *"Don't eat the peanuts."*

Dievs just shook his head in bafflement.

"Okay, what is *up* with the peanut thing?" He got no reply. "And what if I don't wanna ride?"

The attendants looked perplexed by this hypothetical.

"Well… I don't see why you wouldn't, sir. It's… This is… this is the afterlife. This is *it*. There's no reason not to board," said the squirrelly attendant.

"I understand it might be a little scary at first, but I assure you it's perfectly natural…" said the portly man.

"No other options?" interrupted Dievs.

The attendants looked at each other, then back at Dievs. "Well. There is an exit," said the portly attendant.

"To…"

"No one ever uses it."

"Where?" asked Dievs and the squirrelly attendant at the same time. They looked at each other in a brief moment of shared curiosity. The portly attendant just raised his arm and pointed.

Sure enough, just across the lobby, against a huge blank wall of white marble, was a clearly labeled exit door, just like you might find in a school gymnasium, glowing red sign and all. It couldn't have looked more out of place against the massive slab of white wall.

"Huh," said Dievs and the squirrelly attendant in unison.

"How did I not see that?" said Dievs. He turned back to look at the attendants. "Well. Thank… you. For all your *help*. I guess," already beginning to slide slowly away from the desk. "S'pose I'll be going then."

"Hey, before you go, would you fill out my service quality questionnaire?" asked the squirrelly attendant.

The portly man turned around to look at him, indignant. "You didn't even do anything, Kevin, except call me."

"Well… I mean, c'mon, it was a team effort," replied Kevin.

"Okay, thank you. Have a… um, good day."

Dievs slipped away from the attendants while they bickered about the survey and made his way to the exit door. He heard Kevin behind him.

"Hey… my out to lunch sign."

All Dievs could think was, *who was the poor bastard that was murdered with a spoon?* He had to push through a few clumps of ghost passengers to reach the big blank wall, and then he was there. It seemed too simple. Too easy. *Hey, maybe it's one of those times where it's just as easy as it looks. And it's easy because it ought to be easy, and there's no hidden catch or evil twist later on in the story. Maybe it's one of those times.*

Then Dievs pushed the metal bar on the right side of the double doors and walked through.

#

THE attendants watched Dievs disappear through the double exit doors on the opposite side of the lobby. The portly one shook his head as the door swung shut.

"Poor bastard."

"I thought he was kind of cool," said Kevin.

The portly attendant turned to Kevin and shook his head.

"Yeah? Why don't you follow him out the exit then, huh?" he asked.

"And give up these benefits? Heck no. Full dental, 401k, vision… *no way*. Best job I ever had," said Kevin.

"More like *only* job you ever had…"

"Hey, you know I'm sensitive about that. Not my fault they forgot to lock the tiger cage… the zoo is a rough first job."

"Yeah, yeah, boo-hoo… you know, I never understood

the stragglers. I mean, what? *Best case scenario*, the exit leads back to where he came from. Why would he, *why would anyone,* want to go back there? He was murdered with *a spoon*. Oh, wait… no… different guy… Still, I dunno… It's like asking to repeat high school or something," said the portly man, more to himself than to Kevin. He shook his head in wonder.

They stood together in silence, staring at the exit doors.

"Hey… um, excuse me? I think… I… I may have… had an accident," the next man in line said.

The attendants both looked at him and blinked.

PART TWO:

Workin' Man

CHAPTER FOUR

Quite Hankly (Part 1)

HANK sat up in his single bed and wiped his eyes. *Too much vodka, not enough peanuts.* The mattress groaned with the sound of dead and dying springs. In the stagnant heat of the small hotel room-turned-apartment, it sounded particularly sad. *Claustrophobic.* The air was muggy and stale, smelling faintly of B.O. On the small bedside stool, a Sears radio alarm clock blasted into life. Hank didn't even glance over.

"Goood morning, folkss! Big Chaz here on KAMP 90.9 — Jazzy Chazzy baby — beaming straight into your brain-veins out of *B-E-A-utiful Cam-pai-yo-tay*, Texas. Today we're blasting that number one summer hit I'm sure all your friends have been listening to… it's the Eye of the Tiger by those Survivors. Hey Jim, ever wonder what they survived?"

"Hey, hey, Chaz, how about these freakin' gas prices, eh? They're killin' me, no kidding, no joke. Freakin' buck twenty a gallon."

"Hot dog, you're sure right about that, Jimmy. Spin it, baby."

Now playing, Eye of the Tiger.

Hank sat in his bed, head down, rubbing his throbbing temples. About halfway through the song, he reached over and gently pressed the black plastic stop button, attempting to cut Jimi Jamison off mid-verse. The alarm, however, did not stop, and The Eye of the Tiger continued unimpeded. Three times, Hank pressed the button before accepting it was broken. He sighed. *7:15.*

He rose slowly from his single bed, feeling a little like he might vomit, and shuffled over to the kitchenette in the corner of the chubby, L-shaped studio. Kettle on. The metal plate at the bottom was rusty from years of remaining half full. Three scoops instant coffee in the stained plastic Texaco travel mug. The insta-Folgers looked like fertilizer. Water in. *Smells like dirt and metal shavings.*

Hank turned and leaned against the plain particleboard countertop, surveying his kingdom, as his daily custom demanded. The apartment comprised a bed, a nightstand, a loveseat (though it had only ever had one occupant), a small T.V. and several large cardboard boxes, crammed in the corner. The bathroom was little more than a closet: a standing shower and a toilet. Hank went to take a sip of his coffee and burned his lip.

"SHHffuuu… sufferin' succotash… Fuck me."

The Eye of the Tiger came to its conclusion, and the voice of Jazzy Chazzy returned to fill the void.

"Welcome back friendlies, that was Eye of the Tiger, by Survivor — topping the charts all summer. Next we've got Come on Eileen, from a band out of Birmingham going by the name Dexy and the Midnight Runners. I like this one, Jim. Whaddya think?"

"Never trust the British — song ain't too bad though."

"Cheerio, spin it."

Now playing Come on Eileen.

Hank's eyes fluttered closed, and he began to wilt, still standing against his kitchenette counter in the wrinkled black boxers he'd slept in. Just as his coffee started to spill out of his drooping hand, the ring of the telephone cut through his brain like a frosty knife. He jolted awake, sloshing his coffee and spilling half of it on his bare feet. *Hot.*

"Son of a…"

Hank swallowed the pain and turned his attention to the ringing in the corner. He hated that phone. Hated the way it sounded. What it meant. It sat in the corner of the room, emanating a black force. *E-ville. The hotline of death, baby.*

Hundreds of little yellow post-it notes containing long disconnected phone numbers, hastily scribbled addresses and directions littered the little wooden stand that the phone sat on. It rang again, vibrating so violently that it shifted on the table. It looked like some kind of Japanese *O-fuda* shrine, designed to seal some cruel electro-god in an eternal prison of yellow plastic. *Bound and trapped in BIC-branded sticky notes.*

"BBRRIIINNNGG…"

Hank looked down into his half-empty coffee morosely, then over at the yellow phone in the corner.

"BRRBRINNNGGG…"

He sighed and set his cup down on the counter, stepping gingerly over the steaming puddle of coffee on the floor.

"BRRINGGNNGGGNNGG..."

"Alright, alright, I'm comin'... fuckin' bastard..." Hank walked over to the phone stand.

"BRRII-"

"Hank Cooper, Lone Star CSC."

"Howdy, Hank."

He knew that voice. He wished he didn't. A chill ran down his back like a clammy little salamander. He froze for a moment, then spoke.

"...Jenine... I wasn't expecting a call."

"I wasn't expecting to make a call, but you know, sometimes shit happens... As they say. I'm in need of your... discreet services."

"I don't work for..."

"Oooh, I think ya do, *son*. Otherwise, it's gonna be big problems... *Big. Problems. Hank.* And you — *no, we* — don't want that, eh? *Listen,* do a good job, just like last time, and the time before that..." The woman on the other end of the phone let out a curt, gross cackle. "Easy-peasy, my Hanky-panky, and we won't have any issues. I don't know why you try n' fight all this. You're like the Mr. Miyagi of this shit, could make a fortune. Just... *just...* help me out — *help Mr. B out* — eh? He said there'll be a big bonus in it for ya."

Hank stopped and glanced around his apartment. The peanut shells on the floor seemed to whisper to one another like spectators of the world's worst one-man play. The radio was still playing music, but the signal was fading in and out. Hank let the buzz of silence hang in the air for another few seconds, then closed his eyes.

"What's the address? And how many?"

Now playing Theme from Ghostbusters.

CHAPTER FIVE

Quite Hankly (Part 2)

HANK found himself wishing he had something to look forward to. Anything.

At the moment, only unpleasantness lay ahead of him. *At least I have vodka. That, at least, I have.* The last day he could remember being actually excited was the premiere of the second Star Wars movie. But even in a life full of nasty biz days, today was going to be one of those *really, freakin, no-joke-Chazz, nasty biz* days. *Nasty biz. It's that god-damn telephone. It's that phone's fault.* As it had been many times before.

Instant coffee drained. What hadn't spilled on the floor, anyway. Breakfast served. A large helping of unshelled peanuts, and a bowl of cornflakes with warm whole milk. The peanuts were kind of driving Hank mad, but some small part of him just couldn't let them go to waste.

The boxes had arrived on his doorstep almost a month ago. Four nondescript, plain ol' shipping boxes. And stranger still, they'd had no labels. Absolutely nothing detailing the contents of the box. Which turned out to be peanuts.

Hank had given it a few days. Even gone so far as to put them out on the main catwalk of the third floor of his little hotel community (a generous description of the Texas Inn). Eventually he'd gone to his landlord, a man named Won Park. Won hadn't even entertained a conversation.

"Don care," Won had said without even looking up from his desk in the back room of the hotel lobby.

"But I…"

"Don care, Hank. Rent due on 1st. Unless is problem with rent, don care."

Hank had left it at that. In the end, he'd opened one box just to satiate his curiosity about what might be inside. *Just… full of peanuts. Must be thirty pounds of unshelled… peanuts…* From that realization, there hadn't been much to do except eat them. Or not. Hank did. The first one he'd eaten hesitantly. Now, a month later, peanut shells littered Hank's floor like bodies on a battlefield.

Dusting off the bottoms of his feet, Hank slid on some plain black socks and a heavily stained white T-shirt. The shirt bore a logo on the front right breast: the star of Texas, bound by a circle, with the words "Lone Star Crime Scene Cleanup" ringing the outside of the icon.

"…Oh, I keep my nose to the grindstone, mmhmm, drink a little beer…"

Hank hummed under his breath as he found his way into his old steel-toed boots, wormed into a light canvas jacket (also stained and branded), fished his keys out of the pocket of the pants he"d worn the day before and grabbed his black plastic sunglasses off the floor by the bed.

"N'sing a little of these workin' man blues…"

#

THE sky burned blue and stretched wide, like some great upturned breakfast bowl. The heat hit Hank like bog water. Hot and sticky. Though the rush of semi-truck traffic flowing by — Hank's very own blacktop diesel river — provided some breeze, it was a hot kind. He was used to it, but oppressive is oppressive, and a little of Hank's already nonexistent enthusiasm for the day left him.

He took a moment to survey the state of his home: a hotel overlooking Interstate 35 East, just outside of the city of Waxahachie, Texas. The white sign, turned brown by dust and time, read THE TEXAS INN in faded red lettering.

Still beige. Hank was the hotel's only permanent resident, aside from Won, the landlord, his wife, Kim and the lady next to Hank in room 334. *What was her name again?* Hank had never asked for it, but preferred to think he'd just forgotten. He'd met his neighbor briefly on several occasions, but had gone no further towards conversation than a polite nod. What he *did* know about her was that she smelled strongly of weed and chemicals. Sometimes the scent was potent enough to seep in through Hank's wall and turn his sweaty apartment into what felt like a Jamaican sock. *Just Vodka for me, thanks.* Aside from the few permanent residents of the Texas Inn, the Renaissance fair two miles down the road from the Texas Inn brought a cast of regulars during its months of operation. Which happened to be now.

An overweight man wearing yellow boxers that might have once been white, a wife-beater and fuzzy, white bunny slippers was leaning against the walkway's metal railing smoking a cigarette. Five long, tangled dreadlocks hung down over his neck like turds. He looked like he smelled positively fresh. His clown makeup had smeared badly from a night of drunken sleep and the morning's sweat. He looked at Hank with lizard eyes. Hank looked right back, digging into his pocket for a crumpled pack of Hillsborough cigarettes.

"Mornin'," said Hank.

The man nodded and took a drag of his own cigarette. Hank lit one for himself. Together they watched the morning traffic roll by and listened to the never ending scream of rubber on road.

#

A beaten old bulletin board at the Texas Inn reception displayed an ad for a lost puppy. *Looks like a rabid skunk.* It'd been there for several months. Hank had made a habit of checking the board, even though he really had no reason to. *Sometimes the motions are enough.* Today he only glanced at the board. A few new notices had been tacked up crookedly: *Judo classes. Lost cat. Garage sale. Scorpion bourbon tasting. Weed. Babysitting, 7.50 an hour.*

He continued on towards the bright orange Power Wagon in the parking lot. *My baby.* In the back were several blue barrels and locked metal chests full of cleaning equipment: a consolidation of a decade's worth of specialty supplies.

Won Park, the owner of the Texas Inn, knew what Hank did for a living. He didn't much care. Nor did anyone, really. Hank provided year-round income for the Parks (Won and Kim), so not too many questions ever got asked. *Or any questions, really.* Although he had gotten the occasional complaint from Won about digging holes in the barren field behind the Inn, a space Won insisted would be occupied by an expansion in the near future. It wouldn't.

Hank made his way across the small lot to his Power Wagon, unlocked the door and slid in. The ignition was loose, and the key jiggled into its slot like a fish into an oven mitt. But that engine purred, baby. *Never fun to be pulled over by the police and have to explain why you have a bunch of dead bodies in the back of your truck.* Even if they were *supposed* to be there.

Reverse. Hank didn't even need to turn to get on the highway; he just drove straight to the on-ramp. *Perk of living in a roadside hotel.*

CHAPTER SIX

Beethoven

A woman, two men and a St. Bernard. Christ.

It was the St. Bernard that worried him. *Big dog. BIG dog. What kind of shitshow…* But he didn't really want to know. He'd stopped wanting to know after the first time he'd done this. He shivered at the memory of that experience, even after all this time. The old woman's shrunken face and peeled-back eyes. It tickled the back of his throat.

Hank was going south on I-35 (15 over 70) when he realized he was out of cigarettes. He knew 'cause he'd started biting his fingernails while thinking instead of smoking. A quick grab at the crumpled pack in his pocket confirmed his fear. He veered across the two right-most lanes to a Texaco just off the highway. *Handicap spot. Park. E-brake.*

He could already see heat lines shimmering over the concrete of the Texaco lot and on the highway, which stretched out to either side of him like some earthly, black fruit roll-up. A little bell rang as Hank pushed through the caged glass door. The sound made him think of sunflower seeds. He went straight to the counter, though it took the single on-duty cashier a good minute to put down her magazine and shuffle lazily over to the register. A short, stout middle-aged woman, dressed in a stained black Texaco shirt and positively radiating cigarette fumes. *I'll have what you're having, lady*, Hank thought. Her name tag read "Barbara."

"Hillsboroughs, please."

"Black, Red, er Menthol?"

She sounds like she swallowed a piece of sandpaper covered in snot.

"Red. Always."

The cashier did not reply to Hank's declaration of character, as expressed through his affiliation with an Antiguan tobacco brand and its red and white packaging. She tossed the pack onto the counter and punched a couple buttons on her register. The little rotating fan in the corner of the plexiglass booth whined like a sad robot.

"52 cents, baby," rasped Barbara.

Voice of an angel.

Hank pulled his brown leather wallet out of his pocket and fished down in the bill section for any change. He found two quarters and one penny. The *take a penny* dish sitting on the counter was empty except for a piece of hair and a paper clip. Hank looked pleadingly up at the cashier, holding his fifty-one cents. Her eyes showed no mercy.

He had to break a five.

#

THE day was hot and still, like an old, congealing bucket of rainwater and algae. The three cigarettes he'd smoked between his stop at the Texaco and the big white ranch house had made his throat sticky and raw. He hadn't had the bandwidth to think of buying something to drink either, and so found himself slurping at the spitty dregs of an old sixteen-ounce bottle of Coke he'd found under his seat. *Warm and flat. Just the way I like it.*

Hank sipped his Coke and looked out the windshield at the job waiting for him. If what Jenine had said was true, this was going to take him all day. *Maybe two.* Without even entering the house, Hank saw some bad signs. The screen door was off its hinges and leaning haphazardly against the outside wall. There was a big hole in it as well. *Maybe a foot… or a shotgun blast.*

Above the house, the twirling black tower he'd seen all the way from the exit, circled in a column several hundred feet tall. *Vultures* — at least ten of them. Big, black, bomber silhouettes. Shadows in flight. Hank peered up at the birds from the driver's seat. *Hello, comrades. Wish I could just take the roof off of this place and let you do my job.*

Aside from the broken-down door and the circling vultures — like some gnarly omen out of a Stephen King novel — the ranch house still had a decidedly uninviting vibe. The windows of the house were dark. Black, actually, against the bright sunshine of the day and the gleaming white siding. *They look mean.* As if they warned of something inside that was best left alone. *Or burned. God, I wish I could just burn it.*

Not today, though. Mr. B needs this place, so no arson. Why am I taking a job from this lunatic anyway? I said never again. Never again. But here I fuckin' am. Somewhere down at the bottom of

Hank's brain stem, Mr. B's voice whispered, *because you're a coward, Hank.*

Oh, shut it. Hank killed his soda and shoved open the driver's side door.

#

HE looked like a pro gardener turned astronaut.

Hank wore a full-body hazmat suit of white Tyvec, a face mask, black rubber boots and yellow dish gloves. He squeaked like a dog toy as he walked up the sagging front porch steps. They creaked out a reply like a set piece in some cliché western. Framed against the bright doorway of the ranch house, Hank made a terrifying silhouette. *The man in white cometh.*

He carried nothing in his hands. The first part usually required both free. Outside, Hank had prepped a work area, a large blue tarp and several blue fifty-gallon drums, half-full of sulfuric acid. The smell coming from inside the house wasn't too bad. Not yet. But it had that *meatiness* Hank had come to know and dread. The smell that signaled the beginnings of rot and decay.

Stepping inside, it took Hank's eyes a moment to adjust to the dim lighting. The first thing he saw was a trail of blood running through the main sitting room and trailing into the open door of the first-floor bath. It was crusting from the heat and dry air. The deep redness reminded Hank of the color of overripe cherries. Almost purple.

He walked slowly beside the trail of blood and followed it into the bathroom.

#

SHE was sitting on a low stool with her back against the wall, facing the vanity cabinet above the sink. Though the trail of blood leading into the small bathroom was minimal, the scene inside made up for it. Red smears covered everything but the ceiling.

She'd left the light on, and in the fluorescence, Hank could see clearly enough of what had happened. The woman, wearing a shredded blue suit, had been shot in the stomach. *With a shotgun, by the looks of it.*

But it was evident that she'd had some time between being shot and actually biting it. Enough time to convince herself that maybe she could sew up all those little holes and be alright after all. It looked to Hank like she'd lost consciousness in the middle of a stitch. *Valiant effort, lady.* He stood in the doorway, just looking. It took him a moment to notice that on the floor next to the woman was a blood-covered shotgun. He wondered if she'd had time to use it. *Probably.*

Hank turned from the grizzly scene in the bathroom, squeaking in his Wellies. *Business-lady, check. Two men… and a dog…* He followed the trail of blood away from the bathroom. It wound around the central loop of the house, through the kitchen and up the old wooden staircase. *Two men and a dog. Two men and…* Hank could hear faintly, even through the fabric of his hazmat suit, the sound of buzzing flies. *Someone left the window open.*

He made his way up the stairs, being careful to avoid spreading the blood on the steps anymore than it already was. Once at the top, he faced two doors. One was closed, and the other ajar. A bloody handprint stained the right door. *Blue-suit lady, maybe?* He turned and nudged open the door with the handprint with his boot.

Inside he found a man lying flat on his stomach at the foot of a crisply made bed. He had also been shot, Hank judged, by the stagnant pool of blood underneath his stomach. He couldn't help but try to put together the scene in his mind, though he didn't want to. *Blue-suit lady shot this guy? He must've gotten one off at her before he went down though. Still another guy… and a dog…*

The man here looked much more peaceful than the lady downstairs, though still not exactly ready for a Sunday drive. He was lying flat on his face, one hand stuck under his chest, and the other down by his side. He might've been sleeping, or maybe getting ready for a deep tissue massage, if not for the odd position and the black-red circle underneath him. Still, it was pretty clean, all things considered. *Almost like he fell on a gun.* Hank decided he'd wait to flip this one over and see how accurate his assessment was. He took another quick look around, then turned to venture into the neighboring room.

What he found there was considerably more gruesome. *This was no gunfight. Man vs… good boy.* Somehow, the last member of this triple — *no, quadruple* — homicide had come to be trapped in the upstairs bedroom with a St. Bernard. *250 pounds of St. Bernard, at least.* The dog was massive, lying on its side on the king-sized bed. *That's the biggest dog I've ever seen.* And Hank had seen some pretty big dogs (that's not… innuendo, by the way). *What kind of loony keeps a St. Bernard in this kind of heat? Texas? In August? Jeebus Crisco.*

The man must've lost his gun somewhere in the struggle, because the evidence of their fight was all over the room. It hadn't been a quick thing. It was like a meat tornado had spun through the bedroom, or else someone had let their tomato-and-beet smoothie get a little out of hand. Hank stood in the doorway and sighed. *Fuuuck.* A flash of green metal caught his eye, and he moved closer to the bed. *The collar tag. Beethoven.*

Then a hand came down on his shoulder, and Hank screamed like a little girl.

CHAPTER SEVEN

Workin' Man Blues

FEAR spun Hank around like a top. He slung the hand off his shoulder and jumped away. In his Tyvec suit, face mask and gloves, he looked like some strange dancing alien.

"Hey… R' you… who are… I thought… I… I was just… talking to someone in a suit. But his was different… Train? Say… where am I?" The man looked around, confused, like a child waking from a nap.

Hank stood in shocked stillness. He'd put his arms up in a mock karate pose, but his mouth hung open. It was the man from the other room. The one who'd looked like he'd fallen on a gun. Hank could see the hole in his chest clearly now. A deep bowl of exposed tissue and bone, with what looked like his heart, pulsing in sluggish rhythm. The man seemed not to notice his wound. Not one bit. He looked around the bedroom and its fresh coat of red paint.

"Jeezuss… That's terrible there. Who's gonna clean all that up?" asked the man, casual as someone talking about taking out the trash. A dribble of thick blood pulsed out of his chest. "Hey… yeah. Yeah! I remember this place. Mr. B sent me and… Johnny… to… to… and then that woman…"

The man's eyes widened. He looked down at his gored chest and gasped. He started hyperventilating and let out little moaning sounds.

"Oh, shit… oh, *fuck*… Hey man, I… I… I… this is… you gotta get me to the hospital. Am I gonna die? I'm gonna die! I *was* dead!"

The man was yelling now, and though there was no one for miles around to hear, it made Hank uneasy. He was used to working in silence. Hank himself was still in shock, but he gathered himself enough to spit out a few words of comfort to calm Mr. Chest Wound. Or something like that.

"Hey… um, just… be… calm. Just *chillll*, alright. I'll, um. I'll… get someone to…"

"Hey! I… I… I know you! You're the fuckin' cleaner! The goddamn cleaner! I was dead! Oh, Christ- oh, *God*!"

This was the last straw. He wheeled and walked over to the top of the staircase. It was only then that Hank realized the man was holding a pistol in his right hand. Even in shock, he had enough time to think: *Oh, please don't shoot me. Hank Cooper, 1953-1982: killed by a dead man.* It was more apt than he wanted to admit. The man stopped at the top of the staircase, looked down, swayed, then turned back to Hank.

"Hey… don't you come following me. Hmm?" He sounded drunk now. Or sleepy.

The man hoisted his gun up with one arm. Hank raised his hands in innocence. As they eyed each other for that brief moment, Hank thought he saw the instant the man died. A flicker, like the last bits of battery in an old flashlight being used up. The man's eyes sparkled. He fell forward, pistol and all, and flopped down the old wooden stairs. The sound was awful. Like a bag of puppies being thrown down… *well… being thrown down a flight of stairs.*

#

HANK stood still for a few seconds after watching the man fall out of sight. His brain was having trouble processing what he'd just seen. It was coming. Slowly. At the moment, all he could think was, *at least now I don't have to drag him down the stairs myself.* It wasn't the way Hank had always thought, but as Jenine had wisely observed, *shit happens.*

It sure does, Jenine.

Hank had thought he might be a comic book artist as a child. Or a teacher. *Then one day you wake up and you don't recognize any of it.* That was how he'd felt staring into the eyes of the man as he'd died. Just like he'd said: *Say, Jack. Where am I?*

But a golden beam of sunshine coming through the open window of the upstairs bedroom interrupted this thought. It bounced off Beethoven's tag briefly, casting a green strip of light across the red-speckled wall. *Day is going. Still a job to be done.*

Hank got on with it. Just like he always did.

#

FIRST came the man at the bottom of the stairs.

It was the heavy lifting that usually made him wish he'd hired some help. *My lower back would thank me.* There was Cody, but Hank hated calling him. And he couldn't bring himself to ask anyone else to share in the horrors of this job. *No, better it's just me.* He'd made it this far alone.

A few thuds and thumps later he got the man out the front door, down the front steps of the porch and onto the blue tarp. Hank stood back and took a breather. The man looked like a strange Picasso painting there, red on blue, sprawled, like a jumbled-up stick man. He laid him out as he'd found him, real peaceful-like. *He won't be getting up again. Probably?*

Woman in the blue suit next. She was considerably lighter. He followed the red trail she'd made through the living room and had her out on the tarp in no time. *Blue on blue. Well, a little red.*

He stood once again over the bed that was Beethoven's final resting place. The dog was in good shape aside from the bullet wound that must've taken out his heart. Hank didn't like dogs, or cats for that matter, but he had to admit, Beethoven was a pretty noble-looking animal. *You didn't deserve this, big buddy.* Hank often found himself more distraught at the sight of a wounded or dead animal than at humans. And he'd encountered a wide variety of both.

First, he tried to lift the dog up by its back legs. It didn't take long to realize how futile that effort was going to be. He glanced back at the hallway and the flight of stairs. Under his face mask, sweat was pouring down into eyes. The sun was in full bloom now, and the Texas heat was no joke. Especially in a Tyvec onesie.

Hank turned and looked at the open window, then down at Beethoven. He grimaced.

#

IF anyone had been passing by the Werner ranch house on Sunday morning, August 12th, perhaps taking a nice slow stroll through the brush, they would've had the unfortunate pleasure of watching 250 pounds of St. Bernard fall from a second-story window. And shortly afterwards, a similarly sized man.

Hank wondered what he would've done if there hadn't been a window, one big enough to squeeze the bodies through. *Would've had to call Cody.*

The second man had been on the floor on the other side of the big king bed, hidden from view. Beethoven had inflicted a gruesome series of wounds before this poor sap had fired his shot. A short, stalky man, with a buzzed head and fat arms. One of which was barely attached. After his tumble out the window, it wasn't.

Pockets of red in the arrangement of a dog's jaw pimpled his clothes. *Thigh, arms, crotch.* The wound on his neck was the one that had killed him, though. The big St. Bernard must have gotten a good sink on the man's gullet, and that was that. *Game over. No do-overs. Thanks for playing.* That, and one shotgun shell had been enough to put them both out of commish.

Once Hank had pushed the dog out the window, he thought he might as well save himself the time and hassle and just push the man out the same way.

It's just a… garbage chute. Yep. That's all. An open-air garbage chute.

#

OF course, this entire ordeal was not the norm for Hank Cooper. It was a sight *looser* than the average day's work. Though, *a normal day's work* can vary quite a bit in the business of crime scene cleanup. This was a *Mr. B* job. A *James Brackington* Job. *Illegal*, in other words. A call from James Brackington's assistant, Jenine, meant these people had no one coming to look for them. No family. No friends. No *inquirers*. And so, everything had to go. All trace.

It happened that Hank was very good at this particular thing, putting aside the fact he'd just pushed a St. Bernard out a second-story window. That skill-set was what had brought Brackington to Hank in the first place, though it had taken a fair amount of bullying — *and enticing* — to get Hank to engage in this illegal partnership. In the end though, he had. *And apparently, I still do.* Thinking back on those first jobs, he had had little choice. At least, that's what he told himself.

James Brackington was a killer. Hank Cooper was a coward.

#

HANK spent the next several hours managing mass. Managing mass into fifty-gallon drums halfway filled with sulfuric acid. Beethoven was the most troublesome.

Hank did the thing he so often did when it came to this job of his. He left himself, and let his body take over. Like a really terrible carnival ride. Some people might call it dissociation. Or just *work*. But he was thankful that when the end of the day finally came, he would have trouble remembering the details. Just vague colors and shapes would remain, as well as the ache in his muscles from…*whatever* he'd had to do.

It was an especially valuable tool on days like today. Days when he did things that nobody should have to do. Crime scene cleanup was gruesome enough when it was just hauling bodies to the funeral home. This was different in the worst possible way. But Jenine's words clawed and pecked at the back of his head like a relentless crow. *Big problems… big problems, my Hanky Hanky.* Hank did not doubt there would be. *But what is it that you're scared to lose, Hank?… Nothing. Then why keep doing this to yourself?… I don't know.*

Hank hadn't done much traveling in his life, but he often thought about his trip as a young man to the Caribbean. He'd met a Brit there named Saul, who'd told him a story about a friend he'd had back in Southampton. A friend who'd worked in an industrial slaughterhouse for pigs, and whose sole responsibility had been to drive a pressurized metal rod into their brains. Hundreds of times a day, this man would pull a trigger and take a life. And was paid to do it. *Like pig Hitler. Or at least, a high-ranking Pig-nazi.*

Food for thought.

CHAPTER EIGHT

Chevrolet Steak

IT was late into the night before Hank headed home. *1:25.* The power wagon was groaning down the highway, considerably more laden than it had been going the other direction that morning. That additional weight had been the hard part. *They,* had been the hard part. Cleaning the house was easy as pie, comparatively speaking. *Burn everything you can without taking the whole house down. Bleach the rest.* Someone seeing the smoke was a risk he'd been willing to take, even in the current drought.

Hank was smoking a Hillsborough with the window rolled down as he passed the Texaco he'd stopped into earlier. He took another drag on his Hillsborough and saw briefly that it was the same woman sitting by the register, still reading her magazine. *Long shift, eh? Wanna switch?* Hank chuckled at his own private joke, turned back to the road and clicked the radio on.

"-y out there, this is DJ Millz, on 90.5 KLMS, The Drive. That was Come On Eileen by Dexy's Midnight Runners. Next we've got Eye of the Tiger by…"

Hank turned the radio off.

\#

THE highway was still busy, even at near two in the morning. *These are America's veins. The blood pumping. If it's ever quiet, there's a problem.*

Freight trucks heading across the country to who knows where. Shady cars with shady drivers. Maybe some people coming home from the late shift. Some going in for the later shift. Or early shift, depending on how you look at it. Certainly some cars going to places one might not expect. A serial killer on his way to see his Gam-gam in St. Louis. A Taxi driver going to buy a handgun, then a birthday present for his young daughter. A congressman going to a dank motel to visit a 'friend.' A man with three bodies liquidating in the back of his bright orange Dodge Power Wagon.

The man who'd woken up back at the ranch house was still in one piece. Hank had underestimated the size of Beethoven and run out of barrel-space. It didn't help that Jenine, when asked what size dog to expect, had said, "I don't know, *man*. Medium-sized? Fuckin' dog, just a dog. That's all I know."

Thank you, Jenine. So… pal was still *tout en un* in the back of the power wagon as it chugged along down I-35, all wrapped up in a black bag. *Lawn clippings, officer, just lawn clippings… So many stories on the highway, all passing Barbara in her little Texaco cubicle.*

Hank's cigarette burned his fingers. Hank realized he'd just been staring out at the road, not actually paying attention — a side effect of fourteen hours of brain-frying-gore-clean-up-duty. He flicked the butt of his cig towards the window before he realized it was shut. The smoldering yellow filter came careening back from the dirty glass and into his lap.

"Oh, shit. Ah... God..."

The red cherry rolled down to his crotch, promptly burned a hole through Hank's jeans and left a minor burn down under. He nearly swerved on the road but got it under control before anything catastrophic occurred. He heard the barrels rolling and sloshing in the back of the truck. The thought of one of those drums coming unsealed on the highway made him nauseous. He straightened out the car and, looking in the mirrors, saw no leaks or oozes. *Nice. Real professional.*

Oooooooohhh, who's got a load of bio-waste? This guyyyy, this guyyyy. And gon-na dump it in a tank...

Ooh da-doo-da day.

#

HE was almost back at the Texas Inn when he passed the wreck. A Chevrolet Caprice lay in flaming tatters by the side of the road, burning a deep orange against the black of night, like some strange lantern, guiding automobiles across highway purgatory.

The police had cordoned off half the road, but luckily there wasn't enough traffic to cause a real jam. Even so, Hank had to slow down to pass through the bottleneck. He could see the station wagon lying broken on its side in the grassy median, but before he could get a good view, the smell hit him.

Steak...

As he got closer, the smell intensified. *Smells like a freakin' 4th of July barbecue.* But as he rolled past the wreckage, with dawning horror, Hank realized what he was smelling. It *was* steak. *A lot of steak.* The station wagon had hit a steer. A thousand pounds of bovine colliding with four thousand pounds of Chevrolet at highway speed.

Passing as close as he could to the flaming station wagon, Hank could see what remained of the steer's enormous body, lodged deep in the car, like some hellish, oversized pig in a blanket. The flames obscured much of the interior of the car, but he wondered if some part of that juicy, savory smell wasn't something other than cow. *No. No, thank you. No.* Hank gulped.

The impact had obliterated the driver's seat. Hank saw several firefighters and policemen standing around the wreckage, not doing much. Just watching. He supposed there wasn't much they *could* do. He knew they were all thinking the same thing he was.

Smells good.

The rest of the ride home was uneventful. Hank rolled off the highway and turned towards the Texas Inn. He wanted nothing more than to park and go to bed. *After a drink and some peanuts, of course.* But there was more to do before this day could end. *Finally end.* And this part was always better done under cover of night anyway.

CHAPTER NINE

The Vault

HANK pulled the orange Power Wagon around behind the Texas Inn to a barren field of dead grass and molehills. The field Won Park promised would one day become an expansion of the Texas Inn, though it never would. Hank had been out here more times than he could remember, not that he *wanted* to remember any of them.

This place, almost more than anywhere else, was firmly locked in his brain vault: the secret spot where Hank put memories he never wanted to see or hear again. A nice, cozy nook in his neural stem where he tucked away all those unpleasant experiences, nice and neat, so they couldn't stroll around free in his consciousness causing unwanted mayhem. Hank was logging this experience there now.

In the beginning, when he'd taken his first job from James Brackington, he'd dug holes with a shovel. *Just this once,* he'd told himself. And then, for the second time, *just once more.* By the fifth job, Hank realized he was going to have to come up with a more permanent solution. With Won's begrudging permission, he'd commandeered an underground sewage tank, left abandoned by some previous attempt to build on the land. *Failed Attempt.*

A tank for what? Good question, Jack! For all the things people didn't want to see other places, and that wouldn't go down the drain. *Viscera, body parts, blood, certain **fluids**. Maybe the occasional tangle of hair. And a lot of sulfuric acid.* A place for the by-products of a crime scene cleanup business.

It was an unassuming hatch in the middle of the field with a rusted circular handle, like the door to a submarine. A passerby wouldn't look twice, *but boy, oh boy*, if they did… They'd find it did *not*, in fact, lead to a sewage tank or a water main, but to a private swimming pool for the dead.

Hank turned off the gravel road behind the Texas Inn and veered towards the hatch in the ground. The bumpy earth made the truck sway and waggle like the butt of a Corgi. Hank could hear the blue barrels sloshing in the bed. He pulled forward to bring the truck in line with the hatch entrance. The wheels of the Power Wagon slipped into two deep ruts in the grass, evidence of repeat visits.

Hank popped the shifter into park and cut the engine. The metal click of his door opening rang out into the night. Quiet, save for the faded scream of the highway and the buzz of a single street lamp posted in the corner of the field, a lone fluorescent soldier in the dark. It made Hank look like some kind of moon creature, outlined in soupy halogen light.

Now fully cowering in his brain vault, Hank walked to the back of the truck, unlocked the tailgate and lowered the ramp. It took him several minutes to get the heavy barrels out of the back of the truck and lined up by the hatch. He wanted them ready to go. *Don't want to leave it open any longer than I have to…* Though he would lock these memories away, a part of Hank was still present, and that part of him dreaded the next step.

Mr. Chest Wound remained in the back of the wagon. Hank considered hauling him out of the bed, sack and all, and tossing him down the hatch, but something stopped him. Mostly the gritty, grinding pain in his knees, but there was another thought too: *Nobody will know if I take him to Smiley. I'd get to see the gang, and she can give him the unclaimed special. Brackington'll never know. I'm his employee of the month, his ace. He won't care. Decided, then.* He'd take Mr. Chest Wound to Smiley's tomorrow morning. It wouldn't be the first time Hank had left a body in the back of his truck overnight either. He tried not to think about it too hard.

The metal wheel on the hatch squeaked and scraped as it turned. *It doesn't want to be opened. I don't want to open it.* The sound spiraled out into the silence like fingernails on blackboard. When the turning was finally done, Hank kicked the hatch open. A black pit opened up like the yawning jaws of the man in black himself — *Lucifer, Death.* The wall of out-gas hit Hank like a truck. Rank decomposition turned the air to sickly butter, so *thick*, he felt he couldn't breathe.

Hank steadied himself, then grabbed one of the blue barrels. He lowered the lip of the first one as gently as possible to the edge of the hatch, reached into his pocket and found a quarter to loosen the clamp that held the lid shut. *Turn, turn, turn…* then, suddenly, the lid burst off like a cork off a champagne bottle. A vile, *vile*, champagne bottle.

Scrambled Beethoven came tumbling out and down into the black pool waiting fifteen feet below. Hank turned away and tried not to breathe. When the barrel was mostly empty, Hank picked it up and tapped out the remainder. *The dregs at the bottom of the coke bottle.* As he resealed the empty barrel and moved on to the next, Hank began to sing a tune in his head. *Anything to get away from here. From this moment.*

I'll drink my beer in a tavern…

N'sing a little bit a these workin' man blues.

#

IT was 3:30 when Hank finally finished in the field, parked the Power Wagon, covered the remaining body in the back of the truck (*Mr. Chest Wound / The Reanimator*) and walked, exhausted, up to his corner room of the Texas Inn, *333*. He heard a metal clang from behind the door of 334, his neighbor's room, and got a strong whiff of musty marijuana. *Howdy neighbor.* In his exhausted state, it almost smelled good. *Something other than death.*

When Hank opened his door, he realized he'd left the lamp by the telephone on. Yellow light lit up the piles of sticky notes there like little squares of gold. The telephone too, made of yellow plastic, seemed almost to glow. *Fuck that thing.* Hank knew there were probably several messages waiting for him. He wouldn't be checking them tonight. *No.* As much as he wanted never to check that answering machine ever again, it would be the first thing he did in the morning.

I should hire someone. A secretary or something. So I don't have to touch that phone. Could bring Cody on full time, a voice whispered in the back of Hank's brain. *No, please, God. Not worth it.*

Hank stripped his clothes off, all except for his jeans, as he walked towards the low bed in the corner. He detoured to turn the lamp above the telephone off, then fell into bed. He was asleep before his head hit the pillow.

PART THREE:

The Monkey House

CHAPTER TEN

Mr. Mojo Risin'

"I been singing the blues ever since the world began."
                                                    Jim Morrison

\#

HE stood on the raised back porch, still as the night. Smoke from his cigarette rose in undisturbed paisleys into the stagnant air. The porch overlooked a valley of sorts — a steep wooded area, level with the house so that when one looked out the windows, all was green. The last house on a dead-end road.

The man was tall and lean, not muscular, but with a dark, sort of youthful, vitality. Like there was a nuclear reactor hidden inside his chest running on cigarettes and whiskey. Though one got the sense, looking into that unlined face, that he was older than he looked. Maybe… a *lot* older. Orange light from the house behind him cut the side of his face into a crescent of fire. Long black curls of hair hung over his neck like a rock star, glistening in the light.

He didn't move. Only the slow exhalation of his smoke gave any hint that he was alive. That, and the electric green twinkle in his eyes. Eyes in which burned far away sulfur campfires. He looked peaceful there, leaning on the porch railing, gazing out into the wooded blackness.

But something stank.

The faint sweetness of rot and burning rubber. Gasoline and death. Highway smells. Hot sun and cooking blacktop.

Then the man didn't look terribly peaceful at all, and neither did the night. It began to come alive with snapping twigs and creeping shadows somehow blacker than the evening itself. He was calling the monsters out to party. To come out of the black and dance to rock and roll music. *To eat.*

The man in black cometh.

#

ROCK n' roll thumped against the air like a beating heart. A woman wearing something that couldn't quite be called clothing put her palm on the man's lightly stubbled cheek.

"Oh, baby. Why the long face?"

The man did not respond, though he lifted his head off his fist and turned to look at the woman. Those green eyes sparkled. The woman gasped and pulled her hand away, as if he'd poked her with a hot brand. She gazed open-mouthed for a few seconds, paralyzed, then turned and waded nervously back into the human sea of the house party. The man watched her go, smiling and silent.

He sat in a chair with a high, ornately carved back, like a throne belonging to the king of Scotland. He leaned heavily on one armrest, and slung over the other, lounging like a cat. A lazy cat, lean and slippery, like black water. His chin sat on his propped palm. It was the posture of boredom, yet his eyes were alive, scanning the scene playing out in front of him with delight. A sea of flesh and sweat and substances. It squirmed and bounced and swirled to the electric-metal sound of the band.

A different woman came crawling out of the twisting mess of people and up to the man in the chair. She was sweaty and panting. Her eyes shimmered with pleasure and an unsettling sense of presence- intense, aggressive awareness of the moment. Her pupils were pinpoints. The man looked over to where she sat on the floor and smiled.

"My my, chère, you look exhausted." That sly smile. Like there was some joke only he was in on.

"That. Is. Fuckin' *MUSIC*, right there!" The woman had to yell to make her voice heard over the stomping of the crowd and the roar of the speakers. The man's voice, however, cut through the noise like a hot knife, even though he appeared to be only whispering.

"Glad you like the band," he said.

"Where did you find these guys, Mr. B? They're like The Doors reborn."

The man turned away from the woman to gaze back over the crowd. His smile faded.

"No. Not quite the Doors. But they're not bad." He let the warm hum of the party hang in the air for a moment, then turned to the woman again, green eyes locking on hers. The woman stiffened.

"Is there something I can... do for you, Mr. B?"

"Have you received any word from Monsieur Hank?"

"Nossir. I expect he'll contact me in the morning. He always..."

"YES… yes. *He always*. He… always," the man grumbled.

Something about the phrase troubled him. *It's too easy with that one.* That's what it was. *Too easy.*

"You want me to call him?" asked the woman. Mr. B waved his hand in annoyance.

"No. I'm sure he knows the deal…" *Refuse and we'll rip your toes off one by one, kinda thing.* "Just… too easy nowadays. Where's the risk? Where's the *flavor*, Jenine?"

The man looked at her with a longing that seemed to cover up amusement. Like hidden behind his skin somewhere was another face. One that was always smiling.

"I… know what you mean, sir." After a moment she said, "I could… arrange something for you later. If that might… *help.*"

"Yes… That would be nice, Jenine. Thank you."

The man stared out at the crowd for a moment, then rose lazily from his throne and stretched like a teenager, hands raised high over his head. "I think I'll dance." He sauntered down into the meaty crowd, wearing only black jeans and a battered vest, stitched with the stars and stripes of the American flag. The sea of people parted, then swallowed him.

(HAPTER ELEVEN

Ms. Smiley Davis

MS. Smiley Davis sat in the driver's seat of her beige Ford Pinto, in the parking lot of *Mrs. Smiley's funeral home and crematorium.* *Her* funeral home, though she was no *Missus.*

Mrs. has been shown to be more marketable than Ms., rang the voice of her former business advisor. *Whole lotta help that's been.* She hung both her hands on the worn steering wheel of the Pinto and pressed her forehead against the back of her hands. The American prayer position, only possible in the driver's seat of an automobile. It was early morning, and the sky was still deciding whether to brighten. The sky was a steel blue color, and the air was cool, though the concrete still shook and shimmied with heat lines from the previous day's sunny beat down.

Smiley lifted her head and looked out the front windshield. She was the only one here. *Unsurprising,* considering the only other employees of Smily's Funeral Home were a mopey teenage white girl and an ex-lumberjack with neurological issues, neither of whom ever showed up on time.

The parking lot was small, but still bigger than what some of the other businesses in Campaiyote had. A 'crime' for which Smiley had been harassed repeatedly by those same business owners. Those same *white* owners.

The building itself had been many things in its years. Most evidently, a bowling alley. *God knows what the place was before that. Lucky Lanes… Lucky my ass.* A sign rose high above the squat little building, glowing dimly. She had changed the words to "Mrs. Smiley's Funeral Home", but the shape was still that of a bowling pin. It was a strange combination, but somehow charming. She'd thought other people might think so at least, though now she knew she had overestimated the power of that charm.

The building was perched atop the edge of a natural plateau, southeast of Fort Worth, giving it an expansive backdrop of brown-ery and highway. Beautiful, in a squinty sort of way. *Campaiyote, Tejas… How did I end up here?* Smiley Davis scanned the quiet parking lot and gazed at her building. *Another day, another dollar.* The voice of her mother. *Just keep going.* She took a deep breath and opened the door.

#

IT was two hours later when Karina finally waltzed in.

Smiley had already done most of her day's paperwork by then, minus dealing with the stack of foreclosure notices and overdue payment slips she had locked in the lowest drawer of her desk. She was determined to ignore those for as long as possible. *Not until a man shows up and makes me leave this place.* She'd already drained an entire pot of coffee.

Smiley looked up from her desk as Karina threw open the glass door and trudged inside. The little bell over the door tinkled sweetly. A sound that brought the smells and memories of Waffle House leaping into Smiley's mind.

Karina certainly did not share any of those warm, fuzzy, Waffle House memories. The bell just made her more disgruntled. And she was always, to some extent, disgruntled. Smiley thought she was far too morbid for a high schooler. *Like Wendy Adams or something. At least she shows up. And for two bucks an hour.*

"Morning, Ms. Davis."

"Mornin' Karina. Get enough sleep? You're lookin' a tad… sleep deprived."

Karina stared at her, a zombie dressed in all black, dark eyeliner accentuating tired eyes.

"This… this is just the way I look, Ms. Davis."

They blinked at each other.

"Well… just, *ahem*, make sure you're getting enough sleep, honey. Don't want my receptionist falling asleep at the phone."

"You look a little tired too, ma'am. Want me to make some coffee?"

Smiley looked at the empty pot of coffee that she had already finished by herself then smiled.

"Yes, please, that'd be wonderful."

#

ABOUT thirty minutes after Karina's entrance, Joe made his lumbering way across the parking lot. He carried, as always, his red lunch pail in one hand and his change of clothes under the other. His thick mustache and heavy brow made him look like some cartoon miner. *If only he were wearing a headlamp.* The bell again. *Waffles. Maple syrup. Eggs. Coffee. Bacon.* Smiley's stomach rumbled.

"Mornin' Smiley."

"Mornin' Joe. How's the knee?"

"Ooh, alright. Not too bad, I guess. Still waddlin' like a toddler, but it's better with taking some of the weight now."

"Well, be careful. Glad to hear it's not too painful. Think you'll go back to chopping down trees when it's healed?" Smiley grinned. Joe laughed loudly.

"No, Ma'am, don't think so."

"Well… nobody's called in yet, so it may just be another day with what we've got."

Joe nodded.

"I can handle that. Just holler if we get busy." No one said anything, but they knew *getting busy* wasn't a likely event. "Forecast says rain, but I don't mind taking the Beast out. Do some pickups."

"Okay, Karina, you hear that?"

"Yeah," Karina answered from the other side of the small lobby, her black boots kicked up on the desk.

"Hey, what'd I tell you about feet on the desk?"

Karina sighed and took her feet down, with an only slightly dramatic huff. Smiley shook her head and looked up at Joe.

"I'll be down in just a few to help you."

"Take your time, Ma'am. You're lookin' a little run down… I can do most of everything if it's just what we've got already."

"Thank you, honey."

Joe nodded and walked through the door that led to the back of house. Quiet fell over the lobby again. Smiley resumed her paperwork — *busy work* — and Karina slowly put her feet back up on the desk. The only sound was Smiley's pen scratching on paper, and then…

The phone rang.

A noise like a cold plunge. It shattered the silence like lake ice.

RRRIGNGNNG

BRBRIGNGNGIG

BRRIGIINGGG

IIINNGGG…

It took Karina a few moments to comprehend what was happening. Despite being the sole secretary of Smiley's Funeral Home for the past three months, this was only her third time answering the phone. Smiley's wasn't exactly a popular spot. *Yet.*

Karina snapped out of her surprise and picked up the phone, looking over to Smiley for reassurance. Smiley gave her a small nod and went back to her paperwork. Inside, she was screaming. *God, yes! Shiiiet, that's what I'm talkin' about! Whoo… fine day for profiting off of some death.* But, on the outside, she betrayed nothing. She'd read recently in a book titled, *The Secrets of the Keepers of the Structures of Business, and what we can learn from them,* by Jim Farlow, that not getting excited about success was good for keeping employees at their best. *Just act normal.*

But it wasn't normal. This was only the fifth call in the six months since Smiley's had opened, and she was counting. Smiley had made a few deals, namely with a couple of crime scene cleaners, to keep them afloat, but the noose was tightening. *We need more customers. The Dallas and Forth Worth markets.* Smiley had no illusions about what more business meant. *More death.*

"Hello, this is Smiley's Funeral Home and Crematorium, corner of Fairfax and Stockton, how may I help you?"

Karina answered in an uncharacteristically cheery fashion. It sounded wrong coming out of her mouth, but Smiley was glad she was at least *capable* of being a normal-ish secretary. Karina took a moment and nodded. Nodded again. And again. Began to speak, then paused. Her eyes widened a little as she glanced at Smiley. After a moment of hesitation, she said,

"What's the address? And how many?"

CHAPTER TWELVE

Hank Sinatra

HANK woke with a headache, despite not having drunk any alcohol the night before, nor having indulged in any peanuts. Three days had passed since he'd finished the job at the white ranch house. Three days since cleaning up Beethoven.

I really should try to polish those off though, before the mold gets in. And the mold *would* get in. Hank's hotel room was always stale from lack of proper ventilation and several leaky pipes and windows, which Mr. Park refused to acknowledge, let alone fix. *AC's broken again.* It seemed to be broken more often than not nowadays. *Cheap bastard.*

Hank sat up and let his head swim for a minute. *Why do I always feel like shit. Do I need a chiropractor? Acupuncture maybe…* He stood and stretched, not unlike the long, lean Mr. B. *Coffee. Peanuts. Toast.*

Hank stood, leaning on his kitchenette counter, and looked reluctantly over to the last place he wanted to look, the yellow telephone in the corner, and the answering machine that sat underneath it. Sure enough, the little green light on the machine was blinking. All at once, Hank felt like crying. He wondered how he'd come to this place. *Why am I still here, and where is my wife and family? What if I die here?* The answers to all those questions, all plainly accessible in his mind (*you clean up crime scenes, you've never gone on a date, you live in a hotel, you're weak, you're a coward*) were swept aside by the emotion best suited to that task: despair. He wanted to drown in the victimhood of it all. *Why me, God, why me?* Think. Nick Cage (not the bees).

Then, another voice, Mr. B's voice, said, *You know why.* And suddenly, Hank felt a little tingle in his tailbone. He didn't cry, but he *did* stew in his own pity for a while as he sipped his instant coffee. *Maybe I should get a dog. No. Cat? No, definitely not... well...*

After he finished his coffee and peanuts, Hank gathered his courage and went to the phone. He would undoubtedly have a few messages from yesterday, but what he was really dreading was the call with Jenine. He didn't like that lady, and he got the feeling she didn't like him much either. And he especially did not like the guy she worked for, *James Brackington.* Her boss. *His* boss. He'd promised himself that he would never work for him again, no matter what. Then, he'd crumpled like a piece of origami paper. Just, *Yes ma'am, how high would you like me to jump? Oh, this high? Yes, I do massive canine removal too... That's it, man. That's it. No more. I won't do it.* Hank whispered a pep talk to himself.

"No more. I won't do it. Not for that headcase, and I don't care if there'll be *big problems.* I'm not doin' it, *Jenine.*"

He picked up the phone and dialed. The receiver buzzed with cosmic dial tones. He finished punching in the number he'd received on the back of a matchbook. BEE-BOO-BOP-BEE-DO-DA-DII.

Mmeememm. Mmemmem. Meeeeee...

"Hello, Hank."

The voice that came through the phone was not Jenine's, as Hank had been expecting. It was a warm, soft voice, but somehow icy cold. The voice of a liar. Of someone who acted like a friend, but in truth, kept no such things. Honey poured over a knife. *James Brackington.*

"Mr… Brackington?" asked Hank hesitantly.

"Please, Hank. Call me James. I suppose Mr. B's alright, if you prefer."

"Mr. B. I… was expecting to reach Jenine."

"Ooh, well. Guess I'll have to do. Jenine is occupado at the moment. I'll try to perform her duties as best I can, though I will admit, I'm not as gifted a secretary as she is."

Hank did not laugh.

"Well… I…"

"I have another job for you, Hank."

Hank's blood ran cold. In the still and quiet air of the hotel apartment, he began to sweat. The smidge of confidence he'd worked up with his self-delivered pep talk fled like a rabbit from a coyote.

"That's, uh, just the thing I wanted to speak to Jenine… about. I… *ahem…* I won't be cl…"

"That's funny. It sounded like you were about to say, '*I won't do it.*' It's funny because I know you would never say that. Right, *Hank*? You don't want any problems. *We* don't want any problems. Right?"

Brackington's voice was low and calm, but there was a *heat* to it. Hank could feel hot air coming out through the receiver's speaker grill. For a moment, he couldn't speak. He just crouched by the telephone in silence.

"…No."

"Of course not, Hank! I know you, baby. *Better than you might think.* I know you don't want to cause any trouble. So just do the jobs I give you, and everything will be just hunky-dory. Mm?"

"…Okay."

Hank had dulled himself. He couldn't do anything but be dragged along by the voice on the other end of the receiver. *Such a loser. Grow a spine. Stand up for your…*

Brackington sighed.

"You know, you're a good one, Hank. So agreeable. That's what I like. Agreeable people. *Reliable* people. And *you. Are. Reliable,* my friend. I know I don't even need to ask about the ranch house the other day… that little mess. Cuz I know how thorough you are. I'm sure the dog wasn't too much trouble, not for Hank Cooper, the best damn cleaner in Tejas! Anyway, we've got a big one for you my man. I hope you got some sleep."

Hooray.

#

THE first time they get you is easy.

Rosco says, "Hey you, Hank, whatever the fuck, clean this shit up so sparkly I can eat off it, or Joey and I are gonna facilitate a little conversation between this here baseball bat and that perty skull a yer's."

And Hank says, "Yes, Rosco," because, well, Hank doesn't want to have that conversation.

Hank had cleaned up two bodies that day. That first time. The first time James Brackington had coerced him into cleaning. *And so much blood…* Afterwards, he'd been so exhausted, the thought of going to the police hadn't even crossed his mind (What-A-Burger had though).

A week later, and not only had he not gone to the police, he was *scared* of going to them, scared that he was too late, that he might be arrested for concealing evidence, *or… or…* he wasn't quite sure. He had a suspicion that Brackington owned most of the PD anyway. He'd found himself trapped between two undesirable options, and the longer he'd waited, the worse it had gotten. That was three years ago.

When Brackington had come a'knockin' the second time, Rosco didn't have to threaten violence. All they had to do was dangle Hank's accessory to murder over his head.

"You cleaned a crime scene illegally. And we have proof, Hanky Panky. Now come, little doggy, we have another job for you."

And so here he was again, for the who-knows-what-number job, reeled back into working for James Brackington. Only this time, he thought he might just implode. He wasn't sure he could handle what he'd just absorbed from the terrible voice on the other side of that yellow telephone.

Hank sat on the floor next to the phone stand, his back against the wall. He stared into deep space, boring a hole through time, the universe and his empty yet messy hotel room. Suddenly, the answering machine clicked over, and the messages played unprompted. Hank turned to look at the machine. *That's new. Wonder how many voicemails I've missed that way.*

"…Um, hi. This is…" It was an elderly woman's voice. She sounded a bit like a turkey that could speak Texan.

"Tartina Walker, I was hoping to reach… Hank… Cooper? At Lone Star Crime Scene Cleanup? *Gosh, hope I'm calling the right number…* I'm down at 607 Brockhiemer, just outside of Campaiyote. My Nephew…"

The woman choked up for a second, and the answering machine went quiet.

"…My nephew, Darryl… well, we… There's just no easy way to say it. He wasn't answering his phone, and he always calls me on Monday nights about Family Feud, so I knew something was wrong, but he's a grown man, so, I waited, you know… I *waited*. But when Monday came around again, and he didn't call, I knew that wasn't like Darryl — *I knew it* — so I went with Kathleen… uh, my neighbor, over to his house to check on him… and we… we… found him…"

The old lady was really struggling now, obviously having a hard time with the words.

"We found him in the bathtub. I… I… I guess… *Drowned…* drowned in… *butter.*"

Hank turned to the answering machine and blinked.

"So… *ahem*… please, uh, give me a call back… help. Please. Thank you."

The woman tried to regain some of the pleasantries of a normal phone message at the end, but it was pointless. *Pointless, after mentioning your nephew drowned in a bathtub full of butter. Hard to recover from that one.* Hank couldn't help but imagine what this cleanup process might entail, and it did *not* promise to be pleasant. Not many ever did.

None, actually.

CHAPTER THIRTEEN

Ann Hank

THE other two messages left on Hank's answering machine were pretty standard. *Stain removal. Decontamination. Easy money.*

Hank figured he could start his day off with the easier of these and work his way down the list, though the conversation he'd had with Brackington that morning was still weighing on his mind like a heat blanket. *Last. I'll do that one last.*

The orange Power Wagon hummed down the highway, unburdened, with four big, *empty*, fifty-gallon drums. Texas rolled by lazily in the steely morning light. Cows and grass and road and sky. Driving was when Hank felt most at peace. In the bubble of his own personal automobile, with no-one to talk to, no-one to listen to, and nothing to do but press the gas pedal.

He flipped on the radio.

"…ought to you by NPR, national public radio. I'm Michelle Norris, and this is *The World Today*. Guatemalan General Efraín Ríos Mott is under international scrutiny again today for his ongoing campaign against North Mayan rebel forces. The international community is labeling Mott's killings, genocide, though General Efraín still enjoys a close relationship with President Regan, who this morning annou…" Hank turned the knob. "…njoy Dream-Cola! All new Grape and…" Again. "…investigators say the murder weapon appears to have been a *spoon*…" Again. "…*you don't care about what I think… I think I'll just stay here and drink.*"

That's what I'm talkin' about.

\#

"HEY, are you… the cleaner?" the man in the pink polo shirt asked, sounding a bit like a lost child.

"Yep." Hank pointed to the logo on his stained T-shirt.

"Oh, thank Christ. We gotta get back in the house soon." Pink Polo scratched his head. "Can't afford the hotel much longer. But the smell… is… real bad. We didn't know he'd um, *ahem… passed.* We went on vacation, he didn't want to come, so we left him here by himself… and… ya know…" The man made a little explosion with his hands in front of his heart. "Thought he was just enjoying his *alone time*, my father-in-law, but, umm… turned out he'd gone on… without us."

The man in the pink polo said all this without a hint of remorse. Hank nodded along. He'd already heard this story on the answering machine, though this was usually the way it went. People wanted to… *reiterate* themselves, *make it make sense.* To make him *understand.*

This schmuck didn't seem all that distraught to Hank, though. He sounded like he was reading off a teleprompter, or maybe in a rush to get to a golf game. *Probably is.* It was often the case, Hank found, that people were more concerned with how a death would affect their own lives than with the death itself. *Guess it makes sense. They're dead; we're not.*

"Don't worry about a thing, sir. I'll get it done. You said someone already removed the body?"

"Yeah, that's right. Smiley's funeral home, I believe."

"Oh, I know Smiley. Good people there. Good people. So, only the bedroom has…"

"Yes, only the bedroom. It's gotta be… all clean. We're putting our daughter in there, and my wife is already on the edge of a meltdown. I think she might just keel over if there was any reminder that her father died in the room where her daughter is gonna sleep, ya know."

"I understand. No worries. It'll be spotless. I've been doing this a long time. I'm *thorough*."

And just two hours later, by around nine o'clock, Hank *did* have the bedroom spotless. *Move in ready, unless you want to get some priest to bless it with sage or something. Clear out the bad voodoo.* Hank didn't really go in for all that, but he knew many people did. Something told him Mr. Pink Polo wasn't too much of a salt lamp worshipper.

Something like this really just came down to hauling away the mattress. *Always a pleasant surprise when someone dies on a mattress. Like a human-sized sponge.*

Mr. Pink Polo was happy with the service. Less so when he saw the bill.

#

A few hours after wrapping up with Mr. Pink Polo and Hank had already swung through Maypearl to wipe down a kitchen that had been the scene of an unfortunate narcoleptic episode. The guy had fallen asleep while walking into the kitchen and slammed face first into the granite countertop. The KitchenAid had fallen on his head afterwards. *So it goes.*

He was now on his way to the third scene of the day. *The human butter-sicle… That's terrible. I should really have more compassion.* But he didn't. It was his job. And he asked himself, not for the first time, *is something wrong with me?* Except it wasn't really a question in his mind, but more of a feeling. And the feeling was: *Yes.*

He'd returned Tartina Walker's call and discovered that Darryl's abode was close to his existing route for the day, and he'd committed to coming by. The *house* turned out to be a trailer. Hank hated trailers. They never had enough room to move around or bring things out. He was always hitting his head on a doorway, or bumping into a plywood counter or something. His experience with trailers, *being extensive*, was that it was usually better to burn the thing down than pay to get it cleaned. *Hey, if the price is right, it's right.* The voice of Hank's father whispered in his ear: *Just do it. Money's money, kiddo. Job's a job. Not everyone has the privilege of being employed.*

Fuck, *I don't want to clean out a bathtub full of butter and rotting flesh though, Dad. Pause. Well, tough shit, son. You already said you would. It'll be easy. Like cleaning out a butter dish. Or wiping out the bacon lard at the bottom of a pan. Pause. No. No, I don't think it will be easy. But I did say I would do it. Why? Why did I say that?*

#

"YOU must be Mrs. Walker."

"*Ms.* Walker. Howdy."

"Howdy."

Tartina Walker stood on the front porch of her nephew's trailer — more of a pile of rotting planks than a porch — shifting nervously. She'd watched Hank walk up the drive like a cornered Chihuahua. It was clear this whole ordeal was making her supremely uncomfortable. It seemed Ms. Walker didn't get out much, and having to meet a stranger about, *well,* extracting her deceased nephew from a bathtub full of congealed butter, wasn't an activity she seemed thrilled about participating in. Hank and Ms. Walker shared this sentiment.

Behind Ms. Walker, sitting on the saddest stand-alone porch swing Hank had ever seen, was another woman, smoking a cigarette. She was the closest thing to a backwoods Buddha Hank had ever seen. Or maybe a redneck Jabba the Hutt. A cigarette dangled between her fat, stubby fingers, half consumed, and her head sat on her round body like a melting scoop of banana ice cream.

The woman on the porch swing wore an expression Hank knew well. *The face of the dead.* The face of someone who lives for the next cigarette. A face that said clearly, to Hank's eyes, "*I'm gonna sit my ass right here the whole time while you pull that sucker outta there. Because… I'm comfortable.*" Backwoods Buddha raised her cigarette hand a whole inch and a half in greeting.

"Kathleen," was all she said.

After shaking Ms. Walker's hand, Hank waited for either Ms. Walker or Kathleen to say something, *anything*, but

they didn't. They just looked at Hank like two frogs choking on
hot air.

"Well… a pleasure… I'll just pop in and have a look
then."

Ms. Walker seemed to snap back into frantic motion at
this.

"Oh, yes! Please, uhm… Let me… I can…"

"It's alright, ma'am. If you could just direct me to the…
the bathroom, right?"

"That's… right. The smell is really jus…"

"I'll be fine, ma'am."

"Go in and turn right. It's the last door on the left, before
the bedroom. The door with the little angel sign hanging on it.
The live, laugh, love one."

"Thank you."

As Hank turned to enter the trailer, Kathleen spoke.

"You got any help witcha?"

Hank paused. Turned.

"Ma'am?"

"Got eny help witcha?"

"Ah, no ma'am. Just me."

Kathleen nodded slowly, lips pursed.

"Darryl's a big boy."

Hank let out a quick sigh of defeat. Turned to glance at
Ms. Walker and nodded. Then he was inside the trailer, drifting
through the life of a stranger who would no longer be calling
his aunt about Family Feud. And yet, he felt like he knew this
man. *Darryl. Darryl, Darryl, Darryl.*

The mountain of un-recycled Bud Light cans in the
kitchen corner said a lot. The general state of the trailer said
more. The place was small, one of those shotgun-style mobile

homes where everything lay in one line, beginning with the kitchen and ending with the bedroom. Stepping through the front door put Hank directly in the living room, where a three-seater couch faced a large, boxy television. General debris and garbage seemed to be the main furnishings.

The smell hit him almost immediately, as he'd known it would. *Whoo, doggy. She wasn't kidding.* Spoiled meat. Except this had a fat, airy *greasiness* to it. *That would be the butter.* Hank was surprised Ms. Walker had made it as far as the bathroom. People usually tapped out at the first whiff. Most unattended deaths were discovered solely because of that rank, fruity odor. That same smell was usually more than enough to keep them away.

Carpet squished under Hank's boots as he stepped inside. The screen door slamming behind him made him jump. *Chill thoughts. Calm like still water, Hank.* At first, he thought the floor was wet. *No, it's rotting from the bottom up.*

The plywood bowed under Hank's weight. He scanned the kitchen and living room quickly and let his nostrils adapt to the smell for a moment. Already his eyes were watering, but there were other smells here too, like old pizza and a couch turned B.O. machine. He started walking back towards the bathroom.

The hallway was short, with three faux-wood doors lining its walls. The ceiling sagged under years of neglect. *Maybe just the weight of time.* The first door on the right was open, and Hank took a peek. *Guest room, maybe.* The room consisted of a moldy bed and the same general detritus that was strewn everywhere else in the house. There also looked to be a few big boxes of un-developed film rolls. Hank thought about his peanuts. His tummy rumbled, despite the horrible stink in the trailer.

At the end of the hall was the bedroom, just as Ms. Walker had said, and to the left was the last door. The little sign hanging there did not say, *live, laugh, love* though. It read, *God, Family, Guns. Close enough.* There was an angel painted on the sign above the words: a little, scantily clad, curly-haired baby with big wings and clothes made of flowing strips of white cloth. With one hand he played the trumpet, and with the other, he held an assault rifle.

Hank blinked and pushed the door open.

#

BEHIND door number three was a small bathroom. The sink and the toilet were immediately to the right as Hank entered, and against the back wall was a bathtub. It wasn't full-sized exactly, but big enough to cover most of Darryl Walker.

She wasn't kidding. No freakin' lie. What were you doing, man?

Darryl Walker had filled his entire bathtub with butter. So much of it, in fact, that it had run over the edges of the tub and onto the floor. The entire room glistened with butter and grease.

It also seemed that replacing the butter every time he'd wanted to take a special bath had gotten a little too costly for Mr. Walker. *Or maybe he just couldn't be bothered.* All the same, the butter was a deep brown-yellow. *Soiled,* Hank was sure, with all kinds of secretions. He could see hundreds of little curly black hairs sprouting from the half-solidified butter. Hank swallowed the toad climbing up his throat.

The smell was really something. The butter lent the stink of rotting meat a fuzzy fullness, kind of like moldy Velveeta Cheese. Hank looked down at Darryl. Only his head and his stomach were above the butter line. The congealed mush covered the rest of his body in an opaque blanket. Hank thought of carbonite from Star Wars.

Darryl was just beginning the worst phase of the decomposition process. *Liquefaction*. His eyes had rotted out, and his stomach looked like it might burst at any moment from bloat. Hank stood in the small, hot bathroom and tried to imagine the next several hours of his life. He decided this would be one for the vault.

Click.

CHAPTER FOURTEEN

704 Emerson

HE was already on the highway, driving into the setting sun, when Hank emerged from his brain vault. He found himself holding a lit Hillsborough with the window rolled down. Glancing in his rearview mirror, he saw not a barrel in the bed of his truck, but a casket. *Darryl.* He brought the cigarette to his lips and took a drag. *Ahhh.* His fingers left a grease spot on his lips.

The Power Wagon bounced on down the highway towards Campaiyote, and Hank thought about the last job of the day. *And the vacation I'm gonna take afterwards. Vacation* meaning, two to three days of getting really, thoroughly, properly, absolutely toe-tinglingly drunk, with a few bowls of peanuts sprinkled in between drinks.

Hank realized with a jolt that he didn't know where he was going, but just as quickly, it came rushing back. The important bits usually did. *Smiley's.* He was heading to Smiley's. To prepare Darryl for his appointment with the worms. Personally, Hank was in favor of cremation. After some of the things he'd seen, fire always seemed like the answer. *Clean. It does my job better than I ever could.*

Hank took another drag of his cigarette and gazed out at the evening highway. The sky was wide and turning a bloody orange. He rubbed his fingers together again, feeling that buttery grease on his skin. A picture of Darryl, naked in the bathtub, half excavated, flashed in Hank's mind. The congealed, grimy butter, the softness of his rotting skin…

NO. No. Not that, please. That stays in the box. In. The. Vault.

#

FIFTEEN minutes later, Hank pulled off the highway into Campaiyote. A small town, but with a uncharacteristic wealth of businesses, including a funeral home, laundromat, dry cleaners, taco stand and greeting card shop. Not to mention KAMP 90.9 and Jazzy Chazzy.

Nothing about the town screamed *glam*, but the view certainly made up for some of the shabbiness. The whole town overlooked a sprawling scrubland. It wasn't even that Campaiyote was that much higher in elevation than the surrounding area; it just happened to be placed perfectly for the view. And Smiley's Funeral Home and Crematorium had the best of it.

Pulling into the parking lot, Hank saw the Beast wasn't there. *Joe must be out. That's good.* However, Ms. Smiley's beige Pinto occupied its usual space. Hank had always been wary of that car, and he swerved wide to avoid it now. It always looked to him as if it might just spontaneously combust. The incidents where Pinto gas tanks had exploded after being rear-ended had only confirmed Hank's feelings. He'd told Smiley as much, and she'd agreed.

"You wanna buy me a new car?" she'd asked, and Hank had said, "Well…"

Hank pulled the Power Wagon around to what Joe called *backstage*. Though he'd entered through this back door unannounced many times over the past few months, he felt it was probably a good idea to at least go say hello. To Karina, most likely. Smiley was usually occupied. *Anything* to delay going to his last job of the day. *Brackington's house party. Or the remains of it*. He shuddered. Hank parked the truck, *bed facing the back door*, and walked around to the front of the building. Karina didn't even look up when Hank pushed open the glass door.

Brinnngbrigtink.

The sound of that bell always made Hank hungry. *Waffles and Coffee*.

"Hey, Hank. Smiley and Joe are out on a pickup," said Karina, without looking away from the very important business of filing her nails.

"Yeah, saw the Beast wasn't here. What's the scoop? Hospital pickups?"

"Actually, we got a call," Karina said, still filing.

"Oh?"

"Yeah, some woman called… She was a real bitch over the phone, said I sounded high." Karina scrunched up her face at this, like she was smelling something foul. "Said there was a pretty nasty scene at a house party the other night out in Corsicana. Already cleared by the PD, so they wanted us to come get the bodies, three, I think, report the deaths and all that. Basic burial package. Some big shot's paying for the whole shebang. Guess none of them had families that cared enough to bury 'em. Woulda called you in for this one, but Smiley said she and Joe could handle it."

As Karina explained all this, in her characteristically nonchalant tone, Hank's blood ran cold. Then colder. *Jenine. Brackington. This is bad. He's already got me under his thumb, guess I'm not enough. He wants a whole funeral home for himself. His own cover-up shop.*

"You… uh, know the address of this house party?" asked Hank, trying to keep the concern out of his voice. It didn't work. Karina looked up at him suspiciously.

"Uhh, yeah… I think it's… let me take a looksie." Karina hoisted her feet off the desk and shuffled a few papers on her desk. "Here… 704 Emerson."

Hank dug in his back right pocket, where he'd stashed a sticky note with the address of the job Brackington had given him that morning. He already knew the address, but he pulled it out anyway, hoping it had changed — hoping he was misremembering. He wasn't. Written on the sticky note was *704 Emerson, Corsicana.*

"Damn," Hank whispered under his breath.

"What?" asked Karina, only mildly interested.

"Hey, would you help me unload? It's the one I called about earlier. Darryl Walker. His Aunt'll be by later today. I think… I should go help Joe and Smiley. They… well, never mind. Just come help me, would ya."

Karina looked up at Hank like, *you what?*

"Uh, Hank. I, uh, I don't do the whole… I don't touch the… bodies. I'm the receptionist. That's Joe's area of expertise."

Hank looked down at Karina and blinked. The silence in the lobby seemed to grow. Hank looked around at the emptiness and then back at Karina.

"Five minutes," he said.

Karina looked up at Hank, and for once she didn't look bored.

"Umm…"

A few minutes later, Hank and Karina were on opposite ends of a Darryl sandwich. The box he was in was light, but Darryl was heavy. It was a struggle, but they got him out of the bed of the truck, through the back door and into the storage room. Karina left quickly when Hank popped open the box to move Darryl to one of the cooler cabinets. Karina yelled back in a concerned voice as she made her way back to the lobby.

"Haaaankk… why is everything greasy?"

"Go wash your hands."

#

HANK was no storybook hero. Not even close. His list of heroic achievements extended to having two sober nights in a row.

He was a person. Not even a particularly brave person. But for some reason, a heroic urgency had struck him when he'd found out Jenine had called Smiley's. Hank didn't really have *friends*, per se, but he supposed that Smiley, Joe and Karina were about as close to that as anyone in his life.

Before Smiley opened up her funeral home half a year ago, Hank had had to drive all the way up near Dallas to find a reputable parlor — *not that he always did business with reputable people* — but Smiley's had changed that. She ran a good place. A nice place. And Hank marveled at her ability to mix business and humanity. She took care of people. *Dead and alive.*

Perhaps it was seeing a little goodness brought into the world that made him feel the way he did about Smiley and her two employees. A goodness that he could never hope to match. He was the person no one wanted to see. He hid things. Burn things. Smiley, at the very least, had a face that people would remember. The owner of a business that said, *it'll be alright now.*

Hank was pretty sure someone had changed the neon phrase below "Smiley's" on the bowling pin-shaped sign from "low rates, and quality lanes" to "low rates, and quality service," but it remained true. Their rates were reasonable, and the service was good. It doesn't sound so revolutionary, but Hank was continually surprised by how vicious death profiteering could be — price gouging, coffin upgrades, cemetery spaces, exotic flower bouquets, embalming — the list went on and on. Smiley's was simple. *Texan.*

It really wasn't his business to be going around telling people not to work with Brackington, but Hank felt a sort of allegiance with Smiley, and he'd been around enough times to know this was bad news.

Big problems, the voice of James Brackington whispered somewhere in the back of his brain. This was a job she would be better off without. He didn't want to lose that sliver of normality they brought to his life. Every day was different, and uniquely horrible for Hank Cooper, but Smiley and Joe and Karina would be there afterwards to say, "Howdy, Hank. Busy day?" He liked that. He didn't want to admit as much, but he did.

And *that* is why Hank found himself hurtling down the highway towards Corsicana, to his last job of the day, and hopefully to stop another person from falling into the black pit that was James Brackington.

To 704 Emerson.

CHAPTER FIFTEEN

Smiley and Mr. Mojo

JOE eased the Beast (a raging yellow Ford Granada with a giant smiley face on the hood) into a gravel spot on the side of the dead-end road. The house at the end of the green lane had no driveway, only a walking path to the front door. Smiley could see why it was used as a party house. *Nobody around for miles to hear the music. Or screams. Nobody who'd complain, anyway.*

The dense trees seemed to fold over the narrow road and the house itself, making a green tunnel that was increasingly foreboding. There were no other cars on the street, yet Smiley felt watched, as if the trees were peering at them with a thousand, thousand leafy green eyes.

Joe slotted the shifter into park, clicked the engine off and pulled up the emergency brake. For a moment, they sat together in silence. They were both thinking the same thing, and they could feel it. *I don't want to go into that house.* And at that moment, the wind blew through the trees, making an airy shuffling sound, muffled by the car windows.

Joe looked over at Smiley.

"Well?"

"… Let's get this shit over with," replied Smiley, feigning a sort of professional comfort.

They both took their time unbuckling and getting out of the car, however. There was a palpable uneasiness about this place. *This road. This house.*

Once out of the car, they opened up the back of the Granada and began suiting up. White Tyvec suits — the kind Hank would've been quite familiar with — yellow gloves and booties. They looked like mad scientists escaped from a secret underground lab.

Joe had never minded the getup, but Smiley hated the way it locked in the sweat and the heat. *Sweat my fuckin' ass off in this thing.* Still, much better to go into something like this with a suit than with nothing. It gave Smiley a small sense of clinical protection. *Armor.* She didn't want to go into this place regardless, suit or no.

Just before they could start making their way down to the house, when they'd gotten all their clothes on and their equipment gathered together, a car pulled around the corner at the end of the lane behind them. The wind blew again, causing the trees to dance overtop the dark blue 1967 Shelby GT 500 heading towards them with alarming speed.

A low hum vibrated down the empty country lane, mixing with the papery sound of wind on leaves. It was a deep engine, like the purr of a tiger. Joe and Smiley turned around to watch it approach. Something about the car seemed to both scream and whisper at them. *RUN. RUN. RUN.* Both Joe and Smiley felt it, yet neither vocalized their instincts, lest the sound of their voices make it real. As the dark blue predator sped down the lane, Smiley felt like she was watching one of those dolly zoom shots out of *Jaws*. The trees were *parting* for this evil car, thrusting it towards them. She squinted, trying to see the driver's face, but the heavily tinted, almost black, front windshield obscured it.

"Hey, uh, Smiley… I, uh, don't feel very good. I…"

"Me neither. Something is… very bad. Just be cool."

Smiley looked up at Joe, who had begun to sweat profusely. She told herself it was the heat of midday in Texas and the Tyvec suit. But it wasn't. And she herself had begun to feel sick. A kind of airy nausea. *What is this, a Stephen King novel or something? Pull yourself together.* As if to confirm that hypothesis, her legs started trembling, just slightly, as the car pulled ever closer. Smiley felt better standing by her beefy six-foot-six former lumberjack employee, though the knowledge that Joe would almost certainly die rather than fight another person wasn't overly comforting. *Pacifists.*

Only when the car was fifty feet away from them did the driver slow down. Smiley was sure the car wouldn't be able to stop in time. She even started to move off the road, but somehow it stopped in time, and without sliding or screeching a bit. The low rumble of the engine, *the quietness of it,* was unsettling. As were the black windows. But as the car pulled up next to Smiley and Joe, they held their ground (unconsciously scooching slightly closer to each other).

At least ten seconds of silence passed before anything moved. The wind moved through the trees again, but the sound was somehow far away. Joe and Smiley's eyes were focused on the passenger-side window. Finally, the pane came sliding down, slow and silent. Behind the black glass was a young man with curly black hair and piercing green eyes. He was smiling, one hand laid casually on the black leather steering wheel, the other on the gearshift. He was leaning over to look up at Joe and Smiley from the driver's seat, giving him a sort of lankiness. A leanness.

It was clear as soon as she saw him that this pretty man was the source of all the uneasiness in the air. His smile was chilling. Cold and straight and clean and there for all the wrong reasons. A voice in Smiley's brain began frantically repeating, *this is normal. This is normal. A normal man in a normal car. A normal man in a normal car. He's not going to hurt anyone. A normal man in a normal car.* But he wasn't. And another voice told Smiley that he just might hurt someone. Just might hurt someone *bad*.

"Hey there, friends," the man said.

His voice was jovial, and a little nasally. Then it hit her all at once. *Jim Morrison. He looks just like Jim Morrison.* He sounded like him too. Joe went to give a reply, but could only gasp. Smiley took a small step forward, with more confidence than she'd thought possible.

"Howdy, there. Something we can do for ya?"

The man chuckled. The sound was no more comforting than his smile.

"Oh, I just wanted to drop by and make sure you had all you needed. I'm the one that…" The man flipped his hand on the steering wheel, searching for the right word. "… *requested* your services." Something in his tone had turned condescending. Like the thought of *requesting* anything was below him.

"Oh, well… We got a call from someone named Jenine? I don't know if you…"

"I'm in the right place, love." The man's smile was gone. "Jenine is my secretary, you might say. My name is James. You must be Smiley. And I see you brought your lumberjack along."

The man was smiling again, just a little, and looking at them in a way Smiley did not care for. Almost like a butcher sizing up a piece of meat. For a moment, she didn't really know what to say to that, and Joe wasn't any help. He was still gazing slack-jawed into the car, frozen.

"I see… pleasure to meet you, James… but we should be fine here on our own. We provide professional services, so you don't need to worry about anythi…"

"I heard you're making some waves in Campaioyte."

"Pardon me?"

"Well, I just… I have a few business connections out there, and they've mentioned how inspiring it is to have a young… *black* woman start a business in their town. They're just tickled."

A hot shiver ran down Smiley's back. She knew this banter. She'd heard it her whole life, and though they sounded exceptionally slimy coming out of this man's mouth, the words were the same. He'd said *black*, but the word was *nigger*. That shiver turned into a steel rod of disgust and anger that straightened Smiley's back, and suddenly, her fear was gone. It must've shown on her face too, because James' smile wavered. In her eyes then, he looked small and thin. A hollow, broken thing, hiding behind a pretty face and a prettier car.

"Well… it's good to hear my neighbors like having me around. They certainly haven't been showing me much love."

Smiley took another step towards the car and leaned down into the passenger window, riding that wave of confident anger.

"Maybe next time you see your business connections, you can tell them to stop bitching about my parking lot. And also to stop vandalizing my building."

James had leaned away from Smiley, but had regained that knowing smirk.

"I'll be sure to do that… listen, *Ms. Davis…*"

That was when the popping sound of yet another engine came bouncing down the green lane. The pop of an engine attached to a blazing orange Power Wagon.

CHAPTER SIXTEEN

Party at the End of the Lane (Part 1)

AS he turned onto the long dead end lane, he could see in the distance, two figures in white suits standing by a blue Shelby. *Brackington.* He wouldn't ever mistake that one. *That dark blue snake of a car.* And his stomach dropped. *He's actually here. His car is here.* **He's** *here.* A deep nausea twisted his stomach, and suddenly all those thoughts of being a good friend to Smiley and Joe, and about saving them from the same fate he was suffering, vanished from his mind. Vanished as if they'd never existed. The idea of facing Brackington like this produced only one thought:

RUN, BETTER RUN!

He'd thought that if it were Jenine, maybe he could talk her into letting him have the job and letting Smiley off. But Brackington… he wasn't in it for the money, *or anything actually,* besides the joy of making other people suffer. He wouldn't let them go, even if they managed to slip away today. *Not now that he's zeroed in.* Hank knew this. He knew from experience. Though when you looked into those green eyes, you didn't need any experience to see the truth. He just hoped it wasn't too late to keep Smiley out of legal trouble. Maybe they could still have an ally in the police, though Smiley would probably laugh at that idea.

Hank eased his foot off the gas at the sight of Brackignton's Shelby, but he realized they'd all surely seen his car now, so there would be no turning back. He had a job to do here anyway. It occurred to Hank in this moment, strangely enough, this was the first time in years he was about to meet three people who all knew him, all at the same time. He wished they didn't.

Brackington did this on purpose. He called me here so that I would know he got his mitts on Smiley. As narcissistic as it sounded in his brain, he knew it was true. *Nothing to do about it now but move forward.* So he did.

#

THE country lane seemed to stretch out forever. Something about the trees and the wind made Hank uncomfortable. It ought to have been beautiful, but the place was *tainted. Anyplace Brackington goes is.*

He did though, after what seemed an eternity, finally reach the gathering at the end of the road. He pulled up behind the Beast and put the Power Wagon in park. The three cars were a bit of a sight when parked so close together. A yellow hearse, an orange Power Wagon, and a blue Shelby GT500. A car enthusiast's wet dream about forty years in the future. *Or maybe like the Bophuthatswanaian flag?*

Hank killed the engine and got out of the car. The metal crunch of the door closing seemed loud in the breezy silence of the lane. Joe and Smiley were looking at him as he approached.

They weren't smiling. In fact, Joe looked like he might faint, and Smiley looked angry. As he got closer, Smiley called out to him.

"Hey honey, didn't know you were comin'. You cleaning up?" she asked.

Before Hank could answer, Brackignton had opened his door and stepped out.

"Oh, yeah. Hank is like my right-hand man, *sugar*." Brackington laughed. *So… empty.* "Not that I have this problem a lot… *well*… a bit more than the average, I suppose." He flashed that perfect smile over the roof of the Shelby at Smiley. She didn't return it. "Business ventures, you know. And just plain bad luck. The services of a *professional crime scene cleaner* are more valuable than a lot of people know. Very useful indeed, and required more frequently than most would like to believe. Isn't that right, Hank?"

"… I guess that's right, Mr. Brackington."

"You know him, Hank?" asked Smiley, ignoring Brackington's interjections.

"Well…"

"I said he was like my right-hand man, didn't I, *honey*?" The way Brackington said *honey* sounded more like *bitch*. "My business associates in Campaiyote told me you two've been working together. So I thought we might do a little, what? Team-up? Collab?"

"Well… I was actually coming to say that I don't mind doing this job myself. I don't need any he…" said Hank.

"Oh, Hank, relax, would ya? You don't get to keep all the fun to yourself, my man. I hired Smiley here fair and square.

You just take care of the last part. The, uh, scrubbing and whatnot." Brackington waved his hand as if shooing a fly. "I really don't understand why you're so down all the time. You oughtta take a vacation."

Brackington smiled that wolfish grin at Hank, his green eyes twinkling. For a moment, Hank thought James might kill them all right there, just commit a daylight triple homicide (though that wouldn't be new territory for the man). There was an electricity to him, a black vibration, like live power lines buzzing in morning mist. The feeling that if you touched him, you'd regret it. Joe was big, Smiley was fierce, and Hank was… Hank… but he had no doubt that Brackington could do it. Could take them all. He just could.

"… I just meant…" Hank trailed off. What little confidence he'd had coming into this conversation was gone. He was once again a tack under Brackington's thumb. But before he could be beaten down any further, Smiley broke in.

"Well, honey, we can always use an extra hand if you want to come in with us. You look pretty bushed already, maybe we can help each other out, eh?" said Smiley.

Her tone was one of genuine compassion. She meant what she said. Hank appreciated that. And though he knew it was already too late to avoid getting them involved with the psychopath standing between them, he thought they might be better off together. At least for the moment.

"Yeah, alright." Hank said, more confident than he felt.

Suddenly, James clapped his hands and rubbed them together. The sound was piercing in the late afternoon quiet. Hank and Joe actually jumped at the sound. Smiley didn't flinch, though Hank thought he saw a flash of anger in her eyes.

"Good! Good! I wish you all the best of luck! I was going

to give you two," Brackington said, gesturing at Smiley and Joe. "A brief introduction to how I do business, but now that Hank's here, I'm sure he can fill you in. Right, Hank? You know the drill."

Hank nodded, keeping his eyes on the ground.

"Great. I'll leave it to you then. Don't forget to have fun."

Brackington gave each of them a big cheesy smile, then reopened the car door and climbed back inside. He started the engine, rolled the window up, then proceeded to peel out, gassing the Shelby into a full tailspin and kicking up a monstrous cloud of dust and rubber smoke. He was gone in a moment, speeding back down the empty lane.

Though he knew things were far from over, it felt like a cinderblock had been lifted off Hank's chest. The air itself felt lighter without Brackington around. Hank suddenly realized that he hadn't been breathing, and he gulped down air, ignoring the dust.

He saw Smiley watching the blue Shelby speed down the lane, a hard look in her eyes. Joe was doing the same thing as Hank. *Just breathing*. Smiley turned to Hank.

"What the fuck was that?" she asked.

CHAPTER SEVENTEEN

Party at the End of the Lane (Part 2)

SMILEY watched the exchange between Hank and Brackignton intensely.

She knew Hank, though not that well, she had to admit. But she liked him well enough. Even if he was a little strange. Brackington was right about one thing. *He should take a vacation.* As far as she could tell, the guy worked pretty much all the time. *And to run a crime scene cleanup business solo…* it was pretty grim stuff. Still, he had been good for the funeral home, and after a few months, had warmed up to the team.

Sometimes she'd come in to work to find him smoking a cigarette out back with Joe, or in the middle of a staring contest with Karina. She didn't like the idea that he worked with that… *man? Brackington.* In truth, Smiley thought he seemed more like some kind of demon in disguise than a real person, and she could see that Hank suspected the same, but was too scared, or too *beaten,* perhaps, to fight him. Or even to say as much.

"What the fuck… was that?"

Hank looked up at Smiley, fear in his eyes, then turned to look down the lane, apparently to confirm that the Shelby was actually gone and not just pulling some cruel fake-out.

"Look, you two should get out of here. But you can't take the Beast. They'll see you leaving, and they'll know. You can go on foot out the back and then follow the highway…"

"Woah, woah," interrupted Smiley. "Slow down, Hank. *They*? Who are you talking about?"

"James Brackingon, the guy you were just talking to, his people."

"Something was definitely wrong with that… *guy* … but we need this job. This removal fee alone is going to keep the home going for another few months. I'm not just gonna leave, Hank. *Can't*. And if you think I'm gonna walk my ass along the highway in this heat… boy…"

Hank stepped forward, panic still in his voice. "I'll pay you for the job, for everything. He's already picked you out. He's… he won't stop… ever. The best shot you have is to just leave town, leave the *state*, actually. And never come back."

"Yeah, *okay*, Hank, let me just pick up and leave everyth…"

"I know it's crazy. But he's…" A deep sense of sadness washed over Hank's eyes while he searched for the right words. "Bad. He's very bad."

Joe talked for the first time since Brackington had rolled up in the Shelby. He gulped.

"That… that wuddn't no goddamn *man*. That… that was some kind of… *demon*. Did you see his eyes, Lee?" It seemed like Joe was still in some state of shock. He was watching the fading cloud of dust down the lane like a mouse that had just narrowly avoided being eaten by a hawk.

"Oh, come on, Joe. It wasn't that bad," said Smiley.

"Not that bad?" Joe asked, incredulous. "I don't know how you were even talking to him. I could hardly breathe."

"He's human," said Hank, somewhat unconvincingly. "But that doesn't make him any less capable of *terrible things*."

"How do you know him?" asked Smiley.

"He hired me, years ago. On a job similar to this… and he… has been a *repeat customer*, I guess you might say. Not that I want his business."

"Why don't just say no?"

Hank checked the lane once more, then stepped close to Smiley and Joe, almost whispering. "He's a mob boss, or some kind of… of, I don't know… criminal overlord or something. He looks young, but he's not. All I know is that if you *displease* the guy, you're likely to end up like the people in that house." Hank pointed at the empty and foreboding party pad. "And I don't even need to go in there to know what we're going to find. A freakin'… *massacre*."

Joe gulped again, though he was looking somewhat recovered from the whole interaction with Brackington.

"I believe you, Hank. I think we should go, Lee."

Smiley was looking hard at Hank.

"So, you're sayin' if we leave here, that fella is gonna have us killed? Why? We haven't done anything to him."

"If you don't do the job… *yeah*. You don't have to do anything to him. I can't claim to know what he wants… but you just met him. Does he seem like someone to let things slide? He plays with people… like *toys*. If you refuse the work, he'll replace you with someone who will *cooperate*," Hank said gravely.

"What does he have on you, Hank?" Smiley asked, now half concerned and half angry.

She'd thought she'd known Hank, at least a little, but it turned out, not so much. *Just when you think ya know somebody, they turn out to be working for a criminal overlord.* Hank seemed to grow a little paler at the question.

"I don't… it… it's best you don't hear about that."

"I agree," said Joe.

Smiley turned and looked disapprovingly at Joe, then back to Hank.

"So what? You want us to sneak outta here, leave town and never come back?"

Hank looked up at the sky quickly, as if he were trying to remember a phone number, then back down at Smiley.

"Yes. That would be ideal."

Smiley just looked at Hank like he was crazy, then turned and started walking towards the house.

"Wait!" said Hank, skipping to walk along beside Smiley.

"C'mon Joe, we got a job to do. You can leave town and run away to wherever you want to go after we finish. I know you need the gas money."

Joe's jaw dropped incredulously. He looked at Smiley's turned back like, *how dare you?* He turned, as if to walk back to the Beast, then stopped, lowered his head and sighed.

"Yeah," he whispered under his breath. "Yeah. God." Then Joe turned and began walking behind Smiley towards the house.

"You too?" asked Hank, unbelievingly.

"Yeah. Me too. She's right. I do need the money."

Hank shook his head.

"Not good. Not good," he said.

"You coming?" asked Smiley without turning around.

Hank stood for a moment, then muttered, "Fuck," and joined the conga line descending towards 704 Emerson.

CHAPTER EIGHTEEN

Karina and The Dead Man

KARINA was sitting at her desk in the lobby of Smiley's Funeral Home and Crematorium reading Frankenstein when she heard the sound. Like someone banging their head against a metal desk. The sort of tarpy sound thin metal makes when bent.

It was faint, and at first, she wasn't sure she'd actually heard anything at all, but just as she'd resumed her reading, it came again, louder this time. Then stopped. Then started. Then stopped. She rested her open book on her knees, still reclining with her feet on the desk. She cocked her head to listen to the sound. *The back. It's coming from the back room.*

The ceiling fan turned lazily overhead in the silence, shifting dust motes around in the evening sun of the lobby. The coffee machine gurgled quietly. Then the banging came again, and Karina thought she heard some kind of muffled *scream* buried in the metallic thumping. She looked around the quiet lobby and saw nothing. Nothing moved except the ceiling fan.

Slowly, Karina set her book facedown on the desk and rose from her chair. All the tropes from all the horror stories she'd ever read or seen came rushing into her head. *Teenage girl hears a noise… Investigates by herself, all alone, telling no one… gets murdered with an axe.* But she made her way to the door that led to the back of house anyway and opened it. *They all end with 'gets murdered with an axe.'*

The sound was much clearer back here, and she could hear what sounded like a muffled voice. *Why are you doing the thing that all horror movie characters do? Literally the opposite of the sane thing. Go call the police, or Mom, or Joe, or Smiley… anyone.* And yet, Karina stepped through the door and started slowly down the hallway to her left.

Though her internal monologue was screaming *why?* She knew why. She was bored out of her goddamn gourd. A little excitement, even if it involved *axe murder*, would be a stimulating change of pace. She couldn't help herself.

Her heart was racing now as she neared the door to the cold storage room, clearly the source of the noise. She quietly put her ear up to the door. The banging was coming in brief spurts. There would be a loud metallic warping sound, then a muffled voice, then quiet. Again and again, for different lengths and different intensities. And then it stopped completely. Karina waited at the door for what seemed like an eternity, then ever so slowly, grasped the doorknob and pushed open the door.

Inside was the cold storage room. Or the *powder closet*, as Joe called it. It was small, and stacked on either side with large horizontal lockers that ran the entire length of the room. Only a few of these lockers were occupied at the moment. People who had no one to claim them, or were unidentifiable.

Smiley's had been in business for six months now, but people still hadn't given their trust over to her just yet. At least not for *family affairs*. For now, Smiley's was the home of the unclaimed. Of those whose names the living would forget rather quickly. Smiley would talk about marketing and *getting into the community*, but the truth was that Campaiyote was racist. *Shit*, America was racist. And people here didn't like the idea of a black woman owning a business. Or of taking care of dead relatives. That made Karina sick. Joe too. But there was nothing to be done except move forward. For now, making deals with crime scene cleaners was the best way to bring in steady income. Thus, the bodies in the back were *family-less. The lonely dead. Like Frankenstein's monster.*

Karina opened the door slowly and looked around. Silence. She stepped inside and tip-toed her way around the big stainless steel island in the middle of the room. *Quiet. Guess it ought to be.* Karina stopped and looked around. *Maybe it was just the AC banging around or something.* After another fifteen seconds of silence, Karina let her nerves relax. She let out an enormous sigh (almost out of disappointment), and was about to head back towards the lobby when one of the metal lockers exploded into movement, like there was a rabid raccoon locked inside. Karina screamed.

Karina wasn't exactly the most girlish girl, but the scream she let fly then certainly was — the whole nine yards — hands to cheeks, 100 decibels, glass shattering, horror movie scream. The shaking in the locker stopped abruptly. Karina could only gaze at the locker. Then, came a voice, muffled by the little metal door that kept the coffin-style cabinet in place.

"Um, hello? Is someone out there? Could you let me out, please?" Karina stood in shocked silence, staring at the locker.

"Hello?... It's uh, a little cramped in here."

#

IT was a good minute before Karina could bring herself to move. Not knowing what to do, she looked around the room to the open door, hoping Joe or Smiley would come running in to help. *Totally normal, Karina, they'd say. Just a zombie, no big deal. Why don't you let us handle this and go back to the lobby.*

But they didn't.

She froze in place, unable to move. *I just need to wait… wait for…* she didn't quite know. After a while, the voice came again. Karina could only stare at the metal coffin in horror and awe.

"Hey out there. Not sure exactly where I am, but I'd appreciate it mightily if someone would let me out. I heard a scream… I know someone's there. Unless this is… Hell, I guess. That would suck… I'm not gonna hurt anyone… I just wanna stand up and stretch… It's cold in here."

Karina raced through the possibilities in her mind. As she emerged from shock, her thoughts cleared. *Someone is trapped. In a cold storage locker. For dead people. But. But he's not dead.* Even with the muffling, she recognized the voice as male. She'd heard of this happening, had read tons of stories about people that'd been buried alive, but never dreamed it would happen to her. Her horror was slowly transitioning to a kind of perverse giddiness. *It's like when they used to put bells on strings down to buried coffins so that if the person woke up, they could signal for help.* If she opened the locker, would she find a guy with half his head blown off who had miraculously regained consciousness? She suddenly wished she'd brought her camera.

Even in her excitement, it was hard to move any closer to the locker door. She forced herself to take a step, and then another. Then she found herself standing at the locker door, reaching out for the lock. She hesitated for a moment. Again, those horror movie clichés came rushing into her brain: *girl is curious, trusts a stranger, gets murdered with an axe.* Each thought invariably ended with: *murdered with an axe. I should go call Smiley.* Instead, she reached up and clicked the lock.

With a metallic springing sound, the locker popped open to reveal two shoed feet. They clicked together.

"Hey! Thank you! Pull me out!" came the voice.

Karina did.

As she slid the locker out from the wall, she became more and more certain something gruesome was waiting for her. *He'll be missing his face, or there'll be an arrow sticking out of his eye or some shit.* After revealing a normal set of legs and a torso, she finally came to his head. It was all there, all *intact*. It was just… *a guy.* He looked older, maybe in his late thirties or early forties. But there was no axe buried in his skull, or missing facial features, or obvious injury. He looked fine. When he was fully out of the locker, he looked up at Karina and blinked. They stared at each other for a few moments, then the man sat up. Karina stumbled backwards, wide-eyed.

The man swung his feet down from the locker and rubbed his eyes with the back of his hands, obviously struggling to adjust to the fluorescent lighting in the storage room. He looked at Karina through one eye as he rubbed the other, then shivered violently.

"Um, hello," he said.

Karina's mouth hung open in shock, but she managed a squeaky response.

"Hello."

"Where… am I?"

"… You're at a funeral home."

The man looked around at the grim, clinical storage room and at the other lockers.

"Huh. That's weird… I could've sworn I was just in a… a big… train station?" The man stared down at his hands and arms, looking confused.

Karina was still frightened, but the man's easy demeanor was putting her at some ease. She didn't think he was going to hurt her, or anyone else for that matter. *He doesn't even seem to know who he is.* The man looked up from his hands to Karina.

"You wouldn't happen to have any coffee, would ya?"

#

KARINA sat at her desk in the lobby across from the dead man. *Or the undead man?* She was staring as he sipped a cup of black coffee with a smiley face printed on the side. She'd also given him a little throw blanket done in the Navajo style, which he'd drawn around himself like a poncho. Despite it being a bajillion degrees outside, he'd been shivering with the cold. He looked like a little old babushka that had accidentally wandered through a portal to the middle of Texas. Maybe he was. The man looked up at Karina.

"Hey… I appreciate the coffee, but uh, could you not stare at me like that? I feel like I'm being examined."

"Sorry."

Karina kept staring. The man sighed.

"What did you say your name was again?" asked Karina.

"Dievs. Robert Dievs."

"Why were you locked in a cadaver cabinet, Robert?"

"I told you, I have no idea. I was in some *place,* some weird train station, with very unhelpful attendants. I went through an exit door… and that's all I remember. Next thing I know, I'm in that box, in the dark. Thought I was buried alive for a minute there."

Dievs shivered. Karina just stared and blinked.

"I should've taken your picture in the locker. Maybe I could've sold it to a magazine or something."

Dievs looked at Karina uncomprehendingly.

"You're a weird girl. And that's coming from someone who may have just risen from the dead. *Apparently*. I don't feel very dead though…"

"What's your unresolved business?"

"Say again?"

"Your unresolved business? Why did you come back and not… *erm… pass on?* All ghosts have a reason for haunting shit. Not that… you're a ghost, or I mean… kind of, but…"

"Please. I ain't no ghost."

Dievs took a moment to consider Karina's question. "I can't remember anything. So I guess that's my business. To figure out who I am… who I was, I guess?"

Karina considered this.

"Kinda boring. You sure there's not anything else?"

"… I think there was something about *peanuts*… and…" Images came and went like lightning inside Dievs' head. *A briefcase filled with dark blue light. A man in a white suit. A dog. A gun. And a pair of terrible green eyes.* Then they were gone. "…uh, not really, no."

"Hmm… Well, I can help get you started if you'd like. You're lucky I'm the one who found you."

"Lucky?"

"Someone else might have turned you in to the looney bin. But I, my friend, happen to be a connoisseur of all things creepy, and I pledge, on my honor as a supernaturalist, to help you fulfill your unresolved business on this earthly plane and return you to the great above!" Karina had raised her hands into the air and grinned maniacally at the ceiling. Her smile faltered. "Or the great train station above, I guess."

Dievs watched Karina in silence and sipped his coffee.

"Sound good?" asked Karina, smiling.

"Well…"

CHAPTER NINETEEN

Party at the End of the Lane (Part 3)

IT was rare that Hank went to a crime scene with other people. Exceedingly rare. In fact, this was only the third time ever. He spent the overwhelming majority of his days at work (and at home) alone. *Easier that way.* Even though deep down — *and he hated to admit it, even to himself* — he was happy to have comrades to share his misery with. The current situation made him supremely uncomfortable. *People. With mouths and brains. That I have to talk to for longer than ten minutes. Gulp.*

Smiley's angry confidence was also making him nervous. She was a smart lady, Smiley, and she could handle herself. But she didn't know Brackington like he did, and she wasn't in the mood to listen to Hank. *Nobody ever listens to poor ol' Hank. No, no… what does he know? Only what a psychopathic monster James Brackington is.* This was the beginning of the end. He would trap her in his fucked-up murder web, and use her — *and use her, and use her* — until there was nothing left. *Then, what do you do with used things?*

Still, he understood where she was coming from. It was partially how Brackington had gotten him in the first place.

Money. She had started a business, and she needed money. *Customers.* Brackington was playing the part well. *Money talks.*

704 Emerson was, despite its gloomy aura, a beautiful house, large, surrounded by big oak trees and tastefully decorated. The path down from the dead-end lane led straight to the front door, which opened into a large airy living room with exposed wooden beams running along the ceiling, German bierhaus style.

It was clear as soon as Smiley, Hank and Joe stepped in that there had been one hell of a party here. Trash littered the floor: solo cups, bottles, shattered glass, vomit and plenty of other unidentifiable stains and debris. Hank stepped over a mannequin torso that appeared to have been burned and or beaten like a piñata. A big stripe of red paint ran around the entire room and all over the floor. It was as if someone had emptied a paint can by spinning around in a circle with the lid off. *Probably what happened.* For Hank, it was a reminder of all the other times he'd seen something similar, only, those times, it hadn't been paint. Beethoven's green name tag glinted in the back of his brain.

Hank had seen this kind of party before. *One of Brackington's bashes.* He'd suspected that most of his *parties* ended with one kind of bloodshed or another. The red paint slung about the living room was a warm up — *an advertisement* — for what was surely awaiting them upstairs.

#

"...JEEZUS, they wrecked this place. No gettin' that paint out now. Need a belt sander or some shit," Joe said to the silent living room.

"That's not our business, Joe. C'mon, upstairs. Lady on the phone said master bedroom," said Smiley.

"Smiley. I won't stop you from going up there. *Can't* stop you, obviously. But if you do this, he'll never let you go. Now's your shot to get out. Just… leave…" said Hank, looking down at the floor.

Smiley turned and gazed at Hank.

"…What has he done to you, honey?" When Hank didn't answer, she continued. "Running away is no way to live a life, and I don't intend on letting some punk white boy threaten me, even if he's as bad as you seem to think he is. Now. You helping, or not?"

"I'm here, aren't I?" Hank replied, somewhat sulkily.

"Let's go then."

Smiley was first up the stairs, followed by Joe and Hank. The wooden steps creaked subtly under their weight, somehow making the house feel even quieter. Hank noticed Joe had begun to sweat. The dark stains under his armpits were growing larger by the second, and sweat slicked his hair down against his forehead. *C'mon Joe. No worries, baby. Picture a beach in Cuba. That's what I do.* Hank didn't say this out loud. He knew that if Joe had a Cuban beach hiding in his brain, he was already there, sipping an ice-cold piña colada.

They crested the stairs and made their way down the hallway. Joe wiped nervously at his face with the sleeve of his uniform. Several plain wooden doors lined the walls, but at the end of the corridor was a closed red door, wider than the others. Someone had left the lights on in the house, and though sun was filtering through several windows, a single lamp hanging above the red door was the primary source of light at that end of the hallway. It was almost too obvious that the red door was their destination. *Like some Kubrick-Lynch nightmare door. I mean, fuck.*

They walked in silence, not needing to communicate their thoughts, and eventually reached the end of the hallway. Smiley, who had been moving briskly, still filled with that angry confidence, gripped the door handle. For a moment she faltered, and Hank thought she might turn around. *Just leave. Quit and never come back. Please.* But she didn't. And before he could prepare himself for what lay on the other side, she had pushed open the door. He heard her gasp before he saw for himself what Brackington had left them.

#

AT first, Hank thought the bed was one of those velvet love pads at those fancy Tokyo love hotels, all red and plush and heart-shaped. He saw then, the girl lying on her back, shoulders away from the headboard, and realized that what he'd thought were folds in a red blanket, were her insides. Her insides were… *outside.* And where her head ought to have been was air and a stump, though some of her neck hair remained, draping down to the carpeted floor. Two more women lay on the floor on either side of the bed. They were not decapitated, though neither were they un-mutilated.

Smiley stood in shock, still gripping the door handle with white knuckles. Joe looked only for a second before turning and throwing up. Hank moved aside as fast as he could, but the vomit still splashed all over his shoes. Joe didn't even try to apologize. He was too busy riding the vomit comet to speak. Joe put his hand on the wall to steady himself while Hank stepped around him to get a better look into the room.

"… What… in God's name," whispered Smiley.

Hank stepped forward to stand beside Smiley. *This is one for the vault*, he thought, but he couldn't shut down yet. *Not yet.*

"Welcome to the monkey house."

"This was no *accident*. The woman on the phone said, *accident*. She told Karina, *accident*… This… was no God damn *accident*!" Hank watched as a tear welled in Smiley's eye. She shivered subtly, as if something had touched her tailbone.

"This is James," said Hank. "Did he say the police had already cleared it?"

"…Yeah… how…"

"Been here before. I know how it goes."

"You mean…"

"Yeah. I've cleaned… *stuff like this*… several times… I'm sure there are a lot more I haven't seen."

Smiley pulled her eyes off the decapitated woman on the bed and turned to Hank.

"…Why don't you tell anyone? The police, the… the… the state police?"

"He'd have me killed before I even got close… or maybe he'd let me tell them, just so he could have his guys on the force frame me, or put me in the looney bin."

Smiley didn't reply to this, just let her jaw hang open. Eventually, she turned back to the gruesome scene laid out before her. Joe got his technicolor yawn under control and stood up, though he kept his back to the room.

"…Hey," *Gulp*. "I, uh, dunno if I can help you guys with this… That's… that's too much for me. You gotta get me a blindfold or something."

"Close your eyes if you have to, Joe. But you're helping. Hank says we really have no choice in the matter."

"I tried to get you to leave…" Hank interrupted.

"So we're just gonna have to get it over with," said Smiley.

And with that, she took a shaky breath and stepped into the room. Hank watched, half in sadness, half in awe, then followed. Joe moaned.

"Oh… God."

CHAPTER TWENTY

The Supernaturalist

KARINA sat criss-cross applesauce on the carpeted floor of Smiley's front lobby across from Dievs, also sitting cross-legged, the blanket she'd given him still draped over his shoulders. His coffee had gone thoroughly cold. Their attention was turned to the floor space between them. Karina had drawn out a DIY Ouija board on a piece of manila folder paper and was currently humming *Break on Through* by The Doors in low tones while touching her fingertips to an upside-down shot glass resting on the paper. Dievs was also touching the glass, though he didn't recognize the song, nor did he really understand what in holy hell was supposed to be happening.

Karina's eyes were closed, but Dievs' were open, and he was looking at her like she'd lost her cow-tippin' mind. He thought maybe she had. Maybe *he* had. *Aren't I the one who was supposed to be strange? Having just risen from the dead and all? How is she weirder?*

Karina's eyes sprang open.

"You're not channeling, Robert. You must channel your body-spirit connection; otherwise, the souls of the damned can't speak through us. Mm?"

"Well… uh, let me give it another try."

Dievs closed his eyes and tried to… *channel his body-spirit connection.* For a moment, he thought it might be working. He felt strange. A tingling sensation wormed its way down from his chest into his abdomen.

"Hey… hey! I think something is happening," he shouted. Karina just kept humming The Doors. Dievs squinted his eyes together and held his core tight. The sensation grew and grew… and then dropped right down into his bowels. *Oh.*

"Uh… is there a bathroom here?"

#

AFTER Dievs had relieved himself of a *whopper*, Karina insisted they try the Ouija board again. And so they sat back down on the floor criss-cross, hands together on the shot glass. Karina didn't hum this time; they just sat together in the silence of the lobby. Above them, the ceiling fan swung lazily, like a ladle through old soup.

They didn't move for at least two minutes. Dievs was growing tired of the whole exercise. *I mean, I can't even remember who I am. What am I doing here? Who is this girl? What's going…* but just when he was about to give up and take his hands off the shot glass, it moved. Karina's eyes burst open. Above the pair, the ceiling fan stopped, as if it had hit a brick wall.

"Body-spirit connection," she whispered. "You aren't moving it, are you?"

"No…" Dievs replied.

They watched the shot glass glide over the yellow paper, past *h, g, f-* to stop abruptly on *D.* "D," said Karina. The glass paused, as if making sure they had enough time to read the letter and remember it, then it moved on to the next, and then the next.

"O… N…. T…. E… A…"

And after three minutes of this, the glass stopped moving. It was clear that whatever had sent the message was done. They both felt an invisible hand lift from theirs.

"T, H, E, P, E, A… *Don't eat the peanuts*," said Karina. She looked down at the note she had been jotting on and blinked. "Don't… eat. The peanuts." She sounded utterly nonplussed.

"Well… what the hell." Dievs watched Karina shift on the floor a bit, as if something had tickled her tailbone.

"Hey, I said there was something about peanuts, didn't I?"

"Yeah, but what does it mean?" asked Karina.

Dievs considered the question for a moment.

"Well. Maybe, *and this is just a guess*, should the opportunity to eat peanuts present itself… We… don't eat them," he said.

Karina looked down at the board again, looking for more answers.

"*No*… doesn't seem quite right. Who sent this, anyway? Who's tellin' me I can't eat peanuts? Who are **they** to tell **me** what legumes I can and can't consume, huh? I think we should go find some peanuts and eat them. See what happens."

"We… are just *not* on the same wavelength here."

#

THIRTY minutes later, Dievs and Karina stood in the grain aisle of Campaiyote's Piggly Wiggly. Karina hoisted a jumbo container of shelled Planters peanuts up from the bottom shelf, smiling wickedly.

"Bounty secured. We're gonna resolve your unfinished business lickity split, Mista, get you that eternal peace and rest you need. Don-chu worry bout nuthin'."

Dievs raised an eyebrow.

"Hey wait, doesn't that mean I have to die agai…"

"C'mon. Let's go."

The store had only a few customers milling about. Karina recognized a few of them.

"Mrs. Jibbenwald… Sarah Thompson… *that bitch.*"

Karina lived in Campaiyote, Dievs had learned, only a twenty minute walk from the funeral parlor, and before getting the secretary job, had worked for a few months at this very Piggly Wiggly. Though she didn't have many fond memories of it, it seemed to Dievs. She recognized the woman running the cash register too.

"Peggy… God almighty she's slow."

A woman far too old (in Karina's opinion) to be charged with the one duty in a grocery store that required some amount of speed. Despite the sleepiness of the place, there were already two people waiting in line to check out. And of course, only the one cashier, Peggy, who seemed more closely related to a three-toed sloth than a homosapien. Her back arched *just so* she might look right at home clinging to the underside of a tree branch and letting moss grow on her stomach.

"She's only 55," said Karina.

"No way," he said, giving Karina an incredulous look. Karina shrugged.

"She liked to party." Dievs was still unsatisfied. "Hard," Karina added.

Karina stood and watched Peggy for a few moments, then turned to Dievs. She said nothing, but while making eye contact, slowly stuffed the box of Planters peanuts under her oversized black T-shirt. Dievs realized what she was doing too late, and Karina spun towards the exit. Dievs looked around frantically to see if anyone had noticed, then reluctantly followed her towards the door, trying to walk as normally as possible. *First day back from the dead and I'm already shoplifting. Good start.*

Though no one was paying them any mind whatsoever, when she got close to the door, Karina ran. She pushed through the door and bolted out into the parking lot. The little bell hanging above the door tinkled loudly. Dievs cringed and turned around. No one was even looking. Peggy continued to scan cans of Campbell's soup with the speed of a thousand snails on slug-back. Dievs found Karina around the corner of the building, about to shovel a handful of peanuts into her mouth.

"Hey!" he said, and moved to take the box from her.

"No! This is America, goddammit! I shan't have my legume rights infringed upon, especially not by a ghost! I ain't afraid a no ghost!"

Karina tried to pack a handful of peanut into her mouth, but Dievs grabbed her arm before she could smush any in. They wrestled this way for half a minute, peanuts spilling out all over the parking lot.

"It said not to eat the peanuts!" said Dievs, still holding Karina's arm back.

"Who said? People eat peanuts all the time!" Karina shouted in reply. "We'll never get your soul to be at peace if we don't break the rules a little!"

"What are you even talking about?" Dievs eventually got the bucket of peanuts away from Karina and staggered back, sweating and panting.

"Jeezus…" Dievs' tailbone twitched a little. "…You're stronger than you look."

Karina looked at Dievs with squinted eyes and lifted a single peanut up to her mouth. Dievs stepped forward and slapped her hand. The peanut went flying over the blacktop. Karina watched it go.

"What is *wrong* with you?" Dievs asked, unbelievingly.

"My mom says I'm a natural born risk taker."

"…Ya don't say."

It was then that Dievs noticed the three figures standing in the parking lot to his left. They were standing in a row, watching him and Karina: a big tall white fella, like a lumberjack, a kind of sad-looking guy, and a younger black woman. All three were staring at them with a look that went beyond public concern. Following Dievs' gaze, Karina turned to face the three figures.

"…Oh, hey boss. I just, uh… stepped out for a second. This is… Mr. Dievs."

The three figures all turned to look at Dievs, who was breathing heavily and holding the jumbo container of peanuts. He raised his hand, smiled sheepishly and gave a little wave. The sad-looking guy returned the wave halfheartedly, but no one said anything. Dievs noticed the trio looked rather pale, and they all had red stains on their shoes and clothes.

"Uhh… what happened to you guys?" asked Karina.

CHAPTER TWENTY-ONE

Palaver at Denny's (Part 1)

SMILEY was the one who brought the meeting to order.

An hour after finding Karina and Dievs fighting over a tub of Planters Peanuts in the parking lot of the Piggly Wiggly, all three employees of Smiley's Funeral Home, as well as Hank the crime scene cleaner, and Dievs, the undead amnesiac, all sat together in a six-person booth at the Campaiyote Denny's.

On one side sat Dievs, Hank and Smiley, and on the other, Joe and Karina. No one spoke, and somehow the clatter and clank of the overheated coffee pots and fellow diner's forks and knives on stoneware plates failed to provide the American comfort Smiley was searching for. *Craving*, actually.

She sat with her face folded down into her hands. *What a day… And it ain't even over yet. It was already hard… and now I might be the next target for some crazy-ass psycho mob boss? Just my luck. Maybe I should go, like Hank said. I certainly never want to do something like that again.* She shivered as the image of a small intestine sliding onto a flat rusty shovel blade flashed in her mind. Smiley didn't have a vault yet, like Hank did. She would. The red faux leather squeaked as she shifted in her corner spot of the double-wide booth.

Around Smiley, the other members of the *what-a-day* club sat quietly, eyeing one another — though Dievs was certainly drawing the most attention. It had taken a bit of convincing from Karina to let him come at all, and no one was really sure what his deal was. Karina had said she would tell them the story, but had revealed no details yet. When prompted, she'd said that Smiley and Joe just didn't share the same enthusiasm for the *supernatural* as she did, which had puzzled them all even more. Dievs sat quietly, hands folded in his lap, looking down at a pink sugar packet lying on the table.

A young waitress with a messy fountain of blonde hair on her head walked briskly up to the table, smiling, notepad in hand.

"Howdy! How ya'll doin'? I'm Betty, I'll be your server. Can I start ya off with some drinks?"

This question was answered with silence and lowered heads. The waitress's smile faltered. Karina looked up and grinned darkly at the waitress.

"Five coffees, please… and the All-Star Meat-nado breaky burrito for me, with a triple scoop of vanilla ice cream brought out as soon as I take the last bite… and I mean, *as **soon*** as I take the last bite. Like an Olympic baton handoff, get me? I want to feel like I'm in a calorie marathon; no breaks, no…"

The waitress was no longer smiling and was instead writing furiously on her pad while nodding. Smiley lifted her head out of her hands.

"Not on my tab, missy. You want the meat-nado or whatever, you can buy it yourself. Just the coffees, please, Betty."

"But Ms. Smiley, I *neeeed* the meat-nado to grow up big and strong like Joe. Ya know, protein n' stuff."

Joe turned his head at the mention of his name, but could only manage, "Huh?" It appeared he was still lost somewhere in the shock and horror of the last few hours.

"Just the coffees," reiterated Smiley.

"Ah… man…" Karina said dejectedly.

The waitress nodded at Smiley and rushed off to get the coffee. Smiley put her hands down on the table, sat up straight, took a deep breath and tried to compose herself. *Eyes closed. 1…2…3… Eyes open.*

"*So.* Let's get all this straight. And I don't want to leave anything out now, especially if this is all as serious as you say, Hank. I mean, I talked with that creep, and sure, he was… *well, creepy…* but I can't imagine he would do anything…" But even as she said it, Smiley knew she didn't believe it.

Maybe I can imagine it. She remembered the way he had looked at her from over his car, that evil-looking blue Shelby GT. The dark laughter in his eyes, way down, hidden somewhere underneath that pretty face.

"*Well,* never mind what I think. Why don't we start with you, Mr. *Dievs,* was it? Who are you, and why were you wrestling over peanuts in the parking lot with my secretary?"

Dievs coughed and shifted in his seat.

"Well… uh, I…"

"Okay, listen," Karina broke in. "Mister…" *Cough.* "Dievs, is my… my new friend." Karina flipped her head from Dievs to Smiley, in a gesture that clearly showed she'd settled on her angle for this explanation. "He's my new friend… that I met…" Karina faltered and looked back at Dievs who stared back at her blankly, like a portrait on the back of a milk bottle. "That I met at work."

Smiley raised her eyebrows. Hank and Joe were hardly paying attention, despite being in the middle of the conversation. *Literally*. In fact, Hank had drifted off in his seat. A little vine of drool worming its way down from the corner of his mouth had nearly cleared his chin. Joe was watching its progress like a baby staring at a rattle.

"You… were looking for burial services, Mr. Dievs?"

"Well… not exactly…"

"Ya know…" Smiley squinted at Dievs from her end of the booth. "You actually look really… familiar. Have we met before?"

"No! Uh, no, no, no, Definitely not. I would know. Definitely haven't met before," Karina interrupted again, a bit nervously this time.

"Uh, Karina, that was rude. I was asking Mr. Dievs."

"Uhm, well… not that I can recall, Ma'am. But I'm pleased to make your acquaintance."

Dievs reached over Hank to offer Smiley his hand, carefully avoiding the lengthening strand of drool coming from his mouth. She took it slowly, still trying to place him. After a firm shake, she gave up and flashed him a bright, if not tired, smile.

"Pleased to meet you. So, if you weren't looking for burial services, what can we help you with?"

"*Well,* he was actually looking for a bowling alley, and he saw the sign, right? Remember that one guy who came in the other day? Same thing," Karina interjected.

"That guy was flat out drunk, and probably homeless too, Karina."

"*AND…*" Karina said this word as if it were two syllables. *Eh-yund.* "We got to talking, see. He asked me for some advice on mind-body dualism applications, and also about my thoughts on the Firth Solway Spaceman…"

Smiley collapsed into her hands again like a crumpled piece of paper.

"Oh, God, Karina." Smiley shifted as if something had tickled her tailbone. "Please… no more of the UFO stuff, and the spirits and the demons and the Ouija…"

"Hey! They proved the photo genuine! And it's incubus…"

"And all the ritual hoodoo voodoo, it's all bologna. You're being swindled by these crazy-ass, paranoid tabloid writers. They just want your subscription money, honey. Did you bring another nut into the funeral home? No offense, Mr. Dievs, but…" Dievs lifted his hands up in a sort of *I totally get it* kind of way.

"Scam," said Joe, still staring at Hank's drool droplet. Which was now entering phase three: descent onto the front of his shirt. Smiley and Karina both turned to Joe, stupefied that he had been listening at all. He looked up.

"What? They are. All scams, I mean. I got a subscription to a magazine about big foot, Sasquatch ya know, always liked that stuff. After a couple of months I saw a program on NBC that said they'd been faking the whole time. Just photos of someone in a big suit made of badger hair. Though, I'll say, the Firth Solway thing is compelling… What?"

Smiley blinked at Joe for a moment in silence. Karina raised her hand towards Joe, like '*see?*' then turned back to Smiley and broke the quiet.

"Bigfoot is a scam, but what I do with my paycheck isn't anyone's business. That's my right as an American citizen. I'll spend it all on virgin blood candles if I so please. And I was *connecting* with a potential customer, just like you told me to, Ms. Davis," said Karina.

Smiley let out a big sigh. "Oh, go ahead," she said, with a small wave of her hand. "But try not to get too deep into all that conspiracy shit when you're on the clock. *Please.* Especially to the more *average* customers, eh? No offense, Mr. Dievs." Dievs raised his hands up again. "Hey, and what were you doing at Piggly Wiggly, anyway? I seem to recall you were *working* when I left. You locked the home right?"

"I might ask you the same thing," said Karina.

"Careful now. I am your employer. *Well, for now.* And I also know your mom," said Smiley.

Karina shrank a little at that.

"Sorry," she muttered. "We just… after our chat, Mr. Dievs and I, that is… we had a real craving for peanuts. So we went to get some. And yes, I locked up the shop."

Smiley looked as if she was having a really hard time swallowing this particular pill.

"A craving for peanuts, you say. And this couldn't wait?"

"Not even for a minute," answered Karina confidently.

Smiley turned to Dievs, who had been watching this exchange with a confused kind of wonder. He met Smiley's questioning gaze, shut his dangling jaw and nodded.

"Yes, ma'am. Unsalted. Peanuts," he said. "It's part of that… mind-body dualism thing she mentioned. Very… *critical*… for all that."

Karina nodded along and pointed at Dievs as if he were exhibit A at the *told-you-so-museum*.

"You know." Smiley paused for at least five seconds, just staring at Dievs. Her eyes darted away for a moment to check the status of Hank's drool bomb (almost touching shirt). "We can just pretend I buy all that and move on."

Karina threw out two big thumbs up and smiled.

CHAPTER TWENTY-TWO

Palaver at Denny's (Part 2)

"HEY y'all…"

Hank vaulted awake, abruptly severing his spittle rope and rocking the table violently with his knees. He let out a short, throaty scream. A sound like when someone jumps into ice-cold water, like the air had just been forced out of him. He'd been having a terrible dream, but then, most of his dreams were terrible. It took him a few seconds to remember where he was and who he was with. Then his day came rushing back to him in gritty detail, and he wished he hadn't woken up at all. The waitress with the blonde hair stood looking at Hank with an open mouth.

"…Gotch'er coffees."

Hank smiled up at her, dried spit still clinging to the side of his chin, and reached for one of the steaming cups like a baby reaching for a bottle. She handed it to him, pretending she hadn't just scared a stranger out of a nap.

Hank's nightmare was already receding into the brain mist that swallows up forgotten dreams, but he did recall it having something to do with peanuts. *And speaking of… didn't this guy… what was his name, Dievs? Didn't he just say something about peanuts?*

Hank thought he'd recognized the guy when they'd stumbled upon the kerfuffle in the Piggly Wiggly parking lot, but after a moment of contemplation he'd dismissed it. *Probably just passed him on the street or something.* But now, sitting next to him in the Denny's booth, that familiarity hit him again. *Something to do with peanuts…* Something barked at him from his brain vault, and he gave Dievs a quick sideways glance. Still, nothing helpful came to him. He thought about mentioning his own supply of mysteriously abandoned peanuts, but it was still a little coincidental to put any importance on it.

"So, now you know what I was up to, what happened with you guys?" Karina asked as the coffees were distributed.

Smiley opened her mouth to reply, but Hank cut her off as he lifted his coffee cup to his lips, blowing at the surface.

"Ah-ta-tatatata, please… let me have a few sips of my coffee before you start telling this story. I just… I think that if you talk about it, my coffee is gonna go bad."

Karina looked at Hank, almost angrily.

"I think you're in the wrong profession, Mr. Cooper," she said.

"Jeezus, what am I, 80? *Hank*, please. And you don't know the half of it, son."

Karina seemed about to speak again, but saw that Smiley had also bent her head down to gaze into the blackness of her cup-a-Joe and subsequently closed her mouth. The waitress finished handing out coffees, gave them a look that said *Jeez, you guys are weird*, then hurried off.

It was at least three minutes before anyone broke the silence, but after a while, Hank had had sufficient sips of his coffee to allow Smiley to tell the gruesome story. She didn't seem eager to re-live it. At all. Dievs and Karina sat silently, listening to the tale. Hank interjected only when she mentioned Brackington and the interaction they'd had through the window of his car. She didn't exaggerate Brackington's evil aura, the sense of doom that seemed to hover around him (and not in the self-pitying kind of way, but in the, *I **bring** the doom*, sort of way), but also didn't leave it out.

"He's a monster," said Hank.

"Wait, I thought you hadn't gotten to the house yet?" asked Karina.

"Hank here has worked with Brackignton before, apparently."

"Whaaatt… plot twist," said Karina.

"Not voluntarily," said Hank, gazing down into his coffee. "And like it or not, you all do too now. The guy's got his fingers in so many pies… it's like he's untouchable. I don't know what he does, or who he even is, really. But what I can tell you is, I've done what we did today enough times to know he's got people in the force, in the courts. In the *government*. Enough people to make things go away. *Terrible things*. And we're a part of the very important process of cleaning up the evidence." At this, Hank's voice dropped. "I used to be enough, but I guess… he's looking to expand."

"You make him sound like Michael Corleone or something," said Karina, shrugging off the gravity in Hank's voice. She turned to Smiley for backup, then saw how grave she looked. Hank lowered his voice even further.

"This was a trial run. I'm serious when I say he could have someone listening to us right now." Hank glanced briefly at the patrons sitting in the booths and tables around them. They looked alright, but he guessed that would be the idea for a spy. "I wouldn't put it past him. He needs a reliable cleanup service, but if we don't cooperate… *well*. We wouldn't be reliable then, would we."

Smiley looked at Hank with an expression that said, *I really want to call you crazy, but with what I've seen, that's getting harder to do.* After a moment, she continued on with the story, and, sparing the goriest details, described the scene they'd found in the bedroom of the party mansion at the end of the wooded lane.

When Smiley finally finished, Karina had turned a shade or two paler than when the story had begun. And for once, was quiet. Dievs had digested the story in silence and now seemed to be lost in thought. Though whether it was about their situation or something else entirely, Hank couldn't tell. He felt terrible for dragging these people into this. *The orbit of a criminal lunatic. I tried to stop it. I did.* But, as his mother used to say, *here we are now. Yeah. He we are now. And what to do…*

"Karina, you're fired," said Smiley, with no playfulness in her voice.

Karina looked up, shocked. "What? You can't be serious. I…"

"You heard all I just said, right? And what Mr. Cooper said too?"

"*Hank*, guys… jeezus. *Hank*," Hank put in quietly.

"You might still have a chance to get out of this if he doesn't know you work for me. Or maybe he might not care if the sixteen-year-old secretary quits. I don't want you dragged into anything. *Anything*. Even if it is bologna. According to our resident criminal overlord informant, Joe and I have already been marked.

"The most exciting thing that's ever happened in my whole life, and you want me to quit?" asked Karina incredulously. She was still pale, but there was a blackness in her eyes that kind of scared Hank. *Kind of like Brackington*, he thought, then shoved the idea away.

"No. I'm firing you," said Smiley, matter-of-factly. "Honestly, I couldn't have afforded you much longer anyway."

Karina's jaw dropped. It looked like she might try to argue again, then the pointlessness of it seemed to settle over her like a heavy blanket. Joe reached over and patted her on the back.

"Hey, could be worse. Better you get fired than *not be able to quit*, right?" he said.

"Easy for you to say," Karina grumbled, looking down into her empty cup.

Smiley leaned over the table to look at Dievs.

"Mr. Dievs. I hope we haven't scared you too much. It'd probably be best if you went on your way too. You've heard more than you wanted to, I'm sure. It was very nice to meet you, though."

Dievs lifted himself out of the cloud of thought he'd been lost in and nodded to Smiley.

"Likewise, Ma'am."

Karina shrugged down in her seat, as pouty children do. A raised eyebrow from Smiley made her roll her eyes dramatically, and she slunk reluctantly out of the booth, sighing heavily as she did so. Dievs followed, minus the attitude. They stood at the edge of the table.

"Well. Guess I'll see you guys around," said Karina.

"I'll mail your last paycheck," said Smiley.

"It was a pleasure to meet you all," said Dievs, holding the now half-empty bucket of peanuts under his right arm. Everyone seated at the table nodded, with half-hearted smiles.

Hank watched as they turned and made their way out the front door, Karina almost stomping. *That Dievs is a strange one. Swear I've seen him before…* Hank didn't know it, but Joe and Smiley were thinking the same thing.

When Karina and Dievs were out of sight, Smiley, Hank and Joe looked plainly at each other in silence. Hank recognized the look on their faces. It was the same one he'd seen on his own face so many times in his cracked bathroom mirror: hopelessness. *What have I done.* The thought raced through his brain like hot lightning, and he felt sick. *Karina was right. I might be in the wrong line of work.*

CHAPTER TWENTY-THREE

Suburbia

KARINA let out a big, *woe is me*, sigh.

"Guess I have to come up with *another* explanation for my mom as to why I lost this job. I can't freakin' believe it. You know this isn't the first time this has happened to me? I got fired from the library because they were *'concerned with my intense interest in the subject of witchcraft.'* Like, when did reading become a fireable offense? It's *IN* the damn library. It's not like I wrote *'A History of Ritual Sacrifice.'* Though, I did do a pretty excellent report on it, if I say so myself."

Dievs walked beside Karina down a sidewalk in a small suburb of Campaiyote. He was listening to her, but his eyes were trained on the new world around him. It all seemed familiar, but somehow strange. He watched as a car came rolling down the road towards them. A woman with blonde hair, a bob cut and cartoonishly large sunglasses was behind the wheel. *That seems right,* he thought. *I've seen that before. I've seen neighborhoods and houses and people and Denny's diners.* But something was wrong, and it was bugging him. Though the message from the great beyond would suggest it had to do with the bucket of peanuts tucked under his arm — *or peanuts in general, I guess* — Dievs thought it was something else.

The sounds. It was the sound of the breeze rushing through the green leaves above him, and the feel of it against his face. It sounded like life. And some dull instinct in the back of his brain told him he shouldn't be hearing those sounds. The quiet, purgatorial hum of the train station came back to him in a wave. He got that tight, panicky feeling in his chest again, and it only got worse when he groped in his mind for an identity that wasn't there. A suitcase, filled with dark blue light, opened briefly in his mind.

"Are you listening?" asked Karina. Dievs snapped out of his daze and looked down at the teenager who had saved him from that cold metal coffin, and probably much more than that.

"Sorry, I got kinda lost there for a moment," he said.

"Well, better pull it together. We're almost at my house. I'm gonna see if you can stay for dinner."

"Oh, that's okay, I don't know if I should…"

"Don't know if you should go with the only person who knows you rose from the dead earlier today? You have somewhere better to be? A business meeting at five, perhaps?"

Dievs was going to open his mouth to object, then shut it.

"You… You have a point," he said.

Karina nodded like *Than-q you very much*. Dievs took a moment to think about just how right she'd been about… well, lots of things since he'd met her this morning. *Smart kid. Maybe I should have let her eat the peanuts*. The bucket under his arm seemed to grow heavier.

"C'mon, we're just a couple of blocks away. I'm going to warn you… It is liver night. Might take you a minute to, er, *get acquainted with the flavor*."

At the mention of dinner, Dievs' stomach let out an audible growl, and he realized just how hungry he was. Karina laughed.

"Resurrection is hungry work, eh?"

Dievs chuckled for the first time since… well, he couldn't remember. It felt good.

"Yeah, s'pose it is."

They walked another couple of blocks through the suburban neighborhood. Hank looked at the low houses with well-kept yards and little metal signs that said "TEXAS" or "GOD, FAMILY, COUNTRY." He wondered how someone like Karina, a girl who couldn't set down the topic of death and the afterlife for more than two seconds, (and also looked like a walking ad for the color black) could bear to live in a place like this, though it seemed she was right at home. Eventually they came to a low, wide brick house with a big maple in the front yard, covered in English Ivy and a large bay window.

"Home, sweet home. Just wait here for a few while I go talk to my mom, okay?"

"Alright," said Dievs.

Karina ran through the yard, up the steps to the concrete porch and flung the glass door open, not bothering to close it behind her. Dievs could hear her shouting inside, and the angry reply from (presumably) her mother, telling her to close the door, that she was letting the AC out. Dievs smiled, though he wasn't sure why.

As he stood on the sidewalk by the road, gazing up at the telephone wires and the neighboring houses, he heard a low rumble. The growl of a muscle car. But something in the rhythm of the engine was sour. *Mean*. It was how Dievs imagined a car that ran on blood might sound. *Hell's chariot*. He turned to see a blue Shelby GT with black-tinted windows rolling down the road towards him.

When Karina came running back out the door to tell Dievs he could come in for dinner, all she found were a few unsalted peanuts scattered on the sidewalk.

CHAPTER TWENTY-FOUR

333

HANK drove home from Denny's after another half hour of sitting in relative silence with Smiley and Joe. There had been nothing more to say, really. *Sorry*, had crossed his mind, but he didn't think it would've helped much. He wasn't sure if they blamed him at all for involving them with Brackington, but he certainly blamed himself. *Work alone. This is why I work alone.*

The orange Power Wagon trundled down 35 East towards Waxahachie, the radio buzzing in and out. Hank hardly noticed. The highway was working its hypnotic magic on him, as it so often did.

"Bzbzbbszzz… bbzz-Azzy baby! Streaming straight into your dome home. This is KAMP 90.9 blasting out of stunning Campaiyote, *Te-jas*. Got an oldie here that could use some love."

Hank rolled through fields and farmhouses and along brown highways, as he had hundreds of times before. He knew this place. He knew this road like his own driveway. Figuratively speaking, of course, he'd never had his own driveway. But it had all changed. *No. Never quite that simple, is it? A place might feel different, but it isn't the place that's doing the changing, it's you.*

This was his ninth year in Waxahachie. His eighth year at the Texas Inn. He had never been one to get itchy after staying in a place too long, Hank. He probably wouldn't have left his hometown if not for the rise of certain *circumstances*. But as he powered down the highway, Hank found himself dealing with an unfamiliar sensation in his stomach. An unpleasant one. Claustrophobia without the tight space. An itch without a way to scratch. Too much caffeine and a long car ride. Too hot for a sweater, too cold for a t-shirt.

He was uncomfortable. Suddenly, the song playing on the radio burst into clarity.

"*…Successful hills are here to stay. Bahbum-bum-bum. Everything must be this way. Dlaouda-ducka-dunk-dunk. Gentle stream where people play. Dlaouda-ducka-dunk-dunk. Welcome to the soft parade…*"

Hank clicked the radio off. Something about that sound scared the shit out of him. *No, not the song… the voice.* It sounded like *him*.

And then he knew what that feeling in his stomach was. It was a lust for change. And… *anger*.

#

HANK walked up the iron-grated stairs to his hotel apartment. It wasn't the first time he'd wanted to do *literally anything else*, rather than go home. But the feeling this time was bad. Real bad. He just didn't know if he could take it much longer. Any of it. *Jesus. I don't want to walk into that room. I don't want to look at that telephone. I don't want to eat peanuts. I just…* And yet, he kept walking, heavy boots clunking on the suspended metal stairs. His steps sent vibrations into the beige stucco wall of the Texas

Inn, a building held together by luck and some unseen God of broken things whose only apparent purpose was keeping shitty old buildings from collapsing back into the dust from which they'd come.

Hank was looking down, but as he crested the top few steps, he raised his eyes to find a *gargantuan* man dressed in a pair of split green and purple tights, and a jester hat with four-foot long, dangling foam tentacles. Gargantuan, meaning in *all* dimensions. He had a couple of red and white diamonds painted over his eyes, but the day's sweat had obviously had its way with them, and the paint ran down his face in greasy pink streams.

The big man wore no shirt, and hanging on his massive, flabby arm was a tiny Asian woman. Hank thought she couldn't be more than a hundred pounds. She was dressed in what looked like a collection of multi-colored rags, though the colors had been dulled from time and use and dust. Mud covered her from the waist down. They were both smoking cigarettes, though the woman held a white ferret in her off hand.

The smell of menthol hit Hank like a brick wall. The strange but somehow fitting pair turned to look at him as he finished his ascent. Hank didn't even blink, just nodded and made his way past them towards his room. The ferret squeaked as he went by.

Arriving at his front door, Hank stopped. *333.* The leftmost 3 of the number plaque hanging on his door, wrought in dull, rusted metal digits, had come loose and was dangling lopsidedly. Hank thought this only a little strange, though he wondered what it had been about *today* in particular that had finally cut it loose, after absorbing all the long years of abuse it'd taken from the Texas sun and elements. He reached out, touched the number and felt that it was loose. As he shifted the 3 back to its original position, he saw that there was a mark scratched into the wood underneath. Hank slowly flipped the 3 all the way around so he could see the writing clearly.

B.

God. Like I'm some little boy's claimed piece of property. His favorite climbing tree or some shit. Then another voice came from deep down in his brain. *His* voice. *Mr. B's voice: Aren't you?* Hank couldn't tell if someone had made the mark long ago, or carved it earlier that day. He thought the first was more likely, though he wouldn't put it past Brackington to have someone come by and loosen the number. Just so he would see it. Just so he would *remember* all those *big problems* he would have if he refused to work.

He suddenly got the feeling it was about time to start having some *big problems. Might be past time, actually.* He just hoped that when he saw Brackington next, he could keep that nerve.

Hank looked at the mark blankly for a long time. He couldn't say how long, but when he finally broke out of his stupor, the giant clown and the petite ferret lady by the railing had gone. Hank sighed, flipped the 3 down back to its normal spot, and shoved his key into the lock.

CHAPTER TWENTY-FIVE

Peanuts from Beyond

SMILEY Davis crouched behind her desk in the main lobby of her funeral home. *Her* funeral home, Dammit. Nothing moved except the dying ceiling fan overhead, and outside, framed in the big tilted bay windows, the night was black and quiet. It filled up the panes like black ink in glass beakers. The only light came from Smiley's desk lamp, which shone with a kind of yellow that only a dying incandescent light bulb can produce. Cozy, with a certain melancholy to it.

Outside in the parking lot, Smiley's beige Pinto sat underneath a lone streetlight, like a bomb in a spotlight. A twirling mass of moths and June bugs swirled around the bulb like Schrodinger's model of the atom. One of them rammed itself into the plastic casing a little too hard and went careening off into the void that was Sycamore Street at night.

Smiley was not paying the least bit of attention to the insectile battle of life and death outside her windows. Her face was firmly planted in upturned palms. She was thinking only of what her life was going to look like in the coming years. *If I make it that far.* She wanted to sleep. Joe had left hours ago, though he had been reluctant to leave her alone. She would hear *"none of that bologna,"* and finally, all but pushed him out the door. She wanted to be alone. Maybe she could think up some kind of magical plan to dig herself out of the troubles that seemed to stack themselves on top of her like toddlers piling on the kid with the ball. Except she didn't feel like she even had the ball. *Did I ever have it?*

She wanted to sleep, but sleep did not want her, and she knew it. If she went home, it would be silence, emptiness and a sleepless night. At least here was a better kind of silence. *More…* she couldn't put her finger on the thought exactly, but it felt more like home than her actual *home* at the moment: a studio apartment near Red Oak — though that wasn't a place she'd ever felt was really a suitable burrow. She'd loved this building from the first time she'd seen it, and she still loved it. It had an undeniable charm that seemed to reach back into her brain and pull out the best memories of childhood. *Roadside diners with runny egg yolks and hot waffles, days so hot you would go to the bank just to feel that sweet, sweet AC on your skin. The little bell hanging over the door that tinkled like the Waffle House Fairy.* And more than that, it represented her ambitions as a business owner. She'd fought for this, *goddammit.* A little tingle in her tailbone made Smiley shift in her ancient office chair. *I **worked** for that down payment, and those bastards at the bank did everything they could to block my loan. But I still did it, didn't I, bastards? Yessir. I still…*

And yet, here she was, apparently, at the mercy of another scrawny white man. And a guy she'd only met once, at that. It stung. *No. **No.** It makes me angry. But what to do?* She still wasn't sure how much credit she ought to give Hank's warnings. He was a strange guy, Hank. And, as she knew after a few months of working with him, had buckets full of his own problems. But he wasn't a liar. At least not that she knew. The more she thought about the whole deal, the more nervous she became. There had been no threats, not really. No weapons brandished, or insults lobbed. But his *eyes*… those eyes were terrible. They had grown in her memory like two green, sulfurous fires. She couldn't believe she'd leaned down into his window. In hindsight, it seemed insane. Smiley was sure her mother would've been appalled that she'd put her hands on any white man's car without an invitation… and a nice car, at that.

Oh, fuck' em. Smiley was sure her mother would've warned her of the dangers of that attitude as well.

Even aside from the problem of James Brackington, she had other things to worry about. Namely, the imminent foreclosure of her business. *Should have listened to Uncle Rick. 'Don't open unless you have a year's operating costs, young Lee. Better to have two.' A bit too late now, Rick.* She'd thought she was ready. She *had been ready*. But maybe this town, this place, wasn't. Now that Karina was gone, she'd have to be around all the time to answer the phone. Though she didn't exactly anticipate that being a huge time-suck, it was another thing to think about.

Smiley raised her head out of her hands and rubbed her groggy eyes. She blinked them open to several notices of overdraft on her debit account, credit card bills and the real *bad-news-bears*, a letter from Wells Fargo (the first of what she was sure would be many) notifying her of her most recent missing payment on her mortgage for the home. It. Was. A. *Bummer.* And now she faced the prospect of not only being boxed out of owning her own business — *likely forever* — but just maybe being *killed* for it too. Smiley wondered briefly why it was always the little guys who got shafted. Then she remembered she lived in America. A piece of a song from a George Carlin special came to her out of that great ether of half-remembered jokes and bits in the sky. *America, America, man sheds his waste on thee, and hides the pines with billboard signs, from sea to oily sea...*

The image of the upstairs bedroom at Brackington's party house — and what remained of the woman who had been sprawled there — struck in her brain like a rattlesnake. Smiley closed her eyes and let out a spirited sigh, trying to avoid the nausea that came with that memory. She glanced up to her right to check the clock hanging on the wall. 9:37. Smiley rose slowly from her chair and stretched out. Her back popped several times in the effort. *Slightly better.*

Suddenly, a faint click came from the door that led to the back rooms of the funeral home. It sounded to Smiley like a paperclip hitting concrete, or maybe a safety pin. Her blood ran cold, and for half a second, she felt her heart stop beating. Thoughts of paid assassins and mafia thugs coming to rob and beat her came stampeding through her brain. *Hold it. Hold it. Calm down. Probably just a mouse or something. So jumpy.*

She managed to calm herself down, though it took a bit of controlled breathing and self-assurance that it was just paranoia working its terrible magic on her. She made her way over to the door.

#

PUSHING through the back door, she saw nothing out of the ordinary. Only the hallway that led one way to the cadaver storage room and the other to the back exit. Smiley leaned into the dark hallway and turned her head left, then right, like a child checking for traffic at a crosswalk. The faint light from her desk lamp in the lobby gave her an electric orange halo. She flipped the light switch to the left of the door. The fluorescent lights came flickering on, painting the plain hallway in crisp blacks and whites.

Smiley furrowed her brow and looked around again. Nothing. Stepping into the empty hallway, she felt a crunch under her foot. She jolted at the unexpected sound. Lifting her shoe, she saw a little pile of cream-colored crumbs under the sole of her yellow flats. *A peanut?* For a long time, Smiley just stared down at the crumbs, stared like when a computer is given a line of code that it just can't comprehend, running the same program over and over again until someone comes along and turns it off or reboots it. Smiley did eventually reboot, but it took a minute.

It wasn't the peanut itself that surprised her, but that she knew there had been no peanut here when Joe had left. She was sure of it. She'd gone out back to sneak a cigarette (a Hillsborough, of course) after Joe had gone, and she thought she would've noticed it then. *I would've noticed. Would I have noticed? I would have noticed. Maybe not. Maybe I'm just going crazy.* And then, at that moment, there came another faint clicking sound, the same as before, this time coming from behind the door at the end of the hallway labeled "COLD ROOM."

Smiley snapped her attention to the door. The light above the entrance seemed to grow dimmer, lending the door an ominous, *doomy-gloomy* grayness. She was getting a little angry now, though it was partially to cover up her fright. She suspected that was what had happened when she'd leaned into Brackington's car window. Anger can swallow fear whole.

But there was more to this than irritation. Smiley was tired of it all. Of the world seeming to conspire against her. Of old white bankers and shitty neighbors and mob bosses and *peanuts*. She turned and stomped down the hallway towards the door, not hesitating for even a moment to fling it open and flick on the light. Waiting at her feet, like a patient pet rock, was another shelled peanut. Unsalted, by the look of it, and rocking back and forth ever so slightly, as if it had just been gently placed there.

Smiley looked around the brightly lit room and saw nothing but the many metal coffins lining the walls and the center chrome table. There was nowhere to hide *except…* Frustration mounting, Smiley waltzed slowly into the room. Her eyes narrowed, and she scanned the metal boxes along the edges of the room. She knew exactly which ones would be full and empty. And she ought to. She was the one who'd put them there.

Though she knew on the surface level of her consciousness that it would be almost impossible for someone to slide themselves into one of the mortuary cabinets so quickly and quietly, her deeper anger and fear said that it was completely plausible. So she started on her way around the room from the right side. She clicked open the first cabinet. *Empty*, just as she'd known it would be. The next, *empty*. Then a new guest, one of the women from Brackington's house party. She closed that one quickly.

On she went, opening each of the metal boxes in turn and finding exactly what she had expected to find… nothing. The last coffin, just to the left of the entrance, had the name DERRICK V. SWISS written on it in small black letters. She had written the name herself, and yet, when she looked again at the tag, there was something *off* about it. Some lone neuron in her brain was screaming like the first person to notice a house fire. The tag was reminding her of something. *Of what?*

The box was being used for a man that Hank had brought in a few days ago, under *strange* circumstances, to say the least. *No family, no friends. To be burned and dispersed, as the literature says.* Taking into consideration recent events, she was becoming more and more certain that this fellow was another piece of collateral damage in the wake of James Brackington, though she couldn't be sure. She knew that when she opened the box, she *should* find a set of ten blue toes and a little name tag attached by a piece of string, but some sliver of intuition was telling her she wouldn't. That the thing was empty. *Well, not empty.* She pushed the box in towards the wall until it clicked, then let hidden springs push it back out. The cabinet was empty. Instead of the body that ought to have been there, was a singular peanut.

PART FOUR:

Action!

CHAPTER TWENTY-SIX

Old Blues Man

A dark blue 1967 Shelby GT 500 hummed down Main Street in Dallas, Texas. Above it, the sky was blacktop. No clouds. No stars. Electric lights buzzed over the road in nice orderly rows, sending liquid yellow reflections streaming and slipping over the black glass of the Shelby. There was something deeply unsettling about those windows, more than just the fact that such a heavy tint was illegal. No one would pull this car over. *No one*. On either side of the wide street, tan buildings stood like some colossal child's building blocks, square and solid, dull in the shade of night.

For a moment, although the street was busy, the Shelby cruised alone on the road. A cat in its very own cement jungle. A deep blue panther, with lines and form made for America. For killing. The only sound it made was the purr of satisfaction. The rumble of a perfectly honed V8 burning dinosaurs and getting in return, *speed*. *Power*. Though the rumble of the engine was plain enough, for those who heard it, it seemed to whisper… whisper something profound and dangerous. It made them sweat and squirm. It said, RUN.

The moment passed and once again, the blue predator shared the road with the grazers, the Pintos and the Studebakers and the Ford Escorts. The Shelby cruised on, all the way up Main Street, before taking a right onto South Field Street, and then another right onto San Jacinto. It slipped quietly into an alley there, just behind the first building — the one on the corner — another big beige cube with small windows and drawn shades. It rolled up to a green metal door, illuminated by a single light, and stopped.

For a few seconds the alley was quiet, then the driver-side door popped open. Out stepped brown leather boots with worn, slanting heels. A cigarette dropped between the two shoes, burned to the filter. Faded black jeans came down around the tops of the boots and led up to the lean body of James Brackington. He was wearing an old patched leather vest patterned in what might have once been the stars and stripes of the American flag. It looked more like a bleeding thing now, with brown patches obscuring the stars and navy blue, leaving only rust-colored streams of red.

James stepped out of the Shelby and did a big stretch, arms raised to the sky and fingers interlaced. Cat-like. The lean muscles in his arms rippled subtly, almost as if he weren't really a man at all, but a fleshy vessel for a thousand-thousand squirming snakes. He finished his stretch and shut the door of the Shelby gently, walking lazily around the hood of the car over to the green door. He sighed in mock annoyance and knocked. A small hatch at eye level opened quickly. James flashed a big grin. With teeth. The door opened.

#

JAMES didn't have to say a word. This was his palace. Or one of them, at least. He had many. The eyes behind that metal hatch had been hard and angry at first, but one glimpse at Brackington's smiling face had been enough to turn the doorman's blood to ice. James kept his eyes closed as a courtesy. They sometimes… *hurt* people. Not that he minded much, but replacing a good bouncer was annoying.

As he stepped inside, a young man with his eyes pointed firmly at the ground scurried up to Brackington to take his keys. James dropped them into the kid's hands without so much as a sideways glance. The young man practically ran outside to valet the Shelby. James knew he didn't have to emphasize the care with which the task had to be done. The kid didn't need to hear it either. He knew he was taking his life into his hands just by *holding* the keys.

Though outside the plain green door, the alley was silent; once inside the bare concrete hallway, a heavy beat began to drum against his chest, muffled by cinderblock walls, but strong enough to make his ears buzz. It felt good. He smiled.

The doorman stood stiffly aside to let Brackington pass. He was sweating, and as James walked past, the man seemed to catch the smell of James: *gasoline. Burnt rubber. Roadkill roasting on two hundred degree, sun-baked highway.* The man shut his eyes and held his breath.

The short, plain hallway led to a set of stairs, then to a set of push-bar doors, like one might find in a school gymnasium. Brackington waltzed down the hallway, doing a little spin and skip. The bass was really thudding now. *Oh…*

yes. He bounded the stairs, two, then three steps at a time and pushed open both doors at once. The music hit him like a wall, along with those most wonderful smells. Human smells: *old beer, sweat, hot breath and dried blood.* The doors opened into a large room where four hundred people bounced as one to the beat of a kick drum and the rumble of an out of tune electric guitar playing blues rock. *Hello.*

He let the doors swing closed behind him, and although many did not see him enter, they felt him. The crowd parted as he moved forward, like a leopard slicing through jungle thicket. He began to dance and jump with the crowd. Though from far away he might have blended in with the rest of the partygoers, he was *not* one of them. Just as a wolf does not blend in with sheep, even when it's wearing its best Merino coat.

#

IT was sometime later when James Brackington made his way up to the private quarters of his club on San Jacinto, a simple, but finely furnished room overlooking the main floor, with the standout features being a large red-felted pool table and the thick cream-colored carpet underneath it. A few men in suits were playing a game there and chatting. One was smoking a cigar, giving the room a smoky haze. The sound of the door opening turned their heads, but the sight of James made them gulp hard and quiet down.

"Hey boys," said James, as he walked lazily, and somewhat stiltedly, into the room. The men at the pool table knew the ruse by now. Lasting a few years in the company of James Brackington meant having a good eye for detail. A *very* good eye. He might look drunk — *sweaty, lazy, strung out, tired*

— but one overstep, one wrong word, and all that would vanish. It was his way of keeping his lieutenants relaxed and effective, but still on their toes. He wanted them to be unsure of how lucid he really was. It worked. Though by all accounts, it appeared he *really did* enjoy dancing. Especially to rock.

The men at the pool table stopped their game and nodded towards Brackington.

"At ease," he said, his voice a little slurred.

"Hey Mr. B," came the voice of Jenine, the Harley Quinn to James's Joker. The Andy to his Conan. The tail of his dog. She was sprawled on a big leather loveseat in the corner of the room, legs and head draped over the arms. She looked bored, but the sight of Mr. B seemed to cheer her right up. Jenine was perhaps the only person ever to have this reaction to Brackington's presence. It was why he liked her... *well...* *tolerated*, more like. She was also, *occasionally*, useful.

"How's our guest doing? Have you been showing him Hyacinth House hospitality?" asked Brackington, smiling just slightly.

"Oh, you bet," replied Jenine, matching his smile, though after a moment, her grin faltered. "Though... he really doesn't seem to know what's going on. He's playin' it up real good. You know, the old, '*I don't know who you are or what you're talking about*' routine. Even after the thumbnail, he..."

"Now, now, we don't want to disturb our gracious partners," said Brackington, gesturing to the men by the pool table, who had resumed their game (though all of them were keeping one eye on James). "Let's go have a chat with him and see what kind of... *persuasion* he needs."

At this, Brackington spun and headed to a door at the opposite end of the room from where he'd entered, labeled "OFFICE." After a second, Jenine hopped off the loveseat and followed him, skipping just a little. Once they'd reached the door and gone through, the men at the pool table collectively let out a little sigh of relief.

CHAPTER TWENTY-SEVEN

The Case

WHEN the man in the American flag vest entered the small office room, it was as if someone were blowing into some silent, but deafening whistle, as if the air itself had come alive with crackling electricity. It made Dievs' hair stand up and his brain hurt. As *if I weren't already having a hard enough time focusing.* After the beating and maiming he'd received from the woman who seemed to be this man's assistant, his whole body was throbbing, especially his fingers, which were now short three nails. The rope that secured him to the wooden-backed chair was also digging into the meat of his chest and waist.

"Hello, Mr. Swiss," said the man in the American flag vest. His voice sounded smooth and rich. *Melted chocolate* was all Dievs could think. But there was something incredibly unpleasant buried in those soothing tones.

Dievs lifted his head to meet the eyes of James Brackington. He had suspected it was Brackington who'd snatched him from Karina's front drive, but now he was sure. It'd happened so fast, he hadn't been able to get a look at the driver's face. They'd shot him with some kind of tranquilizer or paralytic from out of the window. Now, in the man's presence, he realized why everyone had been so distraught at that Denny's luncheon. *This guy is bad news bears.*

James smiled down at Dievs, those green eyes twinkling, as he pulled up a chair. The room was small and hot, filled with a big oak desk strewn with papers, and a few low bookshelves scattered haphazardly around the room. Three windows lined the far wall, but someone had drawn all the blinds, and they cast lines of orange light around the office like tiger stripes. Dievs had been blindfolded when they'd brought him here, and only half conscious, but he could still feel the thump of loud music playing somewhere in the building. *A club. Maybe his club.*

It was hard, but Dievs forced himself to keep eye contact with Brackington. He licked his dry and swollen lips, flashing a glance at the woman who had come in behind him. She'd split his lip in several places with a few extremely unpleasant punches. *Small fists.* She smiled now, watching his discomfort.

"Like I told your *secretary* here…" The woman let out an indignant snort and moved to punch Dievs yet again. He flinched, but before she could make contact, Brackington grabbed her arm. His motion seemed slow and effortless, but Dievs could see the pain in the woman's eyes from his grip. Brackington never stopped smiling. "I don't know who that is," finished Dievs.

"Well… she is a secretary of sorts," said Brackington, letting go of Jenine's arm, which she immediately pulled to her chest to rub. "This is Jenine. Though I'm sure you two are acquainted by now. Please excuse her violent proclivities." Brackington leaned in to Dievs' ear and in a mock whisper said, "She had a rough childhood."

Dievs just blinked at Brackington. *Sure.*

"But. As for who *you* are… *You, friend, are Mr. Swiss.* Derrick V. Swiss. Born 1952 in Portland, Maine, into a family of three, an older brother, a father and a mother. Nothing really *too* special about you, except maybe a good immune system… good cheekbones," Brackington leaned forward, right into Dievs' face this time. "But, Mr. Swiss… you have something of mine. And I want it *back*. Something that has made you much more special than you have any right being." Brackington leaned back, eyeing Dievs cooly. "For the record, I do believe you. Amnesia is a curious thing. And dying, *I would imagine,* could shuffle up some memories. Maybe even make you change your name. Though I liked Swiss better than Dievs. What is that, by the way? Nordic or something? Russian?"

The smile widened on James Brackington's face, and the sense of electricity Dievs had felt before returned. Gone was the casual, cat-like coolness from moments ago, and the faint sense of inebriation. All replaced with pure green madness. *I was about to eat dinner. And now I'm here. And they ripped off my freakin' finger nails. Who do they think I am? No… who am I?*

"I-I wish I could help you, Mr. Brackington…" Dievs said slowly. "But I really don't know anything about all this. I…"

Brackington leaned back in his chair and gave Dievs a moment to finish his sentence, but there was nothing more to say.

"Well, let me assist you. *Jog your memory…*" said Brackington, obviously getting annoyed. "My *employee,* Hank

Cooper, scraped you and your charred guts off the floor of a ranch house outside of Milford about a week ago. He promptly delivered you to Ms. Smiley's Funeral Home and Crematorium — *ignoring my explicit instructions*, I might add — where they put you in a cold metal box and gussied you up for a date with the incinerator. Following along?"

Dievs just looked at Brackington, mouth slightly agape.

"Good. Buuut, the day before you were to be roasted, *two days ago now*, one of my associates in Campaiyote saw you playing board games and shopping at Piggly Wiggly with the girl who works for Ms. Smiley Davis. And *then*, as if those activities weren't proof enough of your resurrection, you went and got coffee at Denny's… with the *whooole gang*. Now. I don't know how you did it, Swiss, and I will admit, it was an impressive trick… it takes a lot to fool my guys… but unless you want to return to the land of the dead, *permanently this time,* better spill some beans."

Dievs gulped.

#

"YOU *will* tell me where the case is," said Brackington, all playfulness vanishing from his voice.

Dievs searched his brain like someone frantically looking through their dirty laundry for the EpiPen they thought they'd never need. There was nothing. Before Karina let him out of that metal coffin, he had been in a… *Where was that? A train station? That sounds right. There was an annoying guy at a desk…* but the memories of that place were already fading. Only a vague impression remained, white lights and ghosts. He had been *somewhere* before waking up in the back of Smiley's

Funeral Home, that was for sure. *But before that?* There was a void. Open air. There were, however… those images that had come to Dievs in quick flashes, mere glimpse of memories. There *had* been a case. One that glowed blue on the inside.

"A… a case, sir?" Dievs replied, not confident enough in his memory to admit that he might have even an inkling of what Brackington was talking about.

"*The* case. I think you know the one I mean," said Brackington, still without a smile. His smooth, youthful face had turned ugly without that little smirk. It was a hard face, with hollow, burning eyes.

"I… really don't."

Brackington sighed and rubbed his face with his palms. A sigh of fatherly exasperation. He leaned forward to bring his face level with Dievs. Dievs' hands remained bound to the armrests of the wooden chair. Zip-ties strapped his wrists tightly, faced down to expose his fingernails. His right hand showed the work Jenine had done over the course of the last couple of hours. She had pried the thumb, pointer and middle fingernails off, leaving bloody, flat stumps. They throbbed terribly now, pulsing with every heartbeat, but it had been much worse when she'd first taken them off. *Much worse.* In fact, he'd passed out twice in the process and also vomited a little. She'd done the first one with a playing card.

Brackington met Dievs' innocent and frightened eyes. He brought his left hand up and pointed his finger, then dropped it slowly, digging into Dievs' exposed hyponychium (under the fingernail) with his own nail. Dievs couldn't help but scream.

Brought back to life, apparently, just for this. What luck! This thought scampered across his brain behind the tsunami of pain that was flashing up his arm like red lightning. Dievs couldn't remember anything, anything at all, but he thought that if he'd ever experienced any kind of pain like this before, he wasn't sure *forgetting* it was an option. Brackington twisted his finger, and Dievs saw stars, those nice fuzzy white dots around his vision that meant he was going to take a little nap. Passing out would be a welcome relief, but before unconsciousness could take him, Brackington let his finger off.

"Woah now, hey," Brackington snapped his fingers in front of Dievs' face and whistled. "Heyy partner. You can't go yet, you didn't tell me where the case is."

Dievs' lips felt numb, and his stomach gurgled with pain. He answered groggily.

"I… don't know about… any case."

"Oh, but you do. You're the *only one* who does, actually."

"If I knew… I would tell you… what do I have to protect?"

Brackington recoiled slightly at this. Dievs saw a momentary expression of doubt in those green eyes.

"Plenty," said Brackington and once again stabbed his finger into Dievs' exposed thumb.

The thump of bass coming from the main room of the Hyacinth House pulsed through the beige building on San Jacinto until dawn came to Dallas. And no one heard the screams coming from the office above. *Well…* a few people did.

CHAPTER TWENTY-EIGHT

Joe Shmoe

JOE Karipassius walked like a man returned from war. He stumbled through the aisles of Tim Dillards's hardware store in a haze. He picked up tools and read their labels and warnings, only to realize he couldn't remember a word of what he'd just looked at. *Put it back down. Look at another. Be normal. Everything is normal.* Except it wasn't all normal, and there would be no escape from that.

It wasn't even that Smiley was in debt up to her ears, a fact which Joe was only privy to because he had once been in such a situation himself and he could see the signs, or that his knee was causing him worsening pain every day. *Life is a rollercoaster, isn't that the phrase?* A year ago he had been in Bend, Oregon, with his wife, chopping down trees and enjoying the fresh northwestern air. Given his current circumstances, the thought that Oregon had only been a little over a year ago seemed ridiculous. But it was true. It was also true that the 'happily married' portion of his life was over, and unlikely to be resumed.

It wasn't any of the misfortunes that had befallen Joe in the last year, or even that he now cleaned up dead bodies for a living, a line of work he'd never imagined he would be in. None of this. It was those eyes. *Those green eyes.* When James Brackington had visited him and Smiley on that dead-end lane, Joe had seen something in those eyes. Something that Smiley seemed to have forgotten, or maybe disregarded. Hank was more on the money — *more scared* — but still not as terrified as Joe had been. There was something *supernatural* going on in those sulfuric eyeballs, in that brain… or *whatever* was behind that smiling face. *Maybe just a bunch of rats, or snakes… or both.* Smiley had been right on when she'd said he looked like Jim Morrison. He did. But Joe had now opened his mind to the possibility that some kind of alien bug had inhabited Jim Morrison's cadaver and was now haunting Dallas, Texas, killing people like a little kid smashing toy soldiers. This didn't sound half as strange as he had felt in the man's presence. It was as if Brackington's eyes had opened up his skull and had had a look around.

He'd thought about running… *in fact*, was still thinking about it. *Maybe I'm not important enough to him. Maybe he'll just forget about me and let me go.* But logically he knew that wasn't likely. *You saw that house. You saw that… girl. His murder. You're not going anywhere without his knowing it. Not now. Does a cat let a mouse go when it's in its jaws?* And so he was at the hardware store. The safest place he knew. Looking at blue five-gallon buckets and paint rollers.

The only employee in Tim Dillard's Hardware store, a scrawny local kid named Cole Brown, asked Joe if he needed any help about six times over the course of the next hour before Joe finally made his way to the register. The answer was the same each time. *"Hmm? Oh, no. Just pursuing, son."* In the end, Joe bought exactly one roll of black electrician's tape and a black iron quarter-inch fitting for capping off a gas pipe. He couldn't say why he got these two items, other than electrician's tape being his favorite kind of adhesive. He still remembered wrapping up the steering wheel of his first car (*an Impala*) with it. Mostly to cover up the spots where the previous owner's dog had chewed through the rubber. As for the fitting, it felt good in his hand.

Stepping out of the store into the warm Campaiyote night, he was just as lost as when he'd entered. Except now he had tape and a weight in his pocket. A clicking sound coming from behind him made Joe turn. It was Cole Brown locking the doors behind him. The kid shot Joe an exhausted glance, then walked off towards his car, one of only two in the parking lot.

Joe stood in the parking lot under the light of a yellow street lamp for a few minutes, just breathing in the night air and listening to the faraway sound of cars on the highway. A big June-bug slammed into the side of his head, having deflected off the street lamp at high speed. Joe swatted at the bug, shook his head, then made his way to his car.

That *lost* feeling was still strong as he slid into the driver's seat of his beat-up Corolla. He didn't want to go home. He didn't want people *watching him*. And the experiences of the day made him feel like he was being watched. He didn't think he'd be able to sleep anyway, he felt better with a steering wheel under his palm. He wondered if Smiley was feeling anything similar (at the moment he had this thought, Smiley was following a trail of mysteriously appearing peanuts into the cold room). Joe started the car and put it in drive.

Thirty minutes later, after a bit of aimless driving, he found himself at the Sonic drive-in, a couple of blocks from Smiley's. He was absentmindedly sucking down a double chocolate shake and priming himself for the foot-long chili cheese dog that was waiting patiently in the passenger seat. There were only two other cars at the Sonic, and their drivers looked to be rather occupied. *Teenagers.* One car was rocking back and forth rather aggressively.

Joe had grabbed his favorite spot, which afforded him not only a view of the main strip in Campaiyote but also, through a strange twist of city planning, a straight shot view of Smiley's. It was a splendid building, and since Joe had come to Campaiyote, he had enjoyed looking at it and imagining its history, sometimes fantasizing about starting a diner there. It would be perfect, though his prospective customers might appreciate him leaving out the part about it having been converted from a funeral home. Dead bodies and pancakes rarely sell well together, though Joe thought both industries could probably do with a little innovation. Who knew, maybe he could call it *Joe's Final Destination Flapjacks.*

As Joe stared down at Smiley's Funeral Home and sucked on his chocolate shake, he saw two things. First was Smiley's beige Pinto peeling out into the street and screeching off towards the south side of town. He watched it go, and thought about following, but decided against it. *She has a lot going on. Not surprising she can't sleep. Probably going on a thinkin' drive… I could go for one of those too.* But the chili cheese dog in his passenger seat said it could wait.

He drained his shake and was about to take a bite of his dog when he saw another car pull into Smiley's lot. An old beat-up Escort with a dragging back bumper. It bottomed out as it sped into the empty lot, muffler sparking badly, and though Joe was a good three blocks away, he could hear the heavy thump of American steel on concrete.

He paused, mouth open, chili dog at the ready, and kept watching. The car maintained its speed and circled in the lot, back wheels blowing up rubber smoke and sliding out in a donut. Joe debated going and trying to stop the donutters, but memories of his own youth and donutting days gave him pause. *They're not hurting anything, just leaving some tire tracks, that's all.* But a few moments later, the car stopped, and the doors opened. Out stepped four young people. It was difficult to discern their ages from this far away, but Joe's guess was college students. *Young enough to be stupid, and old enough to cause real damage.* It looked like two men and two women, and they were without a doubt heavily intoxicated. In fact, one girl actually fell to the ground as she stepped out of the car. He could see the others laughing, and the way they stumbled like toddlers around the car made their inebriation even more obvious. The girl who had fallen got to her knees and promptly vommed on the blacktop.

Joe sighed and stared longingly at his chili dog. *I should probably go tell them to scram. Right?… right.* And so he set his late-night meal back down in its wrapper, started the car and put it in reverse.

When he pulled up to Smiley's lot, the kids were in various states of stupor. None of them had volunteered their help to the girl vomiting on the ground, who was now sitting in a puddle of her own making. The other girl had passed out on the hood of the car spread eagle, while the two boys had produced a can of black spray paint and were halfway through writing the least creative word in their undoubtedly small vocabulary on the front glass of Smiley's Funeral Home.

#

"NIG-"

#

Upon seeing this, Joe smashed the gas pedal on his Corolla and slammed his hand into the horn. It came out sounding like a small duck in distress, but it was enough of a shock to send the two boys into a blind, drunken panic. The one with the spray can promptly dropped it, and they both sprinted back to their car. One boy tried to wake the girl passed out on the hood, but she didn't respond, and he quickly abandoned the quest.

Joe was now fully in the parking lot and circling back around to face the boys in their car. They jumped in and, doors still wide open, slammed the car into reverse. Joe watched as the girl on the hood's eyes opened wide and she went tumbling off onto the concrete *hard*, mini-skirt ripping as she rolled. The Escort kept reversing. *Too fast*. Joe could only watch as the car slammed into the streetlamp across Sycamore. The impact bent the pole and caused the light to flicker. Joe saw the shocked look on the boys' faces, and the subsequent return of panic. The driver shifted the car into forward, and then they were speeding off towards the main strip of Campaiyote, a back bumper and two young ladies lighter than when they had arrived.

Joe stared at the aftermath of what he'd just witnessed. Two college girls were sprawled in Smiley's parking lot like bodies on a battlefield, yet more victims of that most favorite American drug, alcohol. The one who had been spewing technicolor ooze was now staring up at the black sky, mouth wide open. The other girl, the one who had been thrown from the hood of the car, sat up and stared at her arm, which now had a bend of about 45 degrees in a place where there *definitely* should not have been a bend. She just stared at it with wide, unbelieving eyes.

Two girls, a scattering of beer cans, glass shards, papers, and other random pieces of trash lay strewn across the parking lot and the road, dropped cargo from a dismal drunken adventure. Joe sighed a big sigh and parked. He looked over at the chili dog in his passenger seat longingly.

#

JOE spent about thirty minutes trying to calm the girl with the broken arm before the ambulance finally arrived. The pain-numbing effects of shock only lasted a few minutes, and after that, the girl made no attempt to stop her wailing. It was so loud, in fact, a few people in the neighborhood came to see what the commotion was. They found a mess, trash everywhere, a pair of young women in a sorry state, and what appeared to be an ex-lumberjack trying his best to deal with it all. Though Joe saw little sympathy in those gazing eyes.

Joe came from a different part of the world, a place where racial discrimination existed, but was seemingly less on the brain than here in Campaiyote. *North.* He hadn't even considered the realities of the South before moving here. He remembered seeing the march in Selma as a kid, and the assassination of Dr. Martin Luther King, but all those problems had seemed more *abstract* when he'd watched them in black and white on a television screen thousands of miles away. *Isn't that why we thought World War 2 wasn't our problem?*

But being here, watching first-hand the walls people put in front of Ms. Davis for no reason other than the color of her skin, and how she just… *kept going,* had changed him, and his ideas of what kind of country he lived in. The people who had come to watch the meltdown happening in front of the funeral home probably wouldn't mind finishing the work those delinquents had started, wouldn't mind completing the word that was only halfway scrawled across the front glass like a big ugly target. He couldn't help but despise them. And maybe for the reasons Joe thought, or perhaps not, no one volunteered their help. Not one person.

He couldn't help but smile when an old rusted-out Chevrolet Caprice came careening down Sycamore Street and nearly hit several of the bystanders. The driver looked to be terribly drunk, and only barely made it down the street without running completely off the road. *American freedom at its finest.* He knew he shouldn't wish ill on strangers. *On anyone.* He was trying to be a pacifist, *goddamnit.* But he was suddenly just so *angry.* Though he resented the feeling, knew it was not *him,* he wanted to punch somebody, wanted a piece of meat to take his frustration out on. *Maybe I'll get the chance.*

With no offered help from the bystanders, Joe called the police and hoisted the woman up out of her vomit to sit next to the girl with the broken arm. It was in the process of moving vomit-girl that he noticed something curious about the trash that had flown out of the Escort and now lay all over the parking lot. Shattered glass, scattered papers, metal cans and plastic bottles… but in between all of it lay hundreds of…

peanuts? *Yeah, peanuts.*

Then he saw the container. It was empty and lying way over in the lot's corner. For a moment, he just blinked at it. It appeared to be the same container that Karina and that weird guy — *what was his name again? Dives? Dillan?* — had been fighting over in the parking lot of the Piggly Wiggly just earlier today.

"Huh."

How bout' that. Joe walked over to the Planters container and picked it up. Behind him, broken-arm girl kept screaming, though it had come down a decibel or two from when she'd first started. When he lifted the container, he saw a flyer that had been pinned underneath it. He snatched it up and flipped it over. It read:

"7TH Train and Spark-plug Brigade, live, July 15th, Hyacinth House on San Jacinto. IF YOU KNOW, YOU KNOW."

It was an ad for a concert at a place called the Hyacinth House. Joe had never heard of San Jacinto, or either of the bands, so, he guessed he was one of the people who *didn't know*. But something struck him about the artwork for the poster. At the bottom of the page, which was mostly inked in black, were two green eyes. The face of James Brackington flashed in his mind, and he suddenly got a cold, empty feeling in his chest. He looked the poster over once more, then folded it and put it in his back pocket.

Joe carried the Planters container back over to where the two girls sat, then joined them on the pavement. He tried to talk to them, but vomit-girl was pretty much zombified (she seemed just lucid enough to puke and blink), and broken-arm chick was too busy staring at her nearly exposed bone to speak.

Smiley's gonna love this. He gazed out at the few people watching the scene, standing under the bent and now slightly dimmer streetlamp across the way. They were watching him, and he wondered if the commotion was the only reason they were spectating. Joe got the awful feeling that one of them might be watching for a different reason. He surveyed the crowd and thought for a brief moment that he'd seen a pair of green eyes flash in the darkness. He gulped and thought about how soggy his chili dog would surely be before he could take that first bite.

CHAPTER TWENTY-NINE

Peas and Potatoes

KARINA sat with her back to the three-paneled bay windows that afforded an expansive view of a chain-link fence and some kudzu. All shaded a deep blue under the darkening night sky. The clock on the wall opposite her read 9:55. *Can't believe we made it before 10.*

To her left and right at the round kitchen table sat her two brothers. The younger of the two, ten-year-old Jojo, was attempting to fold his pile of mashed potatoes into some kind of abstract modern art piece. Of course, he was also implementing the other materials at his disposal (peas and pre-cut pieces of steak) to adorn his masterpiece. He was, to put it another way, not eating. Karina's older brother, eighteen-year-old Tommy, had just finished devouring his second plate of food like some starved rabid animal, and was about to ask for thirds when Karina's mother grabbed the plate out from in front of him.

"I told you not to talk with your mouth open," said Karina's mother.

"I didn't!" replied Tommy, ejecting a potato-lathered piece of steak onto the table.

Jojo laughed at this, and in the corner, the spread newspaper that was Karina's dad came down for half a second. Just long enough for those eyes to make sure nothing was required of him, then the paper went back up.

Karina rolled her eyes and picked listlessly at her plate. Looking down, she spied the ever-present rectangular shape in Tommy's pocket. *That's what we need. A little excitement. Firecrackers.* Tommy always had some sort of flammable or otherwise explosive material on hand. Though she'd never caught the pyro-bug herself, she respected Tommy's conviction that if something didn't explode or couldn't be eaten, it was of no use. Karina occupied herself with less destructive hobbies, though she had occasionally joined Tommy for the destruction of a fire-ant hill or two.

Despite this small shared appreciation of things that went *boom*, Karina felt out of place in her family. *Like a bat in a rabbit den.* She wore all black and looked as if she might just spontaneously combust out of pure annoyance. Her two brothers had taken after their father, and they both looked like (she thought) human crayons, wearing brightly striped boyish t-shirts and khakis. Though, unlike her father, both her brothers seemed to have made it their life missions to push her to her absolute mental limit. And they didn't have to do much more than simply exist. But tonight, this was only half the reason for Karina's sullen attitude.

Karina's mother sat thirds down in front of Tommy, who returned to his meal with the same vigor and speed he'd had the first time around. Karina looked at Tommy and watched as he shoveled peas and potatoes into his mouth like some new-century caveman. He even held the spoon like a baby, full-fisted. She rolled her eyes over to Jojo and saw that he at least had some creative impulses. The potato-pea-steak pie was now in a rough smiley face shape. He looked pleased with himself. Karina pulled her gaze away from Jojo and up to meet her mother's eyes.

"So… your friend didn't want to come to dinner?" asked Karina's mother, a bit sympathetically.

"I guess not," Karina replied flatly.

"Where did you say you met him again?"

"At work. He… we talked about ouija boards and… stuff."

"Oh, is that so?" replied Karina's mom, having sat back down to take a bite of her peas.

Suddenly, a spoonful of mashed potatoes went flying across the table, narrowly missing Karina's mother, only to splat against the foot of the refrigerator. There was no hesitation.

"Jojo!" screamed Karina.

"Jojo!" screamed Karina's mom.

"Joseph!" yelled Karina's dad, newspaper coming down halfway.

"Joe!" yelled Tommy.

"Sorry," replied Jojo. He didn't sound sorry.

It took conversation a moment to resume after this, but Karina's mom eventually started things back up.

"Well, his loss, eh? Missing out on my world-famous peas and potatoes." She could see Karina's despondent face and was trying to lighten things up, but it wasn't working. "Maybe he can come another day?"

Karina nodded and looked down at her untouched plate. "Yeah, maybe…"

Just my luck. I meet and befriend a genuine, bona fide, zombie, and he ditches me on the first day. Went off to find some brains to eat, I guess… I didn't even get to test my electroshock kit on him.

But something wasn't sitting quite right with Karina about this thought. First, she didn't think Dievs was the type to just leave like that. At least she hadn't pegged him as someone with *other plans*. And second, *where would he go?* She'd found him trapped in a freakin' metal coffin. He didn't even remember his own age, for Christ's sake. And it had happened so *fast*. She'd only run inside for a minute *tops* to talk to her mom, and when she'd gone back outside, he'd been gone. Even if he was a fast runner (and he didn't look like one), it would have been difficult to get away without a trace that fast. The curiousness of it opened up another possibility…

As Karina pondered the disappearance of Dievs, the doorbell rang. All heads turned towards the front door except Jojo, who continued molding his artwork and also sneaking pieces of steak to the cat hiding under his chair.

"I'll get it," Karina's mother said, getting up.

"No, Mom, eat. I'll go," said Karina, scurrying out of her chair and around the table before her mother could protest. She was still thinking about Dievs when she opened the front door to find an out of breath Smiley Davis waiting for her. As soon as the outer glass door was open, Smiley grabbed Karina by the shoulders and whisper-screamed into her face.

"Dievs? Where's Dievs?"

Karina didn't know what to do except answer the same way Smiley had asked the question. It came out sounding kind of whiny instead of urgent, how she'd intended.

"I don't know."

At this, Smiley looked around, and even peeked inside the house, as if she were being watched. Karina thought it was a funny thing to do. A little paranoid, maybe. But then she remembered the lunch they'd shared earlier in the day at Denny's, and thought *maybe they weren't kidding about all that. Maybe it's bad. That bad.*

Returning her gaze to Karina, Smiley asked, with definite anger in her voice this time, "Did you know?"

From behind Karina, her mom's voice came ringing out, "Who is it, K?"

"Know what?" Again, Karina's voice came out whinier than she'd intended. Smiley's eyes narrowed. Besides her mom, Ms. Davis probably knew her better than just about any other adult.

"Ohhh, you better not be lying to me right now, girl."

"No, I... wouldn't, uh..."

Suddenly, Karina's mother stepped out from the dining room to look at the front door. She smiled at the sight of Smiley, even though she was gripping her daughter with both hands by the shoulders.

"Oh! Ms. Davis, what a surprise! I didn't know you were dropping by... we have room at the table if you want to join us. Bit of a late dinner."

Smiley tried her best to relax and smile at the sight of Karina's mother, but she couldn't quite erase the anxiety that was all over her face.

"Oh, hi Mrs. Blake! No, no, no, thank you for the invitation, but, uh, I'm just here to talk to Karina about some work… matters."

"Oh, yeah? What's going on?"

"Well, ahem, just some…" Smiley shot a quick glance down at Karina. "…Paperwork stuff. Nothing too important, just, you know, getting ready for tax season. Karina's just been such a wonderful help. I really don't know how I'd keep track of everything without her."

Karina's mother seemed to take all this at face value, even though to Karina, Smiley was clearly speaking under distress.

"Ah, well, we appreciate you saying so, Ms. Davis. And Karina does too, right?" Karina's mother elbowed her in the back. It spurred Karina out of her stupor.

"Uh, yes. Appreciated. I… yes, I appreciate you saying so, Ms. Davis. Even though earlier today you said I was fire…" But before she could finish, Smiley stomped on Karina's right foot, all while keeping her smile trained on Mrs. Blake. "Hey…" Karina's mother didn't seem to notice.

"Well, just let me know if you change your mind about dinner. We always have a spot open for friends. And don't keep Karina too long, she hasn't finished her veggies."

"Thank you, Mrs. Blake, I won't." Smiley flashed her kindliest smile and waited for Karina's mom to walk back out of sight. Karina was the one to whisper-scream first this time.

"Why are you acting so freakin' weird, dude?"

Smiley was calm this time in her response. "Dievs' real name is Derrick V. Swiss."

"How do you know that?" asked Karina, surprised.

"'Cause I read the label on the fucking box he came out of, *dude*. I also wrote it. You think I wouldn't notice? One of the dead people I keep in my closet goes missing, and I'd just go,

'Oh, too bad. Wonder where he went?' What did you think was gonna happen?"

"Ohh…" Karina nodded at this and grimaced like, *oh yeah, guess that makes sense. The first time I've experienced a crack in the fortress that is my super-genius detective intellect. Shit.* "Why didn't I check the label on the box?" Karina asked, more to herself than to Smiley.

"I don't know, Sherlock. But what I do know is that *mother, that guy,* was dead. I *saw* him dead. Hank brought him in from God knows where…" Smiley shifted as though her tailbone had tingled a little bit. "…about a week ago. We'd been prepping him for burial, but I guess he didn't feel like waiting around for that. Tell me you didn't know all this."

"Well… I…"

"You did!" Smiley yelled this, and Karina could almost hear her mother turning her head in the other room.

"Hey, shush," said Karina.

"You knew, and you didn't say anything? Is that why you were so weird at Denny's? It is, isn't it? I *knew* I recognized him!"

"Okay, listen… meeting a real-life zombie, slash undead person, isn't an everyday thing. I was going to tell you all… just slowly, so that you wouldn't freak out…"

"I'm freaking out, Karina."

"…Like this. Yeah, I can see. But listen, he's not dangerous. He doesn't remember anything. If he *was* Derrick V.

Swiss, he's not anymore."

"I just… I'm still having a hard time digesting what you're telling me. You found a man, a *stranger*, in one of **my** cadaver storage cabinets, assumed he was a… *zombie*… and proceeded to take him to Piggly Wiggly for, what was it? Peanuts?" asked Smiley.

"You make it sound so blasphemous."

"That's insane, Karina. And also, he ain't no freakin' zombie. I don't know how he did it, but he must have recovered, or used some kind of drug to fake like he was dead or something, which is even crazier, because the guy had had a *hole* in his chest. He ain't a *zombie*. *That* I can tell you for sure, and even if he remembers nothing, he's still dangerous. We need to ask Hank where he came from. I don't really *want* to know, but I think I need to. I have a feeling he was one of Brackington's goons. A *criminal*."

"Well now you're making me feel like the kid in the Iron Giant, like, 'nooo, don't shoot, he's actually a good robot! He doesn't remember that he's a murderous death machine!' What was his name? Something weird, like Hogarth…" said Karina.

"I can't even… what are you?" Karina opened her mouth to speak. "Don't answer that," Smiley cut in. "Now you listen to me…" Smiley lost the anger in her voice and knelt down so that she was closer to being at Karina's eye level. "You're still fired. This is all craziness, and I don't want you mixed up in any of it. That guy…"

"He who shall not be named," said Karina spookily.

"Yeah, him. He's no joke, and I don't think he's above hurting children. So you gotta stay away. I shouldn't have even come here. And if you see Dievs, or Derrick, I guess, you call me or the police. Don't talk to him, okay?"

Karina looked as if she might protest, but in the end, she

knew it was pointless. She didn't know where Dievs was anyway.

"Okay, Ms. Davis."

"Good. Also, get a job at a mini-golf course or something. Or the theater. It's weird for a teenage girl to work at a funeral home… You were an excellent secretary, though."

"Thanks. I guess."

"So… you don't have any idea where Dievs might have gone?"

"No… He was supposed to stay for dinner, but he kind of disappeared. It was actually pretty strange…"

From behind Karina came another volley of shouts as Jojo had apparently hurled another pea-laced potato ball across the room. Karina turned for a moment, and when she turned back around, Smiley was already hustling over to her car, yellow flats sliding on pavement.

Weird day. Not just for me, apparently. She stood in the doorway as Smiley sped off in her beige Pinto. *Doesn't she know those cars explode?*

… I don't want to work at a theater.

CHAPTER THIRTY

The Mess (Part 1)

THE woman in the two-piece blue suit sat primly on the stiff old loveseat, waiting for her guests. Beside her, Beethoven was panting loudly. *Too hot for a Saint Bernard out here. Too hot for me.* Adopting the St. Bernard had been her husband's idea. She didn't particularly like dogs, and the loose fur all over the place gave her awful sneezing fits. But now this dog was all she had to remember him by, and so she kept Beethoven around. The dog didn't seem to have any idea that he was in fact a living memory of her dead husband. He just panted and slept. And ate, of course. Ate a lot.

Resting on the floor beside the woman in blue was a brown leather briefcase. She was sitting with her legs pressed against the side of the case. She could feel its presence there, like a hot egg. Underneath that heat, she thought she could feel the faint ticking of a machine… *So much riding on an empty box.* The briefcase was empty — *well, mostly empty* — but there was another one, just like it, stored away upstairs, except this other briefcase wasn't empty. *Oh, no. Not empty.*

She tried not to think about what was inside that other case, but it was a futile effort. She hadn't been able to take her mind off that subject since she'd opened it yesterday. *Just a peek,* she'd thought. In fact, that case had become the focus of her entire world. Or rather, keeping it out of the hands of James Brackington, had become her mission. That case was the reason for the imminent meeting with Brackignton's goons, and the reason she, in all likelihood, would be dead within the hour.

It was a strange feeling to know she would die before 2 o'clock in the afternoon. There was a certain *unreality* to it. Like maybe this was all a dream and she would wake up in her childhood bed, stretch out and stumble downstairs to some breakfast. But the heat of the air, the sweat rolling down her forehead and Beethoven's incessant panting told her this was no dream. *It's the right thing to do. It's the right thing to do…* She'd been repeating this mantra to herself since she'd devised the plan she was currently executing, but the *right thing* felt a whole lot harder when it meant you had to take a bullet. *Or ten.* She just hoped it wouldn't be any more gruesome than that.

The sound of an engine. A big one. *SUV?* The old front door of the ranch house, covered in cracked white paint, was open, but the screen door was closed. The woman in blue sat still and watched as a baby blue GMC Jimmy with a white bed topper rolled up and parked in the dusty lot. All the windows were all heavily tinted, but the woman in blue could see the shadow of a driver and someone in the passenger seat. And… a glimmer of *green. So, he came. All the better.*

If she got lucky, *very lucky,* maybe she could get him, though she doubted it. He would be protected. The woman in blue tried her best to believe in that idea, that she was *glad*

Brackington had come — but in reality, she was terrified. Truly terrified. An image of those piercing green eyes flashed in her mind like the Jack of Diamonds might jump out at you when riffling through a deck of cards. But the woman in blue was a professional, after all. Years of dealing with psychopaths and killers had taught her to, at the very least, keep the fear from showing.

The Jimmy was framed perfectly in the screen door, and the woman in blue watched as two men stepped out of the back seats of the car. One tall, the other, short. Both wore dark clothes, and both had pistols strapped to their hips. The taller one had dark shades on, but his face looked somehow kinder than the shorter man's, whose face was scrunched up into a terrible grimace. *Not popular with the ladies, that one*, the woman in blue thought. *He looks like Joe Pesci.* The shorter man was also carrying a sawed-off shotgun by his side. As they approached the screen door, the two men saw her sitting on the loveseat and slowed down. They also saw the shotgun resting across her lap and the briefcase by her leg. Once the two men reached the porch, they stopped.

"We said no weapons," the short man grunted. He had a nasty, nasal voice.

"Yeah, me too," replied the woman in blue. "Guess that didn't exactly fly with Mr. B though, did it?" She nodded to the guns they were making no effort to conceal.

"Put your gun on the ground, and we'll come in and talk," said the shorter man.

The woman in blue couldn't help but let out a quick burst of laughter. "Oh yeah, I'll just put my gun down and we can *talk*. Why don't you put yours down first, and then I'll consider your offer."

The two men looked at each other. The woman in blue thought she could feel the eyes of the other two men in the Jimmy through the black glass watching this exchange. *His* eyes.

"There's no need for violence, Loretta," said the shorter man, with a bit of impatience in his voice.

"Did I say otherwise, shorty?"

Probably shouldn't have done that.

The short man's face turned red, but before he could say anything more, the taller man put his hand out and said, "Hey, I think we got off on the wrong foot. Let's start over, hmm?"

"Alright. Let's start over," replied Loretta, not intending to start over at all.

The tall man spoke again.

"I'm Derrick Swiss, and this is my associate, Joe Pesca. We're here on behalf of James Brackington, whom I'm sure you already know."

"He's here, isn't he? Over in that car?" asked Loretta, glancing again at the blue Jimmy.

The tall man kept his gaze on Loretta.

"The location of Mr. Brackington isn't something I'm at liberty to disclose, ma'am. Even if I knew."

"Okay, then… Should we get to it?" asked Loretta.

"I assume you're referring to your… message? May we come in? And I'm sorry, but we won't be putting our weapons away. And I won't ask you to put yours away either."

The short man looked surprised at this, and it appeared he might argue, but the tall man made it clear there would be no discussion.

Loretta took a deep breath, and said, "Come in. Slowly."

The two men stepped up onto the porch and walked to the screen door. Swiss came in first, followed by Pesca. Loretta kept her hand on her shotgun and the barrel aimed just shy of the two men. She swiveled it slightly and flashed a hard, tight-lipped smile (more like a grimace, really) as they sat down on the couch opposite her. The screen door bounced a few times against the door frame as it swung shut. Beethoven wagged his tail at the two men and lurched up from his spot on the floor to go sniff them, but Loretta held his collar and pulled him back gently. The shorter man had grown pale, seeing Beethoven up close.

"…fuck me. That's the biggest dog I ever seen. Mutt's gotta be 200 pounds," said Joe, under his breath.

"245," replied Loretta. Joe seemed to turn green at that figure.

"So, where is it?" asked the tall man, flatly.

Loretta reached down with her free hand to the briefcase resting by her leg. She gripped the handle and slid it forward over the rough wooden floor. It stopped at the tall man's booted foot. He shot an annoyed look at Loretta.

"That easy, huh?"

"That easy, baby," replied Loretta. "Open it."

The tall man's eyes narrowed as he gingerly reached down and picked up the case. He laid it in his lap, keeping his eyes on Loretta the whole time, and clicked the two brass buckles that secured the lid. They flicked open with a springy sound. Only when he lifted the lid did he take his eyes off Loretta.

From inside the briefcase came a dark blue glow, like moonlight on the bottom of a pool of water. It was starting in the hot daylight of the ranch house. It almost seemed to make Derrick's face darker, like it was casting a shadow instead of light. Joe leaned over to look inside the case. Both men stopped and stared down into the open box. Joe stopped breathing. Another fifteen seconds passed in silence this way. It was Joe who broke the quiet.

"Oh, God."

Loretta knew what they were seeing, and she knew they were thinking the same thing she had when she'd first seen what was in the case. *He can't have it. He can't.* She wondered if Brackington had told them what to expect. She doubted it. He'd never been one to share information.

"That's just a piece. A *small* piece."

"Where's the rest?" asked Derrick, eyes still fixed on the open case.

"There's a folded note taped to the lid of that case with the location of the rest of… *it*. It's written in code. When I'm safely out of the country, I'll place a call and give you the cipher. But *only* when I'm safe and clear."

The tall man clicked his tongue. "That's not gonna work for us. For Mr. B." With obvious reluctance, Derrick shut the case and snapped the metal buckles. Loretta had been expecting such an answer. Although a small part of her was still holding out hope she might actually escape all this, she knew that ship had sailed the moment she'd opened the briefcase and laid eyes on what was inside.

"That so? Well, looks like we have a bit of a pickle on our hands," replied Loretta. "I put that piece in there as a payment of good faith. I've done enough deals with people like your boss to know how this goes. Now… you can have that, kill me, and lose the rest, which is an outcome I don't think your boss would like very much, *or*… you can take me at my word."

"Or we could just blow your…" Joe said, leveling his shotgun. But before he was even close to having it pointed at Loretta, she had her own gun aimed right at his nose.

"What was that?" asked Loretta. Joe slowly lowered his gun.

"Loretta… we, nor our boss, want any bloodshed. You tell us where the case is, we take it, and go on our own way. That was the original deal, wasn't it? We'll even forget the part where you looked inside, against the *express* direction of Mr. B… He does, believe it or not, have the power of forgiveness within him."

"I doubt that. And the fact is, I *did* look inside. And there's no *unseeing* that. As you now know," said Loretta, still aiming her gun at Joe.

"Well…" Derrick chuckled. "You're right about that." Derrick looked at Loretta for a moment and scanned her. His eyes paused on her hands. Her *fingernails*. Loretta felt his eyes sticking there and closed her fingers into fists.

"So what's it gonna be? I've got a lunch date in an hour, so if we could move this along…"

"Okay then, Loretta… okay. When should we expect your call?" asked Swiss.

No way they took the bait.

"Don't you worry about that. I'll call when I call."

"Let's go," Derrick said to Joe.

"But…" protested Joe.

"Let's. Go," repeated Derrick.

The two men stood and turned to walk out the door. Derrick went first, Joe following. Loretta watched them walk out, and began to think her plan might actually work, that she might actually survive this afternoon. Those hopes were dashed when she glimpsed Joe's face turning away from her. *Angry.* His eyes were wide. *Adrenaline. The small emotions of a small man. He's gonna snap… no, he already has…* And just as he reached for the screen door, he turned and raised his shotgun. Loretta was ready. Time seemed to slow to a crawl.

Joe lifted his eyes to see the barrel of Loretta's Remington aimed right at his squinted little face. His angry expression morphed into one of horror. *Thought you were fast enough? Not quite.* Loretta pulled the trigger of her shotgun, bracing for the recoil.

The gun clicked, but no report came. No shot.

The safety. I forgot to turn off the safety. Joe, processing this development as fast as a man with his intelligence could, saw his opportunity and took it. He fired, launching a spray of birdshot into Loretta's stomach. The force knocked her backwards and sent her gun flying.

Derrick Swiss had time only to say, "You idiot…" before 245 pounds of brown and white fur came flying at Joe Pesca.

Joe lifted his gun up like a shield to block the St. Bernard's jaws from closing on his throat. He screamed as he went to the floor, fighting off the giant dog as best he could. It was like trying to wrestle a bear. Derrick jumped back from the fighting and watched, fascinated.

Joe, now screaming, "HELP ME, SWISS! GET IT OFF!

GET IT OFF!"

Derrick looked at Joe for a moment, but instead of raising his pistol to shoot the dog, turned and walked out the screen door without another word.

CHAPTER THIRTY-ONE

The Mess (Part 2)

DERRICK V. Swiss walked out of the old ranch house to the soundtrack of his partner's frantic screams and made his way over to the blue Jimmy still parked in the dusty front lot. The dark passenger window came rolling down to reveal the smiling face of James Brackington. He held his hand out, obviously waiting for the briefcase. There would be no '*good job, Derrick*' or '*you'll get em next time,*' from James Brackington. *No.* Rewards came only to those who succeeded. To those who did their job. This was only a partial success.

"Did you retrieve the case?" asked Brackington, in his slightly slurred voice.

"*A* case," said Derrick, handing the slim briefcase through the window.

James took it and opened its lid slowly. From inside the house, Derrick could still hear Joe screaming and struggling with Beethoven. When that strange blue shade hit Brackington's face, he did not smile. But he did look for a good five seconds, in silence, just as Joe and Derrick had. *Awe.* Derrick wondered what Brackington could possibly have planned for it. Every scenario he could imagine was more horrifying than the last. He thought then that maybe Loretta had been right to keep this from Brackington. *She wasn't ever going to make that call, and she knew it*. But it didn't matter. Brackington got what he wanted. *Period. End of discussion*. If it didn't happen now, it would eventually. It was just a matter of playing for the winning side. At least, that's what Derrick Swiss told himself.

At this moment, a blast was fired from what sounded like Joe Pesca's shotgun. The shot was loud, and a few pieces hit the Jimmy, sending some small sparks flying. Derrick ducked, then checked himself over for any wounds. Nothing. He looked up to see that a big hole had been blasted in the screen door. Joe and Beethoven were still wrestling, though it looked like the dog was winning. Derrick turned back to a thoroughly unamused Brackington.

"There's a note on the top of the lid there. Loretta said it's some kind of code or something. The location of the rest," said Derrick.

Brackington closed the briefcase and turned to Derrick. "Is she dead?"

"Loretta? Probably soon… Joe just shot her in the stomach."

Brackington sighed, "Fucking idiot… Search the house. If the woman is still alive, make her talk. She didn't have much time to hide it. The Peruvians only brought it in yesterday. *Find it*. We'll send a team later to get you."

Derrick didn't like how that sounded. *A team to get me, or a team to make sure I don't rat?* Brackington rolled up his window and a second later, the blue Jimmy with the white top was peeling out down the road from where it had come. *Asshole*, thought Derrick. *Guess I'm stuck with ol' Joe Pesca*. Not a fun prospect, considering he was about to be really quite angry with Derrick. If he avoided becoming a Beethoven-sized snack, that is.

Derrick made his way back into the ranch house to find that Joe and Beethoven were no longer in the living room, though a considerable amount of blood had been spilled on the floor. He could hear what sounded like an amateur wrestling match going on upstairs, as well as Joe's continued shouts for help. On the floor by the couch was Joe's shotgun, the wooden stock and pump now adorned with a myriad of teeth marks.

Loretta, the woman in blue, was also gone, though it wasn't hard to see where she'd gone. A thick trail of blood and viscera led into the small bathroom. Derrick followed the trail and cautiously pushed open the door. Loretta was sitting on a low stool, trying to keep her guts from falling out of her stomach. It wasn't going well. She still held the shotgun in one bloody hand, but Derrick could see that the safety was still on. It was clear she didn't have the strength to lift it and pull the trigger, even if the safety had been off. *Lost too much blood.* Derrick knelt down to Loretta, and their eyes met.

"You… can't let him have… *it,*" said Loretta, wheezing.

Derrick, with genuine sympathy in his eyes, said, "He's gonna get it. One way or another. It's just a question of when." Loretta didn't answer this, just kept looking at him. "The last thing you can do is help save my life. Tell me where you hid the case."

Loretta looked away and managed a small laugh. "Eat shit," she said.

Derrick reached out and grabbed Loretta's hand. She tried to pull away, but her strength was gone, and she couldn't stop him. Under her bloody fingernails was a deeper red color. It looked like paint to Derrick. It was harder to see now, but earlier, he'd spotted the stuff under her nails and marked it. She'd been scraping at something. *A painted floor or fence?* Loretta looked at Derrick with a dash of fear now, but she still said nothing. From upstairs came the shot of a pistol and a guttural bark. *Sounds more like a roar.* Derrick and Loretta both turned their eyes up to the ceiling to listen for more shots, but none came. After a moment, Derrick stood and looked down at the ruined bathroom.

"Last chance," he said.

"Do the right thing…" said Loretta, chest heaving now. Derrick gave her one last look, then shut the door.

The commotion in the upstairs bedroom had ceased, and an eerie silence had fallen over the ranch house. He made his way up the creaky stairs to the second-floor landing, pistol in hand, just in case Beethoven decided Joe was just an appetizer. Looking left, then right, he saw a bloody handprint smeared on the door. Derrick walked over and pushed the creaky door.

Jesus. The room looked like some terrible man-dog smoothie gone wrong. He wouldn't miss Joe Pesca. *Not one bit.* Though now he felt just a *little bit* guilty about not helping the man. *Too late now.* Man and dog had locked one another in mortal combat, and the result had been a tie. He shut the door and walked across the hall into the other bedroom.

It was a plain room… simple. One double bed, neatly made with an old-style quilt on top. A dresser in the corner and a little rug, partially covered by the end of the bed. Derrick paused and looked around the room. *There's something here.* That deep maroon color under Loretta's nails flashed in his mind, but he didn't see it anywhere. *Yet…* Derrick walked slowly into the room, dragging his hand lightly over the wall and doorframe. He lowered his pistol as he sauntered over to the rug.

Something had caught Derrick's eye at the corner of the rug. Under the blue painted floor, there looked to be a scratch of some kind. Under the navy blue paint was another tone. *Loretta's fingernails…*

But Derrick V. Swiss didn't have time to investigate this discovery. Indeed, he didn't get any farther than the rug at the foot of the bed. What he failed to see, in his focus on the maroon scratch, was the nailhead protruding from a board on the floor. No one had used this bedroom in years, and repeated drying and wetting without maintenance had caused nails in the floorboards to be pushed out of their beds. One of these nails grabbed Derrick's boot by the rubber sole and tripped him.

The unexpectedness of it made Derrick to reach out with both hands to block his fall, except one of those hands had a Smith and Wesson Model 645 pistol in it. The gun twisted in his hand, and in terrible slow motion, Derrick watched his finger fall on the trigger. His mother, who had taught him to shoot, whispered in the back of his mind. *Finger off the trigger, Swiss. Finger off until you're ready to pull it.*

But it was too late. And suddenly Derrick was envious of Loretta's unfortunate incident with the safety. The gun went off, and he felt the bullet bury itself in his chest. His body jumped as if it had received an electric shock. *No way,* he thought. Shock gripped Derrick in the way only a dying man can know. *No way I just shot myself. That doesn't happen. It doesn't. Not to people like me. That only happens to kids and drunk people.* Then came darkness, and… *a train whistle?*

CHAPTER THIRTY-TWO

The Mess (Part 3)

IT would be a few hours before the secondary team would discover that no one had survived the kerfuffle in the old ranch house and make the report to Mr. B. James Brackington was about as concerned with Derrick Swiss's death, as Derrick had been about Joe's fight with Beethoven.

But long before that, as Derrick sighted the splotch of maroon paint and took the step that would kill him, James Brackington was speeding down an old two-lane country highway towards Dallas in the passenger seat of the blue Jimmy. He was happy… *No*, but he should be. The deal hadn't gone as planned; that was true, though with something like this, he hadn't expected it to. Not exactly. There were always *hiccups* in this business. But at least he'd gotten some of it. *Yes, some. Not enough, but some…* And she would give up the rest. *Oh yes,* she would. And if she died, as she was apt to do, he would still find the rest. That was a guarantee.

But something was still wrong. Felt wrong. Brackington held the case close to his chest and watched the highway. The driver beside him kept his eyes straight ahead, focused on the road. Brackington tried to conjure his usual smirk, but it wouldn't come. *Something's wrong… too easy.* He brought the case down onto his lap and opened it, clicking the brass buckles free. He set his eyes on the bounty inside once again. The driver's eyes glanced down to his right, and the car swerved a little… he quickly glanced away. *No faking that. It's real.* But there was something else.

Brackington lifted his eyes to the underside of the lid. Taped there was a small white envelope. He pulled it free and tore off the tape. No writing on the outside. He took his nail and cracked open the top seal of the letter. Inside was a piece of plain yellow notepaper folded into thirds. Brackington slowly unfolded the note. Drawn in pencil in the center of the page was a small smiley face. Then he heard it, as if the sight of the smiley face had amplified his senses. *Tick, tick, tick, tick…*

There was no time to think. He knew that sound. He had made that sound many times, and he couldn't believe he'd been stupid enough to fall for it. Without a word, he flung open the car door and hurled the case out. It exploded midair. The car swerved and nearly ran off the road. The driver cursed and tried to get the Jimmy under control.

Brackington hardly noticed. He was filling up with rage, like a beaker of baking soda and vinegar. He screamed. It came from the gut, and to the driver's ears, it sounded louder than the explosion. Like an angry, wounded animal.

Brackington's mind was a cauldron of bubbling, murderous thoughts. A soup brothed with the blood of his enemies. He wanted to kill someone. He wanted to kill Loretta, even if she was already dead.

She thought she could kill ME? Arrogant bitch! I will find the rest. I. Will. Find. It.

CHAPTER THIRTY-THREE

Hanky Panky

HANK slept as well as usual. Which is to say, not very well. Though the fifth of vodka and half-pound of peanuts he'd consumed at around midnight had helped get him on the carousel of sleep. His hotel room felt particularly sweaty and damp this morning, also the usual state of affairs, though the growing spots of mold in the corners of the room *were* concerning.

The morning light coming through the small windows felt hot in the most unpleasant way. He didn't want to move, didn't want to get out of his bed, but the Hank-shaped puddle of sweat that had soaked into the bedsheets below was itchy and sticky. *Please… just… I don't want to do it anymore. Not the cleaning, not the driving, not anything. I'm done.* And for a few minutes he thought it was true. Then the phone rang and reminded Hank Cooper who owned him.

#

"HELLOOO, Hanky baby," came the playful yet cold voice of Jenine through the small speaker of that *God forsaken* yellow telephone. Hank didn't know her last name, and he had no desire to learn it. He thought for a moment he would just put the phone down. *Just hang up. It would be so easy.* But then that other voice, the one buried deep in the back of his skull, *his* voice, *Mr. B's* voice, spoke. *I don't think you wanna be doin' that, kiddo.*

Why not? Hank asked himself. It wasn't as though he had much to lose. No family, *really*. No friends besides Smiley, Joe and Karina, though he didn't think getting them inadvertently dragged into the web of a homicidal-maniac-mob-boss had done much for their relationship. *Maybe Barbara, the Texaco cashier*, if you really wanted to stretch it. But life was still *worth living, dammit*. The thought of just rolling over and quitting was at once immensely appealing and repellent. Somehow listing off the reasons he ought to just give up the ghost and let Brackington kill him didn't make the thought of it any more appealing, though the list was extensive. And yet, when he tried to come up with a collection of reasons to continue living, it was pitifully small. Survival instinct was number three.

Hank's job, the whole business of crime scene cleaning, had beaten his emotions like Kermit the Frog might get beaten facing off against a couple of baton-wielding SWAT officers. *Pulped,* that is. But he was still human, and on his list of cares, Smiley and the gang were reasonably high, just under making sure there was always enough vodka available to get swimmingly drunk. If he were to upset Brackington, who knew what he would do to them. Certainly not give them a gold star and a pay raise.

That said, Smiley and Joe and Karina were beyond Hank's help or protection at this point — what little he could provide, anyway. It wouldn't matter what Hank did, they were under

Brackington's thumb, just like he was. *And yet…* he couldn't bring himself to just *hang up the phone,* to accept whatever punishment Brackington had in store for him. It wasn't the threat of death that kept him pulling the plow either. *I'm just like that horse with a broken leg that won't stop trying to get up and walk. Or the blind, deaf dog who spends the last five years of its life looking for a place to die, to slip into that never-ending puppy nap.*

"Hey, Jenine," answered Hank. All that numbness inside him made the words fall out of his mouth like bricks. The audio equivalent of blank copy paper.

"Jesus Hank, you sound terrible… you got the flu or something?" asked Jenine, as if they were co-workers standing at the water cooler. Hank didn't respond, just closed his eyes and breathed into the phone. "*Okay, then.* Well, boy howdy, have I got some good news for you! Another job! *Yaayyy…* I know how much you enjoy the work we do together," said Jenine.

Hank shoved aside a mass of scribbled yellow sticky notes and finally found one with enough space left to write on.

"Addresses and counts." Hank waited expectantly for Jenine to read off the assignments.

"Really not in for the small talk today, are we… Okay, first is…"

Hank listened to the deranged sidekick of James Brackington list off several crime scenes and 'accidents' that would require his attention today. Three houses with a total of 4 persons. *Easy shit.* As tired and mixed up as Hank was, he couldn't help but take some small pride in his work. He was the *best*. He was the *one*. The guy people called — if for no other reason — to make death disappear. Jenine finished her list, and Hank was about to hang up, but she stopped him.

"Hey, wait a second. Change of, uh, what shall we say? *Protocol*? You can take all the bodies to Smiley's. No need for the… *off the books* method anymore. We've gone legit, baby!"

Strangely enough, Hank got an urge to laugh at that statement. *You and Mr. Green Eyes are about as far from legit as a giraffe's head is from its ass.* It took a second for the chuckle to start rolling, but then he found he couldn't stop. It gained its own momentum. As the laugh grew into a howl, Hank realized how insane he must sound to Jenine, but he didn't care. *Maybe I am insane.* This continued for at least a minute. When Hank got himself under control again, he thought Jennie would've hung up, but her voice came through the yellow telephone once again. *Cold.*

"I'm glad you find that so amusing, Mr. Cooper." Her voice no longer had any playfulness in it. *This is you. The real Jenine. This is why he keeps you around.* 'Mr. Cooper' came out like ice. It was clear she didn't enjoy laughter all that much when she wasn't the one making it (preferably via inflicting pain on others). "Do the job."

The phone line clicked and hummed.

I should've been the one to hang up, not her. I'm still in the habit of living, as they say. Self-preservation. He was a coward, and that was about all there was to it. But fortunately for cowards, there is a simple, easy-to-follow, multi-step-plan for ending the misery. More on that later.

Hank pulled the phone away from his ear and looked at it. The giggle attack was gone, and the emptiness that had hollowed him for so long returned like stagnant air resettling in a hot room when someone turns the fan off. He put the phone gently back down on the receiver and looked at it. He felt like a man sitting in the middle of a seesaw. *Could go either way, and neither side looks very inviting… Maybe I'll just get a little crazy.*

"Oh… man."

CHAPTER THIRTY-FOUR

Trains

BACK in the Power Wagon, Hank was thinking no thoughts. The highway flitted under his wheels as if the earth was the thing moving and not his truck. Maybe it was. The other cars on the freeway flickered by him like ghosts. *Maybe I'm one myself.*

About fifteen minutes into his drive, muscle memory and a potent chemical addiction made Hank grab for his pocket, where he did not find what he was looking for. *No ciggys. What a life.* He looked right and was hit with the sight of the Texaco he knew so well.

Peel off. Park. E-brake. Little bell above the door jingles. Barbara awaits me, like a toad on a lily pad.

"Hillsboroughs," said Hank, sounding particularly drained.

"Black or Red?" responded Barbara.

"Red. Por…" Hank paused, wondering why he'd felt the need to insert Spanish into this conversation.

"Favor," said Barbara. Except it came out like 'Fay-ver.'

"That's the one."

Barbara already had Hank's cigarettes and had punched their price into the register.

"Buck-fifty, hun."

Buck-fifty? What is this, the freakin' commissary?

"Price go up?" Hank asked.

"Tobacco shortage. Apparently," said Barbara, and without moving her head she pointed to a poster beside the register. More of a note really. Black Sharpie on white printer paper:

"DEAR CUSTOMER,

THE MANAGEMENT AT TEXACO NEAR ITALY TEXAS REGRETS TO INFORM YOU THAT DUE TO A DISRUPTION IN SUPPLY CHAINS, ALL TEXACOS IN AND AROUND THE GREATER DALLAS AREA ARE EXPERIENCING SHORTAGES OF TOBACCO PRODUCTS. AS A RESULT, PRICES MAY FLUCTUATE. SORRY."

"Huh," said Hank. There was something else that grabbed his attention on the flyer. A little pair of dark green dots at the bottom of the page. They looked almost like… *eyes*.

"I get mine off the reservation. Cousin gives me a deal. I'm quarter Cherokee."

Hank took a deep inhale of the true American perfume coming off of Barbara. *Tobacco, gas and heat. Glorious.* Though it reminded Hank of another smell, one that he'd prefer not to think about. The smirking face of James Brackington, those green eyes, flashed in Hank's mind. *He smells of those things, but also… death.*

"That's smart. Your cousin do business with strangers?" asked Hank, realizing as he said it, that this, *right now*, was the longest conversation he'd had with Barbara, though they'd known each other going on eight years. Barbara just blinked at Hank. "Never mind," said Hank, as he dug into his pocket for his wallet.

He found a lone dollar crumpled up in the slot where normal folks might keep a twenty or two. There he also found a quarter, a dime, two nickels and four pennies. He laid it on the counter and looked up at Barbara, who had already counted it with her eyes. She looked at Hank like a goldfish looks at its prison walls, then glanced down at the *"Take a Penny, Leave a Penny"* dish on the counter. In it was exactly one thoroughly greened penny, and a peanut.

Hank stared for a moment, then gingerly reached down, plucked out the penny, making sure not to touch the peanut, and plopped it on the counter.

"You need a receipt?"

"Can I return this?"

Barbara just shook her head. Then Hank was out the door, ringing that little bell again. Barbara watched him go unenthusiastically, but with eyes that had seen a lot of folks come and go. She thought Hank looked like he was going.

#

THE first assignment of the day was at a private residence. A little house outside of Frost at the end of a cul-de-sac. Hank was looking at the plastic wreath hanging on the front door. There was a wooden sign in the middle, adorned with a little clay angel, that read, "BLESS THIS HOUSE." *Wasn't enough, I guess,* thought Hank. He knew what was waiting for him inside, and it was no blessing. The key was under the mat, like Jenine had told him.

Just dropping in to water the plants. Ha… kidding, kidding… Maybe I am going a little nutzoid.

The woman was sprawled in the kitchen, still wearing her nightgown. Around her head was a deep maroon puddle, undisturbed and perfectly round. *Nice level floor*, was all Hank could think, though somewhere, on a deeper level within himself, he registered that something might be very wrong with that thought, *with him*. The only oddity, aside from the inherit strangeness of death, was the lightbulb that had somehow made its way into the thick puddle and stopped above her head, giving her the image of a cartoon character having a simply fantastic idea.

Hank stood still in the hot, quiet kitchen and stared. It wasn't the first time he'd felt the absurdity of being alone in a stranger's house with death peeking over his shoulder. In the beginning, he'd felt like there ought to be police or medical staff, or like… *the governor or, or, or something, somebody, anybody.* Someone who could make it all kosher, and right, and sound. Someone who could tell Hank that '*this was all part of the plan,*' *and that he 'ought to step back behind the yellow barrier and let them deal with this*'. But those people never came. They never came because **he was** those people. The others, *the police, the priests, the politicians,* dealt only with death's shadow, not what he left behind in this world. That was Hank's job. To sweep up the reaper's leavings.

What seemed like a lifetime ago, when he'd started this job, he'd thought there would be people wailing at every crime scene, crying for their loved ones who'd made it to the clearing at the end of the path. And *surely* other officials would observe him removing the body, document it, and rate his work. That expectation had been shattered like a pane of very thin glass almost immediately. He was always alone when he cleaned, and it was usually quiet as the grave (no pun intended). And hot. There were no documentarians watching him, no rating, no flashbulbs. Just Hank and death. And though he knew what to expect by now, he still wasn't *used to it*. He didn't think anyone could ever really get *used to it*. Just numb, maybe.

He sighed, bent down and grabbed the sprawled woman's legs like the handles on a wheelbarrow. *One, two, buckle my shoe.*

#

THE first job was easy enough. Hank was outta there in under two hours. Three Hillsborough cigarettes later, he arrived at the next house. A big two-story, plantation-style, white-paneled ranch house with a wrap-around porch at the end of its own lane. A fence running along the drive penned in a few cows, lazily munching on brown grass. Hank parked the Power Wagon and looked out at the front porch. *People.* Two men in dark jackets and throughly gelled hair. They were each smoking a cigarette and gazing at Hank through black sunglasses.

Hank knew goons when he saw them, and these guys were *goons. Mr. B's goons, most likely. Probably responsible for whatever I'm gonna find in this house.* They were. And they were. Hank got out of the car and walked over to the porch. The men in black suits watched him approach silently. When he finally reached the porch steps and was about to walk up, the one on the right spoke up.

"Whoa now, friend. Can we help you?"

Hank really wasn't in the mood for this little game. An overwhelming urge to be reckless came over him. *And why not?* He stopped and looked over at the man who'd spoken.

"No, I'm here to help you, actually. You fellas the dingleberries that dropped two bodies in there?" Hank watched with more than a little satisfaction as their faces soured, and he could tell he'd hit the nail on the head.

"Hey pal, we work for James Brackington, and we ain't…" interjected the other man in black, sounding like a spoiled child.

"OH YEAH?" Hank replied, almost yelling it. "AIN'T THAT JUST SO DAMN INTERESTING… Sorry, *sorry*… I shouldn't shout. My patience just runs so thin with *dingleberries* sometimes. Ya know, I work for a guy named Brackington too…"

Hank was on the porch now and walked over to where the two goons sat. Hank realized as he moved towards the men that this was a bit — *okay, more than a bit* — out of character for him, but he just couldn't bring himself to care. Something was snapping. That little twig in everyone's heart that holds up all emotions, all hopes and worries and dreams. Hank's was all dried out and bent to the breaking point. He could almost hear the *crackle-pop* of it.

"Yeah, he's a real charmer, Mr. B." Hank was standing over the man on the left now, looking down at him with shark eyes. "Hey, maybe we work for the same guy, huh? How bout' that? It's funny, cause the Mr. B I know doesn't like fuck ups, doesn't *tolerate* them, actually. So, I wonder why you two are still just *hangin' around* here fondling each other's sacks. Maybe a thumb or two up the butt?" The suited man on the right made to get up, but Hank cut him off. "*If it were me*, I'd find something else productive to do before big boss decides he could do with two less scarecrows on payroll."

The porch went silent. Cigarette smoke curled up into the stagnant air in hot paisleys. Hank couldn't see their eyes under those dark glasses, but their mouths were clearly hanging open in shock. Hank got the feeling these guys weren't exactly used to being spoken to like this. *Good.* He wasn't sure if the threat of Brackington would be enough to get them to leave, and he didn't really care. But he wouldn't clean up their mess while they laughed or mocked or threatened him. *No, ma'am.* He'd seen the type before, and he wouldn't endure it. Sure, he'd clean up dead people all day long, but somebody talking to you while you did it… *Just too much. I may not have the balls to deny Brackington, but by comparison, these guys are cheese-puffs.*

The two men looked at each other, and Hank saw they'd gone a little pale. *Oh, suckers.* In that moment, he realized he was one of them. *We're the same. I just have a different job title.*

"Whaddya say, comrades? Wanna get lost and let me clean up your mess?"

The two men gave Hank another look, then silently rose from their chairs and walked off the porch. Hank watched them go. It was only as they pulled out of the driveway that he realized he was smiling. *Oh, man.*

#

WHAT do we do with a murder scene, doo-daaa, doo-daaa- tryyy not to think too hard, doo-da, doo-da- about their brains on the floor, ooh da-doo-da-dayy…

The two goons Hank had scared off were an hour gone. He sat inside the sparsely but well-furnished plantation house on a beige couch. A pair of great big horns hung on the wall above him, pointing east and west with deadly sharp points, likely from a long-expired bull named T-bone, or maybe Beefsteak.

Splayed on the wide living room floor in front of him were the two bodies he'd mentioned earlier to the assholes on the porch. A man and a woman. *More strangers.* It seemed these two had been caught off guard, doing God knew what. They lay together on the floor, posed like those chalk outlines in murder mystery movies, except these were filled in. *Probably just said, 'Brackington's shit stinks' a little too loud.*

He was beginning to wonder if all this death was *real*. If his life was *real*. If maybe he was trapped in some cruel ring of Hell where death and misery played an unending joke on poor souls like Hank Cooper. He suspected it was indeed all real, but that didn't necessarily mean he *wasn't* trapped in some ring of Hell. *What to do, what to do… nothing.* Nothing except clean. Yet, Hank's rump remained planted squarely in the middle of that beige, faux leather couch. The man on the floor looked up at Hank with black, glassy eyes, and seemed to say, *"Hey, what's a matter, Rich? Somethin' got ya down? Long day? Your monkey die?"*

That's one way to put it.

Hank lifted his eyes to the ceiling and rested the back of his head on the couch. It was there he noticed the ceiling beams:

stained wood against white popcorn. One of the thick beams was partially detached from the ceiling, allowing for — *if one were so inclined* — the wrapping of some material... perhaps a *rope.*

Hank looked down from the ceiling and towards the kitchen, which was attached to the living room by a large, double-wide opening. On the table was a big twisted pile of yellow extension cords. Hank blinked, and the cords suddenly morphed into an Indiana-Jones-Tomb-Raider-style pile of hemp rope. *Huh. How bout' that.* Hank imagined his two friends on the floor had had some kind of plan for the extension cords, but it seemed they wouldn't be in urgent need of them anymore.

He hadn't started this day off with any particularly suicidal urges, but Hank wondered if anyone did. *Probably. Probably a lot of people,* though he hadn't imagined it would ever be him. Even as he rose from the couch and made his way over to the kitchen table (stepping around the puddles of gray and red matter scattered about, courtesy of the folks on the floor), he didn't think he would follow through. *I'm just seeing what it might be like. That's all. Just... seeing what it would be like...*

By the time he had tied the extension cords firmly around the exposed ceiling beam, and stood with his neck inside his own poorly constructed slipknot, his illusions of *'seeing what it would be like'*, were gone. He looked down from a wobbly kitchen stool at the two bodies he was supposed to be collecting into bags and barrels. *Just a moment, fellas, I'll be with you shortly. Ha, get it?*

Hank thought briefly about the poor bastard whose job it would be to clean up the cleaner. *What an idea.* It occurred to him then that it would probably be Smiley, or maybe Joe. That idea soured his growing sense of relief significantly, though not enough to halt him. And the thought that he might anger Brackington with his death was the perfect thing to balance out the scales. *Last card I have left to play.* As he stood there in the silent living room atop his wobbly wooden stool, Hank Cooper's mind wandered towards his brother, whom he hadn't seen in nearly fifteen years. He hoped Brackington wouldn't be spiteful enough to track him down after Hank was gone, but something told him that's *exactly* how spiteful James Brackington was. *Sorry, little bro. Wish I could help.*

The flimsy stool underneath him wobbled on the uneven hardwood. Hank stumbled, leaning hard into the extension cord. He recovered, but just barely. The stool legs squeaked under his shifting weight.

That was close. As he stood, primed to end his days on this earthly plane, the comedy of that thought made him chuckle. *Oh, was it close, Hank? Not like you were about to jump anyway, right? Just seeing what it would be like?* And he began to laugh. A full-bellied, deep-lunged cackle. *Oh, man… I need a drink.* The first giggles gave way to rolling, gut-pumping coughs of laughter, and he found he couldn't stop. The laughs were a curled fist, aimed at life- aimed at the absurdity of all life. *His life, especially.* It felt good, better than any peanut or gulp of vodka, and a hell of a lot better than the usual long days of silence.

After two minutes of uncontrolled, diaphragm-wracking giggling, there were streams of tears rolling down Hank's cheeks. He lifted his hand to wipe his face. *Whoo, dawggy… that was good.* He almost wished someone had been around to hear his little fit, to share it. Though he realized he probably would've come off like just about the looniest loon in the greater DFW area. He wiped the final tear from his cheek and shook his head. *Much better.* Suddenly he thought maybe he *had* just wanted to know what it would be like. He reached up to loosen the slipknot from around his neck, still smiling with amusement, but it was at that moment that the poorly built stool underneath Hank decided to break.

The glue that held the front leg of the stool in place had been loose to begin with, and the rocking and bouncing from Hank's laughing fit had been the *final wafer-thin mint* that broke it completely. The leg slipped, and suddenly Hank was dropping and *stopping.* The extension cord cinched tight around his neck, and the last thought he had before his windpipe was crushed shut was, *hey, wait.* Then came the panic.

The tips of Hank's steel-toed boots brushed the floor, but only just. He dangled from the beam, legs flailing, hands grasping frantically at the loop around his neck. In the fading light, Hank could hear the wail of… *what? A train whistle? Yeah.* And the soft, full whoosh of billowing steam, the *chugga-chugga* of American steel turning under the power of a coal engine. *Oh… that's kinda nice.*

CHAPTER THIRTY-FIVE

Lumber-SMACK!

SMILEY slotted her key into the lock of the funeral home front door like a caffeine-less zombie, which, in fact, she was. She'd spent the entire night in a state of adrenal panic. When she'd sped off from Karina's house the previous evening, she'd been filled with purpose: *find Robert Dievs*. But about five minutes later, she'd realized that she had no leads, nothing to go on, *nowhere to go*. And more than that, *no real reason* to track the man down. *He's gone, so what? What do I care? I don't know the guy.*

But she'd found that she did care, for some indefinable reason. Priorities have a way of shuffling themselves around when a homicidal criminal overlord suddenly waltzes into one's life. Her experience with magically appearing peanuts had impacted her as well, and left her with a sense that Dievs might be important somehow. *Like I'm living in a Tom Robbins novel.* Though now, thinking back on it, she wasn't entirely convinced that had been *real. Real enough, I suppose.* Going home hadn't been an attractive option either, however. She'd known that all she would've done was pace around her living room like a methed out maniac. *Probably wake up the neighbors.* And so, she'd done what so many Americans had done before her when they didn't know what to do or where to go. She'd driven. Driven nowhere in particular, and with no plan.

Though her night spent on the highway hadn't been terribly productive, she had discovered at least one thing. First being that she was indeed being followed. Followed by a pair of men in a beat-up brown Ford Escort. They'd tried to conceal themselves at first, but by the early hours of the morning, they'd given up on that rouse entirely and had made no further efforts to hide. *Brackington. Am I that important? Makes me feel kind of special, actually.*

Smiley didn't even notice the huge black lettering adorning her front windows, nor the word they were attempting to spell, as she stepped inside her funeral home. She'd given a brief shake of her head to the mess in the parking lot, namely the scattered peanuts and other scraps of trash there (and what appeared to be several piles of dried vomit), but no more than that. *Coffee. Now.*

The sun was rising quickly, but the crisp coolness of night still lingered. A steel-blue sky shone against the brown Campaiyote horizon. A few stars still hung around, like the last spaced-out drifters sitting at the bar. Smiley turned to watch the brown Ford Escort cruise slowly down Sycamore Street and come to a stop on the opposite side of the road underneath a lamppost that was leaning somewhat crookedly. *Huh.* She almost felt like whoever was driving the Escort deserved a coffee as much as she did, though she wasn't about to go offer them one.

Smiley went directly to her coffee machine and set a pot brewing. She pressed the big BOLD button, then proceeded to sit her ass down in the yellow office chair behind her desk. The fatigue from lack of sleep was really settling in now, and she asked herself why she hadn't just gone home. *Even trying to sleep would've probably been better than driving all night.* Through the grogginess of sleep deprivation, the thought occurred to her that she might never go home again. Not really. When was the last time she had been *home? Really, at home?* Maybe not since she was a child. It certainly wasn't this place — *this shit town* — though she had tried to make it one. *Yes*, she'd tried *hard*. But Campaiyote didn't want her. It kept spitting her out like an undercooked Brussels sprout. These thoughts swam in her mind like lazy, zoned-out koi fish. Smiley closed her eyes and leaned back in her chair, listening to the crackle of the coffee machine. She was out in seconds.

#

THE jingle of the little brass bell hanging above the glass door jolted Smiley awake, and she slammed her knees on the underside of the steel desk.

"Shit…"

It took her a few seconds to remember where she was and how she'd gotten there. She thought for a moment that the man coming through the doorway was one of the men who'd followed her all last night, but then she recognized the tall, stocky, lumberjack figure of Joe Karipassius. He stepped inside the lobby, looking nearly as bad as Smiley herself, though he grinned when he said, "You look like shit, boss."

Rubbing the sleep out of her eyes, Smiley replied, "Thank you," *yawn*. "Joe."

"Did you go home yesterday?" asked Joe. "Looks like you didn't sleep a wink."

"What time is it?" Smiley asked, looking up at the clock hanging on the wall, which appeared to have stopped dead at 9:37. *9+3+7= 19. Huh.* The sort of passing thought that happens when the brain is out of glucose and on the verge of having sleep-deprived hallucinations.

"Almost noon," replied Joe, sitting down behind what was once Karina's desk.

Smiley tried to gather herself, but the fog of a sleepless night still clung to her brain like glue. She had that vague sense of urgency that had clung relentlessly to her all last night, like she *ought to be doing something, God dammit.* Her tailbone tingled slightly, and she shifted in her chair.

"There was a bit of a kerfuffle here last night. Thought you might like to hear about it," said Joe, rubbing his tired face.

"Oh? Wait, I sent you home last night."

"Yeah, well… I went and got a chili dog, and just happened to see some… *delinquents* pull in here. Trust me, I wish I hadn't." Joe gestured to the front window. Smiley followed his hand and finally saw the black spray paint on the window. She didn't even need to read it to know what it said. On her list of worries, this ranked pretty low. It didn't surprise her. "I also saw you peel out of here like your hair was on fire," said Joe.

"I told you to go home," said Smiley flatly.

"Mmm. Did you go home?" Joe asked with the same dullness in his voice. "I… I couldn't stop thinking about those eyes, Lee. Those green eyes. They're *in* my head. I can't shake the feeling that I'm gonna… that *he's* gonna kill me."

Silence hung between the two for a few moments, and they both looked away from one another. The sound of the refrigeration system for the cold room kicked in, a muted thump of metal followed by a low hum. *At least the electricity hasn't shut off yet*, thought Smiley. Finally, she broke the silence.

"What happened?"

"A few drunk college kids… well, I guess I don't know if they were actually in college. Probably not. Two guys and their girlfriends for the night. They started spray painting the front windows and causing a mess, so I drove over and scared em' enough to make em' leave in a hurry. You see the lamppost out there?"

"Oh, yeah…"

"*In their haste*, they forgot the two young ladies they'd brought with em'. Not that I think they woulda remembered their names tomorrow morning anyhow. One of the girls fell off the hood of the car and broke her arm. I ended up having to go down to the police station and talk with Phil Morris."

"*That cunt…* Sorry," Smiley interrupted. She'd had dealings with Phil Morris, the police chief of Campaiyote, and he hadn't exactly been sympathetic to her cause. Her *cause* being reasonable punishment for the vandalization of her property. Some of the cops here were good, personable folks. Morris wasn't one of them. And he was the biggest piggy in the yard. Smiley had a feeling she wasn't gonna like the next part of this story.

"The one and only. He said that the girl might want to press charges for having," Joe put up air quotes, "'sustained physical injuries on Ms. Davis' property and place of business.' He said you might be liable."

"Oh, Jesus. Give me a fuckin' break. I wasn't even here," replied Smiley, with no small amount of exasperation.

"Hey, that's what I told him. He also offered me that spot in the department again."

"You know he's trying to force me out. Wants to steal my workers, well, *worker*." Smiley sighed and followed it up with, "You should take it, Joe. Take the job."

"What?" Joe said incredulously. "No way, I wouldn't ever work for that piece of shit, racist bas…"

"You said it yourself, Joe. Brackington is watching. If you join the force, he might leave you alone."

"I doubt that, Lee. I'd probably end up doing even more messed up stuff than I already am. And this is *plenty* messed up for me… God, I miss cutting down trees."

Smiley was quiet for a second, lost in terrible thought, but she giggled at that.

"I drove all last night. Didn't go home. I was looking for Dievs."

"The guy at the diner?"

"Yeah. His real name is Derrick V. Swiss."

"Wait, Derrick… That's the guy Hank brought…"

"Yeppers."

"But how is that possible?" Joe's eyes widened as he tried to picture the man who'd sat across from him at that Denny's booth just yesterday. "Oh my God." Joe seemed to twitch, as if his tailbone had tingled him. "How did I not recognize him?"

"Generally speaking, I don't try too hard to remember the faces we put into cadaver cabinets. I don't expect to see their faces again. Usually. And especially not sitting next to me at Denny's."

"Guess not… Holy shit. So… what… wait!" Joe shot up from his seat. "He was with Karina… she might be in danger, we ha…"

"Siddown, Joe. I already checked. She's fine. He got kidnapped, apparently. I'll give you one shot to guess who by."

Joe was hesitant to sit, but looking at Smiley's tired face, he seemed to understand she was telling the truth.

"Brackington… So… what? What now?"

Smiley gave a half chuckle and leaned her elbows on the desk.

"What happens now is, you leave this place and never come back. I won't have another person's blood on my hands. Not yours, not anyone's."

"Now wait a goddamn sec…"

Joe twitched again, and Smiley raised her hand up flat, like a traffic controller.

"I don't want to hear it. We're being watched right now, you know. Maybe even listened to."

"What…"

"That beige Escort parked on the street out there followed me all night. I'm pretty sure it's a couple of Brackington's goons keeping an eye on me. And now you. Listen… I think… If you go fast enough, *if you're careful enough,* you can lose any tails that try to follow you. Go northwest. Cut down some more trees. Go to fuckin' Mexico, just don't tell me where you're headed."

"I'm not gonna leave you here to…"

"You're fired, Joe. End of story. Go on, git."

Smiley waved her hand as if shooing a friendly stray dog. Joe did not move, he just looked at Smiley.

"Ya know, you're a lot like Hank. Always wanna do things alone. Never need any help… *no, not me. I'm a business owner, a strong independent woman, and I don't need shit from anyone.* We *all* need help sometimes, Smiley. *Everyone does.*"

With this, Joe turned and walked out the front door, again jingling the little bell over the front door. Though it was what she'd asked for, Smiley was sad to see him go. He was one of the few friends she had here. One name on a rapidly dwindling list. She sighed and told herself it was for the best, but as she watched Joe stride across the parking lot, limping only a little from the injury he'd sustained long ago, she saw his fists were curled. *Not like Joe…* She watched as he walked right past his beat-up Corolla.

Where… and then Smiley realized he was heading straight for the beige Escort parked across the street, and it didn't look like he was going to sell them cookies.

#

IN seconds Smiley was running across the parking lot, yellow flats skidding over rough concrete, yelling, "Stop!" and "Get out of here!" but it was far too late. She was only halfway across the lot by the time Joe had reached the Ford.

The two men sitting in the beige Escort must've been as groggy as Smiley and Joe, because they didn't notice the six-foot-something, ex-lumberjack in a red plaid shirt until he had opened the driver's side door and seized the driver by the shoulders. *Should have locked it, boys,* Smiley thought as she continued to run across the lot. A part of her was excited that he'd actually managed to grab one of the goons, but even in her adrenaline-laced thoughts she feared Brackington's retribution. She could hear the startled cry of the guy in the driver's seat as Joe hauled him out of the car like a sack of grain.

"What the fu…"

But before the man could finish his sentence, a fistful of lumberjack knuckles filled his mouth. Even from twenty yards away, she could see teeth bouncing over the blacktop like Martha Wayne's pearls. She'd never seen Joe fight before, and it was a shocking sight. So shocking, it made her stop for a moment just to watch, jaw hanging open. It made her feel like maybe she didn't really know Joe as well as she thought she did. *What happened to being a pacifist?* His huggable demeanor was gone, like a candle flame blown out in the wind. He was *scary.* And by the third punch, Smiley thought he might kill the guy. *He's gonna punch a hole right through his face.* Joe was holding the man about three feet off the ground by his shirt collar, and every punch was snapping his head back like a party balloon.

"Joe! Stop, you're gonna kill him!"

Joe seemed not to hear Smiley's warning, but he dropped the guy, anyway. He'd been knocked unconscious on the first punch, and he collapsed into the street in a pile of blood and teeth. The sound he made when he thumped against the concrete was *mushy.*

Smiley was almost to the Ford now, and she could see the face of the other man in the beige Escort peering out the window from the passenger seat, wide-eyed and unbelieving, frozen in shock. The sight of Joe coming through the driver's door was enough to get him moving, however. *Not fast enough,* Smiley thought.

"You… st-stay back! Freak! Stay the hell back!"

The man was fumbling at his crotch for something, and as Smiley finally came up behind Joe, she could see it was a gun. A big silver revolver. The man was frantically trying to get it free of his belt buckle, which was drawn tight over his pudgy stomach. Joe was moving across the driver's seat now, his face like the front of a black-iron locomotive, cold and unyielding. The man finally got the gun free and made to aim it at Joe, but before he could move, Joe's bloody hand came down on the butt of the gun, lodging the barrel right back down into the man's crotch.

The goon went quiet, his face a white sheet of terror. Slowly, Joe cocked the hammer on the revolver.

"Hey, friend," said Joe. "No public parking on Sycamore, I'm afraid. I'd invite you to park in the lot, if you have some business with the funeral home, of course."

#

"HEY, hey, hey! I don't know nuthin' bout all that, man! Honest! Ow… oh, Jesus!"

Joe twisted the cold barrel of the .45 revolver deeper into the man's crotch, like a key in a wind-up toy.

"Oh, churchgoing man are you?"

"Hey… whaddya want from me, man? You crazy or something?"

"Crazy enough," said Joe, staring coldly into the man's eyes.

"Joe, stop this. This isn't gonna help," said Smiley from behind Joe, though she didn't actually sound all that pressed for him to stop.

"Listen, *pal*. Smiley and I have had a couple real unpleasant days, coming off of a hard couple of months, honestly, and I'm just looking for a little *clarity*. I was hoping you could help me with that."

"I can't…"

Joe twisted the revolver, which was now firmly under his control. He felt the soft skin under the man's khaki suit pants twist and tighten.

"Okay!" The man was beginning to turn green, and it looked like he might be sick.

"First, who is James Brackington? *And I want you to listen to me closely before you answer that question.* I will blow your nuts right off your goddamn foopah if you fuck with me, I don't care. Truly. You saw what I did to your friend out there, right? I really hope I didn't kill him. One murder on my record was already more than enough. *So… shoot*, or I shoot. And don't leave out a fuckin' thing. I mean, *A. Fucking. Thing.*"

Smiley stood back and watched Joe interrogate Brackington's goon with an open mouth. It was like finding out that your lovable, crossword-solving dad was actually a secret agent. She wondered which version of Joe was the real one: the gun-wielding, face-smashing, one-man wrecking team, or the guy who limped around carrying his red lunchbox and vomited at the sight of blood. *Astounding*. But deep in Smiley's brain, there was a flicker of something… *hope*. With this kind of muscle on her team, maybe she stood a chance against Brackington. *Just maybe… if we get lucky…*

The man looked like he was going to protest, but after glancing down at the revolver lodged firmly in his most precious of spaces, he took a big gulp and started talking slowly.

"B-Brackington… *James* Brackington, is my employer. He runs a club on San Jacinto called the Hyacinth House. He also sells drugs and weapons, and probably a whole lotta other things too. The drugs and guns are the only things I know about for sure, though. That's it, I swear. I never even met the guy."

"Sounds like you might be leaving some things out… Dave? What was your name? Oh, I don't care…" Joe put his thumb on the hammer of the revolver.

"Wait! Wait, wait, wait… I-I-I know that he's powerful. He's got people in the force and in the courts. The guy's like a Bond villain or somethin'. Things have been… sort of ramping up recently. Rumor is he's got something big planned, but I have no idea what it is, honest to God. I'm just a grunt, real low down. I work at the post office part-time, man… I swear, fella, *I swear*, that's all I know. That's it… please don't blow my nuts off."

Joe turned to give Smiley a quick glance that said, *what do you think?* She didn't know what to think. Not anymore. But the guy sounded like he was telling the truth… though maybe not *all of it*. Smiley stepped forward and poked her head into the car by Joe's shoulder.

"Why were you following me last night?"

Joe raised his eyebrows at the guy like, *you heard the lady.* Now, Dave looked kind of hesitant, but he started talking anyway.

"It… we were assigned to you…"

"By Brackington?" asked Joe.

"No. Well, yes… we got a phone call from someone called… Jenine? I think. Scary lady. I think she's like his assistant or something. Right-hand gal."

Smiley turned to Joe. "That's the woman who called Karina yesterday."

"See! I'm tellin' the truth. I-I wouldn't lie, not me, Dave. Not Dave, no way. Dave don't lie."

"So what? You just follow me around and make sure I do my job? Is that it?" asked Smiley.

"Yeah, that was the gist…" But Dave's eyes drifted away from Joe and Smiley. He couldn't have made his lie more obvious if he'd tried.

"Woah, woah, woah, *Dave*. The fuck was that? I thought we had an understanding." Joe slipped the revolver barrel just free of the man's crotch so that it pointed between his legs and fired. The sound was deafening in the car's closeness. Dave screamed and shut his eyes. He started whispering some kind of scrambled prayer to the god of thugs and sleaze-bags. Joe pressed the hot revolver barrel firmly back into its gonad holster.

"Jesus Christ, Joe!" yelled Smiley. "Someone's gonna hear that and call the cops!"

Joe was cool and collected when he turned, smiled and

said, "I'm licensed to carry. This is Texas, boss. We'll be done soon anyway." He turned back to the man trembling in the passenger seat. "That was a lie, Dave. Why'd you do that?"

"I-I-I didn't lie…"

"*I just didn't tell the whole truth…* Oh, how *clever*, Dave! Jesus, what is this, first grade? **What was your job?**"

The man looked nervous and pale, but he spoke calmly when he answered. "We were told that if *the woman*," he nodded ever so slightly towards Smiley, "Did anything out of the ordinary, or against orders from the *organization*, Jenine, I guess, to… to apprehend her and all known associates for a *meeting* with the big boss. And if it came to it… to use deadly force to prevent escape."

"So, kill us before we skip town?" Joe asked. The man closed his eyes and nodded gravely. "Mailman on the weekdays, are you? And hitman on the weekends. Quite a combo, Dave. You know a teenager worked here. Were they on your list?" The man made no reply. Joe shook his head in wonder. "Wowza. Didn't know it got so scummy here. Texas ain't a place for cowards."

"Let's get out of here, Joe. We need to get someone else involved, the police, maybe."

"How much help have you received from the police around here, Smiley? Think Phil Morris is gonna hang on every word you say like Sherlock Holmes or some shit? No, they won't help us. But… I think Dave here might still be willing to lend us a hand. Right, Dave?"

The man gulped. Smiley hesitantly reached out and touched Joe's shoulder. She felt his body trembling. He glanced back at her, and she could see that the hand holding the gun was shaking badly. He shot her a quick, queasy-looking smile.

Oh goodness.

CHAPTER THIRTY-SIX

Hank Hunting

SWISS still hadn't given up the location of the case by mid-afternoon of the day after his kidnapping. This was frustrating the big man, Mr. B, *the* James Brackington. *The man with the green eyes.* Jennie had continued to practice her art through the night, and Swiss's screams were buried under the roar of the hundreds of party-goers below the office.

James Brackington stood smoking a cigarette at the big bay windows that looked down onto the main floor of the Hyacinth House, his club on San Jacinto. His mouth, for once, was not curled up into that smirking smile, but was a straight, tight line. It seemed that things might not move along as smoothly as he'd anticipated. The man tied up in the office, Robert V. Swiss, was a problem. Either he had far more willpower than James had originally estimated, or he was telling the truth, which was much, *much* worse.

Though Brackington hadn't been present all night, he'd been around enough to hear the man's explanation. *Returned from the train station of the dead. Likely story.* Brackington pictured the blue glow that had emanated from the briefcase he'd held so briefly. *With **that** though, anything is possible…* But his apparent amnesia was more convincing. James thought that if Swiss knew where the case with the rest of… *it*, was, he would've volunteered that information by now. *Probably would have given it up three fingernails ago.* It was disconcerting, to say the least. Jenine was continuing the good work, but even she seemed doubtful that more torture would get them anywhere.

He pondered this as he smoked his cigarette and watched the last stragglers stumble out of his club and into the blinding light of day. He heard soft footsteps approaching from behind. *Jenine.* She spoke quietly.

"Mr. B… it might be time to try a different strategy…"

Before Jenine could finish her sentence, Brackington whirled and sent the back of his hand streaking across Jenine's cheek. She grunted and fell to the floor. She looked up into green fury, and even then, worshipped him.

With a calm voice, like the ocean under a storm, James said, "You don't tell me what it's *time for.*" He lifted his cigarette and took a long pull, keeping his eyes trained on Jenine, who lay on the floor holding her cheek. He sighed and closed his eyes. "Sorry, love. I'm just a little… on edge." And though he did sound on edge, he *did not* sound sorry.

"It's okay Mr. B. I understand," said Jenine, as she lifted herself off the floor. "I… I also have some… bad news."

Brackington turned to face the window again and said, "Shoot."

"Hank Cooper, the clean…"

"I know who the fuck Hank Cooper is."

"He's… disappeared."

"What?"

"He had several assignments today, but it seems he never completed the last one, or maybe he's still there? We had a team at the house, but they left earlier than instructed, for which they were severely reprimanded, *of course*… I just sent a couple guys to see what the situation is. I'll keep you informed."

"I'd hope so," said Brackington quietly.

"And also…"

"If you make me wait any longer, I'll kick your kneecaps in, Jenine."

"Smiley Davis and Joe Karipassius have cut their tail."

At this, Brackington turned around, eyebrows raised. That terrible smile had returned to his face once again. *The schoolyard bully's smile, the smarmy businessman, the criminal running free,* all rolled together into one horrible smirk. He sucked down the last of his cigarette and flicked the butt down onto the cream carpet where it smoldered black.

"Oh, you say so?"

"Yes. Apparently, Karipassius almost killed one of our guys, and another is missing. The paramedics had to scrape the first guy off the pavement like an omelette, and what was left of his face. I contacted our man at Baylor General and gave him the go-ahead to give him the *long sleep* treatment. I know how you feel about… *incompetent employees*."

"Yeah, yeah… good… Seems I got used to Hanky Panky following orders like the beat dog he is. Ms. Smiley and Lumberjack Joe have a little more *spunk*. Fun." Brackington took one last look down over his Hyacinth House and then turned. "Come with me. We're done with Swiss for now. Just make sure he doesn't die while we're gone." Brackington reached down and offered Jenine his hand. She took it like a junkie reaching for a fix.

"We're goin' Hank hunting."

CHAPTER THIRTY-SEVEN

Limbo

HANK was drifting in that blank space between sleep and wakefulness, listening to the sound of trains, and trying to hold on to glimpses of beautiful, white-marbled rooms, which danced behind his eyelids like teensy fairies. He thought he'd seen a chubby man in a baby blue conductor uniform too, but he couldn't be sure.

After some unquantifiable time hanging in this limbo, Hank woke. His first sensation was of floating, and he could feel that his feet weren't touching the ground. *Huh.* He was suspended in the air. The thought came into his groggy mind that maybe he'd fallen asleep in a hammock, or on a swing. It came in that half-awake moment when one is apt to forget who they are and where exactly in the timeline of their life they find themselves.

As he blinked his eyes open… *wait, no… eye.* He saw the big, open-concept living room-kitchen combo of the plantation house he'd been cleaning. He also spied two big red stains on the floor where the bodies of the people he'd been assigned to clean had lain. *Weird.* It all came back to him slowly, like sludge being pushed out of a drainpipe by heavy rain.

The next thing to grab Hank's attention was the pain in his neck and arms. Though in actuality he couldn't really *feel* his left arm, just that something wasn't quite right in that department. His neck though, he could feel, could feel the rough pressure of an extension cord against unprotected skin. *Owy.*

As he blinked open his left eye, he finally remembered what he'd been doing, and the panic came quickly. *The rope. The cord. I… hung myself. What…* Hank tried to speak and found his throat so tightly bound he couldn't, though he got off a shrimpy little moan.

Only then did Hank see the hunched Filipino lady scrubbing at the bloodstains on the floor with a big yellow sponge. At the sound of his moan, she stopped, and slowly raised her head to look at Hank. What she saw was a man suspended by a noose he'd tied himself just a few hours before, with his head and entire left arm up to the shoulder, stuck through the loop of the cord. Most horrifying was his face, blue from lack of oxygen, and bearing a dangling right eyeball, which had popped free of its socket from the force of the drop.

The Filipino lady's name was Angela. She was maid to this house, and no stranger to cleaning up blood and guts. This was, however, the first time she'd found a *living* body in the house after, well, after whatever it was that went on in here. Angela did not ask about such things, though it didn't take a rocket scientist to intuit that it probably wasn't tea parties and crumpet tastings. Whatever it was, it was no business of her's. A few thoughts ran through Angela's mind, including, but not limited to: *bash the hanging man's brains in, ignore him, cut him down, don't cut him down,* and *put his eye back in its socket.* All in Filipino, of course. But the one she settled on was, *take the rest of the day off.* This was usually a solid choice, in Angela's experience. She sighed as she struggled onto one knee, then to her feet. She leaned back, stretching, then wobbled away from Hank towards the front door.

Hank watched as Angela waddled off and realized that he was in dire need of assistance. He moaned again, this time louder, but the cleaning woman just kept walking away. *Probably a good call*, Hank thought, though he wished she'd at least gotten him a stool.

Hank hung this way in silence, unable to move much, and as he became more conscious, the pain and panic rose in his chest. He rocked his legs back and forth, though the pain in his neck and shoulder was terrible. *Gotta get free of this cord.* All the philosophical and emotional components of his suicide had fled Hank's mind. He was reduced to one thing: *live. Live at all costs.* And he wondered if other people had felt like this. *Probably. Probably a lot of people.*

The will to live turned out to be stronger than the pain in his neck and shoulders. After a minute of rocking and squirming, Hank managed to free his chin of the extension cord, and he slid out of the noose, arm and all. His legs might as well have been made of silly putty, the way they crumpled beneath him. Hank collapsed to the floor, sucking in huge gasping breaths of hot air. He lay just like that, breathing, for a good long while.

#

AFTER about an hour, the feeling in his arm came back, though he wished it hadn't. The pins and needles were the worst he'd ever experienced. What did *not* come back, however, was the vision in his right eye. Hank kept blinking, and wondering why he could only see from his left. It was the growing pain emanating from his right eye socket that finally made him feel for his eyeball. What he felt when he put his hand to his face was like a large grape suspended on a small umbilical cord. *Oh.* His eyelid was like an empty candy wrapper.

Hank's first instinct was to push the eye back into place, but something told him that might not be the best idea. He wondered at all the anatomy he'd seen in his life (occupational hazard of crime scene cleanup), and yet how little he knew about the way the body *ought* to be. Hank turned onto his back and breathed deeply. His loose eyeball rolled over his cheek like a paddleball.

I wonder who that lady was. Was she real? Were those train noises I heard earlier… Then he supposed he ought to either get on with this job or leave. The thought did not occur to him at all that his absence of nearly a full day had been noticed by other people. By Brackington himself, actually. He simply didn't think he was important enough.

Something made Hank turn his head to the left, and he saw that on the floor next to him lay a single, shelled peanut, just on the edge of the blood stain left by Mr. Red Fish and Ms. Blue Fish (the two bodies he'd been sent to clean). Hank stared at the legume for a few seconds, then reached over, grabbed it and popped it in his mouth.

Needs salt.

It was as Hank swallowed the last bits of peanut that he heard the front door swing open. He turned his head to look and saw several blurry figures streaming into the old house. Hank, still recovering from lack of oxygen, a dislocated eyeball and a dislocated shoulder, didn't bother to move a muscle… *couldn't*, really. It wasn't until two smiling green eyes were looming close above him that Hank spoke. It sounded like two cat tongues being rubbed together.

"… Hey…" *Swallow.* "I know you," said Hank groggily.

"That's right. Very good, Hank. And I know *you*."

Hank did *not* like the way the man with green eyes said, *you*.

"What, uh… what are you doing here, boss?" asked Hank, sounding like a child when he said it.

"I heard you were having some trouble with your work. I couldn't let my star employee go missing without a *thorough* investigation. Turns out we didn't really *lose* you, but it was a close thing." Brackington chuckled, but it came out sounding more cruel than kind. "Close indeed… Seems you had a wee episode." Brackington clucked his tongue like a scolding mother. "Don't you know that hurting yourself is a real no-no? I thought I'd made it clear, Hank. *You're mine.* Only I give you permission to leave. *To die…* And your poor eye, we'll have to get that looked at… *wait…* you know, actually…"

Brackington squinted and reached down toward Hank's face with his right hand. Hank didn't move, nor did he understand what was happening until a sharp pain shot into his brain from his limp eye socket. Brackington gripped Hank's eyeball with his thumb and forefingers, then pushed it back into the socket, *hard*, like putting a Whopper chocolate ball back into its little plastic sleeve. Hank screamed in pain, but afterwards, found he could shut both his eyelids again, which felt good.

"There we go. Isn't that better?"

To his right, Hank could hear one man who had come in with Brackington vomit onto the floor.

"Not… really," said Hank, who could feel that something was still *very wrong* with his right eye. *Guess it's not as easy as in all the movies.* But Hank's capacity for silly thoughts was running out, and he felt the pull of unconsciousness once again.

He was awake long enough to hear Brackington say, "I'm glad I found you, Hank. I was getting worried. I think it's time we had another little chat, a business meeting, you could say. And maybe we'll invite your two new besties as well." Then to his men, "Get him in the truck."

CHAPTER THIRTY-EIGHT

The Rest of It

THE man once named Derrick V. Swiss, now going by the name he — *for some reason or another* — had put on his pre-afterlife survey card, Robert Dievs, was really quite pooped. He felt like he'd been in this god-forsaken office for an eternity, and nearly all of that eternity had been a *real deal, no joke Chazz, stupid bad time*. He was down eight fingernails and his face, he felt sure, was a mess of bruises and smeared blood stains, courtesy of Jenine… *What's her last name? Oh, who cares.*

And even through the beatings and torture, he was still bitter about having missed dinner with that strange girl, Karina, and her family. *That would've been nice.* A stranger with green eyes, who'd drugged him, thrown him into a van, and tortured him for information he didn't have, had robbed him of that. It was a real bummer, to say the least. Especially after having just been inexplicably resurrected. Though, the part about not having any information wasn't *entirely* true. At least, not anymore.

The first real look had come to him on the back end of one of Jennie's right hooks, a flash of light behind his eyelids. He hadn't understood what it was at first, then he'd recognized it as a memory. Not a memory of Robert Dievs, but of Derrick V. Swiss. And not a pleasant one.

It had been like looking through one of those old-timey stereoscope photo viewers, except the picture was moving. *Eyes*. He was staring out from a familiar yet strange pair of eyes. His eyes… *Swiss's eyes*. He'd seen a rough wooden floor, painted blue, but with… flecks of old red paint showing through from a previous coat. For some reason, that seemed important. A little rug. A twin bed with a quilted cover. Dievs had thought that would be all, then the eyes had dropped, like they'd tripped, and in something like slow-motion, Dievs had seen a hand fumble on the trigger of a pistol. As the vision had gone tumbling to the floor, the short-barreled gun had twisted, lodged its muzzle against his chest and fired. There was no pain, but the thought of something like that was enough to make Dievs scream. Jenine had chalked it up to a really good punch, and Dievs hadn't corrected her.

The vision of Swiss blowing a big ol' hole in his chest had prompted Dievs to take a look at his own solar-plexus. He'd been expecting at least a mark there, but his chest was clean as a baby's bottom (minus the blood dripping from his busted lips and face). *Neato. What a silly way to go… and come back.* The image of that glowing blue case came back to him briefly. He couldn't help but feel that it had something to do with his revival. *It's what Brackington is after.*

More memories had followed, all accompanied by a punch, kick or pull from Jenine. It was like the most exhausting game of self-trivia ever. But by the end of the night, Dievs had gotten at least a vague picture of the man he'd once been. *Apparently*. Though he still didn't recognize any of that personality in himself. *Guess purgatory has a way of rearranging priorities*. It had shocked him, however, that — *if he had his timeline right* — he'd only been dead for a few days. He vaguely remembered moving off of a train platform and feeling *certain* he'd been there a hundred years. *Apparently not*. He supposed time didn't really matter when you were dead. Hadn't someone told him that?

The more he'd remembered, the more of Brackington and Jenine's questions had made sense, though he hadn't told them so. It's easy to say, *"I don't know what you're talking about!"* when you have no idea what someone is talking about. And if the information comes to you later, *well…* it's not that much of a stretch to keep denying knowledge.

Some things were clear in his mind now, however. One being that he'd seen Hank before. There at that old ranch house. Hank had been cleaning up the bodies of Swiss's old partner, Joe. *And a big dog? A St. Bernard, I think*? That was good, because that house was important; he was sure of it. There was something there. *The case*. In fact, Swiss had gone there specifically to retrieve it and had died in the process. *Falling on my own gun. Jeez, that's dumb*. He wondered how such a clumsy idiot could have gotten so deep into Brackington's trust. As close as anyone else anyway.

Surely, Brackington had sent people to search that house from top to bottom, rip out every plank and piece of drywall. But he hadn't found it, otherwise Dievs would probably be dead. Or maybe sleeping in the guest room at Karina Blake's house with a belly full of peas and potatoes. He'd recalled some kind of meeting with a woman in a blue suit, and the case.

Although he couldn't remember *exactly* what he'd seen in that briefcase (only the blue glow of it), there was a feeling around the thing. A feeling of dread and wonder. It was important to Brackington at the very least, Dievs knew that much.

There was more of whatever was in that case, hidden away by the woman in the blue suit. And Dievs thought knew where it was. *Too bad I'm tied to a chair in the supervillain's lair and unlikely to be performing any miraculous escapes.* If they kept at him like they had been for the past 36 hours, he might just crack and tell them where it was, where he *thought* it was, though something in the back of his brain told him that would be very bad. Very bad indeed.

All these thoughts drifted through Dievs' sleep-deprived brain as he listened to the growing roar of party-goers flooding onto the Hyacinth House main floor, some sixty feet below the office where he sat. The band was warming up, and already that pounding bass was chiseling away at Dievs' sanity again, promising another night of one-on-one time with Jenine.

Half an hour later, when the music was in full swing and the scream of the club below was reaching its peak, he heard a commotion coming from outside the office door. He turned and tried to listen. *Brackington's back. Time to start again. God.* Dievs' knees shook uncontrollably, and he feared he might tell them everything before they could do more damage. *All I can hope for is a quick end.*

The scuffling sounds coming from outside the office grew louder. There were shouts, then gunshots. A bullet came streaking through the office door, sending wood chips flying and poking a small hole of light in the door. Somehow it missed the windows on the opposite side of the room, but the bullet must've passed within a few inches of Dievs' nose, because he felt the wind coming off it. *Hot.* Out of instinct, he tried to duck backwards and ended up toppling his chair. He smashed his head against the thinly carpeted floor and groaned.

Okay… Maybe not Brackington. The police? They wouldn't dare… There was a final pop of gunfire, then quiet. The roar of the party below continued, of course. The people below, basking in the vibrations of hundreds of stage speakers, wouldn't have heard even a single shot.

Dievs lay there on the floor for another minute, watching the pinprick of yellow light in the door. Suddenly, an eye came into view there. It scanned the room, then settled on Dievs. He heard a hushed voice say, "He's in here! C'mon."

The doorknob turned and shook, but did not click. *Locked.* He'd heard Jenine lock it when she'd left several hours ago. He wasn't sure if he ought to be happy about that or not, though, just about any situation besides being locked in a dark torture chamber would be a welcome change. Silence again, and the doorknob stopped shaking.

A second later, there was a heavy thud and the whole door shook on its frame. *Again. Again. And again…* then the door finally gave in and swung open violently. Yellow light flooded in, blinding Dievs for a moment. Two figures stood there, one much bigger than the other. He blinked, trying to adjust his eyes to the new light. *That big guy kinda looks like a lumberjack.*

PART FIVE:

Take a Bow, Everyone

CHAPTER THIRTY-NINE

The Hyacinth House

"I can't believe we're doing this," Smiley said into the closed air of the beige Escort that had followed her all the night before.

"You can say that again," said Dave, though that definitely wasn't his name. He sounded angry and scared, and Smiley supposed he had several good reasons to be. One, at least, was the cold barrel of the .45 revolver being pressed into the side of his ribcage by Joe, who sat in the passenger seat.

"You're sure this is the place?" asked Joe, looking out across San Jacinto at a big brick of a building with no distinct features whatsoever.

"You wanna go ahead and ask me that a twentieth time? Make it a nice round number? Yeah. I'm fuckin' sure," Dave said.

Joe made no reply and kept his gaze on the plain building. Smiley did the same from the back seat. Anyone passing by the place might've taken it for an abandoned workshop, or maybe just an out of use office building, but the steady stream of young people which continued to flow into a green metal door down an adjacent alley said otherwise.

"Can I see that poster again, Joe?" asked Smiley.

Joe wordlessly handed back the poster he'd picked up from the kids who'd spray painted the front windows of the funeral home, making sure to keep the pistol firmly aimed at Dave's pudgy guts. Smiley took it and unfolded it. *Hyacinth House.* All black, with a pair of green eyes at the bottom of the page. It gave Smiley the chills, and she prayed again that they could pull this off — *whatever this was* — without hurting anyone, themselves included. *Except maybe Dave. Dave could get hurt.* The trio's brief drive up to Dallas had been revealing as far as Dave's character went. She thought he would try to sabotage this however he could. *This rescue mission.* Anyone prepared to kill a child might be better off in a mortuary cabinet. Or just burned.

Smiley's sense of anxiety had risen steadily since she'd climbed into the back of the Escort, and now she felt almost as if she were living in an alternate universe. *I'm no spy, no vigilante. Jesus, I'm just a failed business owner.* She had accepted that now. *Failure. That,* perhaps, was part of the reason she'd climbed into the Escort. When normalcy falls apart, it makes diving into the absurd a little easier. *And a little easier, and a little easier… and then, before you know it, you're about to rescue an undead stranger from the clutches of a criminal overlord. With an asshole named Dave and a lumberjack named Joe. Rescue mission… Please, more like a death sentence.* The thought of going up against gangsters and armed guards made Smiley want to laugh and vomit at the same time.

"And Brackington's office is upstairs?" asked Joe.

Dave sighed in annoyance. "Yeah. But like I said, I never been *in there;* I just know that's where all the big boys go."

"Alright. You're gonna get us in that door, *Dave.* And you're gonna do it reeeall normal-like. Cause if you don't, I'm gonna…"

"*…Blow my nuts right off my foopah*. Yeah, yeah, man. I got it the first ten times."

"I was gonna say turn your last vertebrae into a nice crunchy salsa dip, but that works. And if you think I won't, I want you to look into my eyes right now."

Dave turned reluctantly, but stared into Joe's eyes all the same. He must've seen something there, because Smiley watched fear rush back onto his face. She recognized the look because she was scared as shit herself. She'd never done anything like this before. Today alone, she'd committed more crimes than she'd ever imagined taking part in, and certainly more than her mother would have envisioned. The last time she'd broken the law was to steal a 100 Grand Bar from a corner mart when she was ten, and she'd gotten caught then. The nervous breakdown that was surely on its way was close, but for now, that sweet wave of adrenaline was whisking her briskly along like a squirrel who'd stumbled upon a bag of crack.

Smiley reached into her pocket and felt the cold piece of machinery there. It made her whole body hot, then cold. It was a Bren Ten automatic pistol, taken from the shoulder holster of Dave's partner, who was, *presumably*, either still baking on the sidewalk of Sycamore Street like a piece of tenderized beef, or being taken to hospital, courtesy of some good samaritan passerby. She'd been concerned about leaving the guy there on the ground, but Joe had made a good point when he'd said, "Oh, shall we take him down to the hospital and explain everything? Sure they'll understand." That had ended the conversation.

Smiley glanced at Joe's hand. The one holding the gun, and the one he'd used to punch Dave's partner. It was shaking, though Joe was doing his best to hide the trembling. The bloodstains on his knuckles made her feel sick.

"We doin' this, or what?" asked Dave, clearly trying to hide his anxiety. He'd adamantly refused this plan at first, but Joe had made a rather persuasive argument from the other side of the .45 revolver.

"Yeah," Joe turned in his seat to face Smiley. "Ready?"

"Ready as I'm gonna get," she replied.

"Ya know… we don't have any business with this guy… Dievs, I mean. *Not really.* We can walk right out of here and forget it. It's not too late," said Joe.

Dave turned and pointed at Joe like, *listen to the man*, but Smiley didn't think that was entirely true.

"And what? Bow to Brackington for the rest of our lives?" said Smiley. "Like this piece of shit?"

"Hey, it ain't so bad," interjected Dave.

"No, we've already done too much. Who knows what he would do. This feels right, doesn't it? Trying to save someone from that green-eyed freak is the best we can do. So let's do it… What is there to lose?"

Joe nodded, then stepped out of the car.

#

IT turned out that getting inside the Hyacinth House wasn't the problem, even when carrying some not so well concealed weaponry. Dave chatted up the doorman for a minute, and the trio had been ushered through the green door without incident, along with the ever-increasing stream of teens and college students flowing into the building.

The main dance floor was thick with people, and already the music was loud enough to give Smiley an instant headache. Once inside, Joe kept Dave close by his side, the .45 tucked in his flannel jacket pocket and aimed at the small of his back.

Smiley couldn't help but be impressed by the interior of the club. The building, plain enough from the outside, was structured like an old hotel, with a big internal courtyard that ran up to a sky-lighted ceiling. Each of the seven floors had a distinguishing feature. One had rows of multicolored, numbered doors. *The pleasure retreats*, thought Smiley. Another had flashing disco lights, which shone down on the main floor, and yet another was filled with people dancing on a metal walkway that ringed the entire building. *Wowza*. She could see why this place was so popular. She herself, back in her early college days, might've come here looking for a good time. *Guess this is Brackington's little side project.*

"There," said Dave, pointing to a pair of ludicrously large men in black suits standing by a grated iron stairwell that zigzagged its way up from the ground floor, stopping on each level of the building, like an indoor fire escape. *Or a prison.*

Smiley could barely hear Joe when he asked, "How do we get past those two?"

Dave shrugged his shoulders in a, *not my fackin' problem* kind of way. Smiley had no ideas either. She looked up towards the ceiling and saw a booth on the seventh floor, which protruded from the wall just slightly. There were windows there, and even before she confirmed it with Dave, she knew that was Brackington's office. Dave had said the office was their best shot at finding Dievs, though it wasn't a certainty by any means.

"We have to make a scene," Smiley shouted over the thumping music.

"What?" Joe asked, barely audible against the roar of the club.

"Make a scene!" Smiley yelled. And as she did, they both turned to see Dave slipping away into the crowd.

The three of them locked eyes as a human curtain closed around Dave, as the mouth of a dance floor dragon, made up of human bodies, swallowed their inside man. In slow motion, Smiley watched Joe raise his gun. His hand was shaking terribly. Smiley tried to speak, but found her throat closed up tight. Breathless. She watched horror dawn on Dave's face, and before she could do anything, Joe pulled the trigger.

#

DAVE'S kneecap exploded like a popped water balloon, spraying the people around him and the floor with warm red. All she could think was, *that's waay too much blood to come out of a knee.*

Dave screamed, but Smiley could barely hear it over the roar of the music. The gunshot had been loud, but still muted from the overpowering hum of the surrounding crowd and the thrumming bass. Dave crashed to the floor, but it took the people around him a few moments to comprehend what was happening. Some tripped over Dave, falling on top of him and into the bloody mess of his knee. The screams started gradually, but as more people noticed the man on the floor with a nearly detached leg, they grew in number and in volume.

Joe was wide-eyed and breathing heavily. He was making no effort to conceal his shaking now, and it looked for a moment like he might collapse. *He's no action hero either.* Smiley knew shock when she saw it and supposed it was her turn to do something. She grabbed Joe's gun hand, shoved it back in his pocket, making sure to take his finger off the trigger, then grabbed him by the arm and shuffled him backwards into the crowd. Dave was out of sight in a second. Smiley stood on her tippy-toes to get a look at the guardsmen by the grated stairs. They were still there, but as she watched, they began to move towards the growing commotion on the dance floor. *One chance.*

She squeezed through the crowd, still dragging Joe along by his right arm. They emerged from the crowd unnoticed, made their way quickly to the stairs and began to climb. The two men who had been guarding the stairs were forcing their way through the crowd to see what the problem was, but their size made it hard for them to move quickly. *We've got some time. That's good,* thought Smiley, and wondered where along the line she'd turned into someone capable of taking advantage of a situation like this. She wasn't sure she was, actually. Her body was moving on its own. Like a puppet on invisible strings.

They were already three floors up by the time the guardsmen got to Dave. Smiley watched them move through the crowd like two hippos wading through mud. They were kneeling by Dave, and as if out of some cheesy spy movie, Smiley watched as Dave pointed his finger up towards the railing, right at her. The faces of the two guards turned in unison, and she knew the clock had started.

"C'mon, Joe. We gotta kick it up a notch here, babe," said Smiley, trying to sound confident, though the words came out in a shaky tenor between ragged breaths. Joe was lagging behind, still wide-eyed and hyperventilating. His limp was more noticeable on the stairs, and it was slowing him down significantly. *Give me some of that secret agent man confidence from earlier, Joe. I know it was fake, but a facade is better than nothing.*

Smiley kept a strong pace on the stairs, taking them two at a time, and watched as the two guards far below pulled out radios and hurriedly made their way back towards the stairs. Dave was forgotten like a day-old toy. *Not good.* Smiley grabbed Joe's arm again and pulled him with renewed vigor. He picked up his pace, but only a little.

The next four flights seemed to take an eternity, though Smiley was glad the music hadn't stopped. It gave her the sense that maybe they had more time. *No cops yet.* Though she wasn't sure if there had ever been, *or ever would be*, cops in this place.

By the time she and Joe crested the last flight of stairs, they were both out of breath and panting hard. The good news was that they didn't have to decide where to go next. At the top of the stairs, was a single hallway with two elevator doors on the left and a turn to the right at the end. The numbers above the elevators were blinking and counting up. *4, 5… Better than I thought.* They wasted no time in moving past the elevators and down the hallway. The duo ran over a red velvet carpet, took the right turn, and raced to the door at the end of the hallway. A red door, with OFFICE painted in bold black letters. It was unguarded.

Smiley reached the door first and yanked on the knob. It swung open easily. She burst into the room, Joe just behind her, and slammed the door shut, putting her back up against it once inside.

It took her a second to realize just what she'd walked into: a big cream carpeted room with a red pool table and seven men in suits, all staring right at her, mouths open, faces confused. The room stood still for what seemed like a full ten seconds, the only sounds heavy breathing and the low vibration of the music downstairs. Smiley broke the silence.

"Hey, fellas…"

But before she could get any further, one man reached inside his jacket and pulled out a gun. Joe was still holding the revolver inside his flannel pocket, and he raised it before the suited man could get his gun free of his jacket.

CLICK, BANG!

The man's right hand, the one that had been going for the gun, was shredded, like a firecracker exploding inside a chunk of brie.

There was a pause of utter astonishment, everyone looking at one another to see what the appropriate response would be, and then the dam broke. The man without a right hand screamed, and the other suits began reaching for their own guns. Smiley grabbed Joe, and they dove behind a thick leather couch to her right. The sound of gunfire became like rain, or a really, *really* loud bubble wrap popping session.

With her eyes shut tight, Smiley slid her hand behind

her back and found her own weapon: the Bren Ten she'd lodged in the back of her pants. Next to her on the ground, Joe let out a grunt, and Smiley saw a hole appear in his left arm. They stared at the wound together as it started to bleed, but only for a second.

The gunfire continued. Bullets tore through the couch like hissing, biting snakes. The couch wasn't actually providing any protection, but it at least obscured the suits' view, so they couldn't aim with precision.

The shots slowed for a moment. Smiley figured at least one of the men needed to reload. She felt the Bren Ten in her hand and clicked the safety off like Joe had shown her. *Am I about to kill someone?* The thought ran through her head like an Olympic sprinter, high on a near-lethal dose of adrenaline. And before she could think about it any longer, she was on her feet. Her vision seemed to recede into the back of her head, like she was watching the action unfold from the back of some dark movie theater. Her body felt far away and funny, her limbs pulled tight by invisible strings.

Smiley thought she would close her eyes, but she kept them open, only blinking at the shocking sound that came from her gun every time she pulled the trigger. The men in suits hadn't moved from their tight circle around the pool table. Smiley aimed at this circle and squeezed the trigger of the Bren Ten as fast as she could. Squeezed until the gun was clicking, the automatic hammer slamming against dead metal. Bullets whizzed by her head, like angry horseflies, but by the time she'd emptied her magazine, all sound had ceased.

Smiley's eyes were open, but she felt as though she couldn't really *see*. She blinked and tried to comprehend what she was seeing. The area around the pool table was no longer occupied by suited men. Instead, unmoving bodies and growing puddles of blood filled the places where they had stood. *Did I… get them all?* Smiley didn't even realize she was screaming until Joe put his hand on her shoulder. She shuddered, as if waking from some terrible dream, and dropped the Bren Ten onto the ground like it had suddenly turned boiling hot. It clattered on the carpet like a cheap toy.

Smiley turned to Joe and saw that his hand was dripping with blood. He looked pale, but otherwise okay. Suddenly his eyes went wide, and he raised his gun up past Smiley's shoulder and fired. Smiley heard the thump of a body on carpet and turned. It seemed that one of the suits hadn't gone down with the others. He did after Joe's bullet slammed into his chest and knocked him backwards onto the pool table, arms spread wide. Her right ear rang from the report of Dave's .45.

For a few seconds they stood in the eerily quiet office suite, gazing upon their work.

"Jee… Jesus. Jesus Christ," said Joe, voice thick with awe and horror, not at all the confident voice of the man who'd been threatening Dave the past few hours.

Smiley heard her voice far away. It sounded strange and unnatural. Her lips were numb.

"What… did I do, Joe?"

CHAPTER FORTY

Piña Coladas

"HEY, hun," said the shorter figure.

"*Woof*, son. They did a number on you," said the lumberjack.

He recognized those voices. Finally, as they approached, their faces came into focus.

"I… Smiley? From Denny's? And… what was your name again?" asked Dievs, groggily.

"I'd tell you, but I… can't remember right now."

"Joe," Smiley said while working at Dievs' zip tie bindings with a pair of scissors she'd picked up off the desk.

"How… how did you find me?" Dievs asked.

"Later, no time right now," said Joe. "We need… *to go.*"

Dievs didn't like the way Joe said those words. His mind was still in a thick haze of pain and sleep deprivation, but he was lucid enough to hear the shock in his rescuers' voices. *They just… killed the guys out there. Oh, jeez.* Relief washed over Dievs when they finally cut the ropes wrapped around his waist and the zip ties slicing into his wrists. Joe and Smiley hoisted him to his feet, but he still needed help walking. His body felt like a boiled noodle, and suddenly, he needed to pee fearfully. The trio limped out of the office, and Dievs got his first look at the scene Smiley and Joe had wrought.

"Wh… what happened? Did you… *did you do this?*"

He asked these questions and got silence in reply. Dievs had glimpsed the outer office when Jennie had opened the door (between fingernail-pulling sessions), but he didn't need any prior information to know the carpet wasn't supposed to be littered with red polka dots. *There must be seven or eight of them. God… How… Luck and bullets.* The question was…

"Why did you come for me?" Dievs asked, expecting no reply. He got none. "I hardly know you. *Why?*"

And then they were out of the office and stumbling down the hallway towards a pair of elevators. Dievs felt about as capable as a chewed piece of gum, but he could feel Smiley and Joe trembling on either side of him as well. *People don't do this. **Normal people** don't shoot up a mobster lair and **win**. It doesn't happen.* But Dievs, reflecting on it for a moment longer, supposed that stranger things happened. *Someone rising from the dead, for example.* He chose not to think too hard about it right this moment. As they rounded the corner, Dievs could see the left-side elevator was on its way up, the glowing numbers above the double doors dinging subtly with every floor change.

"They must've been slowed down by people on other floors," said Smiley, though Dievs hardly heard her as she raced to press the down button for the right elevator. Luck, it appeared, was on their side, as the elevator doors slid promptly open. The wounded trio shuffled inside. Joe, still supporting Dievs, stumbled and fell to one knee. Dievs noticed then that

Joe was bleeding. *Badly.* His left arm was red from the shoulder down, and he was dripping thick blood from his fingertips in slow pulses.

"Joe!" said Smiley. She quickly pressed the button with a big "B" on it before dipping down to get under Joe's arm. "C'mon. Almost done. Almost there."

To Dievs, she sounded remarkably calm for a lady who'd just mowed down seven men, though the impression of shock was still there. *Adrenaline. Lots of adrenaline.* Dievs' head was spinning, and he felt faint. *Probably the missing fingernails.* He looked down at the swollen, bloody lumps that were his fingertips, and felt nausea rise in his stomach. Standing in the elevator with a dying lumberjack and a funeral home director turned septuple homicider, he realized he was peeing himself. *Ohhh…*

Dievs heard the ding of the other elevator reaching the top floor just as the doors to their own closed shut. They began to descend and in the quiet of the ride Dievs heard a song playing over a small speaker mounted in the ceiling.

If you like Piña Coladas, and gettin' caught in the rain… If you're not into yoga, if you have half a brain… if you like makin' love at midnight, in the dunes on the cape… Then I'm the love that you've looked for, write to me and escape.

Dievs looked down at his shoes to see the spreading puddle of his relief. He met Smiley's gaze and saw her dilated pupils. Her eyes looked almost black. *This lady…* In that moment, he wasn't sure if his situation had actually improved much from being tied up in that office.

Suddenly the elevator came to a stop, and the doors opened. Waiting outside was a group of teenagers dressed in tight leather outfits and wearing what looked to be imitation

Indian headdresses made of glow sticks. They gawked at the man bleeding out on the floor and Dievs, who stood alone, swaying in thoroughly soiled jeans. The music hit them like waves on a beach. A tall, skinny man with long dreadlocks, wearing only a speedo and striped plastic sunglasses, pushed through the group of teenagers and stepped into the elevator. The smell of liquor radiating from his body made Dievs blink and shake his head. The man was dancing, bouncing to the beat of the music, which penetrated the whole of the hyacinth house like the breath of a great beast.

"The fuck is that smell?" asked Joe, eyes shut, sounding about as drunk as the man in the speedo looked.

The elevator doors closed, and the car once again moved downward. Speedo man was smoking a cigarette, and as he turned, Dievs could see his crossed eyes under his sunglasses. The man waved his hand up and let it slap back down against his waist. *Howdy.*

Then the doors opened, and they were moving again, this time Dievs was supporting Joe more than the other way around. He was limping badly, and the amount of blood coming from the wound in his shoulder was alarming. Dievs' arm was soon slick with Joe's neon blood.

They were in a parking garage, presumably a floor below the party raging above, though Dievs could more *feel* the music than hear it now. He turned to look back at the elevator just in time to see the doors closing on the man in the speedo, who had fallen into the wide puddle of urine and blood on the floor. He was laughing and somehow still sucking on his cigarette.

Dievs also saw the numbers above the other elevator doors changing downwards, now seemingly unhindered by would-be passengers on other floors. He turned and shambled forward.

#

THEY somehow made it to a stairwell exit and burst out into the warm afternoon sunlight of San Jacinto Street. Cars cruised past the Hyacinth House in casual lines of traffic. *Normal day.* There was no hint of the mayhem that had just occurred inside that innocuous brick building. They all stopped for a moment, taking in the uncanniness of it.

It was Smiley who spurred them on. "Car," was all she said. And across the street, shining like a golden turd, was a beige Ford Escort. Dievs wasn't sure how he knew that model of car, but he was sure that he didn't like it. *Better than a Pinto though. Those explode.*

The six-legged creature that was Smiley (on the right), Joe (in the middle), and Dievs (on the left), waddled into the road. Dievs lifted his free arm in the universal *stop, please* motion towards an incoming minivan. The driver honked, but stopped once he'd seen the state of the jaywalkers. They made it across the road to the Escort just in time to hear a commotion coming from an alley next to the club. Someone was screaming.

"My fackin' knee!"

Joe chuckled, though it came out as more of a gurgle. Dievs helped Smiley lay Joe into the back seat of the Escort, then hobbled around to the passenger side door and got in. Smiley sat in the driver's seat, and Dievs watched as she tried to slot the key into the ignition. Her hand was quaking violently, and she missed the ignition several times. Smiley closed her eyes, took a shuddering breath, then slowly put the key in and twisted.

#

ONLY after about forty minutes of driving did Dievs get his heart rate under control. *They're not following us. Not right now, at least... How is that possible?*

He still couldn't wrap his head around the fact that two regular Joes — *well, a Smiley and a Joe* — had fought their way through the spider's lair and made it out. *Not entirely unscathed, but still...* It beggared belief. Stranger still was their choice to rescue *him*. A stranger. Nothing to them. A dead man walking. *In more ways than one...*

He and Smiley hadn't spoken after getting in the car. She was focused intently on the road, and Dievs got the feeling that a game of twenty questions might not be appropriate. In the back seat, Joe was sitting up, but his breathing had slowed into a shallow, weak rhythm. His eyes were slits, though he wasn't unconscious. *Not yet. Big guy. Lotta blood to lose.* Dievs could see the red wetness of the beige bench seat and shuddered.

He wanted to ask where they were headed, but the highway signs soon answered that question. *Campaiyote.* It was just before the exit that Dievs felt a comment was warranted.

"They're gonna check the funeral home. We shouldn't go there..."

"You have a better idea?" Smiley shot back, venom in her voice.

… *McDonald's?* Dievs was quiet.

"He needs medicine. There's at least some there… If we go to the hospital, they'd, *he'd* find us before we could take a breath… Brackington might not expect us to go back to the home. At least, that's the idea," Smiley said with a bit more softness.

Dievs could tell Smiley was not even close to recovered from her experience at the Hyacinth House. *She didn't expect to kill seven people there. Or anywhere ever, probably. She'll never recover from that. A piece of her died with those men.* It made Dievs wonder about his own past life. Though he didn't have any specific memories of murder, the glimpses he'd gotten of his past self told him he probably had killed. And more than once. *Did I ever recover?*

Smiley's plan made some kind of sense, Dievs had to admit, but it didn't make him feel at ease exactly. Ten minutes later, Smiley pulled the Escort into the parking lot of the funeral home he'd emerged from just a few days prior. *Full circle,* thought Dievs, with more than a little despair. His mind was a swirling fishbowl of emotions and a stranger's memories. And one thing kept rising to the surface. *The briefcase.*

Smiley didn't bother parking in one of the empty spots but pulled right up to the front door. She slammed the gearshift into P and killed the engine, leaving the keys in the ignition. Dievs got out and went to the back seat just in time to catch Joe as he fell over in his seat. Smiley ran around the back of the car and together they hauled him inside, leaving a bright red trail of blood from the parking lot, all the way to the cold room.

CHAPTER FORTY-ONE

Pong

HANK drifted in and out of consciousness for what seemed like days. He was in the back of a car for some time, he knew. He remembered the rushing vibrato of the highway under him. *Could never mistake that.* Then he was on a couch somewhere, and people were yelling. One of them was James Brackington, he was sure. There was music. A heavy baseline beat against his throbbing head.

"HOW COULD YOU LET THIS HAPPEN?"

Brackington's voice was like thunder. *Yeesh, scary.*

Then maybe the road again? He wasn't sure, but when he finally woke for longer than a few minutes, he found himself at home. 333. And he had company.

Someone had tied Hank to a wooden chair in the middle of his small hotel room at the Texas Inn. Around him were several men in suits, and sitting on a chair directly in front of him was James Brackington. All the sly humor in his smirk was gone. He was angry. His green eyes shone like hard chips of emerald, pitted with deep black pupils.

"Hiya… boss," said Hank. He was still in the half-daze of sleep and didn't fully remember the situation he was in.

What *did* come back to him was the pain in his shoulder and right eye.

"Oww…"

But before Hank could say any more, Brackington stood and sent the back of his hand flying across Hank's face. *Hard.* Hank's cheek and eye exploded in pain. He would've screamed, but he had no breath for it. The shock to his system was too much. It felt like someone had scooped out the right half of his face with a spoon. *What… happened…*

When Hank finally opened his working eye again, Brackington was there, inches from his face.

"Did you know about your friends' little rescue plan? Hmm? Hank? I don't know how you could've, but I want you to answer me."

"Wh-what?" asked Hank, still recovering from the first blow, when down came another, even harder than the last.

"DID YOU KNOW?" asked Brackington, his voice seeming to fill the world.

"No… I-I don't know anything about… No. Where… are we…"

"Don't let another word come dripping out of your mouth, Hank, or I swear I'll cut your tongue out."

Even in the fog of unconsciousness and the pain in his head, Hank knew to respect the threat. Though if he had to lose a body part, his tongue was probably on his list of *least used* organs.

Brackington stood and took a deep breath. He ran his fingers through his thick, curly, black hair and closed his eyes. When he breathed out, he was smiling.

"Pardon me, Hank," said Brackington, his voice under control now. "I just get a little frustrated when I'm surrounded by idiots." He paused, looked at Hank, then began to pace slowly around the room. "I know you weren't in on your co-workers' scheme, which worked *marvelously*, by the way. Who knew a woman who wears sunshine flats, and a retired lumberjack had so much *spunk*? But… where we find ourselves now is a bit like a hostage exchange. I need *Swiss*, you see. I doubt you'll be enough of a reward for your friends, *if you wanna call them that*, to care much, but maybe. Of course, they stole Swiss, and they didn't even know the guy, so maybe they'll come for you."

Brackington shook his head in wonder, as if unable to believe such loyalty could ever truly exist. Hank almost asked Brackington if he was talking about *Swiss cheese*, but remembered the previously issued threat to cut his tongue out and decided silence might be more prudent. As if sensing this confusion, Brackington stopped and laughed.

"Oh, that's right, you don't know him by that name. The man that Ms. Davis's young secretary, *a rather morbid girl…*" Brackington shrugged. "…brought to your Denny's bruncheon, *Dievs*, he calls himself, his name is Derrick V. Swiss. You might know him as, *guy with a hole in his chest who fell down the stairs.*"

Understanding dawned in Hank's mind. *I knew I recognized him.* But that was just about the only thing Hank knew or understood. He wondered briefly what Smiley and Joe had done to cause all this trouble. *Must've been pretty dramatic.* He also thought it strange that Jennie wasn't around. *She's always with him. His teniente primero.*

"Please do try and keep up, Coop. It's not that hard. Resurrection and kidnapping and blah-ba-blah-ba-blah… As I was saying… I need Swiss, and the information in his head. *If only I could pull it out like a fortune out of a fortune cookie…"* Brackington seemed to get lost in his own train of thought at this, but he came back to Hank with an even wider grin on his face. A wolf's smile.

"Think your friends will trade a stranger's life for yours? *Were they ever really friends?* I'm not so sure, Hanky. I guess we'll find out. And you know, in these hostage exchanges, the villain always has the advantage. Not that I'd call myself a villain, the opposite, really, but you know, if you want to look at it that way, *sure.* I'm gonna wipe Smiley's little trio right off the map, and take what I want. In all the stories, the good guys win… But that's why we read stories, isn't it? *Reality's a little different."*

#

HANK continued to listen to Brackington monologue for another half hour. It was without a doubt the longest time he'd spent in the boss's presence, and several things became clear to Hank, though his head still throbbed terribly. For one, James Brackington was still a man. Just a man. Like Hank, and Joe, and every other poor sap walking around with a ding-dong hanging between his legs. Okay, maybe not *just like,* but still. He was human. And haunted by the same demons that haunt the rest of the population. *Paranoia. Vanity. Greed. Hubris.* He was suffering from those afflictions now, Hank could tell.

He's isolated. Like me. Like lots of people, probably. What remained a mystery, however, was what he wanted with the man named Robert Dievs… *or, Derrick V. Swiss, I guess? Goll-ee, that seems unnecessarily confusing.*

But, in all honesty, Hank didn't care much. These thoughts trundled across his frontal lobe like ants walking to a capful of honey. He wasn't trying particularly hard to *think* about anything. His mind ran like a teleprompter with no one to read it. *How the fuck did I end up in the middle of a bad crime thriller? We've got a supervillain, a treasure hunt, and characters that just keep coming back despite, I dunno, a gunshot to the chest. Why is it never an episode of Baywatch?* Hank thought back to slipping that extension cord over his neck and wondered how he'd messed even that up. *Maybe I didn't and this is my eternal punishment. Listening to a narcissist talk to himself in a sweaty hotel room off the highway. For eternity ever after. Seems apt.*

Hank's more immediate concern was the fire burning in his right eye. He wanted to scratch it desperately, but he was bound to a chair and didn't dare interrupt Brackington, lest he end up tongue-less. Not that he thought Brackington would untie him if he asked. *Not a chance.*

Mr. B went on for a long time. Hank couldn't have said how long, but he covered quite the range of topics, going as far back as childhood, which Hank would've rather not heard about. He made sure to act as though he were listening intently, but in his brain he was playing Pong with himself. What really kept grabbing his attention was that *goddamn yellow phone* in the corner. His eyes would drift away from Brackington and back to the corner of the room. The thing was like a magnet. *Old habits, I guess. Still just waiting for the next job.* Surprising even himself, he felt the urge to check the voicemails and see what was waiting for him there now. The blinking light on the answering machine started to take over Hank's world. It was a full minute before he realized that Brackington had stopped talking.

"Hank. Are you listening?" asked Brackington politely.

Hank snapped his head back to face those green eyes. He nodded enthusiastically. Brackington smiled.

"You really are such a good dog, Hanky. So well trained. Since this venture with Smiley's Funeral Home and Crematorium did *not* go quite as planned, I may still require your services after this is all settled. Would you like that?"

Hank took a second to think about that question. He nodded slowly. Brackington leaned down to put his face in front of Hank's.

"And don't you worry about that telephone. We'll be getting a call *any minute now*."

CHAPTER FORTY-TWO

Andalusia

SMILEY sat in the lobby of her funeral home, eyes staring into the oblivion below the floor. Blood covered her arms and clothes. Joe's blood. Had a customer come in at that moment, they might've thought Smiley a real *hands-on* boss. Maybe a little *too* hands-on. Nothing moved except the lazy ceiling fan overhead. At Karina's old desk sat Dievs, also staring into the floor, though he was gently massaging his bandaged fingertips while doing so. Back in the cold room, on the stainless steel island, lay Joe. In a big smear of blood. He was breathing, but shallowly. In a metal dog bowl next to him were several bullet fragments and a considerable amount of dark red chunky blood. His arm was bandaged, but already showing signs of fresh leakage.

Suddenly, Smiley became aware, in the dead silence of the place, that a faint ticking noise had started up. She looked up at the wall and saw that the clock hands had begun moving again. *Huh.* Half a second later, the little bell above the glass door rang out like a fire alarm in the silence. Smiley jumped to her feet and turned to face the door. Karina was standing there, eyes wide. She held a pair of headphones in her right hand, with a cord that trailed down to a Walkman clipped to her black leather belt. Smiley could hear the music playing faintly.

Carry me caravan, take me a-way. BUM-BA-BUMP-BUMP, BUM-BA-BUMP-BUMP. Take me to Portugal, take me to Spain. BUM-BA-BUMP-BUMP, BUM-BA-BUMP-BUMP. Andalusia with fields full of grain. BUM-BA-BUMP-BUMP, BUM-BA-BUMP-BUMP. I have to see you again and again...

"Hey… guys," said Karina.

Smiley collapsed back into her chair.

"You look, um… great," said Karina, not concealing the sarcasm in her voice in the slightest. "Whatcha been up to?"

Smiley folded her face into her hands. "I told you not to come here, Karina. It's dangerous."

"You mean exciting," replied Karina. Smiley shot her a tired, very sad look. "*Kidding.* Just kidding. I only came back to get some stuff out of my desk." Karina turned to her old desk and saw Dievs sitting there. "You!" she shouted. "Where the flip did you go, dead man? You really hurt my feelings when you dipped out on dinner like that. *Not. Cool.*" Dievs made to reply, but was cut off by Karina again. She'd turned back to Smiley. "Where did you find him? Was he kidnapped? He was kidnapped. I knew it."

"You need to go, Karina," said Smiley, this time with a little more force.

"Alright, alright," replied Karina, as if to her mother.

But before Karina could turn to leave, the phone rang. The shrill *BBBRRRIIINGG* cut through the dead silence like a jackhammer. Nobody moved. Again, *BBBRRRIIIIIINGG*, And again, *BBBRRRIIIN...* But before Smiley could get a word out, Karina had stepped over and picked up the receiver.

"Smiley's Funeral Home and Crematorium, how can I help you?" She said it as if it were the most normal thing in the world. *Well, she would've made a good secretary if we'd had any business.* Karina looked over at Smiley and gave a big, cheesy A-OK sign. She mouthed the words, *don't worry about it.*

But as she listened to the voice coming over the other side of the phone, her face grew pale, and her smile vanished.

#

SMILEY lifted herself from the desk, walked over to where Karina stood and snatched the phone out of her hand. She put the receiver to her ear just in time to catch the last part of Jenine's sentence.

"*...put that nigger on the phone right now, you little shit, or...*"

"Speaking," said Smiley, flatly.

It took Jenine a moment to process this, then she laughed heartily. An over-the-top, shrill, manic laughter buzzed its way over the phone. Smiley grimaced. It was a laugh that said *I have nothing to lose.*

"Good. Hello, Ms. Davis." She spat the name out like a bad grape, like it actually caused Jenine physical pain to say it. "I wasn't sure if you'd be stupid enough to go back to your funeral home, but I guess I overestimated your intelligence. What I get for thinking one of your kind..."

"What do you want?" asked Smiley.

"DON'T YOU DARE INTERRUPT ME, YOU MONKEY BITCH!" Jenine screamed into the phone.

Smiley moved the receiver away from her ear. She couldn't help but grin a little, even through her weariness and exhaustion. It was funny to hear someone give themselves an aneurysm over the phone. Especially someone like this vile woman. For a moment, the line was quiet. Smiley could picture Jenine composing herself. She heard her clear her throat.

"*Ahem…* what we… what *Mr. B* wants, is to make you an offer."

"Let's hear it," said Smiley, looking at Karina and Dievs who had moved around her to listen in on the conversation.

Smiley could hear the forced restraint in Jenine's voice when she said, "Mr. B only wants the man going by Robert Dievs returned to his care. That's all. If you deliver him to the Texas Inn by nightfall, he's agreed to forget all about the… *incident* at the Hyacinth House… AND, he will no longer require your services. You'll be off the hook, so to speak."

Smiley took a moment to look at Dievs. His face was sullen and blank.

"You smell that, Jenine?" asked Smiley.

"What?"

"I thought maybe I'd forgotten to pay the electric bill and my clients were rotting in the back, but it was actually just a giant load of *bullshit*."

Karina gasped and smiled, putting her hand to her mouth. Smiley couldn't help but smile a little herself, though it vanished quickly. She wasn't sure she could ever feel truly *amused* again after what she'd done at the Hyacinth House. The terrible miracle that had made her a murderer. Jenine was quiet for a moment.

"You'll regret that," she said, voice deadly low. "Just remember I gave you a chance. Deliver Dievs. Oh, and say hi to Mr. Morris for me."

Then the phone clicked, and she was gone. Smiley brought the phone away from her ear. Looked at it and put it gently back on the stand. She turned to Dievs and Karina.

"Guess the '*they won't think to look for us here*' plan didn't work too well. Why do they want you so bad, Mr. Dievs… or Swiss?"

Dievs looked back at Smiley and said, "They think I'm a human treasure map." Smiley and Karina looked back at him in silence. "What?" he asked. "It's true."

"Hey, treasure is good," said Karina, turning and nudging Smiley gently with her elbow. "Hey, BT-dubs, how did you get him back from Brackington?"

"Not right now, Karina," said Smiley, still looking at Dievs. "You know where something is? Something he wants? I thought you couldn't remember anything."

"Well… that woman," Dievs nodded to the phone. "Jenine, sort of *jogged* my memory. With her fist. And yes… I think I do."

"What is it that he wants?" asked Smiley, but before Dievs could answer, three big, black and white Ramchargers came screeching into the parking lot.

#

"SMILEY Davis! Joe Karipassius! Derrick Swiss… or, ehm… Robert Dievs! This is Phil Morris, chief of the Campaiyote Police Department. Come out of the building with your hands up. SLOWLY. We have you surrounded… fun's over!"

The voice coming over the loudspeaker mounted on the frontmost Ramcharger was slurred with mucus and obviously very pleased to be ordering Smiley Davis to surrender. *Phil Morris.* Campaiyote police chief.

The only thing providing cover between the three big SUVs and Smiley was the black spray paint on her front windows. *Gotta call somebody about that*. Aside from that, the glass front of the funeral home was crystal clear, and Smiley could see the grinning face of Phil Morris leaning out his driver's side window. *Bastard*. She could see what he held in his hands too. In his right, the mic for the loudspeaker, and in his left, a big, shiny silver revolver. Cocked. *Thinks he's some kind of gunslinger. He's too fat to be a cowboy. He'd kill his horse.* Smiley and Dievs did as they were told. They raised their hands and walked slowly to the glass entrance.

Smiley was already stepping outside before she realized Karina was not with them. *Where…* but before she could go any further with that thought, the pig-like voice of Phil Morris once again came blasting over the loudspeaker.

"Where is Karipassius?" Morris asked.

Smiley was still a good twenty feet from the small fleet of Ramchargers, now surrounded by armed men in bulletproof vests, so she had to yell.

"He's in the ba…"

"Can't hear you, woman. Speak up!"

Smiley swallowed a *fuck you*, and cleared her throat.

"HE'S IN THE BACK! UNCONSCIOUS!" she yelled, plenty loud this time.

"Jesus. No need to yell," said Morris over the loudspeaker, then laughed heartily, still holding the mic button. *He's enjoying this. I've been on his list a long time*. "I'm just messin' with ya, shorty. Keep those hands raised waaaay up, n' we can keep things nice and friendly."

Phil Morris set the loudspeaker mic down, holstered his gun and slipped back through the window he'd been leaning out of. Smiley could see the pregnant curve of his belly jiggling under a vest he must've insisted fit him, though it looked terribly tight. And that nasty rat smile.

Smiley glanced at Dievs, to see how he was taking all this. His face was pale, but otherwise expressionless. *Guess that's pretty much par for the course for someone who's already died once, and been damn close several other times.* They watched together as Phil Morris hauled his mass out of the parked car and did a little shimmy to pull up his sagging brown khakis. *That poor belt.*

Morris gestured to the officer closest to him, and, never taking his eyes off Smiley, whispered something. He did a little twirl with his fat pointer finger, and the officers from the leftmost car began moving around to the back of the building, guns raised.

Morris sauntered up to Smiley and Dievs slowly, clearly enjoying the circumstance of it all. He didn't speak until he was right up in front of the pair, only a few feet away.

"Well. I'd be lyin' if I said I hadn't been waitin' for this one a good while. I was gettin' ready to charge you on suspected fraud, or some other bullshit…" he chuckled. "Duddn't really matter all that much round here. 'Specially if you get the right judge." Morris's eyes twinkled blackly. "But you went ahead n' gave me all the probable cause I could want. Shootin' up a club in downtown Dallas… A fine establishment, I might add, and still covered in blood." He gave a long, dramatic whistle. "Now that *is* an actionable O-ffense, if I ever heard one. We got you pinned by nineteen witnesses. *Nine. Teen.*" Morris held up nine fingers and smiled.

An officer came hurrying out through the glass door of the funeral home.

"We found Karipassius. Unconscious in the back. Looks like he was shot. Needs medical attention."

Morris nodded to the officer, then turned back to Smiley.

"Thank you for your honesty, hun. 'Preciate it."

Smiley could see the look of total satisfaction on Morris's face. *Here it comes.* That moment when he would really indulge himself, roll around in his power as a man of the law, like a pig rolls in shit. Morris leaned down and put his bloated, stubbled face in front of Smiley's. Dievs watched this with a look of growing disgust.

"You know…" said Morris in a voice low enough that no one else except Smiley and Dievs could hear. "Some of the boys were joking the other night about having themselves a little rollick with a lady of a… *darker complexion.* We got this fancy new surveillance system down at the station, but there are a few nooks and crannies where two people might get away for a time. *Un-watched,* that is. How's somethin' like that sound?"

Smiley didn't have to think very hard about what she did next, which was lob the mouthful of spit she'd been saving up right into Morris's smug face. He recoiled and grunted.

"Ah… you fucking bitch!" But the sound of crumpling metal and screeching tires drowned Morris's cry. He wiped the spit out of his eyes just in time to witness the utter destruction of his little fleet of squad cars.

At first glance, it looked as if a massive yellow fist had come out of nowhere to smash the SUVs. A fist with a big smiley face painted on its back. Then Smiley recognized it as the Beast, her hearse. *How…* Smiley traced the trajectory of the Beast across the lot and found the figure of a teenage girl, dressed all in black, pounding her fist in the air and jumping with satisfaction. Smiley could see the giant grin on Karina's face from fifty yards away. *She must've jammed the gas somehow… Good aim!* She watched as Karina turned and ran. Smiley followed her path and realized she was going for the Pinto. Her pinto.

In seconds, the Beast plowed through the first Ramcharger at fifty miles per hour, crumpling the side panels and bending the whole car into a banana shape. Smiley could hear the increasing thrum of the big V8 engine just before the Beast — first Ramcharger in tow — slammed into the second squad car. The three Ramchargers had parked relatively close together in a sort of fan shape, but the angle was such that the pileup clipped even the back half of the third car. Smiley could hear the hiss of air coming from a popped tire on the last car, and still the Beast didn't stop. The engine hum only got louder and more frantic. The momentum was gone, but the hearse kept pushing, throwing up a vast cloud of rubber smoke and pinning the first two Ramchargers against a light post.

Smiley was still gaping at the chaos when Dievs grabbed her arm and pointed. Karina had made it to the Pinto and started the engine. Then they were running. Phil Morris made a clumsy attempt to stop the pair, but tripped over his oversized cowboy boots and fell hard to the ground. By the time he'd lifted his heap off the ground and began scrabbling for his revolver, Dievs and Smiley were running full sprint to the Pinto.

"STOP THOSE TWO! DEADLY FORCE AUTHORIZED! STOP THEM!"

Smiley didn't turn to see how many of the officers were heeding their captain, but she heard the first pop of gunfire as the Pinto lurched forward and came speeding towards her and Dievs. She could see Karina behind the wheel, her face a mixture of terror and enlightenment. A bullet struck the concrete next to Smiley's foot and sent a spray of stone into her ankle. She hardly felt it.

Then the Pinto was there in front of them. Dievs threw open the back door and they dove inside, falling on top of one another along the faux leather bench seat.

"Go, go, go!" screamed Dievs. Karina did.

Smiley hadn't known her little Pinto was capable of such speed. The back door slammed shut from the acceleration, and Smiley could hear the scream of rubber on road. Bullets shattered the back windshield into what seemed like a billion pieces of glass. It rained down on her and Dievs, cutting her hands where she braced herself. The back passenger side window did the same, covering them in more shards. Smiley closed her eyes and listened to the PING-PONG-PING of bullets hitting the outside of the car. She just hoped they'd miss the gas tank.

Karina was alternating between screams and whispers.

"Hold Shit, holy shit, holy shit. YES! YEAH! FUCK YOU, PIGS! IIAIIA! Oh, man. Oh, man. Mom's gonna kill me." She looked in the rearview mirror. The stream of bullets chasing them had slowed. "FACK YOUUU!" she screamed. A bullet suddenly obliterated the rearview mirror and sent cracks splintering across the front windshield. Karina ducked. "Oh, shit."

Smiley thought she heard Morris yelling from the parking lot. Something like, "Get the spare on right now! You worthless pieces of…" and then he was out of hearing.

When the barrage of bullets finally ceased completely, Smiley slowly peaked her head over the bench seat to look out the shattered back window. They were pulling off Sycamore and onto Main Street at a screaming forty-five miles per hour. She thought the car might roll when Karina jerked the wheel to the right, but she somehow held it, and after a screeching complaint from the back wheels, they were shooting down the main strip towards the highway. Only a few other cars were on the road this afternoon, and Karina swerved around them easily, though quite recklessly.

"Karina! Slow down, you're gonna wreck it!" Smiley

screamed over the whoosh of air coming through the shattered windows. Karina didn't verbally acknowledge this, but she eased off the gas just a dash. Bringing their speed down to sixty.

Dievs and Smiley were tangled together, shoved up against the driver's side door from Karina's quick turn onto the main road, glass cutting them everywhere. They untangled and sat up. Smiley scrambled up to the passenger seat, already nauseous from Karina's speeding.

"To the highway, Karina. The highway. And slow down once you get there, or you're gonna pull every ranger from here to Dallas."

"Not sure speeding is gonna be our biggest problem, chief," said Karina, with a wild sort of excitement. *She's got a point.* But after blasting off Main Street and turning onto the on-ramp, she did slow to five over the limit.

The trio sat in silence for a full minute, letting the wind do the talking. The lack of any sirens or gunfire was eerie. *Wrong.* Karina broke the silence.

"I FUCKING LOVE DRIVING! HOT DOG!"

Smiley reached over and pulled the wheel gently to correct Karina's lane-drift.

"Just keep it in your pants there, Earnhardt," replied Smiley.

"That was insane," said Karina to nobody in particular. "I feel high. Do you guys feel high? It's like…" she lifted her hand and saw it was trembling like a leaf. "Actually… I feel kinda… do you see those little white dots? My head…" and then the Pinto began to slow. Karina's eyes rolled back and she collapsed sideways.

Smiley did, in fact, see those little white dots, but she knew that fainting now would be like failing high school for missing a PE credit. Just dumb. She held onto the wheel and moved into the driver's seat, steeling her nerves and controlling her breathing. *Maybe I'm more suited to this kinda stuff than I thought.* Then the full nausea of what they'd just done came flooding over her, and her arrogance vanished like smoke in the wind.

"Dievs!" Smiley yelled and was relieved to see she didn't have to tell him what to do. He reached up from the back seat, grabbed Karina under both arms and pulled her into the back seat like a big Brats doll.

Smiley slipped behind the wheel and brought the Pinto back up to speed. She glanced back to check on Karina. She was already waking up from her faint, eyelids fluttering.

"I'mmm… the best…" muttered Karina.

Smiley shook her head. *Unbelievable.* But she had to admit, Karina had just saved their asses. *Or doomed us, depending on how you look at it… I was doomed already though.* It didn't take Smiley long to conclude that she'd much rather die in a high-speed car chase than in the Campaiyote jail with Morris's boys. *No rollicks for me, thank you. At least I can die fighting.* It really had come to that, she realized, and it made her sick.

Dievs leaned forward into the front seat and said, "I know where to go."

CHAPTER FORTY-THREE

"Oh"

A flood of unpleasant memories assaulted Robert Dievs as the Pinto pulled up in front of the white ranch house where he'd died. The car almost seemed to sigh as Smiley slotted the shifter into P, as if saying, *Jesus, I was not made for what you just did to me.*

They all sat quietly for a minute, just staring out at the black windows and dusty white paneling. None of them could quite believe they'd actually made it out of Campaiyote alive and unfollowed. It was another miracle they hadn't been pulled over on the road, considering the state of the Pinto. Should Phil Morris corner them again, Dievs didn't think they would be so lucky. Dievs glanced at Smiley and saw she was looking down at her hands, still covered in Joe's blood. The steering wheel was greasy with it. In that moment, he felt immensely guilty. *I'm sorry. This is my fault. I did this.* A memory came to him of the place he'd gone after dying. The train station. *I just walked out of those exit doors, not a care in the world. Why did I do that? Look what happened.*

There was a hole in the screen door of the ranch house. *Shotgun? Yes, shotgun.* A memory of a woman in a blue two-piece suit slammed into Dievs' frontal lobe like a thrown fish.

She wasn't very nice. I remember that… but I guess I wasn't exactly a cupcake either.

Karina had recovered from her earlier faint, and Smiley wasn't quite as pale as she had been, but the mood in the car was *contemplative,* to say the least. *If you thought being dead was interesting, whoo doggy, try life.*

The shootout, more like *narrow escape,* with the Campaiyote PD spelled the end of any freedom Smiley might have had whilst cooperating with James Brackington. She was a fugitive now, simple as that. Dievs supposed he was as well. Karina might be able to escape blame, though he doubted it. He hoped that jail was less *torture-y* than the Hyacinth House had been, though meeting Phil Morris hadn't given him much hope in that regard.

"You guys can stay in the car if you want," said Dievs. "Don't think I'll be long."

Smiley nodded, but Karina spoke up.

"Not uh. I only stay in the car when my mom and I go to the post office. Think I'm gonna miss the chance to see some crazy shit? No way, José."

"You don't even know what's in there," said Dievs, a little unbelievingly.

"Don't need to. I'm getting mad 'crazy shit' vibes from that house. Let's go."

This kid… Dievs thought for a second that Smiley might protest, but she just stared at her hands and the bloody steering wheel in front of her. Her face was blank. *Shock, maybe. Or just… tired.*

Dievs and Karina stepped out of the Pinto, shutting the dented and bullet-sprayed doors behind them. Up two creaky wooden steps and onto the porch. Dievs heard the voice of the woman in blue, and for a moment, he thought she was there.

Oh yeah, I'll just put my gun down and we can talk.

Karina saw Dievs pause, and she turned.

"You alright? Looks like you just saw a ghost."

"Just heard one. This is where I died, you know."

Karina's face lit up. "I knew this was all about finding closure! You're a disgruntled soul, freed from purgatory to fulfill your earthly purpose. And I'm your spirit guide. Your Virgil… kind of. But I guess it's the other way around in this story. Same difference. You know, Jehovah's Witnesses claim the only hell is the one we're living in. Or wait… did I get that right? Eh." Karina pointed her finger at Dievs and raised her eyebrows. "Food for thought."

At this, she turned and opened the screen door. Dievs watched her for a moment, reflecting on the fact that, once again, this strange girl might be more right than she knew. He stepped forward and followed her into the ranch house.

It was immediately clear that the place had been searched. *Thoroughly.* The furniture was in shreds and piled in the center of the living room as if in preparation for a bonfire, including the couch he had sat on not that long ago with his ex-partner, Joe Pesca. *Joe fish.* The furniture wasn't the only thing that had been disassembled. The paneling on the walls had been taken off to expose the studs and old insulation buried in the walls. *They looked. But they didn't find it.* He was sure the floor had been searched as well, though it showed no signs of having been ripped up. Karina took a look around and pursed her lips.

"Booorring," she said, and moved towards the stairs. Dievs followed silently.

At the top of the stairs, Karina turned left and pushed open the door where Beethoven and Joe Pesca had become locked in mortal doggy combat. Dievs took a quick look into the room, recalling how he'd last seen it (i.e. covered in copious amounts of mammal blood). He had to admit, Hank was good. He couldn't spot a single piece of evidence that there had been any kind of out-of-the-ordinary struggle here. *And, oh boy,* a struggle there had been. But Dievs did not follow Karina into that bedroom. Instead he turned left, into the single room where he'd died. *Last week. I died here last week.*

Someone had torn apart the small bedroom in the same fashion as the rest of the house. The floor had several holes in the planking. *Searching for hidden compartments.* They'd found what Dievs had expected they would find: nothing. The floor was too thin to conceal any hidden packages.

The single mattress had been reduced to a pile of fluff and springs, the frame a tangle of metal bars. Dievs took a step into the room and stopped. His boot had bumped into a nail head sticking up from the floor. The nail that had caused his death. Kind of. Along with a bit of irresponsible firearm usage. *Hi, there.* Dievs leaned down and grabbed the nail with his thumb and forefinger. He worked it loose easily, held it up, examined it, then put it in his pocket.

Where the little rug had been was now a big hole. Another search for a secret compartment. He looked for maroon, thinking back to the color he's seen under Loretta's fingernails what felt like an eternity ago (in *a different lifetime* wasn't such a silly phrase in this context). The wooden floor was painted a deep blue, like a child's room, but the maroon underneath was clearly visible in certain scuffs and scratches scattered about the floor. Dievs looked around slowly, searching. *There.*

Whichever one of Brackington's goons had combed this room had done a thorough job, no doubt, but they'd made the mistake of thinking the entire floor was the same. Dievs — or Swiss, rather — had noticed when he'd first walked into the house that where the ceilings of the living room and kitchen met was a dip, a kind of blocky bulge. A space just big enough for something thin and square. *A briefcase, perhaps.* It was hard to pinpoint exactly where that bulge was when looking at the room from above, but near the back left corner, Dievs spotted a line of red along the white trim of the floor. Ever so faint.

He went over to the corner, bent down and ran his finger along the red strip. He noticed then that the glue holding the trim in place was fresher here, more white than gray. *Someone took this off and put it back recently. Carefully. Loretta.* He reflected, as he ran his hand along the rough wood, that there might be more Derrick Swiss left in him than he'd wanted to imagine. *These instincts... I used to work for Brackington. And I was good at my job.*

Dievs was about to pull the trim off when Karina nearly shouted in his ear, "Watcha doin'?"

Dievs flinched and fell backwards onto his ass with a thump.

"Jesus Christ, Karina!" His tailbone twitched, but not from the fall. "Scared the shit out of me. Can you just... not do that, please?"

Karina looked down at him blankly. "Sorry. Didn't mean to. You're pretty skittish for an undead guy." She turned her attention back to the trim Dievs had been about to take off.

Dievs righted himself, gave Karina another annoyed look, then slipped his finger into a small gap along the trim and pulled. It took a little finagling, but the strip eventually came off, taking some of the floor paint with it. Once removed, it revealed that the plank closest to the wall was loose. Dievs yanked it free, and there, in the narrow space he'd seen from below, was the handle of a brown leather briefcase.

"Woah. Some spy shit right there," said Karina. Dievs turned to her and just shook his head. "What?" she asked.

He pulled the briefcase free from its little hidey-hole and set it flat on the floor. It seemed to be... *humming? Yes, vibrating.* Dievs ran his hands over the soft leather to the two brass latches that held the lid shut. *No lock.*

He popped the latches and opened the case.

"Oh," said Karina.

CHAPTER FORTY-FOUR

Dynamite

SMILEY watched Dievs and Karina as they exited the ranch house. Their faces were unreadable, if not a little pale. Neither of them spoke as they got back into the Pinto. *Strange. Karina looks more scared than she did when speeding away from the police, who were shooting at us.* Dievs had a thin brown briefcase in his hand. *Guess he found what he was looking for. What we're looking for.*

The oddly fitting duo opened the front and rear passenger doors and slid inside. They kept their eyes forward and their mouths shut. Smiley looked at them both for a few seconds. Then decided she couldn't take it any longer.

"Okay, you got me. What the fuck happened?" she asked.

Dievs glanced at Karina in the remaining shards of the rearview mirror. She nodded back at him, pale and uncharacteristically silent. Dievs set the briefcase on his lap and opened it. Smiley couldn't help but gasp. A dark blue glow flooded out from the case, like moonlight glimmering at the bottom of a deep pool.

"What… in…" Smiley mumbled.

"This is what Brackington is after," said Dievs, his eyes locked on the case. "And maybe Karina is right. It might be my unresolved business here. Or maybe not. But what I know is that a man like James Brackington cannot be allowed to have this."

"And there was something else," chimed Karina. A little giddiness had slipped into her voice. Smiley had to use all her willpower to pull her eyes away from the inside of the briefcase. She turned back to Karina and saw that she held a bundle of three red sticks, along with a bag of what looked like several little watches and some long green wire.

"Is that… *dynamite?*" asked Smiley, unbelieving.

"*Cause I'm T.N.T! I'm dynamite! T.N.T. and I'll win the fight!*" Karina feigned hitting power chords on an air guitar. "Yeah. It's dynamite."

Smiley held her gaze on Karina for a few more seconds, mouth open. She turned back to Dievs and the open case. *Holy hell…* Smiley's tailbone twitched just slightly. *This is bad. All… very, very bad.*

#

THERE was nowhere to go but to the Texas Inn. She didn't *want to*, that was for sure. The craziness of the past few days was really sinking in now, and the worst of it was the fact that she, Smiley Anne Davis, was a murderer. Yes, a murderer. And there was no way around that minor hiccup. *No, sir-ee Bob.*

I killed… My God, I don't even know how many people I killed. Seven? Eight? Too many. One is too many. And now I'm in my destroyed car with the teenager I fired, and a dead man who doesn't even know his real name. On the run from the mafia and the law. With dynamite, and a case full of… She felt faint. She gripped the steering wheel of her Pinto harder and told herself that she was really past all that silliness. None of it had been a *mistake,* or an *accident* (except maybe their escape from Campaiyote, which had been the definition of luck). She was a killer. And she supposed that her business had been about *death* for quite a while now.

The highway rushing beneath her wheels ran straight and true, striking across the brown land like the path of an arrow. Smiley caught some looks from other drivers who could see the shot-up state of her car. She smiled and nodded, hair waving in the wind coming through the back window, and hoped none of them felt compelled by their civic duty to call a trooper. *Who really wants to be that good of a citizen?*

In the back seat, Karina was quiet. But she kept rolling the bundle of dynamite between her palms like Golem polishing his precious ring. It was beginning to creep Smiley out, but it felt inappropriate somehow, after everything she'd done, to scold her. *Murderers generally aren't the ones handing out lectures about the golden rule.*

Smiley'd contemplated taking Karina home before going to the Texas Inn, or maybe dropping her off somewhere, but Dievs had spoken against that idea. She had reluctantly agreed that, *A,* Karina was a very helpful individual when it came to breaking the law (as it turned out), and *B,* that she might be in more danger away from them, than with them, despite their intention to face off with Brackington.

A line from one of Smiley's mother's old tabloid

magazines came back to her as she stared out at highway and blue sky. A line uttered by a fellow murderer: *I'm the Devil, and I'm here to do the Devil's business.*

CHAPTER FORTY-FIVE

Ya Do You Do the Hanky-Panky and Ya Turn Yourself Around

HANK was pretty sure his right eye was done for, despite it being shoved back into its socket by dear Mr. B. It had a certain *jellied* feel in his skull that was not comforting in the least. He couldn't even crack his swollen eyelid to check if he could see, but he was certain he would not be able to. *All up to you, lefty. My trusty… left eye. Sigh.* Hank wondered briefly if an eyepatch was actually an upgrade in the coolness department. He thought maybe so.

James Brackington was still seated opposite Hank, and it seemed that waiting wasn't something he had much experience with. He was fidgeting terribly with his hands and feet (an odd look for someone usually so imposing and suave), and looking out the window at the whoosh of every passing car on the highway. Hank was tempted, in his punch-drunk, anxiety-free (though not *pain-free*) state of mind, to say, *patience is a virtue, James*, but he didn't really want to be slapped again, or have his tongue cut out. *No, thanks.*

Suddenly, into the quiet of the hotel room, came a

clanging sound from the neighboring room. And again. It sounded like a dropped cast-iron skillet, or maybe someone smashing two pans together like maracas. Brackington jerked his gaze towards the wall and almost snarled. He lifted himself from the chair and walked over to where the sound had come from. He banged on the wall several times with his fist.

"Keep it down!" he shouted, and Hank had to stifle a laugh. In that moment, Mr. B had seemed like just another disgruntled resident of the Texas Inn. A passing Renaissance specter.

There came no reply from the other side of the wall, but the clanging ceased. Brackington nodded to one of his men standing by the entrance to Hank's room, and he immediately turned to go investigate. When the guard opened the door to step outside, he was greeted with a sight very familiar to Hank. Won Park, the owner of the Texas Inn, and Hank's landlord. He'd been about to knock when the door had swung open. The sight of the big man in the suit and dark glasses obviously surprised him, but not enough to scare him off. *It's gonna take more than that to discourage Won Park from collecting rent.*

"Hank! You in there? Where rent? It's the first! I already told you, late again, out!" Won shouted into the room, completely ignoring the guard. For a moment, no one spoke.

"Umm… I'm a little busy right this moment, Won. Might I get it to you… on the morrow?" Hank said timidly, and with a bit of a British accent for some reason.

Brackington doubled over in a big hearty laugh. When finally he regained his composure, he mumbled through after-giggles, "Oh, shit, that's funny." When he'd bent over to laugh, he'd somehow produced a big gray revolver. "Hank, seems like you let time get away from you." He made a *tsk-tsk-tsk* sound and wagged his finger, smiling like the Cheshire Cat. Brackington turned from the wall and sauntered over to the doorway. Won yelled again.

"Hank! Rent! Rent now! No orgies either… Who all these people?"

Brackington put his hand lightly on the guard's shoulder, and the big man immediately moved aside. Hank couldn't see Brackington's face, but he knew what was on it. *That smirk.* He had no great love for Won Park, but in the grand scheme of things, he was an innocent man who didn't deserve to die. And he had *no idea* how close he was getting to that cliff edge. *Maybe if he lives, he'll fix the God-damned AC.*

"Hello… Mr. Park? Wasn't it?" Hank could hear Brackington say from the doorway. "Hank is indisposed at the moment. Perhaps I can be of assistance?" This came out in a sickly sweet, ultra-polite tone. Hank's stomach dropped. *He's playing with him.*

Won Park had obviously not picked up on the vibe coming off James Brackington, and certainly had not seen the revolver in his hand (or maybe he had and was just insane enough to continue pushing), because he shouted again, this time right into Brackington's face.

"No! Where Hank? Too many people in here. Against the rules." Won gestured with his hand as if shooing off a stray dog. Hank heard Brackington laugh again.

"I'm so sorry. I didn't realize there was a rule against parties. You're welcome to join us if you'd like." Won must've finally picked up on his mortal peril then, because he gave no reply. Brackington continued, "You know, on second thought, maybe you shouldn't. I hear *you people* can be a little strict… I'm willing to give you one more chance though."

You people came out casually, but Hank could hear the disgust in it. The memory of that afternoon spent on the dead-end lane came back to him briefly. How Brackington had spoken to Smiley as though she were a dog wearing human skin. Hank shivered. Won spoke again, and Hank could hear the distress in his voice this time.

"N-no. I go back down…"

Brackington interrupted. "No, no, no! Won, you really must come IN!"

Won yelped, and as Brackington turned, Hank could see that he had the barrel of his revolver stuck up Won's right nostril. Brackington led Won into the room like a dog on a choker. Then…

BRRRRINNNGG…

BBBBBRRRIING…

BRRIIIIINNGNGGG…

The ringing was so sudden and so violent, Hank thought the phone might just jump right off the little table in the corner. The collection of years of crumpled sticky notes fluttered from the vibration. Brackington paused, then made his way over to the phone, keeping Won hooked on the barrel of his comically large revolver. He lifted the receiver with his free hand.

"Yellow?" Brackington said into the receiver.

"*Muwmpapon, we wumpon te toe,*" whispered the phone. *Jenine.*

"Ah, huh."

"*Aye bewindey wer hened woo you.*"

"Is that so?" said Brackington.

"Ysm."

"Well… how exciting. Thank you, Jenine. Keep me informed." With this, he hung up the phone. Brackington turned to one of the several guards standing along the wall and said, "J, make a note to mark Jenine for termination."

Hank blinked in surprise and looked up at Brackington. He shrugged his lean shoulders.

"Out with the old, in with the new, isn't that what they say, Hank old boy? She was becoming unreliable. Tiresome even. Can't have that." He turned back to the fish at the end of his revolver and looked him over as if he were inspecting a piece of meat. *Isn't he?* Won closed his eyes and trembled.

"But, there is *some* interesting news. Seems Ms. Davis and her little gang have gone *completely off the rails…* and that bloated idiot, Morris, couldn't even stop them with a whole god-damn police department… Much more metal than I was expecting. Now this whole thing has just gotten waayy, way, way too complicated." It seemed Brackington was almost talking to himself now. Or maybe to Won, in a sort of *pet frog* kind of way. "…All I wanted was a crime scene cleanup business of my own, same as her. Then Swiss had to come back from the dead." He shook his head in wonder at this brief side note. "And what I thought would be a band of pushovers, turned out to be far more prolific killers than my best men!"

Brackington ran his free hand through his curly black hair and took a deep breath. He'd worked himself into a tizzy, and Hank could see the restless anxiety from earlier returning. He wondered what Smiley had done. *Seems like I missed a lot in the past two days. Why do they get to have all the fun?* Then his eye was hit with a fresh wave of throbbing pain, and he regretted even thinking such a thought.

Brackington recovered his cool, and he once again put on that chilling smirk.

"But their luck will run out. Yessir-ee. And now, at least, we have the lumberjack." *Joe.* "Wonder how Ms. Davis will fare without her muscle." And instead of that look of anxiety and consternation, James Brackington licked his lips and smiled. Hank could think only of a wolf. "My intuition is telling me we might have ourselves a little standoff here in a bit, Hank. Excited?"

No… okay, maybe a little.

CHAPTER FORTY-SIX

Oh Joy

JAMES Brackington had discovered the sizable stash of peanuts in the corner of Hank's hotel residence and was munching them several at a time.

"These are good, Hank." He gestured to the large boxes sitting on the ground and raised his eyebrows. "Seems a little overkill though. Couldn't have just gotten a jumbo box like everyone else?"

"I, uh… found them," Hank muttered.

"What? Speak up, kid, can't hear you." Hank looked like a beaten gopher sitting in that chair. His eye was put out, and his shoulder was almost surely dislocated. *At the very least. Well, not like he's gonna be using it much longer, anyway.* Though James had begun reconsidering killing Hank Cooper. He thought his frustrations with Jenine and certain other members of his staff might be clouding his judgment just a smidge. He'd been trying to cut down on his murder streaks. And besides, Hank was a good little dog. Always had been. Though that was part of what made James Brackington so frustrated at times.

*Hank is a good tool. Excellent really. And quite affordable. **And**, he opted to kill himself rather than stand up to me, unlike that* *bitch in yellow. I do love a little fight, but it's nice to have a beat dog around too.*

The hotel room was making him feel cramped. *Can't believe he lives here.* The room was tiny, hardly large enough for a bed and a loveseat. *Smells like shit too.* Like long, hot days, and no showers. Like dirty laundry and unwashed beer cans. It was tidy, relatively speaking, but that was only because there was barely anything in the place.

"I found them," said Hank.

"Oh," said Brackington, looking at the little pile of peanuts in his hand. "Wait, what?"

"Someone left them…" Hank's head drifted down, and it looked like he might lose consciousness.

"Wooah, buddy…" James said as he reached down and grabbed a handful of short brown hair with his free hand. He pulled Hank's head up and smacked him gently on each cheek. He spared Hank's right eye, which had become a swollen, oozing mess. *Should definitely put some Neosporin on that. Disgusting.* "Stay with us, kiddo. You don't want to miss this next part. Gonna be *electric.*"

Brackington straightened up and looked at the peanuts in his palm, but with a little uncertainty this time. He held them out to Won Park, who was shaking terribly and bleeding from his stretched nostril. The landlord looked down past the barrel of the .45 revolver stuck up his sniffer with one cracked eye and shook his head, trembling. Brackington shrugged and tossed the rest into his mouth. *Already had two mouthfuls anyway.* Brackington sighed and looked around the shabby room one more time.

"Yeah… this place is a drag, Hank. Whaddyah say we move outside to wait for our friends, hmm? Yeah, get a little highway air."

Brackington turned to Won and gave him a searching look.

"You feel like calling the police there, Mr. Park? I mean, I'm not sure what you would tell them if you did. *What*? That you assaulted an upstanding, *white,* American citizen in his own hotel room? 'Cause that's what I recall happening. And I really hate to bring violence into anything, *truly*… But if you force my hand…"

Won might've been a leaf in the wind with how violently his legs shook. His knees were almost clacking together with each shimmy. James thought he might fall to the floor if not for the gun propped under his nose. It made him want to laugh.

"Na-nuh-No! No. No police, no police. I-I-I swear." James gave him a disapproving look and stuck his lower lip out.

"You wouldn't lie to me, would you, Won? I can call you that, can't I?"

"Yes-ss-s. Of course… I mean… No, of course not."

"You're confusing me now, Won. Which is it? You feel like calling the police, or don't you?"

Tears were dripping down Won's face now. Brackington felt the thrill of striking fear into someone's heart. He swallowed heavily, but kept his face playful. He could see the reflection of his green eyes in Won's wide black pupils. For a split second he thought he might just pull the trigger and paint Hank's ceiling with poor Mr. Park's brains, but before he could make that decision, that clanging sound from the other room came again.

In one swift motion, before he could give it any thought, James yanked the barrel of his colt from Won's nose (ripping out a piece of nose flesh with the metal bar sight), aimed it at the wall where the sound had come from and fired three times.

BANG!

Click.

BANG!

Ker-click.

BANG!

Click.

"I told you to keep it down," James said casually, as if speaking to a little child. The guards along the wall hadn't so much as flinched. *Good doggies.* There came a conclusive *thud* from the other side of the wall, and then silence. *Just that easy, folks.*

Looking down, he saw Won had curled into a frighteningly small bundle on the ground. He nearly had his head to his crotch, and he was still trembling. *Di-sgusting.* James kicked the human ball with his worn boot.

"Get along, Mr. Park. Seems like you don't handle blood very well. And I could be wrong, but I think there might be more in the near future."

Won lifted his head to meet Brackington's cold gaze. James lifted his eyebrows and shooed him with the gun. That was enough for Won, who uncurled from his fetal position and scrambled out of the room like a cat, skidding and slipping on the laminate floor. Brackington watched him go and laughed. He turned to his guards and put his hands on his hips. The barrel of the Colt stuck out like a chicken wing.

"Alright. Let's get outta this shitty room. C'mon. Bring the gopher."

The seven guards immediately sprang into action. Three of them split off to pick up Hank in his chair, and the rest filed out onto the catwalk. James walked behind them, stomping around like a cowboy walking into a saloon. Once on the catwalk, he gripped the square metal rails and leaned out over the deserted parking lot.

"Mmm… exhaust and dry concrete. Refreshing."

To the right, on the adjacent walkway, was a man smoking a cigarette in full clown attire. They made eye contact, and James nodded, smiling. The clown saw the revolver hanging loosely from James' hand, calmly snubbed his cigarette out on the railing and went back into his room.

Any time now, thought James Brackington. *Any time now. She'll bring me Swiss. Then we find the case. I know he remembers where it is. He was always a liar. But we'll get it out of him, oh yes… maybe I ought to keep Jenine around a while longer…*

Gazing out over the highway, James spotted a beige Ford Pinto with a shattered back window, swerving to catch the off ramp which led right to the Texas Inn parking lot. *Oh, joy.* His men were already carrying Hank down the steps, still bound to the wooden chair.

Party time.

CHAPTER FORTY-SEVEN

Standoff at the Texas Inn

SMILEY was glad they'd stopped at the Texaco while they'd had a chance. For one, there seemed no need to hide her smoking habit from either of her companions at this point, though paying a buck-fifty for a single pack of Hillsboroughs gave her an icky feeling. The two green dots at the bottom of the poster pasted up by the register made her feel cold. *Brackington.*

Nicotine fix secured, Karina and Dievs had had time to explain their plan — *if you can call it that.* Smiley supposed it was better than nothing, but it still sounded like the plot of a really terrible action movie. *Those things never star a black woman. Or a goth teenager, for that matter. They're usually the ones that die in the first scene. If they got hired at all.* But there seemed to be no better alternative. At least Smiley had nothing to offer, and so she'd listened to their idea in the Slim Jim aisle of the Texaco, while Barbara watched them from behind her fiberglass barrier. She'd looked kind of like a big toad, sitting there on her stool. Smiley had taken comfort in the smell of tobacco and dust radiating from the woman. Now, as she approached the Texas Inn in her beaten Pinto, she longed to be back at that Texaco. It smelled of highway and death here.

She thought she saw a flash of violent green, like a piece of metal glinting in the sun, before she'd even pulled off the highway. *He's here alright.* As she veered off the highway and into the Texas Inn parking lot, the absurdity of this whole situation, *this whole week,* hit her, and she couldn't help but laugh. Dievs, who was sitting in the passenger seat, gave her a funny look, and after a moment, he was laughing along with her. Smiley let the Pinto cruise gently into the middle of the parking lot and finally come to an easy stop. *Park. E-brake.*

The two were still trying to shake the giggles as they stepped out of the car and turned to face the gang of suited men that had gathered in the lot by the front office. In the front, loosely holding a large silver revolver on his hip, stood James Brackington. Behind him were seven men in black suits, also holding guns. In the middle of the conglomeration sat Hank, tied to a wooden chair and looking about one sneeze away from dead.

#

HOT wind blew over the parking lot. The highway screamed under the weight of passing semis.

"I love jokes! Why don't you tell me one? Seems like something's really funny."

The sound of his voice transported Smiley back to that day on the dead-end lane, his blue Shelby (which now sat quietly in a handicap spot, like a dark blue jungle cat), the party house and the woman they'd found in the bedroom. *What was left of her, anyway. He did that.* Then Smiley felt red, raw anger swelling in her chest.

"No, really, what's so funny?" Brackington asked again, but the playfulness had fled his voice, and his face might as well have been made of stone. Only his eyes seemed to be enjoying this game.

"Oh, honey. You wouldn't get it," said Smiley, with a coolness in her voice that surprised her.

Brackington scoffed at this. *Business time.* He raised his revolver towards Smiley and cocked the hammer.

"I'm so glad you two could make it. Hank was beginning to worry. Where'd that little rascal, Karina get off to? I'll be sure to pay her mother a visit after this."

Behind Brackington, Hank lifted his head groggily at the sound of his name, and Smiley got a glimpse of his mutilated eye. She couldn't help flinching at the sight of it. *Poor guy. He didn't deserve this.* But, not for the first time since being dragged into all this mess, she wondered how long Hank had been in the service of Mr. James Brackington, how many decapitated women he'd scraped off heart shaped beds and dumped in a septic tank somewhere, how many *murders* he'd been complicit in. *Maybe he does deserve it.* Then the horribleness of that thought chased itself out of her mind. *Don't let this green-eyed bastard bring you down to his level.*

Smiley said nothing in response to the thinly veiled threat. Brackington turned his attention to Dievs, who stood quietly by Smiley's side.

"Ah, Swiss. Good to see you again. You ran off before you and Jenine could finish chatting… so rude, and without even saying goodbye." Brackington clicked his tongue. "We'll have to remedy that."

Dievs didn't move or speak, only looked into Brackington's eyes grimly. Seeing him out of her periphery, Smiley was struck by the image of Clint Eastwood in *The Good, The Bad, and The Ugly*, squinty eyes and all. Brackington returned Dievs' gaze and smiled darkly.

"So… Whaddyah say *Dievs*… you tell me where the case is… *and we both know, you know where it is, so don't bullshit me…* and I give you both a quick death, right here."

"Noo… I don't like that idea," interjected Smiley.

Dievs, still not breaking his silence, took a step back, reached through the open passenger window of the Pinto and pulled out the slim leather briefcase. Brackington's eyes widened at the sight of it. *He's hungry for it.* Smiley saw him lick his lips.

"Well… you've certainly made things a lot simpler. Just… hand it over, and no one has to get hurt. Actually, no, that's a lie. Sorry."

"Let Hank go," said Smiley.

Brackington shook his head in wonder.

"Oh. I didn't realize you actually cared about Hanky Panky here. I thought your showing up was more of a courtesy thing… Unfortunately, I still have some work for Hank, so I can't part with my loyal dog just yet. Wait… now that I'm thinking it over… how about I just kill you both right now and take the case? I like that plan."

Brackington stiffened his gun arm and pointed it at Smiley. *Uh oh. This was not the plan. **Repeat**, not the plan.* But in that moment, just as Brackington's finger tightened on the trigger of his big revolver, the third floor of the Texas Inn exploded.

CHAPTER FORTY-EIGHT

The Future

SUSAN Vessemer pulled into the parking lot of the Texas Inn and parked her maroon Camry in one of the empty spots around the corner of the building. She enjoyed being close to the far staircase, which led up to the second and third-floor catwalks. Not that she thought anyone was going to question her business, least of all Won Park (a client of hers, in fact), but she'd always been one to err on the side of caution.

She sat in the driver's seat and let the AC blow on her a bit longer, just until it lost its crispness. Her wispy blond-white hair fluttered in the gentle breeze. She turned the key and silenced the engine. *This heat is gonna kill me*, she thought, as she sat and looked out at the shimmering highway, and the brownness beyond it, which seemed to stretch out to infinity.

The car immediately began to warm beneath the harsh sun. Susan sighed and gathered her energy. She reached over to the passenger seat and picked up the brown grocery bag sitting there. Metal cans clinked together as she hoisted it into her lap. That always made her nervous. *It's fine,* she told herself, but a bag full of pressurized cans of butane just had a way of making her anxious, no matter how careful she was. And this was the largest batch she'd ever dared to buy in one trip.

She got out of the car, closed the door with her foot and locked it, bending down and slotting her key into the lock with her free hand. She made her way up the grated iron staircase to the third-floor walkway, taking each step slowly and deliberately, then shuffled all the way down to room 334. Susan glanced down at the parking lot as she shoved her key into the lock of the old red door. *No Power Wagon. Guess Hank's not home.* Though Susan kept a room at the Texas Inn for business purposes only, she'd been here long enough to come to know the screaming orange truck and the poor guy who drove it.

Stepping into Susan Vessemer's room was like opening the door to a dive bar expecting to see a worn out pool table and several haggard drunk men, and instead, being greeted with a university-grade drug lab. The walls were clean and white, free of the black mold that so infested the corners of Hank's room. In lieu of furniture or any kind of general living equipment, sat three long, black laminate tables, each stacked with various pieces of glass and metal equipment. To the average person's eye, these items looked like a collection one might find in a high school chemistry classroom. The major difference being the fifty-gallon clear plastic bag sitting on the floor filled to the brim with weed. *Marijuana. Flower. Ganja. Skunk. Pot. Dope. Sticky-icky. The good stuff. Go-go puffs. Oregano. THC.*

Susan tossed her keys onto a small round table by the entrance and kicked the door shut behind her. She moved over to one of the long tables and set the grocery bag down. *Okay. Tea, then work.*

#

THIRTY minutes later, Susan had her white coat on, and a pair of plastic safety goggles strapped over her eyes. She was leaning on one of the laminate tables and psyching herself up for a THC extraction marathon extravaganza. *You're gonna make so much money, Susan. Dabs are the future. Pure, extracted THC. People aren't gonna know what hit em'.* It was then that she heard the opening and closing of the neighboring room's door. *Hank's home,* she thought, but it was a thought that passed quickly. Her mind was focused on the job at hand.

Let's begin.

Susan started by arranging four specialized, two foot long glass tubes in a line (the only four she had) and filling them to the brim with weed from the trash bag. To both her dismay and delight, the filled tubes hardly made a dent in the copious amount of bud in the trash bag. *Gonna be a long one. That's good.* Next came the butane.

Each tube had a screen on the bottom, which would allow for pressure to be released, and a hole at the top for the butane to be sprayed in. She placed the nozzle of one of the butane canisters at the top of the first tube and sprayed. The tube slowly frosted over, like a glass of water left out in the cold, and after the last bits of butane sputtered out, a yellowish liquid began to drip out of the bottom of the tube into a glass dish. She sprayed another can of butane and the drip became a steady stream.

As Susan finished off the second can of butane, the nozzle caught briefly on the tube, and it went tumbling to the floor. She tried to twist in time to catch it, but in her haste, knocked a metal mixing bowl off the table behind her. It went clanging to the floor, shockingly loud in the hot silence of her room. When the bowl finally stopped bouncing, there came a knocking from Hank's room, and an angry voice.

"*Eeb in own!*" it said.

Keep it down. Okay, Hank. No need to be so upset. It was an accident. A small voice in the back of her brain said *that didn't sound like Hank*, but it hardly mattered. She picked up the dropped bowl and can and continued.

#

THREE-quarters of the fifty-gallon trash bag of weed was gone, and one of the long black tables was now covered in glass dishes, each filled with a hardening golden yellow puddle of butane-extracted THC wax. *B-E-A-utiful*. It was. And she'd used far less butane than she'd expected. *I might have enough for a whole 'nother batch of this. Means I have to buy from Cody again though. That cheap bastard…*

Around forty cans of pressurized butane, yellow labels gleaming, sat at the end of the black table closest to the door and the big bay window of the hotel room. Susan took a step back to survey her work and glanced at the small army of butane canisters, all sweating in the swampiness of her room. Although the black plastic tables and chemistry equipment did a good impression of a lab, there was still no working AC in the room, just a lazy ceiling fan. She was certain that Won Park knew what was happening here, but she still didn't want to take the risk of him seeing it, getting scared, then kicking her out, so she managed without AC.

All these thoughts were brought to an abrupt halt when she, for the second time, knocked over the big silver mixing bowl on the corner of the middle table. She'd been walking to the sink at the back of the room, and in the way so many people would be familiar with, slid around the edge of the table sort of lazily. Exhaustion often breeds corner-cutting, and in this case, quite literally. She slammed her hip into the hard black tabletop, causing the table to shift and Susan to cry out.

"Oh… motherfucker!"

She bent over to clutch her throbbing hip, and the bowl, teetering on the edge of the countertop behind her like a prop in a Tom and Jerry cartoon, finally dropped to the floor, scaring Susan so badly she jumped. In frustration and misdirected anger (from the pain in her hip), she kicked the mixing bowl against the far wall. It clanged loudly and skittered across the floor.

That's better…

That was the last thought Susan Vessemer had before her right leg, just above the knee, exploded. The damage was so catastrophic, and so sudden, she didn't even have time to flinch. It was as if her leg had been blown up from the inside. There was no time to scream before the second bullet tore through the wall and slammed into her upper arm. This one knocked her backwards, though she didn't fall. The surprise and shock kept her upright. She looked down at the mess of her shoulder and heard the quiet click of a revolver from the other room. *Hank?*

Then blackness.

#

SUSAN Vessemer was back in freshmen year chemistry class, with her lab partner DeAndre Jackson, who she'd had a terrible crush on until Junior year when he'd been arrested. The K-9 unit found an ounce of weed in his locker. That had only made Susan like him more. But this was before all that. She was trying to get the Bunsen burner to just the right temperature, while DeAndre sat with his chin in his palm and watched her.

She could hear the voice of her teacher, Mr. Lennon, from Wales, trying to guide his child-flock of Texan teens through a comically simple experiment (and failing). Susan was already well beyond caring about the activity at hand. Her mind was working at different problems. Adult problems.

One O five for three minutes… wait until the color changes… But Susan felt that something was wrong. Really wrong. *What is this hollow feeling? I've… I've already been here. This… where am I?* Then DeAndre spoke.

"Susaan," he said, and she turned to face him. He gave her a smirk and pointed to his right eye like, *you have something you might wanna take care of.*

Susan reached up and felt her face with her hands. She found that her right cheek was wet. Her hand came down shiny with blood… *and small flecks of gray and white.* It was then she realized she couldn't see out of her right eye. She brought her hand back up to her face and gently felt for her eye. Instead of finding that delicate bulge, she found a fleshy, wet crater.

Horror and panic spread through her body like a shot of whiskey, hot and fast. Then DeAndre was gone, and the voice of Mr. Lennon was gone, and she was back in her hotel room at the Texas Inn, staring at a stovetop. A glowing red stovetop with a can of butane sitting on it.

This sight didn't register *danger* with Susan Vessemer. Her only concern was her eye. *Was I shot?* Looking down, she was reminded of the bullet wounds she'd sustained, though there was no pain. *How? Someone… Hank… shot me?* She brought her hand down from her face and was once again greeted with the sight of blood and those grayish-white flecks. *Oh… Brain. That's brain. My brain. That's my brain.*

Before she could go any further with these thoughts, the can of butane exploded.

Yet, Susan did not die. As the chemical fire engulfed her body, her nerves, being at the mercy of a terribly damaged brain, but *not dead*, sent her legs pumping. She ran down the length of her makeshift lab and hit the glass window at a stride. By the time she was through the glass and over the railing, she was sure she could hear a train whistle. *Sounds nice…* The sensation of falling was wonderful, like falling back into a big comfy bed and knowing she didn't have to get up for school.

CHAPTER FORTY-NINE

Anthills

KARINA stood on the roof of the Texas Inn, high above the standoff happening in the parking lot below. She felt like some kind of badass cowboy Batgirl… except the height of the drop was starting to make her nauseous, and she didn't think Batgirl got nauseous from heights. *Or maybe she just hides it really well.*

This was, *by far*, the most exciting thing she'd ever done in her (relatively speaking) short life. Not counting the getaway driving she'd done earlier that day, which felt more like the preamble to the daring feat of pyromania she was about to attempt.

As she crept forward to peek over the edge of the slanted roof, she couldn't help but smile at the simplicity of their plan. *Drop of stick of dynamite on em'. Best plan I ever heard.* Except, '*the plan*', was experiencing a few minor hiccups. For one, they hadn't expected Hank to be brought out right behind Brackington. *And,* Smiley had insisted that Karina not be *directly* responsible for killing anyone. Though she'd protested, the sorrow and seriousness in Smiley's eyes had told her it was for the best.

"Just get one stick close enough to cause chaos. That's what we need, chaos and confusion. We just want to get Hank outta there and run. If Mr. B gets the case, he'll be satisfied... *I hope*," Smiley had said.

Karina remembered Smiley's words as she peered over the edge of the roof and looked for the best spot to drop the stick of dynamite. This one was gonna be *live. Oh yes, live like a Roman candle*. The other two sticks were on timers. Timers that Karina hoped she'd set correctly. She tried to visualize the other two sticks, and how far along each of their timers were. She thought she had a good idea, but couldn't be sure. It only occurred to her then that she should've set another clock along with the two timers so she would've known exactly when they would go off. *Hey, first-time bomber over here, give me a break.*

Rigging the sticks of dynamite had been a nerve-wracking experience, to say the least. Her older brother, Tommy, was the pyromaniac, not her, but she'd watched him blow up enough anthills to get the gist. Well, she'd thought so anyway. *Light the fuse, toss and run.* Turned out dynamite was a little different. There were fuses in the bag she'd found at the ranch house, though the timers had presented some interesting possibilities. She hoped she'd done it right. *Stick the clock in the boom-boom stick and twist, right? Right.* She supposed she'd find out if it'd worked soon enough.

Despite it all, Karina thought they were doing pretty well for a trio of regular Joes (though Joe was currently not with them). *We've got a shot at this.* Smiley had obviously gone through something the past two days. She was *changed*, and

Karina got the impression she would never be the same. Karina however, too young and too hungry for excitement to fully comprehend the weight of her actions, was thoroughly enjoying herself. In fact, she wasn't sure she could ever really return to her life after this. *Probably all down hill from here. I have* **school** *tomorrow. What a joke.* Something inside Smiley had snapped, Karina knew. That little piece of soul that can only be broken by taking another life. Inside Karina though, a fire was raging. The fire of rebellion and rage that only the young can understand. And she would not let it go.

Dievs was clearly not having much fun, though he had a good mind for this sorta stuff it seemed to Karina. The longer he stuck around, the more *Derrick Swiss* began to reemerge. Karina still thought there was something up with the whole peanut thing, but they hadn't had much time to investigate it further. She wondered how Joe was doing, if he was being visited by magical peanuts and messages from the beyond. *He's fine. Morris always liked him… bet he's in the hospital right now, gettin' all stitched up… Probably.*

Karina watched the unfolding negotiations in the Texas Inn parking lot below and was pleased with how unmindful the opposition had been, and *continued* to be. She'd snuck around their little circle so easily (having been secretly dropped off before Smiley and Dievs had make their obvious entrance), she thought maybe Brackington had been playing with her. Now she knew he was just that arrogant.

In the lot far below, Karina saw Brackington raise his revolver at Smiley and knew that her window was closing. *Do it now.* She pulled the *Boom-boom, no bitey-bitey, Slim Jim-dynamite* out of her back pocket, along with a mini white Bic lighter. She lifted the curly brown fuse up and was about to strike the lighter when an explosion shook the building.

At first, Karina thought one of her planted sticks of dynamite had gone off prematurely, but then she saw the geyser of flames pouring out of the third floor of the Texas Inn, and something else as well. *A person?* On fire and falling through the air. For a half second, everything froze. The figures below all turned to look at the sudden explosion, hostages and valuable briefcases completely forgotten. All eyes were on the flaming poltergeist which was sailing through the afternoon air like a horseman of the apocalypse. Even from the roof, Karina could see the surprise in James Brackington's green eyes.

Then time resumed its ceaseless flow and the flaming body crashed to the ground, only a foot or two in front of Hank, who remained tied up in his chair. The sound of the impact made it all the way up to Karina's ears. *Wet. It sounded wet.* Karina was not a squeamish girl, though for a second, she thought she might vomit. She swallowed hard and held it down. *Okay, maybe this **is** all a little bit intense for me,* she thought… *Nah.* Then she lit the fuse.

CHAPTER FIFTY

Long in the Dying

THINGS went fuzzy again after Brackington shot through the wall of Hank's room with his big silver revolver. Things had been fuzzy before, but it seemed like the situation was really *escalating* every time he opened his eyes. *Eye.* He was skipping in and out of consciousness in a very unpleasant and disorienting way. Like a scratched VHS tape. His right eye (or rather, where his eye had once been) was a throbbing, pulsating core of pain, beating in his head like a bass drum. His shoulder also screamed at him, though compared to the pain in his eye, it seemed a trifling thing.

The three shots from Brackington's revolver had shocked him awake, for a minute at least. The report from each shot, in the smallness of his room, had been deafening. He'd been lucid enough then to hope his neighbor was alright. *What was her name again…* Hank's wakefulness had waned as they'd carried him down the stairs and set him down in the parking lot. He'd tried to stay awake, really, he had, but the pain was too much. *Vodka… and peanuts… please. And a nap, maybe.*

The thought that Smiley, Dievs and Karina had come to rescue him never crossed his mind. And it was out of this haze of confusion and pain that he emerged to find himself at the center of a terrible vortex of violence and calamity.

He heard his name being called. More out of reflex than desire, he lifted his gaze and saw James Brackington standing in front of him, revolver in hand, and his surrounding circle of bodyguards. Further down the parking lot, in front of her beige Pinto, stood Smiley Davis and… *damn, what was that guy's name? Diego, or something. Cheese guy. I wonder what they're doing here… Don't they know those cars explode?* It took him a moment to realize everyone was looking at something above him. *What'd I miss?* Time froze for a split second, just long enough for Hank to get his bearings, and then his question was answered, quickly, and in red.

A body crashed to the concrete in front of him, wearing a thick cloak of butane-fueled flames. It landed a foot and a half in front of Hank, and before his partially functioning brain could comprehend what had just happened, something hot, wet and metallic smelling sprayed his face and body. *Oh… Jeezus…* He hadn't noticed, but he guessed his mouth had been hanging open, because that same hot liquid came flying into the back of his throat at speed. It tasted like melted pennies and meat. He gagged. When Hank opened his good eye, he saw a small fire on the ground in front of him. Except it didn't appear to be wood fueling the flame.

Hank gagged again, and spat out the foul liquid coating his mouth. He saw it come out red and felt it dribbling down his chin. The rest of him was red too, he saw, and although the liquid appeared to be *smoking*, he could never mistake that shade. *Blood*. His head was whirling. A closer look at the fire revealed a face staring back at him. *Oh. Neighbor. My neighbor*. Hank felt a sudden, overwhelming sorrow. Sorrow for his neighbor, and for all. He just wanted it to stop. All to stop. He knew it wouldn't, though. Not yet.

His perception of time rocked back and forth like a carousel ride, unable to control its speed. The flames of the burning body in front of him seemed to slow almost to stopping, then raced forward, like a scratched VHS tape. Time was becoming meaningless in the living nightmare his life had become. Something was bubbling up from that deep, empty pit inside him. Like the tank that sat silently in the field behind the Texas Inn, filled to the brim with death. The final cry of the child he'd once been, and who had been long in the dying.

He looked into the burning sockets that had once held Susan Vessemer's eyes. He looked there and felt nothing.

Hank screamed.

CHAPTER FIFTY-ONE

SMILEY

IT all happened so fast. Too fast. When Smiley would think back to the events of that afternoon, she couldn't say with any certainty that any of it had happened at all. She regretted giving Karina, an anarchist at heart, the instructions, *"cause chaos,"* though that is exactly what she'd done. *Oh, yes*. With a little help from good old-fashioned luck and dynamite, things in the Texas Inn parking lot had gone from tense and unstable to full-on war-zone, in the space of a few seconds.

The burning body, which had come crashing out of a third-story window, flipped over the metal railing and plunged to the concrete just short of Hank was unexpected. *On both sides*, Smiley guessed, by the look on James Brackington's face. Everyone stopped at that moment to watch the human fireball sail through the air. Smiley cringed at the sound of the impact, the sound of crunching bones and ripping meat. She couldn't help but flinch away at the sight of Hank being violently sprayed with someone's blood, like he'd been in the path of some giant, squished tomato. It was a scene out of a cheesy horror movie. But it was real. So real.

Hank's scream afterward was almost worse than the actual event. She thought they might be too late to save him, even if they all lived through this… and that was a big *if. That scream sounded like someone at the end of their rope.*

In the momentary stillness after Hank's wail had concluded, Smiley saw a small red stick quietly thump to the ground by the foot of one of Mr. B's guards, whose whole, stunned attention was still fixed on the burning body. It was sparking. Smiley had time only to look up to the roof and glimpse an impish smile before the stick of dynamite went off. There was an explosion, like gunfire, except much louder, and something came flying past Smiley's face, just over her right shoulder. *Was that… a shoe?* She felt Dievs putting his arm over her, and they dove to the concrete.

It seemed Karina hadn't exactly heeded her warning not to hurt anyone. *What did I expect, giving her a stick of dynamite? What am I doing?* Looking up, she saw that all of Brackington's men had ducked for cover as Smiley and Dievs had. She also saw that the shoe that had flown past her head had come from the unlucky bodyguard who'd been standing next to the stick of dynamite. His right leg was missing from the knee down. He stared at the remains of his thigh with a look of shocked, unbelieving horror. He screamed. *Oh, Christ.*

And then Dievs was grabbing her by the back of her shirt and pulling her to her feet. Brackington had been caught off guard briefly, just like everyone else, but the effect was gone now. He looked angry. His face twisted into a gruesome caricature of a person, his white lips parted to show gritted teeth, and those green eyes opened wide, *so wide.* It took Smiley a moment to realize she was seeing his face from over the barrel of a gun. A gun he was aiming right at her.

Then he fired.

\#

THE first bullet came slicing through the air just to the left of her head. She felt the bite of it along her cheek, and the rush of hot blood over her chin that followed.

Brackington cocked the trigger of his revolver and fired again whilst walking towards Dievs and Smiley. It was Dievs that saved her this time, pulling her roughly out of the path of the bullet. She heard the tinny twang of the bullet ricocheting off the hood of her Pinto. That's when Brackington switched his aim towards Dievs.

Dievs swung the briefcase up into the air and sent it sailing towards Brackington. The monster's green eyes widened for a moment, and he reached up with his free hand to catch it. Though his attention was focused on the case — *that precious case* — hurdling through the air, he still managed to depress the trigger on his .45. Smiley heard a *PHWUMP*, as the bullet buried itself into Dievs' chest. He let out a small gasp and stumbled back. She turned to see Dievs grabbing at his chest, and the spreading bloom of red which was already soaking through his shirt. They looked at each other, eyes wide, as he fell to the concrete.

Smiley turned back to Brackington, who had caught the briefcase, and was grinning uncontrollably. Something in the proportions of his smile was disturbing, *rotten*. The smile of a rabid dog. He lifted the revolver towards Smiley again.

"Wonder if he'll stay dead this time. I think so," Brackington said through pearly white teeth. He pulled the trigger.

The .45 clicked quietly. He pulled the trigger again. *Click.* Again. *Click. Click. Out of bullets. My God, he's out of bullets.*

Brackington huffed, and that smile disappeared, giving way to almost comical anger. He threw the gun at her. Smiley ducked and heard it clatter over the concrete behind her.

"Well, Ms. Davis, seems you've got at least a little more time among the living. We'll get that taken care of ASAP. You've caused quite a bit of trouble. Though I think this is where it ends." Brackington gave her a contemptuous look and turned away.

He strode towards his blue Shelby, briefcase in hand. Smiley could only watch.

#

SMILEY stared. A man dying, his leg blown to pieces. A smashed, burning body. Dievs, shot and bleeding. Hank, covered in steaming blood, unconscious, tied to a chair. And James Brackington, who seemed to be just about the only one unfazed by the destruction and chaos happening around him. Smiley supposed this was his world. One where the person who could climb in the chaos, *harness it,* could make it all the way to the top of the hill.

But it wasn't over yet.

Brackington was twenty feet from his blue Shelby, and though Smiley could not see his face, she was sure he was smiling. *Think you got it all in the bag, eh? Let's see how you like thi…*

Then, without warning, the Shelby erupted into a column of flames fifteen feet high. Brackington fell backwards, shielding his face from the sudden heat with the briefcase. He screamed in rage. A cry of utter disgust. But Smiley was sure she heard something else in there. *Fear? Maybe.* But the bomb had gone off too early. *It might not be enough. Nothing to do but watch and hope.*

Brackington lifted himself off the ground, briefcase gripped in a white-knuckled hand. He looked drunk, as he stumbled back towards Smiley, discombobulated by the explosion of his car. It seemed a few pieces of shrapnel appeared to have lodged themselves in Brackington's legs. She could see blood there. *So he does bleed. And probably takes dumps too.*

The Waxahachie exit off of I-35, a mile from the renaissance fair, had become a flaming spectacle. The butane explosion on the top floor of the Texas Inn had started a fire that was spreading rapidly to adjacent rooms. Plaster and old wood were catching as if they were soaked in gasoline. Hank's apartment, room 333, was spewing flames from the cracks around the poorly sealed door, and the window seemed likely to burst at any moment from the swirling flames inside. Smiley hoped Karina had found a way down to safety, away from the spreading fire. Then Brackington was standing over her. He yanked her up off the concrete and began yelling in her face, spraying her with hot spittle.

"WHERE ARE YOUR FUCKING KEYS? TELL ME NOW, OR I'LL STRANGLE YOU WITH YOUR OWN GODDAMN INTESTINES. I SWEAR I WILL."

She believed him, and pointed a trembling hand over her shoulder to the golden-beige Pinto.

"I… In the ignition," she whispered.

Brackington let go and Smiley's legs crumpled beneath her and she dropped back down to the ground. Rolling away from the rising heat of the inferno, she watched as Brackington got in the driver's seat of her Pinto and started the engine. For a horrible second, she thought he would run her over, but he backed up quickly, the car rocking on rusted suspension, then floored it out of the parking lot. He was on the highway and disappearing into the afternoon sun in seconds.

Smiley crawled over to where Robert Dievs lay in a growing, though already frighteningly large, puddle of blood.

CHAPTER FIFTY-TWO

Eastbound

"WELL, isn't that something…"

Dievs stood at the front of a long line of lost people. A pudgy man in a baby blue uniform was looking down at a… *a train ticket?* A little yellow perforated square with something written on it.

"Satisfied with your field trip, Mr. Dievs?"

"Huh?"

The pudgy man in the blue uniform laughed and leaned down over the counter, resting his elbows on the marble.

"You went back for some double-dip action, didn'cha? Sounds a little nutters to me, but hey, to each their own."

"What?"

The pudgy man frowned, then nodded, as if realizing something. "Mmm, little trouble with the memory? Happens all the time. Things can get a little fuzzy when you go in and out like that. Well, I've that heard, anyway. Nothing to worry yourself about, should come back to you any minute…"

"Did I… am I dead?"

"Bingo."

"Again, I'm dead again. Was there… was it something to

do with peanuts? Or am I making that up?"

The man in the blue uniform furrowed his brow.

"Well, um, I don't know anything about that… when the western line pulls in, we usually find a couple of boxes in the conductor car. Pretty sure it's somebody's idea of a joke." The pudgy man pointed his finger to the sky and looked up, grinning. "Can't say much beyond that… though, come to think of it, we *did* have a break-in the other day. Got a report that some of the boxes wound up in Texas somewhere…"

"Okay. I've decided I don't care."

Dievs turned to survey the line of people stretching out behind him. He silently thanked God that he didn't remember waiting in it. Things were coming back to him now. *Swiss. My name is Derrick V. Swiss.* Though he thought something about *Dievs* just sounded better.

His gaze veered over to the massive blank wall of white marble that lined the far side of the lobby. Small and out of place, he saw the exit doors he'd pushed open what seemed like long ago, *or not?* He wasn't sure anymore. *Time's sorta funny here*, he remembered the last desk clerk saying. The memory was clearer now that he stood at that same desk once again.

It was like waking from a deep sleep knowing you had dreamed, but not being able to recall *what, exactly*, the dream had been about. But there was enough. He remembered a girl, who liked to dress all in black. A woman who wore yellow flats, and though her name was Smiley, she hadn't smiled all that much. *A lumberjack?* A sad man surrounded by death named Hank. And another man, with terrible green eyes.

A buzzing anxiety gripped Dievs' stomach then. *He got it. He got away with it.* What *it* was, he couldn't quite remember, but it seemed terribly important. *And I'm dead in the parking lot of a hotel off the highway.* But that last thought was enough to bring his anxiety crashing down to zilch. *I'm dead. Not my problem anymore.* He wondered how many times that thought had been thunk. *Probably a lot. Probably a whole lot.*

An image came to him then. A woman's face, dark against an electric blue sky. She wasn't crying, but she looked sad. The woman in the yellow flats. He felt a hole in his chest. *A **big** hole in my chest. I was shot. Again… at least it was somebody else this time. Now I'm back here, dead central station.* He wondered what the moral of the story had been. *What was the point?* He supposed a great many people had had that thought as well, and probably gotten no answer.

Another image came careening out of the aether and splatted against the wall of his brain. A woman with a mean face and a hyena laugh. She was pulling his fingernails off. He shuddered. *Why did I go back? It was just pain… But then again…* he recalled playing with a Ouija board, and drinking hot coffee at a Denny's. *That was nice.* Dievs turned back to the smiling desk attendant.

"So… can I… could I go back again?"

The desk clerk looked down at him and shrugged. "Yeah, s'pose you could… No one's stoppin' you. Do you *want* to go back?"

Dievs turned and looked at the small pair of double exit doors against that massive blank canvas of marble. *No. No, not really.* There were thoughts below that one he didn't want to face, though he heard them, echoing out from the basin of his mind. *I don't want to go back there, because I know what it'll be.*

*What it **is**. But I'm scared to go forward. I'm scared because I **don't** know what it'll be.* As if reading his mind, the clerk in the baby blue uniform leaned over the counter again.

"Personally, I've found that moving forward is usually the best course. But that's just me. You can always stick around here for a while, think about things. There are some nice benches out on the platforms. Good for train watching."

Something about that idea seemed oddly familiar. Dievs turned back to the attendant one more time. "Thank you. Think I may do just that." With this, Dievs turned to walk away, but the attendant called out to him before he could get very far.

"Mr. Dievs! Sir! You forgot this."

Dievs swiveled and stepped back up to the desk, cutting off the next person in line, who looked rather upset that his turn had still not quite come. The attendant held out the yellow ticket stub, smiling brightly. Dievs nodded, took the ticket and moved aside so the next person could step up. Looking down at the ticket, he read what was printed there.

#

EASTERN LINE - ONE WAY
DIEVS, ROBERT

#

Is that different from the first time? He didn't really have the bandwidth to think about what a change in line meant. Something told him it didn't matter all that much. *Can't believe the peanuts were a joke... Very funny.* If the peanuts were just... peanuts, Dievs supposed the train lines might be just that... train lines.

He flipped the ticket over. The back was plain, except for the bottom right corner. Printed there, comically small, was a smiley face. Dievs looked at it, blinked, and after a moment, smiled himself. He put the ticket in his pocket and walked over to the hallway marked "EASTBOUND PLATFORMS."

CHAPTER FIFTY-THREE

The End of the Line

SMILEY sat in the shade of the BP gas station across the highway and watched the Texas Inn burn until only its blackened skeleton remained. She felt no remorse for the building, an ugly, sad thing, but Won Park's frantic yelling (and eventual sobbing) did make her feel sorry for him. *Tough day.* And wasn't it just?

Karina had made it off the roof without injury. She'd waited out the gunfire in the field behind the Texas Inn (as had been the plan, hastily laid out in that Texaco snack aisle), sitting on the hatch to Hank's dump tank, though she hadn't known that's what it was. She now sat beside Smiley, gazing across the highway at the smoldering ruins of the hotel Hank Cooper had once called home.

Smiley hadn't spoken since she'd said those last words to James Brackington and watched the life fade from Robert Dievs. The police questioners had figured she was in a state of shock, and so had abandoned questioning after she'd answered the first twenty with silence and a blank stare. Those police investigators had a hell of a lot else to deal with at the moment. Not the least of which being: *trying to figure out what in the fuck had happened.* Smiley didn't even really know herself. The parking lot of the Texas Inn, which had likely never been the setting for anything remotely interesting or important in the entirety of its existence, was now more of a scene out of a Stephen King novel than a place to park a car. *Blood and smoke and carnage.*

Smiley was thinking (not all that hard, as it sort of hurt her head) about why a man who had been brought back from the dead, presumably by some divine power, would end up bleeding out in the parking lot of a shitty hotel. It seemed random. And stupid. *That's just life though, isn't it?* She hadn't cried when Dievs had died, nor had any wise last words been exchanged. She'd simply sat by his body and looked into his eyes as he went. *This is what I killed those people for*, she'd thought bitterly. *More death. Killing never brings peace, just more killing.* And that was all. What more had she expected? A dues ex machina? A narrator with a deep, rustic American accent to come in and explain the moral? Maybe Sam Elliot? *No.* It all seemed terribly pointless, and worse, Brackington had gotten away with the case. Her future, she knew, was prison. If she was lucky.

"What a day… Who knew cleaning my desk would be so exciting," said Karina, half drowned out by the whoosh of cars on the highway.

It took about ten seconds to get there, but Smiley couldn't help but chuckle. Karina glanced over at Smiley and let out a little laugh of her own. They resumed their silence for a few minutes, then it was Smiley's turn to speak. They watched the firemen across the highway spray water on the ashes of Won Park's legacy.

"He got away," said Smiley quietly.

"The green-eyed guy? Mr. Mojo?"

Smiley nodded and said, "Means it's not over. He'll come back. He said he would. He'll come for me… and you, and

Joe."

Karina looked at Smiley's face for a second, then turned back to the scene playing out across the highway. It reminded Smiley of an anthill, perhaps under attack from a cruel child.

"Nah. I don't think so," said Karina.

Smiley raised her eyebrows and turned to Karina.

"No?" she asked.

"No," replied Karina. "Doesn't feel like it. Does it?"

And though Smiley kept that questioning look on her face, she thought Karina was right. It *didn't* feel like it. For some reason, the thought of Brackington, and those horrible green eyes of his, didn't produce the fear it once had. Still, Smiley didn't trust the feeling. *Wishful thinking, maybe.*

One thing she could surely count on, however, was the load of bullshit undoubtedly waiting for her back in Campaiyote. At her funeral home. Waiting for her in the shape of a very disgruntled Phil Morris. *And I deserve it. I'm a murderer.*

"I'm going to jail, Karina."

Karina shrugged, "Eh, I give it a fifty-fifty, babe."

Smiley couldn't help but grin again, though when the image of those seven or eight men she'd gunned down came back to her mind, *unbidden*, that smile vanished. She thought this would probably never go away, that there would be no forgetting that deed, and no forgiving it either, even if it had been to save herself and someone else. *Even if I don't go to jail, I've made a prison for myself. An inescapable one.*

"You should go home," said Smiley, not turning to look at her ex-secretary.

"Yeah, I was thinking that."

"What did you tell the police, by the way?" asked Smiley.

"Oh, not much. Just that, *'I was so scared, I could hawdly do anythin' officer. I'm just so glad you're here. I don't know what happened. I just heard a lot of yelling and guns and, and, and...'* They ate that shit up." Karina quoted herself in a southern belle voice and chuckled when she finished.

"Good," said Smiley. "You should go home and hug your mom. Please don't tell her about any of this. For my sake. And yours."

"Are you nuts? She'd send me to an institution if I told her about this. She was probably thinking about it already," Karina responded. She turned back to the Texas Inn and put a finger on her lips. "Though it might get me out of school for a while..."

Smiley shook her head and hoped that no one had seen her driving the getaway car back in Campaiyote. Or at least, not well enough to identify her. She supposed they'd find out soon enough.

Smiley herself was letting a gradual feeling of contentment wash over her. Whatever was waiting for her, fair or not, *biased judge or not,* at least it didn't look like Jim Morrison. At least it was under the purview of *the law* (even if the law came in the bloated shape of Phil Morris). Of the American judicial system. That, at least, would just be unfair, not cruel. *Hopefully.*

Her life had changed so dramatically in just a few days, she still couldn't really wrap her mind around it. *Something was gonna break soon, anyway.* But it was over. At least the crazy parts. She would never shoot a gun again, that was for sure... though it crossed her mind that she had never intended to shoot one in the first place. The funeral home would close. There was no getting around that. *No money.* And she didn't think Hank would be returning to the crime scene cleanup business anytime soon. At least she hoped not. The picture of Hank screaming, covered in blood and tied to a chair came back to her, and she shuddered.

The scene that police had initially come upon shortly after Brackington's departure had been closer to a war zone than a hotel parking lot. Several men in suits had been lying in sickeningly large puddles of blood. One had been missing a leg, or rather, his leg had been distributed across the parking lot like bird seed (Karina hadn't seen the result of her bombing, and Smiley was glad for this). Of those suited men, several had been screaming in confusion and pain. One had even wandered out onto the highway, nearly causing a semi-truck to swerve off the road. All this against the backdrop of a bright red-orange twisting blaze of stucco and old dried wood. The Texas Inn sign had even caught, the dye in the lettering making the fire spurt quick columns of blue and green.

It had taken more than a few minutes for the police to realize there was an unconscious man tied to a chair, as well as the still-burning body of a woman in the parking lot. Adding yet another level of confusion to it all was the small stream of renters who had come filing out of their rooms at the sound of dynamite exploding, most of them dressed in some form of Renaissance garb. A clown, a king, a queen, a dog in a butterfly costume, and a couple of confused peasants. It was like the collapse of some strange court of lost time travelers. A man in a stained white Wifebeater threw the look off considerably, however.

Hank had been one of the last people to be carted off in an ambulance. Smiley had pulled him away from the blaze herself. He'd been slick with sweat, pale as a TB patient, and covered head to toe in hot blood, like some sick recreation of the prom scene in Carrie. Except it wasn't pig's blood. *No. Not Pig's blood.* She'd seen the state of his eye up close then and known it was a goner. *Don't have to be a surgeon to see that.* She hoped Hank might recover somehow. His eye was gone, but his life wasn't over. There was hope, though she wondered if he would ever be able to see it. Could she?

It had occurred to her as she'd dragged him across the parking lot that this whole mess was, in a round about sort of way, all a result of Hank. If he hadn't found her funeral home, she might very well be sitting in her office right now, listening to faint music playing through Karina's headphones, and watching Joe eat lunch. *And looking down at all those foreclosure notices…*

The fact was that her business had been destined for failure even before Hank, though his business had prolonged the inevitable end. She supposed she was grateful, but it would be a lie to say she didn't consider just leaving him to burn in that parking lot, for he had also (of course, not directly) made her a murderer. *It helps, when faced with the consequences of your own actions, to blame someone else. Anyone else.* But blaming Hank was wrong. *At the end of the day, my actions were my own. All me.*

Smiley sighed a big sigh. Karina looked over at her, but for once, said nothing. Karina turned to look once more at the smoking ruins of the Texas Inn, then rose and walked over to a pay phone tacked onto the side of the BP.

Smiley watched the firemen do their work over the buzz of the highway.

CHAPTER FIFTY–FOUR

You Know Those Explode, Right?

HE was on fire.

Or that's what it felt like: Green fire pouring through his veins, making his heart pump like a V8 engine. He missed his Shelby already. *No sweat, boss. You can get another just like it. You can have anything you want now. Nothing is in your way, and come to think of it, was there ever anything in your path to begin with? That black bitch? Hank? No. They were speed bumps, that's all. Hiccups.*

James Brackington had thrown the explosives out the window of Smiley's beige Pinto as soon as he'd gotten on the highway. *Fool me once.* He'd checked the contents of the briefcase immediately after fleeing the escalating blaze that was the Texas Inn and found a stick of dynamite with a timer stuck in it. *Not this time.* He'd tossed the bomb, and now his case was full. Full of the right stuff. **The stuff.**

The case had cast that beautiful dark blue glow around the inside of the Pinto. He'd almost crashed on the highway looking at it, but had managed to drag his eyes away and back to the road. He'd heard the faint ticking of the timer then and felt for a false bottom, found it, and subsequently, the stick of dynamite hidden there. *Didn't get the time quite right there, eh, Smiley?* He'd thrown the apparatus out the window like a cigarette butt, not caring that it would probably blow up some unsuspecting minivan passing by in half an hour.

Now he was cruising towards Dallas, smiling madly. And why not? He had it all, and more was to come. His only worry was that the state of the Pinto might get him pulled over, but even then, he wasn't too worried. *I own the cops, and they know it.* He checked what remained of the rearview mirror for smoke from the Texas Inn and saw it was already gone behind the horizon. *Free and clear, baby.* The warm satisfaction of having won (though he told himself victory had been assured from the beginning) wormed its way through his nerves like a shot of hot, high proof, Kentucky bourbon.

#

AN hour later, James Brackington, driving Smiley's battered beige Pinto, pulled off I-35 East and made his way towards San Jacinto and the Hyacinth House. He pulled up to a red light, the only car on the four-lane road. He thought the street seemed a little deserted, but gave it only passing attention. The high from making his escape with the briefcase was still coursing through him, making him *vibrate,* but it wasn't enough to overwhelm completely the pain in his legs. He was littered with shrapnel from his Shelby. *My fucking car…* That still made him angry. He'd loved that car… as much as James Brackington could *love* anything. *Now I have to drive this piece of shit.* Adrenaline had numbed the pain, but he could feel the effect wearing off. He suspected his wounds might be worse than he could feel. *Nothing to do about it now except be careful.*

The traffic light swayed gently in a light Dallas breeze. After waiting for a few seconds, he considered running it, but figured he ought to minimize his risk here. *Most accidents happen within a mile of the home.* He almost laughed. It was a strangely prudent thought for someone like James Brackington, but there was another reason not to run the light.

His eyes drifted over to the passenger seat, where lay the slim leather briefcase. *Irresistible.* It was a magnet that seemed to call out to him. It *was* calling out to him. *Open me… take a look at what your hard work earned…* He was now grinning uncontrollably. *Oh, yes. I'm here. I think I will.* He reached over and pulled the case onto his lap. Glancing up, he saw the light was still red. He turned his attention back down, and though he knew he shouldn't, he opened the case.

That dark blue glow, like the bottom of a deep pool, shimmering in silver light, once again painted the inside of the car. Brackington's wolfish smile faded and was replaced with awe. How could he not be in awe of… *this?*

#

TWO hundred yards behind where James Brackington sat still, gazing down at his glowing bounty, a motor was screaming. It came flying off the highway exit ramp in the shape of a rusted out Chevrolet Caprice, and left long black tire marks where it had nearly slid off the road. At the helm of this creature was a man named Bryan Smith. But that didn't really matter. What did, was that Bryan was drunk. Unlike James, he really *had* felt the warm embrace of some high-proof Kentucky bourbon… a fair bit of it, actually. And he was feeling it now, *oh, yeah, feelin' it.*

Mr. Smith didn't exactly *take note* of the empty road, but even so, he took full advantage of it, swinging the old Caprice left and right across all four lanes of Young Street like a yachter checking the rudder action on his shiny new toy. The Caprice rocked and rolled on old suspension, pitching so violently that the wheel hubs scraped against the rubber of the tires. Bryan, however, did not hear this, *could not* hear it, over the sound of *Green River*, blasting through the car stereo. He was singing along — if you wanted to call what he was doing *singing* — though he didn't really know the lyrics. It all amounted to a drunken slurry of yells, electric guitar and rubber screeching against concrete.

Bryan saw up ahead (more like *sensed* than actually *saw*) a stoplight with a single car parked in the second lane from the left. Even through the whiskey tornado of his vision, Smith could make out the badge on the back of the hatchback. *Pinto.* He snorted.

"Duddn't that idiot know those things explode? Errybody know that."

Smith, quite certain he had plenty of room before reaching the stoplight, gave his Caprice a little more gas. Or rather, what he considered a little more.

As he stepped on the gas, a brown wrapper on the floor of the passenger seat caught Smith's eye. *A Mars Bar. Hey, that's just what I'm lookin' for.* Smith had gone out for a Mars Bar, departing (regretfully) from his favorite seat at Froggy's Roadhouse, but had somehow lost the candy bar between buying it at the gas station and the present moment. *Found youu…*

Smith wasted no time in leaning over and reaching down to the floor with his right hand, abandoning his view of the road completely. The wrapper was tucked up where the passenger floorboard and the door met, at the very edge of his reach. His fingertips grazed the perforated end of the wrapper, and he cursed. His left hand finally came off the wheel. *Just for a second.* He finally grasped the wrapper, yanked it up and smiled. But as he felt it in his hand, he realized it was flat and empty.

"Well, shi…"

The *t* at the end of *shit* was replaced with the sound of twisting metal and shattering glass. Bryan Smith had a half-second view just before his Caprice slammed into the back of that Pinto he'd seen just a few moments earlier. In the shattered remains of the rearview mirror of that car, in those few precious milliseconds before impact, he saw two blazing green fires. *Eyes.* They were looking at him with murderous intent, he was certain, though they would never get the chance. He could see a mouth too. It was open in a scream of rage. A curious blue light, like you might see at the aquarium, played upon the inside walls of the Pinto.

Above the two cars, the traffic light turned green.

Then it was blackness and the sound of train whistles for Bryan Smith.

#

NO one witnessed the accident on Young Street that day, only the smoking, charred aftermath. If anyone had been there however, they would have seen a rusted Chevrolet Caprice slamming into a shot-up beige Ford Pinto at near fifty miles per hour, followed quickly by a black and orange fireball far larger than one might expect from a simple rear end accident, even at high speeds. The gas tank at the back of the Pinto had been pierced, and all it took was a spark (easy enough to come by when two cars slam together) to ignite the whole shebang. With no other cars in sight, on a completely empty street, watching the Caprice slam into the back of the Pinto would've been like watching two lone dung beetles collide in the middle of the Sahara Desert.

The wonders of alcohol.

The driver of the Caprice, later identified as Bryan Smith, died on impact. The driver of the Pinto, however, wasn't so lucky. On impact, James Brackington had flown forward, sending the briefcase toppling to the floor. The airbag failed to inflate, and he hit his head on the steering wheel hard (*another premier feature of the Ford Pinto, only $4,700! Financing available*).

There had been a fleeting moment of relative stillness after the initial crash when Brackington thought he might walk away with nothing more than a bloody nose. Then the fire had come, washing up from behind him in an all-encompassing flood. He screamed, first in rage, then in pain, and last, in fear. He pushed open the door of the Pinto to escape the inferno, but his seatbelt had already melted into the buckle. His fingers melted right along with the vinyl. James Brackington's screams ended, and so too did he hear the whistle of a steam engine and the CHUGGA-CHUGGA of iron on steel.

His final moments had gone as so many other's had, if not with a bit more bang. Had someone been there to witness James Brackington's demise, they might've seen a burst of green flame escape the sizzling heap that was the Pinto, and perhaps heard a ghostly howl to go along with it. But no one was. He did not fill out his post-death survey card happily.

There was one other matter of some importance having to do with the death of James Brackington: the briefcase. The treasure he had been gazing upon when the end had come for him so abruptly, and which had offered no chance for escape. Three explosions followed the crash. The first being the Pinto's gas tank. The second, the rupture of the Caprice's fuel tank, and the third, the relatively small pop and crackle of some unknown substance burning in the front seat of the Pinto.

Though no one was there to witness the impact, later investigators, having sorted through the charred and hollowed out wreckage of both cars, found a collection of curious bumps melted into the seat on the driver's side of the Pinto (mixed in, of course, with the melted remains of the driver). A bundle of shapes that, for lack of any better descriptor, looked like a pile of peanuts.

* * *

www.ingramcontent.com/pod-product-compliance
Lightning Source LLC
Chambersburg PA
CBHW070605300726
48975CB00006B/1718